D0040269

## Advance Praise for
### *Still Life with Monkey*

"Stark and compelling . . . rigorously unsentimental yet suffused with emotion." —*Kirkus Reviews* (starred review)

"In Katharine Weber's new novel, she takes on one of the most challenging subjects we know—the question of how to face a life we never imagined. She does so with great subtlety, tenderness, and intelligence, as well as the beautiful prose we expect from her." —**Roxana Robinson, author of *This Is My Daughter***

"Among the many brilliances of Katharine Weber's new novel is the whole idea of a 'still life.' Painters saw unnatural stillness as a contradiction in terms yet containing a mysterious truth. Here, too, mysterious truth—a car accident, a wheelchair (another contradiction), paralysis, and honest and beautifully drawn people, stopped in mid-passage. To this still life comes the capuchin monkey, the service animal who attends the disconnections of the spine, the spirit, and the species. *Still Life* is life still—the theme of this original, remarkable book." —**Roger Rosenblatt, author of *Kayak Morning***

"*Still Life with Monkey* is a brilliantly crafted novel, brimming with heart. Pairing poetry with wisdom, this is a story about what it means to live, love, and grow." —**Tayari Jones, author of *An American Marriage***

"*Still Life with Monkey* is radiantly tender and piercingly sad. Katharine Weber is a magician of a novelist, one who writes about loss and loneliness with such compassion and humor that we feel enchanted as we read." —**Brian Morton, author of *Florence Gordon* and *Starting Out in the Evening***

## Praise for Katharine Weber's Earlier Novels

### True Confections

"Superb . . . a great American tale." —*New York Times Book Review*

"One of the wittiest, most stimulating novelists at work today . . . wonderful fun and endlessly provocative." —*Chicago Tribune*

"Vividly imagined . . . irresistible." —*Boston Globe*

"Wickedly funny." —*NPR*

### Triangle

"A marvel of ingenuity." —Cynthia Ozick

"An enticing read." —*Washington Post Book World*

"Extraordinary." —*Baltimore Sun*

"A thing of beauty." —*NPR*

"Crackerjack historical mystery." —*Entertainment Weekly*

### The Little Women

"Stops being droll only to be funny and almost never stops being exceedingly smart." —*New York Times*

## The Music Lesson

"Very moving, at times terrifying . . . entirely gripping. A really important novel." —Muriel Spark

"Likely to haunt you . . . a wonderful book."
—*Washington Post Book World*

"Intricate as an acrostic." —*New Yorker*

"Affecting and elegant." —*New York Times Book Review*

"Wonderful . . . a superb book . . . genuinely surprising."
—Kate Atkinson

## Objects in Mirror Are Closer Than They Appear

"Engaging . . . nuanced . . . impressive." —*New York Times Book Review*

An "amazing first novel . . . wise, flippant, deep, witty."
—Madeleine L'Engle

"I much enjoyed this delightfully witty novel."
—Iris Murdoch

"Katharine Weber delivers the goods." —Wally Lamb

A "stunning first novel . . . a fascinating read."
—May Sarton

"Witty, bittersweet . . . [a] meticulously-drawn cast of characters, keen irony, and a flawless sense of place."
—*Cleveland Plain Dealer*

KATHARINE WEBER

# STILL LIFE
## with *Monkey*

**PAUL DRY BOOKS**
*Philadelphia  2018*

An excerpt of this novel appeared in somewhat different form in *Boulevard Magenta* Issue #5.

Grateful acknowledgment is made to W.W. Norton for permission to quote from the Stanley Kunitz poems "The Testing-Tree" (from *The Testing-Tree*, 1971) and "Touch Me" (from *Passing Through: The Later Poems, New and Selected*, by Stanley Kunitz, 1995)

First Paul Dry Books Edition, 2018

Paul Dry Books, Inc.
Philadelphia, Pennsylvania
*www.pauldrybooks.com*

Printed in the United States of America

Library of Congress Control Number: 2018939679

ISBN 978-1-58988-129-7

*For Andrew Zerman*

AND

*Kent and Nancy Converse*

AND

*Farah*

*Secrets, silent, stony sit in the dark
palaces of both our hearts:
secrets weary of their tyranny: tyrants
willing to be dethroned.*

—James Joyce, *Ulysses*

# ONE

## *Her long fingers caressed his cheek*

HER LONG FINGERS CARESSED HIS CHEEK FOR A MO-
ment, as she traced her way down to his jaw, her cool touch
just grazing the stubble of Duncan's five-day beard. She studied his face, seeking his gaze. He met her eyes for an instant
before looking away, strangely embarrassed by his inability to
match the intensity of her insistent stare. Ottoline smacked
little air kisses as she reached up to touch his face again, and
he was surprised by the gentle precision of her tiny fingernails
sorting through his whiskers as she investigated up the con-
tour of his cheek from jaw to upper lip. She pressed two fingers to his lips, and he nearly kissed them, but he didn't, and
then she contemplated her fingertips, sticking out her tongue
daintily for the tiny flake of something she had found on his
lip. She nibbled at it contentedly while continuing to stare up
at him, making a sweet, soft, peeping sound. She repositioned
her springy little body constantly, and now she shifted again,
peering up at his chin, plucking with fascination at the bris-
tles that speckled his face. They had been alone together for
five minutes.

Ignore her, her trainer Martha had advised, before leaving them alone. Act as if you've seen a million monkeys and

you're bored by her. Let her be curious about you. Stay very still. Make no sudden movements. Duncan was very good at sitting still, and he was pretty much the master of being bored, too.

Re-settling herself on his chest, Ottoline began to unfasten the buttons of his cotton shirt, the tufty top of her head brushing under his chin while she dedicated herself to the apparently familiar task of unbuttoning. Top button, done. Next button, done. She breathed out a little sigh of concentration as she undid one more button, but now she was stymied by the padded chest strap of the harness that kept Duncan from flopping forward. She stroked the placket edge of his open shirt and then she touched his exposed chest. She slid her hand into the gap of his unbuttoned shirt and rummaged under the fabric very slowly, moving her hand tentatively, feeling for something, stroking his chest hair, now threading her fingers through it, and Duncan squeezed his closed eyes even more tightly shut as he felt himself moved inexplicably. Her careful, exquisite touch was disturbingly unlike the respectful and routine handling by the various people whose task it was to bathe him and dress him and manage his body. She rotated her fingertip in a tiny circle, gently centering on his left nipple, before moving on to twine her fingers in the surrounding hairs, searching the surface of his body, right there at the equator of his sensory level, delineating the edge of feeling and not feeling. How did she know to trace this line?

She continued her tender exploration, mapping his skin with those careful little fingers. He was barely breathing, but he could feel his heart jumping under her hand. He stayed very still, with his eyes half-closed, feeling her cool, questioning hands on his skin. She had a distinctive, salty tang that was quite pleasant, and as he breathed it in, there was something nearly familiar, yet new. Ah, Milly. Her fur always had a sweet, sunshiny smell when she had been outdoors. This was muskier.

———

Milly and Molly were the grey tiger sister cats of Duncan's childhood, seventh birthday surprises for Duncan and Gordon, his twin. Molly, Gordon's cat, was a hard-luck puss. She had somehow lost most of her tail in her earliest days. Gordon told everyone she was a Manx (which he pronounced "mankth"), but she was really just a cat without a tail. Milly had an elegant, expressive tail, tipped in white. Molly, always timid and fearful, had a short life; she was hit by a car during the twins' tenth birthday party. But Milly lived nearly twenty years, and died, by then a tiny husk of tigery dignity who spent most of her days sleeping in the middle of the big old dictionary which lay open on a stand next to Duncan's desk, only a few months before Duncan met Laura during intermission in the lobby of Long Wharf Theater, introduced by a client of Duncan's who had chatted with Laura at a previous play, because their season ticket seats were in the same row. The client, a banker who was forever renovating his vast Italian Renaissance-style villa on the waterfront in Sachem's Head, had offered Duncan his wife's ticket at the last minute when their sitter cancelled. (Neither Laura nor Duncan could remember the name of the play that night, a tedious modern interpretation of a Greek drama that got terrible reviews.)

When she was young, on hot summer nights, done with her roaming, Milly often came to the twins' bedroom window, leaping onto the shingled front porch roof under their pair of windows from the adjacent maple tree. When she mewed and scraped at the screen, Duncan would tiptoe across the room while Gordon slept, and, despite their mother's admonitions, he would unhook the bottom of the wooden screen frame to push it out so she could slip inside with a grateful chirp. When Milly sprawled purring at the foot of his bed, Duncan liked to flop over beside her, his face pressed into the fur on the back of her neck, so he could breathe in her sweet grassy aroma. He had loved her very much.

Their mother often found him in the morning that way, sleeping on top of his sheets at the foot of his bed with his feet on his pillow, but she never understood why. Identical or not, her boys were quite different from each other. Gordon slept like a stone, and she hardly had to make his bed from one day to the next. Not Duncan, as their mother often complained while she tucked his wildly disheveled bedding together into smooth order. (For thirty-five years, until the day she died, Helen Wheeler was never able to keep herself from making comparisons, and any complaint or praise of one of her sons was inevitably at the expense of the other. Everyone and everything had to be more than or less than someone or something else in Helen's world.) Even when Duncan stayed all night under the covers where he belonged, he twisted his bedclothes into a chaotic vortex. Duncan slept like a windmill, she liked to say. Gordon slept like a stone, but Duncan slept like a windmill.

Not these days.

His eyes still nearly closed, Duncan could see Ottoline's inquisitive gaze through the fringe of his eyelashes. She was done investigating his chest hairs, and now she sat back and reached up to touch his cheek again, peeping softly as she cupped his chin with both hands, turning and angling his face with an insistent pressure until he opened his eyes all the way. She was only inches from his nose, staring at him intently with those pellucid brown eyes. What? She smacked her lips expectantly and tilted her head. He imitated her peeping sound and tilted his head as best he could, and then he smacked his own lips back at her in an exaggerated kiss-kiss, the way he would play with a baby. Ottoline cheeped delightedly, a shrill, joyful sound that nearly hurt his ears, and then suddenly, as if she had just realized who he was—Oh, it's you!—she launched herself against him and hugged him fiercely, burrowing close, her warm body pressed tight against his clavicles, her little fingernails digging into the back of his neck with a pulsing grip. It was oddly thrilling, and flattering, if a little incommodious. He closed his eyes again, feeling strangely peaceful and relaxed. Everything was perfectly still. He hadn't thought about death for at least ten minutes.

This encounter had been billed as an experiment, and Duncan had reluctantly agreed to the visit, though really he had no choice. Laura had been relentless. At first he refused absolutely. He snickered at the bizarre notion of bringing a monkey helper into the house when she first raised it. Why not? How about a mongoose to do the vacuuming, a cockatoo to answer the phone, and perhaps a helper wombat to assist with paperwork? When he realized she was serious, he dismissed the idea as beyond consideration. That, he had thought, was that.

Duncan was angry when Laura admitted she had gone ahead and scheduled a series of interviews behind his back. How long had this been going on? She had been at the Primate Institute three times in two weeks! But even after Laura won, even after he said Okay, fine, I'll do it, I'll meet it, they can bring the damn thing here any time, it's not like I have anything else to do, plan whatever you want, she had continued to sell him on the concept, emphasizing all the tasks the capuchin monkey—the one the Institute thought would be a good match, the monkey absurdly called Ottoline—would be able to perform for him: lights switched on and off, CDs inserted, buttons pushed, pages turned, dropped items retrieved. Wouldn't he like to have this little helper right there to pick up the television remote, or his cell phone, which so often slipped from his grasp? Wouldn't that be fantastic? Yes, fantastic. Whatever. Wouldn't he enjoy having her turn the pages of a book or magazine for him? Sure, why not. Duncan had finally reminded Laura somewhat unpleasantly about the wisdom of his great-uncle Fred, the one with the furniture store in West Hartford, a real holder-forther on a range of topics, who used to say the key to selling is to know when to stop selling.

But now here she was. They had been left together after two hours spent settling in with Martha, the cheerful placement trainer from the Institute who had arrived with Ottoline stuffed inside an incongruous plaid zippered traveling case meant for a cat. Ottoline first explored the room thoroughly. When Martha set up Duncan with a plastic cup, into which she smeared a glob of peanut butter, and a chopstick, Ottoline sprang onto his lap from the coffee table and adroitly seized the chopstick from his loose grasp to dig out her own little helpings.

As Martha clipped the coupling link of the long lead attached to Ottoline's harness to a ring loop on the side of his chair, she reiterated the strategy: Ignore Ottoline. Let her be challenged by his inertness. She might choose to ignore him for a while. Don't force it. Duncan should just let her be curious about him at her own pace. Ottoline had not been very interested in Laura, except when Martha had provided her with some blueberries, which Ottoline snatched immediately from Laura's outstretched palm.

"She's already got it worked out that Duncan is the alpha male in this tribe," Martha murmured. Laura took Martha's cue to sit still on the other side of the room, watching and jotting occasional notes about commands and rules and monkey management strategies, though everything was spelled out clearly in the binder provided by the Institute, and Martha was just reiterating what Laura had already read more than once. After a while, with Ottoline and Duncan engrossed in each other, Martha and Laura had withdrawn to the kitchen, leaving Ottoline alone with Duncan, to whom she was now clinging contentedly, her puppyish warm belly against his chest.

Laura's allergies had kept them from having a cat, though Duncan longed for one and had for years continued to see Milly out of the corner of his eye when he entered a room, only to discover that it was a shadow or a sweater over the arm of a chair. He had never told Laura how often in the night he still felt the phantom weight of a ghost cat jumping up on the bed and settling at his feet. Even since the accident. Especially since the accident.

Now Duncan wondered if Laura's eyes would itch and redden around Ottoline. That would be an easy out right there, putting the whole nutty enterprise beyond further discussion. Keeping Ottoline would already be asking a lot of Laura, not just cleaning the cage and the diaper changes, and the inevitable messes, which were challenging enough, but all the constant maintenance issues, from managing her food to giving her baths, for God's sake. It would be like adopting an ersatz baby, now, after all their hopes.

At the start of the year Laura had begun taking clomiphene every third cycle, and when she began, at the same medical appointment a lifetime ago back in January, they had also scheduled an IUI—intrauterine insemination—for September. If three cycles of IUI failed, they had agreed they would then escalate to IVF—in vitro fertilization—the following spring. And meanwhile, because they had been trying for a pregnancy for more than two years at this point, and because Laura was now thirty-six, Duncan and Laura had been slowly proceeding through all the complicated steps to complete the application materials to meet requirements for approval to adopt a Chinese baby.

Laura had been uncharacteristically superstitious that it would somehow hex their chances of conceiving a baby to apply for a match to a "waiting child," one who would have special needs of some kind, which were the only Chinese adoptions genuinely available in recent years. She knew it wasn't logical, or even nice, but she could hardly bear to contemplate children with cleft palates or missing limbs or cerebral palsy or albinism, while hoping to grow a perfect baby of her own. She was ashamed of her illogical secret fear that being open to adopting one of these imperfect children could invite a defective embryo of her own into existence.

The waiting list for healthy Chinese babies had such a slow clearance rate that approved families now at the top of the list had been waiting since 2007. Laura and Duncan knew several families in New Haven with wonderful, thriving Chinese babies. Well before they had started trying to conceive, the clever Chinese baby girl option had always seemed like their fallback. But now Duncan and Laura tried to persuade themselves that a special needs baby wasn't necessarily one who would be damaged for life. Optimally, her surgery to repair a club foot or cleft palate would be a soon-to-be-forgotten experience of infancy. Two of the adopted Chinese babies in families with whom they were acquainted had undergone such corrective operations successfully.

Well before the accident, they had stopped making casual, optimistic references to their imaginary future twins, or their imaginary future Chinese daughter. And if they were serious about adoption, then it was already getting late to look into adoption possibilities in other countries, though neither of them was quite ready to let go of that phantom Chinese daughter they had kept on reserve all these years, even if she came with a congenital *talipes equinovarus*.

And now the accident had erased the Chinese adoption possibility. China's requirements for foreign adoptive parents not only included strictures about parental body mass index and use of antidepressants, but also forbade a parent in a wheelchair. And there had been so many occasions when they hoped for success, hoped that Laura was pregnant at last;

each time those hopes had been dashed, most cruelly the final time. Instead of the baby girl who might have been theirs, if Ottoline came to stay, Laura would be encumbered with the perpetual care of a grotesque, uncanny, permanently diapered homunculus.

If Ottoline didn't work out, he might actually regret it. Duncan had not expected to care one way or the other. Ending Laura's obsession about the practical possibilities of a monkey helper had been the reason he agreed to the home visit. He wanted to prove her wrong, punish her for having a shred of optimism about the unmitigated disaster of his situation, drag her down into his despair. Duncan had certainly not antici pated Ottoline's complexity. He had not dreamed of her singular presence or how it would feel to be the object of her compelling gaze.

Ottoline began to squirm, and then she clambered up across his collarbone to perch on his shoulder, lifting her leash with her tail as she crossed his body, her diaper rustling. What was she doing now? Make yourself at home, Ottoline. Her breath was warm on his face as she rummaged avidly in his hair. Her attention really was so oddly flattering. Duncan could hear Laura's voice in the kitchen. The coffee grinder whirred and stopped. Martha said something in the chirpy voice she had used when praising Ottoline, which made Laura laugh. The screen door to the back porch banged and the house went quiet. It was an unusually warm October day, but they would need to find someone to come and switch out the screens for glass storm panels on the front and back doors, something Duncan had always enjoyed doing to mark the changing seasons. He would have to explain the way to distinguish the front and back door storm windows. The doors were technically identical, but experience had taught Duncan that the pressure catches didn't line up identically on the panel inserts.

Here in the living room, the faint breeze coming in the open windows lifted the sheer curtains into brief billows and dropped them again. It was getting cooler, and soon someone with ordinary upper body strength and dexterity would have to close the windows. There might not be that many more open window afternoons. The days were noticeably shorter.

If he wanted to, Duncan knew he could roll his chair over to the side bay window and watch the two women walking around the garden. His garden. It was brimming with weeds now. He was the gardener, not Laura, and he had been the last person to prune and weed and mulch, in the middle of June. He had gotten a late start because it was such a cold and rainy spring, and then he had been exceptionally busy with work. The accident was just a couple of weeks after that, when the delayed spring weather had suddenly kicked into a breathtakingly perfect series of hot summer days.

Nothing out there had been touched in four months, except the little patches of grass in front and back which got mowed too short by the indifferent lawn care jockey who came too often and charged too much. Duncan's gardening tools were untouched in the pretty little hexagonal tool shed he had built. Now the leaves had all turned and some of their trees were half bare. Soon enough (Duncan had always liked the satisfying task of raking leaves), the lawn guy would charge them a fortune for the noisy hour he would spend blasting them with a powerful leaf blower into a submissive heap on a big blue tarp.

Duncan's cherished pulmonaria had been ravaged by woodchucks and the feathery pink astilbe was choked with milkweed and goldenrod. The herb beds were overrun by quackgrass and dandelions. Everything had bolted or gone to seed or shriveled. Only the scarlet bells of his penstemon were holding their own, attracting the occasional hummingbird, along with some opportunistic wild blue phlox that had muscled in everywhere. They really should hire someone to tend the flowerbeds. Or, hell with it, they could just pave and gravel, with a few beds of pachysandra. Or forget about it altogether and just leave it decaying and wrecked, a disaster like him. What difference did it make? He toggled the control roughly and turned the chair around with a jerk, and Ottoline automatically tightened her grip to cling to him. He soothed her tentatively, stroking her silky back with the clawed fingers on his left hand, the hand he could use. She was about the same size as a small cat, but without the bonelessness of a cat, more like a coiled spring.

He couldn't bear to watch Laura showing Martha the ruined garden. Duncan hated the way he felt like an abandoned child at these moments, left out, spying pathetically on the grown-ups he depended on for everything. How could anyone expect him to get used to living this way? Who would be satisfied, who would think this was enough of a life?

Ottoline swiveled around toward the open windows that fronted on the street, a questioning click in her throat, suddenly wary of the thudding bass of somebody's music, which swelled louder, the herald of a meandering Toyota moving slowly down Lawrence Street. Duncan toggled the control to turn his chair around in a practiced three-point move and rolled towards the front windows, and Ottoline gripped his shoulder like a seasoned subway rider leaning into a curve. He stared out the window until the source of the booming music came into his line of vision. Would he ever get used to not being able to turn his head more than a couple of inches in any direction?

Michigan plates. Blonde driver, sunglasses, young, yakking on her cell phone. As she rolled by, Duncan observed that the car's rear windows were dark, with what looked like quilts pressing against the glass. A Yale graduate student with all her worldly possessions in the back seat, alive with the drama of this important moment in her special snowflake unicorn life. Every day of the year, somewhere in New Haven a graduate student was moving in or out. Good luck finding a long-term parking spot on this block without a permit, and meanwhile, put down your damned phone and just drive, honey. Both hands on the fucking wheel.

In recent weeks, in his new captivity, Duncan had become an expert on the life of their street. Before the accident, though they had spent the last eight of their nine years of married life in their pleasingly renovated Victorian house on Lawrence Street, he had never bothered to notice much about their neighbors, who didn't interest him unless they made too much noise or parked stupidly, but now he gazed out the window all day long at their quiet block, taking in everything there was to see. When Laura handed Duncan the ratty old bird-watching binoculars that had been her mother's, the better to spy on all the neighbors, she had called him Jimmy Stewart.

Trying to adjust the focus on the heavy, clouded lenses, his weak hand trembling so badly he could barely manage to hold the binoculars steady without dropping them or knocking the eyepieces against his face, Duncan hadn't wanted Laura to see his struggle, and he retorted in irritation that she was no Grace Kelly. He felt bad about saying that when she walked out of the room, hurt. A few days later, the old binoculars were gone from the windowsill, replaced with a new pair of compact, lightweight Nikons that were easier to adjust and handle, with a simple zoom-control focus lever he could manage. Unlike the telephone headset Laura rigged up for him, which he could activate with a whistled note, and which was in its way satisfying, but he refused it anyway—why would he want to have any more of those fakely optimistic, desperately awkward telephone conversations with well-meaning people?—he was willing to wear the binoculars, on a strap around his neck.

Duncan had come to know every car on the street. The dented silver Toyota Camry belonged to the biographer Debby Applegate, who, with her husband, had moved into the tall white house with the steep brick stoop after the elderly retired anthropologist who had lived there for decades moved to assisted living following a bad fall on his own icy steps. The black Audi with the ski rack belonged to Stan Weinberg, the endocrinologist on the corner whose wild beds of cleome going to seed were a visual amenity in Duncan's limited view, though the friendly wife who had tended their flowers year after year, the wife who had traded plants a few times with Duncan—what was her name? Sandy, Sandra?—had been replaced recently by a spoiled-looking young girlfriend, and the cleome had been neither staked nor weeded all summer.

The classic old red Saab in need of a new muffler, usually parked mid-block, was driven by the stunningly beautiful, nearly transparently pale Scandinavian au pair employed to mind the three hectic McCarthy children across the street. She always struggled to extricate them from the car, the baby girl balanced on her hip while she leaned in to unfasten the younger boy from his car seat, while the older boy opened his door on the street side. The au pair would shout Jackson, do not go out your door into the road! while Jackson, who looked to be seven or eight, sauntered to the curb. The parents were self-important criminal defense attorneys whose clients, most of them armed robbers, murderers, and rapists, were often the subject of screaming headlines. Who would defend such people? Dennis McCarthy and Irene Jackson, that's who.

McCarthy & Jackson, Attorneys at Law (their cheesy infomercials that featured them pretending they were stars of a courtroom drama series ran on the local cable channels and had only recently become familiar to Duncan) kept long and erratic hours. Why did they even have children? Duncan had never paid any notice to their comings and goings before now, though Laura had reported to him that their postal carrier was aggrieved by the intermittent sacks of hate mail generated by some of their more notorious cases.

Did McCarthy & Jackson, Attorneys at Law, know or care that nearly every afternoon, when she brought their children home from the progressive day school that was favored by prosperous Yale families and the upper echelon of New Haven doctors and lawyers, Ingrid or Ingvold or Ingeborg or whatever the hell her name was—the boys could often be heard shouting for Ingie—collected McDonald's detritus from the car and dropped it carefully into the next door neighbor's trash can that was tucked behind a side porch before going in the house?

Duncan was concerned about the middle child. He loped after his older brother awkwardly in a way that reminded Duncan of Gordy when they were boys. He was convinced there was something just a little bit off about that kid, though Laura didn't see it. What did Duncan mean, he was like a little professor? He looked like a regular five-year-old kid to Laura. She doubted that Duncan could diagnose from across the street a child with whom he had never even talked. And meanwhile, since his expertise was based on a lifetime with his oddball brother, what exactly was wrong with Gordy? Bartleby Syndrome? Apparently the Wheelers had never been given a specific diagnosis for whatever it was that limited Gordon.

Duncan was the original and his brother was the copy, Duncan, doing his homework at the dining room table, once overheard their mother tell a neighbor over coffee. He had kept this secret knowledge to himself. He never used it, never once in their entire childhood or adolescence did he blurt out the truth to his twin Gordon, no matter how mad his lisping, tentative, unambitious copy of a brother made him. Poor Gordon. Those eight minutes made all the difference.

Starting when the Wheeler boys were seven, about the age
of the oldest McCarthy kid, Gordon stayed after school once
a week to pwactice his consonants with Miss Wyan (Duncan hadn't understood for years that her name was actually
Miss Ryan), the thpeech thewapist, while Duncan, his fluctuating stutter having eluded the cursory classroom screening, had been taken for piano lessons on those afternoons.
While Gordon hissed like a snake and buzzed like a bee, a
futile endeavor that did not end his dentalizing of S's and Z's,
Duncan mastered "The Happy Farmer." Gordon did tongue
exercises that failed to alter his inability to pronounce his r's,
while Duncan learned some of the simpler Bach minuets.
His piano study was under the tutelage of sweet, rabbitty Mr.
Baner, who was, according to Helen Wheeler, a little light in
the loafers, whatever that meant (Mr. Baner kept time by tap-
ping the toe of a sturdy brown laced shoe).

Duncan always did his best to conceal how hard he worked.
This preoccupation had begun when he first learned that he
was the original brother, while Gordy was the copy. It was a
distinction that felt important, one he wanted to maintain and
expand. What if his mother was wrong? What if he was the
copy, and there had been some error giving Gordy the problems that were meant to be his? And so Duncan never wanted
anyone to know how many hours he practiced piano, or how
much time he spent studying for spelling tests. All through
school, he hid or minimized how much time he devoted to
memorizing, rehearsing, practicing his tennis serve, studying
for French tests, learning lines for a play, writing papers. It
was always more thrilling, somehow, if his accomplishments
seemed to have occurred by sheer force of innate talent.

There was a word for this false carelessness, this studied
nonchalance, Laura had told Duncan the first time he admitted to her this chronic habit of his, when they had been
together for about a month. When he revealed the way he
concealed his efforts because he wanted everyone to believe

that his brilliant work and accomplishments flowed naturally from a wellspring of genius, she had nodded and simply replied, *sprezzatura*. He didn't know there was a word for this, that it was not solely his invention and experience. When he looked it up, Duncan discovered that Laura was more than exactly right. *Sprezzatura* can also describe a form of defensive irony, the disguising behind a mask of apparent indifference what one really desires, feels, thinks, or intends. That too.

Whenever Duncan played a new piano piece flawlessly all the way through, the payoff for weeks of diligent practice, Mr. Baner would clasp his hands together prayerfully and tell Duncan that he had a gift. The first time he said it, Duncan had taken him literally and had expected a tangible reward at the end of the lesson, perhaps candy, or a book, but it was just another one of those remarks adults made all the time that didn't really mean what the words meant.

Duncan and Gordon's father Jack Wheeler died unexpectedly when they were eleven, but their world was remarkably little transformed. During the strange week of covered mirrors and no shoes and unshaven Wallerstein uncles from the side of the family that hadn't changed the name, and a grandfather wearing the same torn shirt every day, Duncan overheard grownups repeating certain phrases the way the rabbi had chanted in Hebrew during the funeral service. Helen and the boys have been taken care of very well. Such a good term life policy, the best. Tragic, but Jack certainly did leave his family in a very comfortable situation. Very comfortable. Jack Wheeler knew term life like nobody's business. For something that was nobody's business, they sure were all talking about it.

Sitting dutifully beside his brother in their dress-up clothes, their hands clasped tightly in their laps as they perched on the plump sofa cushions, wedged between two equally well-upholstered, talkative great-aunts from Hoboken and Great

Neck, Duncan listened. At least Rose didn't live to see this day, said the one from Great Neck. The one from Hoboken, who agreed with her, had tusk-like front teeth that reminded Duncan of the genuine ivory keys on the Steinway baby grand piano in Mr. Baner's living room. Duncan was still waiting for the moment he thought the family was going to sit and shiver.

Were they very comfortable? They had been given plates with cookies and little sandwiches all mixed together in a jumble, and it wasn't even lunchtime. A label in Duncan's jacket collar itched the back of his neck. He was not comfortable. Gordy kept swinging his feet, bouncing his heels off the bottom edge of the sofa harder and harder, faster and faster. Nobody stopped him the way they would have on an ordinary day, until Duncan reached over and held Gordy's legs still.

Duncan went to Hotchkiss, where he achieved high grades and played varsity tennis. Gordon went to Wilbur Cross High School, where he missed so many classes he nearly failed to graduate. Duncan went to Yale and Gordon went to the movies. Duncan studied architecture in Florence for a year and then went to graduate school at the Yale School of Architecture, after which he went directly to work for William Corrigan, the brilliant, crotchety architect famous not only for his elegant shingle-style houses that dotted the New England coastline from Cos Cob to Bar Harbor, but also for his bow ties, his outrageously reactionary politics, and his legendary romances with clients (and architecture critics) of all genders.

In those years Gordon lived at home with their mother, where he had lived all his life, and worked happily in a video rental store in Hamden, where he developed a loyal following among customers who enjoyed his encyclopedic knowledge of movies. Before everyone depended on the Internet

Movie Database, there was Gordon Wheeler to tell you in a heartbeat the name of that Howard Hawks movie with Joel McCrea and Edward G. Robinson (*Barbary Coast*). He became an assistant manager, and then weekend manager, and he would have happily worked there forever, but we all know what happened to video rental stores.

Ever since Movie House folded, Gordon had worked loyally, if part-time, at Roxy's Books in Madison, a shoreline suburb of New Haven, where one of his tasks was writing out in his neatest possible handwriting (which was a quirky mix of upper and lowercase letters) all the shelf-talkers, the little folded pieces of paper hanging down from the shelves all over the store with appealing and personal encomia from the staff captioning favorite books. Gordon lived in a rented house in walking distance to Roxy's Books (he didn't own a car), with Ferga, his Border collie, who loved him very much. His mildewed beach cottage had never been intended for year-round occupation, and its charms included insufficient insulation, a deteriorating roof, flapping aluminum siding, and a crumbling front porch. It was perhaps the least nice dwelling in town.

Gordon wore overalls and flannel shirts year round, over red long johns in the winter months. He bicycled everywhere, and otherwise loved to go for long, loping walks with Ferga very early every morning along the beach, which was just two blocks away, down at the end of his dead-end street. Sometimes after a walk they would sit together on their front steps for a while, Ferga leaning against Gordon's leg while he stroked her neck and whispered his devotion into her cocked, trembling ear. The two of them lived on brown rice mixed with stew that simmered intermittently in a big speckled pot on the stove, plus the leftover muffins and bagels Roxy saved for him from the coffee counter in the back of the store. Gordon still had trouble with his r's and his s's, but his overgrown beard and mustache muffled his speech impediments and gave him an old-fashioned air of formal solemnity. There were bookstore customers who thought Gordon might be Amish.

It was now two years since Duncan had taken over Corrigan & Wheeler after Billy Corrigan's death. Duncan was young to have reached this level of achievement and acclaim as an architect, yet all along he had been quite aware that despite having credit on dozens of award-winning projects, despite being a name partner, he had never truly distinguished himself with any recognizable design style of his own. He had developed his identity as an architect dedicating himself entirely to work on houses and additions that perpetuated all the classic Billy Corrigan gestures—the signature grandeur and large-scale intimacy and gables and la-di-da elegance. Did Duncan even really have an architectural style of his own? What exactly would distinguish a true Duncan Wheeler house, unconstrained by all the familiar Corrigan hallmarks? There was exactly one such house, and it had never been built.

Duncan grew up in an undistinguished house on an ordinary suburban street in Hamden, Connecticut, but something about his house had nevertheless always felt just right to him, unlike the houses of many of his friends, which even as a child he had judged for being ill-proportioned or out of balance, with their boring fronts and narrow hallways and disappointing picture windows with fake, stuck-on muntins inside and fake, mis-proportioned shutters outside. Whenever he gazed out his bedroom window at the Band-Aid colored neo-Colonial house across the street, he was made uneasy by the shallow pitch of its gabled roof, which ended without any overhang at all, like fingernails that have been clipped down to the quick. Duncan loved the generous overhanging roofline on all four sides of his own blocky house with its deep front porch, where he felt sheltered and safe.

When Duncan was in his first year as an architecture student, he became intrigued by the subtle distinctions between a hip roof and a pyramidal roof. He adored the pyramidal roof. Of course he did. He had grown up under the generous pyramidal roof that graced his childhood home—that boxy, ordinary, American Four-Square house on Broadfield Road where his mother and brother still lived. Nothing remotely like that house had ever come up for discussion in any of his classes until a guest lecturer from Chicago devoted a few minutes of a Frank Lloyd Wright lecture to the popularity of Sears Roebuck Catalogue kit houses in the early decades of the twentieth century. There on the screen were a series of Midwestern streetscapes with rows of houses that looked exactly like Duncan's childhood home.

The American Four-Square was summarized and dismissed in a few minutes. The lecturer's reason for the digression was to make the point that even if the profoundly original and brilliant work of Frank Lloyd Wright did influence the popularity of these instant Prairie Box homes, he certainly shouldn't be held directly responsible for either their unremarkableness or their proliferation. More than a hundred thousand Sears kit homes were built across the country between 1908 and 1940. They were shipped in boxcars as complete bundles of some thirty thousand elements or more, depending on the style of the house, with everything from roof shingles to foundation bricks. Sears marked the framing members with numbers so builders could assemble them with ease. Sears even sold the mortgages for these houses. Bland, undistinguished, and built rather than designed, was how the lecturer dismissively characterized the Four-Square.

Near the end of his second year at Yale, Duncan found himself a day away from a deadline on an important assignment for an advanced design class that he was supposed to have been working on all semester. Not one of the dozen canonical twentieth-century houses he had been assigned to emulate or oppose had sparked a single worthwhile idea. He had over a period of weeks put hundreds of hours into five different false starts that each deteriorated into an ugly mess of meaningless gestures. When the fifth design failed to come to life, Duncan seized the entire roll of drawings and stomped on it before stuffing the whole thing, weeks of mediocre work, into a recycling bin.

Now, with the presentation a day away, he couldn't even pull out the best of the worst and rework it to make it look like something. He had nothing. He was literally back to the drawing board. The eminent and terrifying Peter Eisenman was that semester's visiting critic, and tomorrow afternoon was the make-or-break for this semester's grade. Without something to put up, Duncan would fail the class and maybe even wash out of the program. Stupid, stupid, stupid!

Beyond panic at this point, Duncan had drawn a square, which he labeled "Square One." And then, without really thinking about it, he started sketching it into a Four-Square house, idly at first, just to give himself something to do, but as it took shape on the paper under his pencil, he had a revelation. This was it. Now, for the first time in months, he was genuinely inspired and eager to work. He set aside the first sketch and started again, with purpose.

Duncan stayed up all night drawing an elaboration on the classic Four-Square house he knew so well. As he bent over his drafting table, alone in the studio (with the exception of occasional rustling in the overflowing trash bin in the corner that attracted mice who lived on pizza crusts and sandwich leftovers), he had no awareness of the hours passing. He was in a trance of invention. Duncan was delighted by this house as it materialized on the paper before him. He loved it with a surge of feeling that he had never before experienced for any of the hundreds of building designs he had conjured and sketched before this. It wasn't an ego trip; he wasn't enthralled by his own brilliance so much as he was captivated by what he found himself revealing and discovering with every stroke of his pencil on the big sheets of drawing paper clipped to his drafting table.

When he had completed the floor plans and the elevations, though he had been drawing for hours, Duncan went on to draw the axonometrics, though they were not required for the assignment. Nothing he had ever designed before this moment had made him feel such urgency and visceral certainty. He was consumed by his desire to render this sublime house with exquisite clarity. The world was sleeping, and he was wider awake than he had ever been before.

The sun was coming up as he swept away the last of the pounce powder with his horsehair desk brush so he could clean up the last stray pencil marks before the final step, inking the plan drawings for what he had decided to call an Explicated Four-Square House. Then he was done. It was a recognizable Four-Square, but his surpassing design made it into something much more than a Four-Square, the way when Lester Young played "All of Me" with Teddy Wilson in 1956 it became something new, much more than just another rendition of the song. This, this—the joyful, soaring feeling of culmination, now that he had conjured and rendered this singular, pleasing house into existence—this was why Duncan Wheeler was an architect.

Everyone was nervous going into the crit. Some of the other architecture students at the nearest drafting tables had laughed out loud as Duncan unrolled his elevations and bulldog-clipped the corners to his drafting table. Some of them had crowded around him as he laid everything out.

"Whoa! Axonometrics!" someone exclaimed, peering over his shoulder. "I admire your nerve, man."

"Did you draw the box it comes in, too?" asked a condescending girl named Sandra who always wore white painter's pants. She had a boyfriend named Cotton who also wore white painter's pants. Duncan never really understood her minimal plans for houses that didn't seem to be three-dimensional.

"Prairie Box, you mean?" added someone else Duncan had liked until that moment.

The Explicated Four-Square House drew quizzical looks from Peter Eisenman, who stood and stared at each element wordlessly for a good five minutes before moving on to look for another victim. Duncan's project wasn't one of the six selected for scrutiny and evisceration during the crit. Anything Eisenman didn't single out for discussion was considered to be tacitly approved. So he had passed. Once it was evident that his work wasn't going to be discussed, Duncan retreated inside himself, sitting perfectly still on his stool, oblivious to the anxious colloquy around him.

There was a lot of apprehension in the room, manifest in frequent bursts of nervous laughter whenever Eisenman said anything halfway witty, even though his cleverest remarks were usually at someone's expense. Someone suddenly got up and fled the room, brushing by Duncan with a suppressed sob, though Duncan hardly noticed. What he had thought he felt, profound joy at this discovery of something truly marvelous in himself, had been nothing more than the deluded self-congratulation of a fool. Or a child. Lesson learned. To succeed as an architect in this world is to sacrifice vision to reality. The field of architecture pretends to be art, and sometimes a house design that is real and true gets recognition, but in reality, success is more often a business. A little seed of brilliance that had germinated and begun to sprout deep inside Duncan withered and died that afternoon.

His sincerely intended Explicated Four-Square House, assumed by everyone to be a witty parody, gave Duncan an erroneous reputation among his peers as both a dark horse and a risk-taker. He was neither. He completed his training by sticking to his former propensity for doing highly adequate and entirely unremarkable work in response to each assignment, neither distinguishing nor disgracing himself. He would never take such a painful chance again. At the end of the semester, when Duncan moved out of his dark ground-floor sublet studio apartment in the building everyone called Trumbull Dungeons near the highway ramp at the corner of Orange and Trumbull, he rolled up all the Explicated Four-Square House material and put it in a tube, which he stored next to the old school papers and notebooks he kept in an old file cabinet in the attic of his mother's house, where he was staying for the summer in order to economize. It was too easy, living there, and he didn't really like waking up in his single bed in his childhood room, across from his snoring brother, though Gordon was delighted to have him back.

While he was up in the attic, Duncan looked for and found stamped numbers on the sides of several rafters. Remembering what he had learned at the Frank Lloyd Wright lecture, he next went down to the cellar and checked under the stairs, where he found, glued to one of the risers, the remnants of a red and gold shipping label with a faint return address on Homan Avenue in Chicago. So it was true—he had grown up in a Sears kit house.

The small mystery of the inexplicable plinth block at the bottom of the staircase in the front hall made sense at last. Though framing members were delivered pre-cut, some of the moldings and baseboard trim were not, because of variations in plaster wall thickness. Sears kit houses came with simplified construction plans that provided the option of a block form at points where complex joints met, so that even an inexperienced carpenter could finish a house neatly.

As a child, Duncan had studied this odd feature with fascination. He had loved to run his Hot Wheels and Match-box cars along the baseboard moldings all the way down the stairs, as he bumped along on the carpeted steps on his bottom, and each time, when he had reached this block at the bottom of the stairs, he would slam on the imaginary brakes, with screechy sound effects that annoyed his mother, in order not to crash.

The demand for a Corrigan & Wheeler house was apparently impervious to economic downturns (Billy always called their prosperous clients "recession-proof"), and had continued unabated since Billy's death. Duncan had never imagined having the kind of money that now flowed his way reliably, in a steady stream, month after month. His money earned a living of its own. He had become one of those people his mother used to call "rich from having money." But it had never occurred to Duncan to move to a bigger house, or design and build a house of his own (which would raise expectations impossibly). He liked everything the way it was. Laura didn't want a bigger or different house either. Neither of them aspired to drive an expensive car. Nevertheless, it felt good, being rewarded with so much money for his work, and being rich was surely an important measure of success.

"That's money in the bank," Billy Corrigan used to say of prime gossip about potential clients, or an A-list weekend invitation in the Hamptons, or a feature in the *New York Times* Home section. But Duncan thought that there was something even better than that kind of money in the bank—actual money in the bank.

At the last partners meeting before the accident, there had been at least three years of contracted projects in the pipeline, providing more than enough work for Duncan, his three partners, and the six associates, along with another dozen employees, from the shop drawing staff and model builder to the office manager. There were five associates now. Todd Walker had not been replaced.

Todd's drafting table by the windows in the stylish Corrigan & Wheeler offices that occupied an old brick ladder factory on River Street had not been touched, Duncan had noted the previous week, on the one occasion when he had let Laura persuade him to make a pitiful visit he didn't think he could bear to repeat for a long time. The office had gone quiet when he rolled off the elevator for the first time since the accident, and everyone had stopped working, and the staff had all been too respectful and cheerful, greeting him warmly but with nervous eye contact that didn't last.

As Duncan motored down the middle aisle of the big central work space, his chair bumping over the scarred floorboards that bore the outlined grooves of the machinery on the ghost assembly line that once filled the space of the ladder factory, he could see, down the row of work stations on the window side, the end drafting table and desk that Todd had inhabited. There was Todd's copper-shaded drafting lamp that had been his grandfather's, and the stool he had made out of a bicycle seat, and his cobalt glass jar of pens and pencils. There were his beautiful stainless steel helical gears that he used to weigh down the curling edges of blueprints, and on the sill, his idiotic collection of wind-up toys—all of it was just sitting there, neatly blank, waiting for Todd, having not got the news that he wasn't coming back.

At their last birthday, when Duncan and Gordon blew out thirty-seven birthday candles together, Duncan had suddenly wished for piano lessons. It just came into his head and he wished for it. He hadn't played since he left home to go to Hotchkiss. This was supposed to have been the year he would take up piano again. That was back in April, a million years ago. He had been so full of resolve and intention, he had even looked up the phone number for a piano teacher one of the associates mentioned when he was raving about his kid's recital, but Duncan had never gotten around to calling her. Too late now. What can you play with two weak fingers of your left hand? Okay, The Happy Farmer had a left-handed melody. Didn't Schumann have something wrong with his right hand? And Scriabin did too, but he was also short and crazy. And Django Reinhardt had a couple of missing fingers, blah blah, triumph over adversity, lemonade out of lemons. Not really.

Ottoline, comfortably perched on his shoulder, sighed contentedly and tugged at his ear as she peered inside, probing delicately, as if the state of his ears was her responsibility. With his head turned slightly, which was as far as it would turn, Duncan could just glimpse down the block where the dark green Subaru wagon was parked slightly nearer to the hydrant than was probably legal. It belonged to the couple next door, Frank and Jesse, who both taught in the Yale English Department. Frank was the Victorianist, while Jesse was the post-Colonialist. Duncan could never quite retain what that actually meant, post-Colonialist, though it had been explained to him pretty thoroughly over dinner when Frank and Jesse first moved in (they called each other "my husband") and Laura invited them over one night for Duncan's grilled butterflied leg of lamb, his perfect summer dinner party specialty he would never cook again.

Sure, he could talk Laura through it step by step, from the butterflying of the whole leg on the big chopping block they had brought back from a Vermont ski trip (no more ski trips), through the marinating with garlic and rosemary from the garden (the herb beds along the wall were overrun by mint and myrtle) and just the right red wine. Roast lamb being very rich and robust, Duncan always used an earthy Australian Syrah, both for the marinade and at the table. This was Duncan's genius theory, that Syrah, earthy and complex, is the lamb of wines. True charcoal, never briquettes, the timing of the coals for perfect grilling—he had all the elements down to a science. How could it possibly be worth the effort that would be required now to reconstitute the kind of careless, easy summer night they used to have? Just getting through each day (never mind grilling a leg of lamb!)

required careful planning and timing, with the myriad details of Duncan's needs anticipated thoroughly, and even then, so many things could and did go wrong, all the time. Every day. This was no way to live.

Jesse and Frank parked their second car, an old Subaru, down the street to avoid the paint-damaging sap from the silver maple tree that shaded this part of the block. Duncan and Laura used to deplore the sap stains eating the paint of their stately gray toboggan of a Volvo wagon, the car that had saved Duncan's life. The car that had not saved Todd Walker's life. Their ugly new hospital-looking van, equipped with a wheelchair lift and a raised roof, now occupied the space directly out front, in the newly-designated handicapped parking space, with the sign reserving it that announced to the world a cripple lived here.

A lucky cripple. Duncan had come to despise that word, lucky, a word many people uttered carelessly in the days after the accident, each one of them certain that this line of reasoning was helpful to Duncan. He should be ecstatic and grateful that he was alive! And that other than having a C6 spinal cord injury, he survived the accident with hardly a scratch! Gosh, he hadn't thought about it that way! Absolutely! Thank you so much!

Good bad luck, Jack Wheeler used to say, when selling comprehensive insurance policies to his clients, is an accident you walk away from, though of course, you might not want to say that to Duncan. His bitterly sarcastic expressions of gratitude for the wise reminders about his wonderful luck for having survived the wreck had not been taken personally by anyone. He was fogged by drugs. He didn't know what he was saying. (He knew exactly what he was saying.) Define luck. Is it an absolute certainty that Duncan Wheeler (why yes, he had indeed become aware of the irony of his last name, but thanks for pointing it out) was luckier than Todd Walker (who had not walked away)?

Ottoline went back to grooming Duncan's hair, sifting her way around the back of his head, pausing from time to time to nibble some invisible particle with dainty concentration, which made him wonder if on top of everything else he had developed some kind of quadriplegic dandruff. Why not? The back of his head was nearly always pressed against a pillow or support of some kind. She tightened her grip on his shoulder and rebalanced as he toggled an adjustment of his chair, tilting himself a little bit further back. Duncan was supposed to change his position often, to ease the perpetual stress on his hips and back, though he also simply liked the way the tiniest pressure on the toggle with one finger made the chair move. It was one of the few things he could do for himself, one of the few satisfactions in his day.

Duncan rotated the chair away from the window, and Ottoline slid down from his shoulder to his lap, where she settled in contentedly, holding onto his curled right wrist with one of her cool little hands. He petted her again, tentatively, with the edge of his left hand, and she seemed to like it. The coffee maker beeped completion in the empty kitchen. Duncan wanted to roll into the kitchen to help himself to coffee (the most ordinary small activity of daily living a man should be able to do in his own house!), but he had made a promise not to try lifting a full carafe of hot coffee ever again, not after the catastrophic incident the previous month which had burned him badly across his thighs, though neither he nor Laura had realized the extent of the burn until many hours after the broken glass had been swept away and his coffee-soaked lap had been blotted. Of course he had not felt it.

His blistered flesh had healed very slowly (there were still dressings that had to be changed daily), because the deep, oozing wounds had developed a vicious infection, which had led to a devastating gut infection which knocked him flat, and it was all a clusterfuck, an avoidable and utterly discouraging setback that had landed him in the hospital again, for ten days. A hospital rabbi had come to call on him one afternoon, because Laura had thoughtlessly ticked the box on the hospital admission form identifying Duncan as Jewish. The wisdom of the Torah has been given to us by God, the rabbi told him, settling in beside the bed for a chat. The only religion that could possibly interest me is one without God, Duncan told the rabbi, before closing his eyes and keeping them closed until he heard the rabbi's departing footsteps. Lying there, developing a pressure sore that was still a problem, smelling the foulness that ran out of his wrecked body, he had made the decision. Six months. He would give it six months.

Duncan wanted his iced coffee. Laura would prepare it for him the way he liked it: fresh, strong coffee poured over lots of ice, with a swirl of milk and a tiny splash of maple syrup. Preferably Grade B maple syrup. He was impatient for Laura to finish her garden tour or whatever it was they were up to out there in the crisp autumn sunshine without him. Didn't they want to see how well he was doing with Ottoline? Surely Martha should be observing their bonding. Was it even safe to leave them alone this way? Didn't Laura want see what was going on so she could be right about one more thing, so she could hoist her invisible flag of moral superiority just a little higher?

Since he had been home from this last hospitalization, she had got into this habit of taking visitors, even, at times, his personal care assistants when they arrived for or departed from their shifts, "to see the garden," which was clearly a ploy to have conversations he couldn't overhear. Was she complaining to Martha about his unpleasantness and gloom? Or was she having one of her noble days, soaking up sympathy and praise for her patience and fortitude in this disastrous situation? She had never before spent so much time in their backyard, except when they had people over, and on those occasions she would always accept praise graciously for the exuberant perennial borders. It was all Duncan's vision, she would demur, which implied, falsely, though she never literally claimed it, that she did in fact have a hand in the hours of planting and weeding and deadheading in the garden.

"What are they doing out there, Ottoline?" he asked experimentally. She cheeped, responding to her name, and hopped from his lap up onto his shoulder, lifting her lead with her tail gracefully, the better to check through his hair some more. He cheeped back, imitating her noises, and she made a clicking, purring sound. Duncan willed Laura to come back in the house and make his iced coffee, and bring it to him with a long flexible straw, and place it on the tray she would clip to his chair. If he was having a clumsy day with his one partially useful claw of a hand, which he was, despite the daily tenodesis grip exercises that were supposed to help, Laura would guide the straw to his mouth and he would sip gratefully and resentfully, because every moment of every waking hour had these patience-requiring complications and compromises. Maybe it was possible Ottoline could make this different, maybe she really could do things for Duncan that he couldn't do for himself. All kinds of things.

He badly wanted Laura back in the kitchen right now, available to fulfill his needs, even as he relished rare moments in a day, like this one, when he was alone in the house and he could just exist without accepting ministrations, without having to ask someone for something he wanted or needed. There were five different strangers who came and went on a schedule that Laura managed skillfully. From one day to the next these personal care assistants—PCAs—each took care of him. Hours of every day were devoted to hygiene, maintenance of his bowel program, the assisted coughing regimen, catheter changes, clothing changes, all the careful, patient maneuvers, the transfers in and out of his bed and wheelchair. Four women and a man, each of them kind and capable. Laura had started saying that thing people say, that Cathy and Darlene and Mounika and Ida Mae and Wendell had each become "just like family."

But what does that mean, just like family? Laura herself was an only child of a single mother who apparently had no relatives she cared to know. Laura had never met a single blood relation other than her mother's father, whom she met once, and he was now long dead. She wouldn't know where to begin to look for her father. Between them, their only living parent was Laura's poor demented mother, who now lived in a nursing home. Other than his weird, semi-functional twin brother, the only family Duncan could claim were a few distant aunts and great-aunts and great-uncles in places like Florida and Myrtle Beach, and a few cousins—their children—dull, unimaginative people who lived their boring, contented lives in Hoboken and Great Neck. Just like family as in just like tedious people with whom you have nothing in common at all, beyond a genetic bond? Just like all the relatives you only ever see at funerals and you don't care if you ever see again? Just like family except pleasant and steadily employed taking care of a smashed, helpless cripple?

Even with the personal care assistants present at crucial intervals each day, Duncan felt that he was perpetually asking Laura for something. She was perfectly willing to do whatever he asked, as she so often reminded him, but even so, he minded the small deprivations of minor comforts and adjustments he didn't feel he had the right to demand continually. She never ground enough pepper onto his food. For some reason she just twisted the small blue pepper grinder (they had bought it years ago at an outdoor market in the Périgord, to take on a memorable picnic hike to see Roman ruins, along with two blue-checked napkins, a jar of duck confit, a local runny cheese in wax paper, a crusty baguette, and a slightly sweet Bergerac they had to drink from the bottle, having made no provision for glasses) a couple of times and then set it down, even though she ought to realize that Duncan had always been a vigorous grinder of pepper at nearly every meal. It was a small thing, but every day was now a broken series of unsuccessful gestures, and there was something ugly about this life that had once been so rich in small quotidian pleasures. What could they still be looking at in the backyard? What kind of conversation were they having so deliberately out of earshot?

He hit the control again and tilted himself a little more upright before rolling over to the side window. Ottoline scrambled across his chest onto his other shoulder, lifting the leash behind her delicately with her tail, like a lady raising her skirts to step over a puddle. They gazed out at the world together. Here they were, the two of them. This is what it would be like. Suddenly, Ottoline uncoiled herself from her perch by his left ear and extended one arm with the expertise of an infielder reaching for an easy line drive, snatching the fly that had been buzzing and bumping fitfully on the window. She hopped down into his lap and pinched the fly between two fingers skillfully to kill it, before rolling it between her palms into a ball—precisely the way Duncan remembered rolling dough balls out of sandwich bread at overnight camp—and then she popped it into her mouth.

As she chewed her pulverized morsel, Ottoline gazed up at Duncan. He praised her softly, Good girl! imitating Martha's nursery school tone, though he wasn't certain if devouring flies skillfully qualified as praiseworthy behavior by Institute standards, and she reached up with one hand and patted his face, chirping softly and looking him in the eye, meeting his gaze, holding his gaze. Duncan was flooded with intense feeling he didn't understand. As tears began to brim in his eyes, Ottoline chirped and touched his face again. She stroked his stubble and then she put her forefinger against his upper lip, as if hushing him, soothing him the way his grandmother had when he was a little boy, when she would come into their room at bedtime and tell her grandsons her Talmudic story about the angels sent by God to every baby.

First the angel teaches each baby the entire Torah, Grandma Rose would say, then the angel hushes the learned baby with a finger pressed right here on the baby's upper lip, right under that little nose, and here she would press her finger first on Duncan's upper lip and then on Gordon's, and in this way the angel would make this indentation we all have, shushing each baby so he will keep his knowledge secret. Ottoline stroked his upper lip again with that gentle and familiar gesture, gazing up at him lovingly, not minding his secrets.

# TWO

## *Todd Walker's gentle touch on Duncan's neck*

TODD WALKER'S GENTLE TOUCH ON DUNCAN'S NECK was a startling and soothing blip of kindness against the hateful burn of the hornet sting just above his Adam's apple. The bold viciousness of the sting shocked Duncan. A moment before, he and Todd had been depositing their armloads of drawings and blueprints, along with job binders stuffed with work orders and town permits, into the oven-like cargo space in the back of Duncan's Volvo wagon after their site visit. Then came the sudden violent injection of fire into his neck.

The car had been parked for nearly four hours in the fifteen-minute zone along Indian Point Road at the top of the Stony Creek town dock, the usual parking ticket tucked under a wiper blade. Duncan got a ticket each time he made a site visit to the Steiner house on Biscuit Island, not only because wherever he went he was always running a few minutes late, but also because of the added complications on this project of the fifteen-minute boat ride to the job site, and the waits on either side of that.

On every site visit, Duncan was inevitably in too much of a hurry to park somewhere a little farther away in a valid street space or in the municipal lot, no matter how often he meant to leave the office early enough to park the car legally. It wasn't clear if racking up parking fines by hogging a fifteen-minute space for several hours a couple of times a week was a positive or negative for his firm's relationship with the village. Found money for the village, yes, but also arrogant flat-lander behavior that was probably resented. The firm should probably make some donations to the town library or the athletic association, and any other civic association they could support, in order to stay in the good graces of residents who frequently sat on multiple town boards.

If pushed, in Duncan's experience, some small town commissions in Connecticut would play the ace—the possibility of a Native American burial mound on the land. Waiting for a state archeologist to inspect the site and research the town records and write an authorizing report before a teaspoon of soil could be shifted could delay a project for a year. As it was, obtaining all the permits and approvals required to start the job had made abundantly evident to everyone working on the Steiner House at Corrigan & Wheeler just how unsympathetic Stony Creekers were to the Steiner family's desire to treat themselves to a home gym, wine cellar, screening room, and poolside entertainment pavilion.

As he shoved the parking ticket into the Steiner job binder already stuffed with an accumulation of older parking tickets and other miscellaneous billable receipts, Duncan was still feeling lightheaded and slightly queasy from the diesel fumes and the choppy ride back from Biscuit Island on the ferry, one of two commercial boats piloted by loquacious captains who provided commentary for tourists about each of the islands as they meandered from one to the next. In the morning they had taken the more efficient charter ferry directly to Biscuit Island, but instead of waiting for the ferry to come chugging back for them, nearly an hour after it had failed to appear at the agreed-upon time, which had happened before (because so many Thimble Islanders used the ferry in season to make grocery and liquor store deliveries as well as haul supplies, which included, for several houses, enormous multiple drums of potable water), they had hailed the next passing tour boat, which was occupied by about a dozen tourists, most of them older couples, sitting complacently in the shade enjoying their five-dollar excursion. The unscheduled Biscuit Island stop was an adventure in itself for the tourists, and several of them took photographs. Duncan and Todd had stood together at the aft railing most of the way back to the Stony Creek marina.

Todd had seemed to enjoy the motion of the boat, standing squarely with his hands clasped behind his neck, balancing effortlessly, staring out into the blue day in a reverie as the sun glimmered in the down on the back of his hands, his half-buttoned white shirt fluttering around him like a topsail.

Duncan had tried to match Todd's precision and grace. He had once skied flawlessly down an entire run in Killington behind an exceptionally beautiful skier, a local guy in his twenties who worked Ski Patrol shifts in the winter and took construction jobs in the summer. They had shared the chairlift to the top of the mountain, and Duncan had skied behind him all the way down, staying in his swooping tracks, following the lovely rhythm of his sweeping turns, exhilarated by this borrowed agility. Now Duncan stood beside Todd, mirroring his insouciance: standing tall, riding the swells, balancing without touching the railing, his hands clasped behind his head. But Duncan couldn't match his equipoise and kept staggering against the railing, knocked off-kilter by the way the ferry bumped over the irregular swells, a losing struggle with awkwardness and nausea. Failed *sprezzatura*.

Finally Duncan dropped his hands to his sides and turned away, unsteadily seeking a bench in the shade with the tourists, hating the glare, the diesel stink, and the engine din. Todd was endlessly adaptable, it seemed. Duncan was just not made of the same stuff as the prosperous denizens of the Thimbles, who took pride in all the complexities and discomforts of daily living in their little New England archipelago.

He never saw the hornet, but Todd, the possessor of a varied collection of delicate, papery shards of honeycombed hornet nests, caught a glimpse as it helicoptered away.

"Big, bad motherfucker of a Vespa."

"Like the scooter? What?" Duncan couldn't think at all for a moment as the bomb of venom burned hotter at his throat. He realized he was crying. He swallowed a sob as he took an unsteady step in no direction, and then another, going in a small circle behind the car, clenching his fists and trying not to panic about the possibility of his throat closing. He heard himself emitting a grunting pant like an animal caught in a trap. His heart was galloping. He had never felt anything like this.

Duncan was known at Corrigan & Wheeler for his reserve and his calm demeanor. He knew his employees liked to imitate certain hesitations in his speech, the vestiges of his childhood stutter, a pause between words and sentences that evinced his thoughtful pursuit of clarity and precision in language as in his architectural designs. (He once overheard bursts of laughter from the copy room accompanying an associate's flawlessly intoned, "I . . . will . . . have . . . a . . . chicken . . . salad sandwich . . . on . . . rye . . . . . . . . . . toast.")

Duncan enjoyed site visit days like this with Todd. He liked the feeling of being in charge, the wise senior architect, mentor to the ambitious, deferential apprentice. Now, in an instant, Duncan felt helpless in front of this twenty-five-year-old junior draftsman who was always trying to impress him.

Todd was a bustling, carelessly graceful young man who moved through every minute of his life as if he was on the verge of careening down a mountain or diving under a wave.

He possessed an innate competence and openness that made people like him. He was unabashed in his desire for Duncan's approval of his work. Duncan was reserved and measured in his approbation, though he secretly indulged himself by being a little more fascinated by Todd Walker than he felt he ought to be or would ever want anyone to recognize. There was nothing more to it. The famous Duncan Wheeler hesitation and reserve created a useful distance. Now, in this moment, he was helpless as he let Todd take him by the arm and steer him a few cautious steps over to the low blocks of Portland brownstone that bordered the little park adjacent to the marina.

Todd pushed Duncan's shoulders gently downward until he was sitting on the seawall, and then he bent over solicitously, carefully tracing the swollen zone around the sting with a delicate touch, just grazing the side of Duncan's neck lightly with his fingers. Duncan sat still with his eyes closed, his hurtling heart insisting and insisting. He tried to remember the correct word for this. Tachycardia. Fibrillation. Arrhythmia. Surely, one of those. His mother's heart condition in her final years had expanded his cardiac vocabulary. A-fib? Not a lion heart but a lying heart. He opened his eyes. Todd was gone.

He was over at the nearby ice locker across from Thimble Marine Service. Duncan watched as Todd fished deep inside along the front edge for something. Oh, clever lad, he was feeling for the inevitable loose ice on the bottom that had escaped from broken bags. Todd grabbed a couple of handfuls of ice and placed them on the grass, no, he was bundling the ice into that big white old man's handkerchief he always carried. Like his pocket watch and his winter galoshes that buckled, the handkerchief was one of Todd Walker's carefully curated details that Duncan found endearing yet also just a little irritating. As was true of so many of his generation, Todd thought he was entirely original in all of his gentleman hobo hipster choices. His architectural design work, the few times he was given opportunities to be wholly original, was actually far more inventive than his personal style, which included mitten-knitting and cigar-box-banjo strumming. In winter there were dizzying combinations of plaid flannel and touching quarts of bizarrely-flavored rhubarb chutney (made with spices brought back from his trip to India). This home-made tracklement, in pale blue antique canning jars with zinc lids, had been placed on every desk or drafting table at Corrigan & Wheeler at Christmas. The previous snowy winter, Todd had arrived more than once on wooden snowshoes; when he walked around the office in his vintage corduroy knickers and woolen leggings, he squeaked. Did he compete in hoop-trundling tourneys on the weekend? Duncan's secret mental nickname for Todd Walker was Penrod.

Now Todd was standing over him, holding the swaddled ice in his two hands. He gently placed the cold bundle against Duncan's neck and held it there. The beginning of relief, or at least the idea of it. After a moment, he switched to one hand in order to pick up one of Duncan's hands from his lap and guide it gently in place so Duncan could take over holding the ice pack himself. Duncan could feel his heart slow down.

"Better?"

Duncan looked for the horizon to anchor himself, but the harsh glare of sunlight sparkling off the choppy water tilted him back and made him feel as if he were still bobbing on the nauseating Thimble Islands ferry. Did he feel better or worse? He nodded anyway, trying to surf the vertiginous sensations and hoping that he was in fact sensing a slight dimming of the nearly electrical pain current glowing down his neck.

Twenty minutes later, the ice had melted, though Duncan continued to hold Todd's wadded, dripping handkerchief against his neck. He had tried to stay focused on observing the plovers picking their way through the marsh grass at the water's edge, while circling gulls occasionally let out raucous cries and dropped down into the water and disappeared, popping up moments later to bob on the swells. His heart rate had returned to normal and now he had started to shiver, even in the baking sun, suddenly feeling drenched in his own cooling sweat. Watching over him, Todd had devoured a coffee ice cream cone from Thimbleberry in precise clockwise bites with a deft turn-bite-turn-bite system.

On their way to Stony Creek that morning, as they passed a Branford farm stand with a big CORN sign out front, just before the turn for the marina, they had chatted desultorily about family food traditions, and had agreed on the best way to butter an ear of corn—namely, a two-handed twirling rotation of a steaming (boiled for no more than four minutes!) ear of corn directly on a concaved stick of butter dedicated to this function.

Duncan's Hoboken cousins made a barbaric practice of rubbing a pat of butter onto the corn with a folded slice of sandwich bread, without apparent sensitivity to the egregious crumb factor. Laura did this too. It drove him nuts. His twin brother didn't like butter on his corn at all, which was probably just as well, since when Gordon had bicycled on back roads from Madison to New Haven in time for dinner a few days earlier, they had had the first local corn of the season, and when Duncan drove him home (it had gotten late, and it was raining), with the bike stowed in the back of the Volvo, he had noticed multiple stray kernels in his brother's beard, which was also startlingly threaded with gray, which had made Duncan realize that his own chin whiskers, if he ever let them grow for more than a weekend, would look exactly the same (minus the corn).

Todd had then told Duncan about his older brother's wife from Kennebunkport, whose family sliced the kernels off the cobs in a crazy synchronized ritual involving heirloom silver fish knives and cobalt finger bowls, and they had laughed together about that. As he continued to hold the melting ice against his neck, Duncan watched Todd unroll the last furl of dunce cap paper from the pointed cone end, which he popped into his mouth and crunched down in a final perfect, disciplined, precise bite.

The elegant Corrigan & Wheeler addition and renovation to the Steiner house, which was called Spartina, were finally underway, despite so many delays and problems that it had seemed an unbuildable, hopeless project more than once. One of three houses on Biscuit, this Victorian wedding cake of a cottage had long ago been the summer home of a minor Jazz Age movie star few people could remember, though she was once famous for the way she wiggled her bottom when she sang, and was said to have been the inspiration for Betty Boop. The house sat squarely in the middle of a granite out-cropping punctuated by tufty clumps of the Spartina grass for which the cottage had been named in 1897 by the first owner, an amateur marine biologist who drowned beside his rowboat under mysterious circumstances, at low tide, a stone's throw from the town dock, just before his house was fin-ished. Spartina occupied the better, seaward half of Biscuit Island and was the grandest of the three houses on the two-acre island. The other two simpler little Capes had been built in the 1920's by the forgotten movie star to house her sum-mer staff. Her legendary weekend house parties were men-tioned in several memoirs of the era.

Spartina was ornamented with Corinthian columns sup-porting the deep porches on every side. The majestic white house was replete with gingerbread trim—pierced frieze boards, scrolled brackets, sawn balusters, and braced arches—and the inventory of Victorian un-subtlety included six chimneys, four bay windows, three towers (one surmounted by a widow's walk that was said to be haunted by the ghost of the drowned biologist's spinster sister), two turrets, and oriel windows galore.

The small patch of mowed lawn beside the house was actually a three-hole putting green, and there was a saltwater swimming pool tucked artfully into a rockery at the edge of the leeward side of the island, below which a swathe of rugosa roses sloped down to the seawall constructed of massive gray blocks of Stony Creek granite. An oversized octagonal gazebo squatted on the end of the floating dock.

Duncan loathed that gazebo, which had clearly come from a catalogue of Amish ready-mades. He thought it was inelegant and disproportionate, a real eyesore, but the Steiners adored it. At their first Corrigan & Wheeler meeting, nearly three years ago (when it was known that Centerbrook was also in a final audition for this plum job), Mimi and Bob Steiner had each told him, in nearly identical words (it was clearly a cherished story they liked to tell about themselves), how a glimpse of the romantic gazebo from the Thimble Island Ferry as they passed by on their way to visit friends on Davis Island for a Fourth of July weekend was one of the reasons they had fallen in love with Spartina before they even set foot on the island. He certainly had no intention of touching it, not now, anyway, though its egregiousness pained him every time he saw it from the water, long before he clambered off the boat onto the pristine, weather-scoured dock where it perched.

"Never shame your client," Billy Corrigan admonished Duncan long ago, when he had been employed as a junior draftsman only a few weeks, after his first disastrous meeting with Meg and Hank Waxman. "Always make the client feel smart and creative. Let the client think he is a design partner whose ideas fascinate and inspire you."

The Waxman Pavilion had been built on the lawn in the backyard behind the Waxmans' original Cos Cob house. The initial commission was for a simple guest cottage, but as the project progressed, it had metamorphosed into an award-winning two-story structure twice the size of the original design. The Waxmans slept in the Pavilion when they felt like it, while retaining their stately, traditional main house as a place to keep all but a few of their possessions, do their laundry, and cook most of their meals. When the many Waxman children and grandchildren visited, they all stayed in the main house, while Meg and Hank slept in the Pavilion, like happy children camping in a pup tent in their backyard.

Within months of its completion, the Waxman Pavilion appeared in various publications (Billy Corrigan employed a great publicist), and it went on to win several design awards. Corrigan's generous yet intimately-scaled spaces were more than a hat-tip to the American vernacular of his miserable childhood in Nebraska. His essential and abiding mission as an architect was to deliberately evoke the barns, detached kitchens, and smokehouses of rural America for his demanding, rich clients who had never forked hay into a loft or butchered a hog and smoked a ham in their privileged lives, though they loved the architectural gestures and references. His clients were oblivious to the deeply cynical sensibility of his work. Before Billy grew fatigued and declared a moratorium on backyard pavilions, nine other Corrigan clients had commissioned similar elegant play houses so they could escape the formal constraints of their main houses, an impulse Marie Antoinette understood perfectly.

The reason for that first regrettable visit to the Waxmen (as they were known around the office) in those early days of Duncan's employment in Billy Corrigan's office was to show preliminary designs addressing Meg and Hank's newfound desire for a dovecote. A dovecote! Duncan had spoken a little too forcefully, almost scornfully, when Meg and Hank Waxman hesitated to accept his elegant plan for a pergola on the west side of the Pavilion that would echo the details of the proposed hexagonal dovecote, thus linking the disparate forms of the two structures. He had spent most of his week-end on the simple elevation drawing. The detail work on this project was Duncan's first significant assignment in the office that was more than rote drafting, and he was anxious to make the most of it and impress Billy Corrigan. It simply hadn't occurred to him that, above all, he needed to please Meg and Hank Waxman, whose fortune derived from a vast institutional food service business that specialized in prisons and hospitals across the country. They were dull, friendly people who depended on artists like Billy Corrigan to make them interesting. They seemed to Duncan more like sturdy public school gym teachers than rich design aficionados.

In that meeting, with his splendid and underappreciated drawing in the center of their original Hans Wegner dining table, Duncan was so eager to make his presentation that he had interrupted Hank and contradicted Meg. By the time they left the meeting, Duncan, as naïve as he was arrogant, was certain that reason had prevailed and aesthetic judgment had carried the day. Billy Corrigan took Duncan off the Waxman Dovecote within hours, a shaming rebuke he never forgot, though in the end, a modified version of his pergola design made them happy, and the Waxman Dovecote became known as a classic Billy Corrigan gesture. Architecture students still studied it avidly.

At Billy's funeral, Duncan felt a rogue wave of that old ignominy wash over him when he saw the Waxmans—the Waxmen—both of them now hollowed out by age and startlingly desiccated and spotted and bleached. They had become relics of themselves. Though they still owned and loved their Cos Cob property, they told him ruefully, their accountant insisted, for tax reasons, that they now spend at least a hundred and ninety nights of each year in Boca Raton, in their spectacular new Hugh Newell Jacobsen house. It was scheduled to be on the cover of the June issue of *Architectural Digest*.

"We really loved working with Hugh!" Meg told him emphatically. "He was inspired by all of our ideas!" Billy Corrigan was right. Never shame your client.

Duncan had made a mistake, remaining out in the blazing sun on the return ferry ride for as long as he did, too long, standing there at the railing with Todd. He hated making mistakes. He had left behind, somewhere at the site, his favorite old Panama hat, one of several brimmed hats he wore prudently outdoors to protect his tender bald spot. Another mistake. He had taken it off to swap it for the borrowed, legally required hard hat when they arrived on the site. Todd had brought along in his canvas rucksack his own vintage coal miner's helmet, complete with a working brass headlamp.

As the ferry chugged a meandering course from one island to another, while the captain name-dropped both past and current owners, Duncan had tried to breathe normally and keep his gaze on the horizon as he fought his rising seasickness. It was so easy for Todd, standing beside him in his beautiful, confident way. Next time they would have to get more of a commitment from Mr. D, the water taxi captain, about their pickup. Or maybe the office should just buy a damned dinghy and outboard to use for the duration of the job, though there were probably all kinds of mooring requirements and permits and fees and rules about the town dock that would tangle them up, plus it would be a disaster on rainy days. As he gave up and staggered over to a seat, Duncan had been irked with himself for being so susceptible to the rise and fall of the swells on this first sublime day of July. It had been an almost perfect moment.

Duncan first encountered Todd when he was in the final weeks of his final semester at the Yale School of Architecture, where Duncan lectured and was a visiting critic from time to time. Todd's prodigious talent dazzled Duncan, though he was measured in his observations of the work during the crit. But he invited him for coffee after class. The invitation did not go unnoticed by nearby architecture students zipping up their portfolios.

Duncan maintained his impassive demeanor, asking just a few questions while Todd did most of the talking as they sat at an outside table in front of the coffee shop in the bottom of Rudolph Hall. Duncan had a pang of missing the crowded little café with a spectacular view of New Haven that in his student days used to be on the top floor of what was then called the Art & Architecture Building, before the most recent blanding renovation by Gwathmey Siegel of Paul Rudolph's brutal concrete monument to himself. But it was nice to be outside. There was something about the spring afternoon on York Street that day which gave it the fresh, optimistic air of a drawing for a presentation of a beautifully successful urban streetscape. Time seemed to slow. He could sit there all day, thought Duncan, as he settled into the spindly folding chair and stretched his long legs out in front of him while he gazed across the street at the tidy west facade of the Yale Art Gallery, mapping Louis Kahn's elegant structure as if he were looking at an axonometric drawing, mentally following the route through the maze of galleries to the conservation lab where Laura was probably working at that very moment.

For more than an hour, long after their coffee was finished, while each of them kept setting aside awareness of impending lateness to afternoon obligations, Todd had rambled from one topic to the next, almost puppyish in his effort to please and impress Duncan, who occasionally prompted him to keep talking. In fact, Duncan *was* impressed.

He offered Todd a position with Corrigan & Wheeler just a few days later. Just as Duncan had been brought in by Billy Corrigan when he was green and inexperienced, stirring jealousies and raising eyebrows among the other architects in the practice, Todd came in as a junior associate, leapfrogging over the usual internship and probationary apprentice slots where he would have worked under one of the senior associates for six months, as was the customary practice. Within a few months Todd had become Duncan's right hand, his sidekick, his protégé, his lightfoot lad, his acolyte, his scrivener, his amanuensis, as one of the older Corrigan partners, Jack Simon, had once sardonically dubbed Duncan himself, behind his back. But there was a significant difference: Todd Walker was clearly a wonderfully bright and ambitious young architect who would have done well anywhere. It was Duncan who might never have risen to the top in any firm if he had not been chosen and anointed by Billy Corrigan. He never knew that Peter Eisenman had named him to Billy Corrigan and suggested that he hire him, specifically because of that brilliant parody of a Four-Square House. It was a calculated and cynical recommendation on Eisenman's part, because he recognized his old friend and rival's narcissistic hunger for just the right reasonably attractive and talented young architect to be his heir apparent. Eisenman saw in Duncan someone who could be content mimicking the Corrigan style flawlessly and perpetually, someone with the necessary talent and polish who could be willing to abrogate his own creative ambitions.

Duncan had tried to ignore his escalating queasiness with each speeding up and slowing down on the swells as the ferry wove through the outer islands and then circled around for the concluding narration of the history of Sheep Nose, Kettle Rock, Butternut, Bean Stack, Big Dipper, Little Dipper, and then finally Little Hodgson, the nearest island to the town dock.

Some of the large islands were dotted with little villages of a dozen or more houses, while others were much grander, with just one or two imposing houses. Three of the inhabited Thimbles near Biscuit were very small, each with just a single house perched on a partly-submerged dome of seamed basalt. The siting of those lone houses made Duncan uneasy. He tried to imagine how it could possibly have seemed like a good idea a hundred years ago to row out into Long Island Sound and erect stately homes in such precarious settings. Didn't anyone recognize that the existence of those dwellings would appear as purposeless and temporary as a dragonfly on a rock?

Duncan was surprised that Todd didn't know how to drive stick shift. He was a New York City kid (Dalton, then five years in the architecture program at Cooper Union), and when he was at Yale for his graduate degree in architecture he had finally gotten a driver's license, but Todd had never owned a car. Todd seemed near tears as he admitted that he had simply never learned how to shift gears and use a clutch. They debated whether to call and ask Lloyd, the summer intern who possessed a ratty MGB convertible he had restored himself (Todd had helped him sew a patch on the mossy soft top), to drive out to Stony Creek in somebody's borrowed car with an automatic transmission so they could swap for the drive back. Was it really necessary? Duncan's head was clearing, the formerly tilting horizon was now staying appropriately level, and he could no longer feel his heart galloping under his shirt. He swallowed experimentally. The welt just above his Adam's apple was still quite painful, but it was no longer charged. Partly out of a desire to protect Todd's pride, and partly out of a desire to enjoy a tiny competitive spark of triumph over this imperfection in his protégé, Duncan decided he was okay to get behind the wheel of the Volvo and make the short drive back into New Haven. The interior of the car was still baking hot. They let the air conditioning run full throttle for a few minutes with all the doors open.

Duncan stood beside the open driver's door for a last moment in the fresh air, looking out over the roof of the car to the shimmering blur of horizon where the sea met the sky, out beyond the hazy contours of Potato, Governor, and Cut-in-Two that punctuated the outer harbor. He watched two Thomas Eakins boys loading a skiff with old rope lobster pots at the town dock. He could smell his own sweat in an unusual way. The back of his shirt was still soaked unpleasantly. Duncan stretched to relieve his tight lower back. He ached all over, as if his entire body had been clenched. He rocked his hips forward and back a couple of times the way Laura had shown him, tilting his pelvis, feeling the stretch, feeling his hip bones connecting to his thigh bones, the longest bones in his body—standing independently with his weight on those long bones for the last time.

At the Stony Creek entrance ramp, as they accelerated onto the highway, Todd apologized all over again for his inability to drive stick shift, and promised he would learn. Duncan narrated the mechanics as he pedaled the clutch and shifted up, and then changed lanes and clutched and shifted up again to reach fifth gear, as they matched the cruising speed of the surrounding late afternoon traffic headed toward New Haven and points south. Duncan had a fleeting hallucinatory sense of the hot steering wheel softening and bending in his hands like a licorice candy rope.

The last thing Duncan could remember of this day, according to the Connecticut State Police accident report, was this moment—this non-moment—of driving through East Haven in a middle southbound lane of Interstate 95 and crossing over the Pearl Harbor Bridge. The police report did not contain any description of the conversation between Duncan and Todd as they headed back to the Corrigan & Wheeler offices on River Street. As they passed through the ugly commercial strip of big box stores and franchises and car dealers that cluttered both sides of the highway, Todd had resumed telling Duncan about his trip to India.

---

On the ferry ride out to Biscuit Island that morning, Todd had started to describe his trip the previous summer, the typical architecture student pilgrimage to Chandigarh, Le Corbusier's capital city of Punjab. Duncan had been distracted by his mental review of the punch list of issues they needed to resolve on this site visit and had not listened closely as Todd talked about his excitement in the dilapidated yet still magnificent Palace of Assembly building, though his attention had certainly been caught when Todd's voice rose with emotion as he described the celestial light flooding down onto the sequence of columns that had made him feel, he said, as if he were in a sun drenched grove of trees.

Now, as they headed back, Todd was telling him the rest of his Chandigarh story, about meeting a group of likeable Scottish architecture students at a hostel who invited him to travel with them. This had led to his crashing (as he called it, a term that made Duncan feel old every time he heard it) for several weeks with rich English people (vaguely related cousins of one of the students) in their beach house in Goa, a region Todd had every intention of exploring thoroughly, armed with his sketchbook and his architect's sensibility and desire to see whatever temples and mosques he could see. Instead, he had found himself just living on the beach from one day to the next, passing the hours with a group of amazing people from every corner of the world. This, this profound experience above all else, was what Todd had found in India.

Duncan wasn't sure what it was that Todd was really telling him when he talked about his days in Goa, though he was aware that there had been multiple references to this interlude ever since Todd had returned to New Haven from the trip at the end of the previous summer looking slightly malnourished, with not much more to show for his adventure than a bad sunburn, a collection of not entirely pleasant spices in tin boxes, and a method for cooking seafood stew in a pot over a fire with coconut milk and kokum. Todd said he still made this Goa delicacy all the time, and offered to make this dish for Duncan and Laura one day soon, with tamarind, the closest approximation to kokum likely to be found in a New Haven grocery store. Duncan wasn't remotely tempted, but agreed that they should make a plan for this dinner one day soon.

"So . . . feeling awed by Le Corbusier in Chandigarh and communing with some interesting people in Goa . . . oh, and a recipe for fish stew . . . these were your biggest takeaways from those lost weeks in India?" Duncan asked, hearing his own patronizing tone and instantly regretting it.

"Not lost weeks, found weeks."

Found weeks, oh no, oh dear. Duncan waited for some further revelation about a mystical encounter with a guru, or perhaps a romantic encounter, but Todd lapsed into pensive silence. A massive car carrier they had passed a moment earlier now slowly slid by them in the fast lane as the brake lights flashed and then stayed lit on the car in front of them. The late afternoon traffic on the Pearl Harbor Bridge that crossed over the mouth of the Quinnipiac River at the edge of New Haven Harbor had slowed to a bottlenecked crawl as they rolled in second gear through New Haven's tank farm. These eight acres of enormous fuel storage cylinders at the harbor edge always reminded Duncan uneasily of a Greenpeace meeting he attended during college at which he was given a photocopied map of nuclear bomb targets, with New Haven's tank farm as a priority bulls-eye.

"The northbound flyover from 95 is bold, but they could have done more with this element," Duncan said, breaking the long silence, gesturing at the rising harp of bridge cables as traffic picked up again. "It could have had a lot more pizzazz, this being the first cable-stayed extradosed bridge in the country. There's not much to show for it."

"Seriously, Duncan. You should go to India. Maybe you know somebody who can introduce you, so you can get inside the Villa Sarabhai. I wish I had gone to Ahmadabad when I was there. You should go. See all the major Corbu buildings and then just see India. And then go to Goa. I could introduce you to my friends there. You would love it."

Duncan shook his head without taking his eyes off the road. He could feel Todd watching him. His answer came out hesitantly as he searched for words and felt the old stammer lurking; it was always there, ready to surface when he was very tired or upset.

"You know . . . I don't think I would love it. All architects are supposed to go to India . . . and commune with Corbu , , , and have that transformative experience . . . but I don't really want to go off and do something like that . . . certainly not now . . . I'm not like you . . . I never was. Not even when I was . . . your age."

"It's not too late."

"It is . . . my heart . . . that's late," said Duncan slowly and carefully, conscious that he was borrowing these words from the lovely poem he had heard read aloud just that morning on public radio by its renowned poet laureate author, who had enunciated with force and verve every word of his poem, "Touch Me," in his elderly yet still robust poet's voice, while Duncan had made coffee in his nice kitchen in his nice house where he lived with his nice wife who might be pregnant. Did Todd listen to public radio in the morning? Perhaps he listened on a vacuum tube radio of his own devising while preparing victuals made from provisions, over a beggar's tin can stove he had brought back from Goa. Duncan signaled and shifted lanes. Trucks walled them in unpleasantly. He felt dizzy again. Traffic started to speed up.

"India changed my life. Duncan? How are you feeling? You okay?" With a careful fingertip Todd lightly traced the swelling of the hornet sting down the front of Duncan's neck.

*When you touch me, you remind me who I am.*
"I'm okay. Not great."
"India changes people."
"So you keep saying. Is change always . . . desirable?"
"We could go to India together."
Those were Todd Walker's last words.

The accident report described how the 2003 Volvo station wagon with Connecticut markers slammed head-on into the orange, plastic, water-filled Jersey barriers at Exit 46, the Long Wharf exit, while traveling at approximately forty miles per hour in the southbound lanes. It then spun into traffic, where it was hit broadside by an eighteen-wheeler from Portland, Maine, that was traveling at approximately sixty miles per hour, hauling a load of turbine engines. The eighteen-wheeler jackknifed as it crushed the Volvo against the concrete median strip. The Volvo was torn almost in two, the report said. The driver, Duncan Wheeler, 37, of New Haven, who sustained life-threatening injuries, was unconscious at the scene and required extrication with hydraulic rescue tools before being transported to Yale-New Haven Hospital. The front-seat passenger, Todd Walker, 26, of New Haven, was pronounced dead at the scene. The driver of the tractor-trailer, Cecil Pullman, 43, of Biddeford, Maine, was treated at the scene for minor injuries. Seven other passenger vehicles were involved in the collision, but there were no other significant injuries. The highway was closed to southbound traffic until 9:12 p.m.

Duncan couldn't remember or explain why they had not taken the downtown exit off 95 before reaching the Long Wharf exit, or for that matter why they hadn't taken the shortcut to River Street through East Haven. He did recall that they had agreed, on the drive out, to stop at a particular corn stand on the return trip, a plan they had both evidently forgotten. The accident report said witnesses reported seeing the car weave just before it struck the Jersey barriers. The shape of Jersey barriers reminded Duncan of Toblerone chocolate bars. The accident report stated that subsequent medical examination of the driver suggested the probability that a bee or wasp had apparently entered the car and stung him on the neck and was the most likely cause of his loss of control of his vehicle.

Duncan had whispered *I don't remember* in answer to most of the State Police accident investigator's questions, including the one about whether he had any recollection of a bee or wasp in his car just before the crash. Bees in cars were thought to be the number one cause of single car loss of control fatal accidents in daylight on dry roads, the investigator told him. The tender hornet sting just above his Adam's apple, protected by a bandage from rubbing against his cervical collar brace, marked the only part of his body Duncan was certain he could still feel.

His one memory of the accident itself was an unreportable fleeting moment of consciousness, after the slam and roar and slam of the collision, when the torn and smashed Volvo had come to its stopped stillness, and he was crushed and suspended in this brief instant of ticking quiet, before relentless actuality swarmed back in and filled up everything around him. In that brief deafening instant of silence he heard only the faint whirring sound of the engine's cooling fan. He couldn't turn his head, but what he could see at the edge of his range of vision, parts of Todd, he would never be able to un-see. An arm not connected to anything. The sharp, white stick of bone stabbed through Todd's white shirt. The enormous incurve chrysanthemums, blooming deep red and spreading across Todd's white shirt, out of season, a harbinger of autumn, in China symbolic of death but surely not here, not yet, expanding and blooming too soon, too soon, too soon, their bitter odor filling the car. And Duncan heard again the elderly poet's reedy voice speaking to him from the radio on his kitchen counter that morning as he lifted his own coffee cup to his own mouth with his own right hand for the last time.

*What makes the engine go? Desire, desire, desire.*

# THREE

## Primate Institute of New England

### New Placement Report

Placement Date: 10.22.14
Name: NORMA JEAN, A.K.A. OTTOLINE
Tufted capuchin # PI06131028
D.O.B.: unknown
Gender: F
Spayed/neutered: YES (date unknown)
Age: unknown, approximately 24–26 y.o.
Prior Placement: YES
Placement Trainer: Martha Peterson
Recipient: Duncan Wheeler, age 37, C6 spinal cord injury,
    complete
127 Lawrence Street, New Haven, CT 06511
Wheelchair dependent since: three months (injury sustained
    July 1 this year)

### Relevant History Summary (see also Leland Morris file)

Tufted female capuchin NORMA JEAN came to the Primate
Institute as a donation from Animal Control Division/
Connecticut Department of Agriculture in March of 1996.

Animal Control took custody of her when notified that she had
been abandoned on the doorstep of the Connecticut Humane
Society facility in Bethany before opening hours. Records
show that she was delivered to the Institute as she was found,
in a small parrot cage, wearing a rhinestone cat collar and a
Cabbage Patch Doll dress.

On examination she was identified as a probably spayed (later
confirmed) female with some socialization, approximately
seven years of age. She had no microchip. Her intake weight
was 3.4 kilograms and she was in somewhat malnourished but
otherwise satisfactory health, though she had a runny nose and
a skin infection on her neck caused by the too-small collar,
her fur was dirty and matted, and her toenails and fingernails
were overgrown. All of her nails were coated in several layers
of pink nail polish. There was no indication that she had been
vaccinated.

There was an unsigned handwritten letter in an envelope
attached to her cage (see medical records file for original),
presumably from the owner who abandoned her, stating the
following unverifiable information:

This tufted capuchin monkey was obtained as an infant
from a breeder (unidentified) in Florida, and had been living
as a pet with a Connecticut family in their home. The letter
stated that her name was Norma Jean and she had been "like a
member of the family," and had always been very friendly and
affectionate "until she changed."

The recent addition to the household of a pair of baby
marmosets "who are very cute and take a lot of our attention"
had apparently upset her, causing her to become aggressive
and uncooperative.

Norma Jean had attacked one of the marmosets and had
also bitten two members of the family.

Although there had been no prior problems and she had always cooperated with being bathed and diapered, she was no longer cooperative enough for baths, and she had recently begun to remove her diaper and engage in what was clearly urine-washing behavior. The family did not understand her behavior and did not like her increasingly unpleasant odor.

The children in the family were now afraid of her. Nobody in the family felt safe cuddling her or playing with her. Consequently, she had not been let out of her cage for nearly two months.

They could no longer handle Norma Jean and had decided to give her up. ("Please find our little baby girl a good home where she will be loved and nobody will do experiments on her.")

Norma Jean was immediately willing to accept care and social interaction. Her canine and incisor teeth were removed under total anesthesia per the Primate Institute protocols. When she had regained full health, after six weeks, trainers began to work with her, and she responded very positively to the training program. She rapidly developed attachments to several trainers, showing a strong preference for women. She acclimated quickly and thrived on the daily routines of learning tasks. She spent 18 months in Classrooms A and B, demonstrating a superior intelligence and ability to learn vocabulary, tasks, and cooperation. She went on to spend two years learning the more sophisticated and specialized tasks and commands in the Household Classroom, where she excelled. In November, 1999, Norma Jean was considered a successful graduate of the Primate Institute Helper Monkey Training Program and was ready for recipient placement. She was the seventh graduate of our Helper Monkey training program, having outpaced three white-faced capuchins

(Lizzie, Marco, and Frankie) who began their training six months ahead of her. Norma Jean was placed successfully with a recipient in January, 2000.

## First Placement Summary

Norma Jean was placed with recipient Leland Morris, 54, a former English professor at Wesleyan University living in Hamden, whose progressive Multiple Sclerosis symptoms had forced him into early retirement from teaching. He had recently become dependent on a manual wheelchair, and his house had been adapted so he could continue living there. His live-in assistant, Dennis McGrath, became Norma Jean's primary caretaker.

Norma Jean bonded well with Professor Morris, whom she readily accepted as her alpha, and with Dennis McGrath, whom she accepted as her caretaker. It was a very successful placement. As Professor Morris's condition advanced, he moved to a motorized wheelchair, and Norma Jean's helping hands became more crucial for his autonomy with his daily living needs, allowing him to maintain a measure of independence. Regular contact with and support from our Institute trainers gave Professor Morris, Dennis, and Norma Jean the opportunity to work together developing an expanded repertoire of commands and tasks for Professor Morris's increasing needs of daily living.

Trainer notes indicate that Professor Morris had by 2005 changed Norma Jean's name to Ottoline (though doing so was a violation of the Institute's Recipient Agreement). It was unclear when this change had been made, and by the time it was observed during a home visit she had habituated and become responsive to this name. (Subsequently, Mr. McGrath explained to a P.I. staffer that Professor Morris had named

her for a friend of the British writer Virginia Woolf, whose
books had been the subject of his classes and scholarship.)
Trainer notes indicate that Professor Morris, far more of a
behavior challenge to our staff than Ottoline, had become
quite difficult and impatient with home visits. By the middle
of 2006 our file notes indicate that his M.S. symptoms had
become more advanced and he was evidently no longer able
to do any of his scholarly work. Mr. McGrath reported to staff
that Professor Morris was depressed, refused physical therapy,
and had dropped most of his social relationships. He rarely
left the house, no longer enjoyed using the telephone, and had
infrequent visitors. At this time Professor Morris continued
to depend on Ottoline every day, though he had stopped
cooperating with Mr. McGrath.

In 2008, Professor Morris became bedridden, and Ottoline's
daily tasks were reduced. Dennis McGrath either resigned or
was dismissed by Professor Morris's attorney. Shifts of PCAs
were employed to care for Professor Morris, and a veterinary
assistant was employed to come in twice daily to provide basic
care for Ottoline, who spent most of her days with Professor
Morris on his bed, simply keeping him company and watching
television with him. (There are numerous home visit check-in
notes after 2007 about her preference for Animal Planet and
her habit of changing the channel on the television remote
whenever Professor Morris was inattentive or had dozed off.
With nobody to correct her behavior, Ottoline apparently
began to make independent choices that are not within the
usual repertoire of learned, command and response activities.)
In this time period, Ottoline's diet deteriorated and despite
repeated attempts at intervention was significantly out of
compliance (in violation of the Recipient Agreement), as
Professor Morris shared his food with her and her intake was
not monitored. (Home visit notes from 2009 and 2010 indicate
that the PCAs were also disregarding our written instruction

sheets, despite several interventions by our staff, and were also feeding Ottoline "treats.")

It was apparent that Professor Morris let Ottoline take her own helpings of whatever he was eating throughout the day, a nutritional disaster for her. He appeared to subsist on smoked salmon, scrambled eggs, and junk food. In addition to being allowed to snatch food from his hands or plate, Ottoline was not required to follow many assistance requests and she was not corrected when she ignored commands or otherwise behaved badly. Notes indicate that her regular diet from 2009 through 2012 included unregulated quantities of Professor Morris's Mint Milano cookies, Krispy Kreme donuts, gummy bears, Cheez Doodles, Pop Tarts, and both peanut butter and Nutella directly from the jar (Ottoline had skillfully adapted to using a pencil as a tool for scooping Nutella and peanut butter from the jar), along with daily portions of her nutritionally balanced monkey chow supplied by the Institute.

Professor Morris died at the end of January, 2013. As had been the case during Professor Morris's previous hospitalizations in 2007 and 2009, Ottoline had come back to the Institute to board when he was hospitalized with what turned out to be his final pulmonary infection in the first week of January. When she arrived at the Institute, her intake assessment showed that she was obese (5.8 kilograms) and diabetic. Three months of proper nutrition reduced her weight to an optimal range (3–4 kilograms), and by the end of six months her blood sugar had returned to normal range and she was no longer diabetic. Her training reinforcement that had begun in this time period was completed in twelve months. (She is very bright and receptive to training, but she is also stubborn, and she had many bad habits to unlearn.) Ottoline has been a candidate for placement since the middle of this year. Given her successful bond with Professor Morris, it was noted that priority should be given to an older male recipient if possible.

*Second/New Placement*

The Recipient, Duncan Wheeler, age 37, suffered a C6
complete spinal cord injury in July of this year (car accident
in July on Interstate 95 with a passenger fatality). Mr. Wheeler
is an architect who heads his own firm. His wife, Laura, an
assistant painting conservation technician at the Yale University
Art Gallery, has reduced her work commitments and will be
Ottoline's primary caretaker. They do not have children or
household pets. They live in a well-maintained three-story
home on Lawrence Street in New Haven. Mr. Wheeler's home
office on the ground floor has been converted into a bedroom
which will easily accommodate Ottoline's nighttime cage
adjacent to his hospital bed without compromising access with
the transfer equipment. There is a second cage for Ottoline in
the large kitchen.

Our placement policy usually requires that our recipients be
stable and fully adapted to their activities of daily living in their
circumstances, e.g., life in a wheelchair. Whether the disability
has been caused by a sudden or gradual loss of lower body
function, it is essential that our recipients have a baseline
"new normal" as a basis for assessing the best options for a
successful placement, which is why we usually require that
placements only be considered after twelve months of living in
a wheelchair.

Mr. Wheeler's situation warrants an exception. Although
his spinal cord injury occurred only four months ago, his
physical health is stable and the household has been well
adapted for his needs. Mrs. Wheeler is knowledgeable and
highly competent. It is she who initiated contact with the
Institute, with concerns about her husband's depression and
lack of engagement with his surroundings since the accident.
She informed us that he has stated the possibility that he
will choose to end his life rather than live as a quadriplegic.
Waiting eight months to begin a placement match might mean

that it would be too late for him to be able to respond positively to a monkey helper and accept an active role in the mutual bonding process. In order to take the first step in considering whether it would be reasonable to make an exception to our policy, I scheduled, with authorization from our placement review committee, a home visit at the Wheeler residence with Ottoline. This was of course another exception to our usual protocol. But as we know, Ottoline is not a standard helper monkey, so it is fitting that her next placement would (like Ottoline herself) bend a number of rules.

The first placement home visit to the Wheeler residence on 10.21.14 was very successful. Ottoline responded well in a potentially stressful and unfamiliar setting and remained organized. Seeing Mr. Wheeler in a motorized wheelchair, she seemed to recognize him almost instantly as the alpha in her new situation. Though it had seemed likely that Mr. Wheeler would not readily agree to the application for a service monkey, he did not resist the introductory meeting with Ottoline and at the end of that meeting he agreed to accept Ottoline as his Helper Monkey. Plans were made to initiate all set-up and support, to begin the placement the next day, on 10.22.14.   M.P.

# FOUR

## *"I couldn't help myself!"*

"I COULDN'T HELP MYSELF!" LAURA DROPPED HER KEYS in the bowl on the table in the foyer, set down her big canvas tote, and threw off her jacket, which she draped on the newel post at the bottom of the stairs. "The entire block of James Street was an intoxicating cloud of chocolate wafting from the exhaust blowers at Zip's Candies. Oh my god! I don't know how your staff can work next door to a candy factory. It's dangerous!"

"Sorry, what's dangerous?" Duncan said over his shoulder. He was in the living room, where he had been attempting to read a British architecture journal which lay open on a rolling elevated table in front of him. Ottoline was helping. He had kept forgetting that the command for turning the page was Page! and instead had kept saying Turn!, which caused obedient, literal-minded Ottoline, poised on his shoulder for his next request, to hop down and turn the entire magazine ninety degrees each time he said this. Page, damn it! resulted in her turning a page of the now-sideways magazine backwards, so first he had to request two more Turn!s, then two more Page!s, and after that a final Turn! in order to find his place and read the rest of the article on uses of daylight in sustainable buildings. The piece was not really interesting enough for all this effort, though Duncan had amused himself noting the occurrences of "fenestration" where "windows" would have been less pretentious. He had just given up and let Ottoline scribble energetically all over the *Architects Journal* with the drawing pen that she had snatched from his desk earlier.

One lens of his reading glasses was smeared with peanut butter, the consequence of having Ottoline fetch them from the kitchen counter, where Laura had put them when she cleaned up after breakfast. He had rolled into the kitchen, remembering that he had his glasses at breakfast, but they weren't on the table. There they were, on the counter, back beyond Duncan's reach. Ottoline had eagerly responded to his Fetch! command, bounding from his shoulder to the countertop to grab them, stopping on the way to fling open the cupboard above her head to forage hopefully for any accessible treat. Ignoring Duncan's Uh-Uh, Ottoline, Down, Ottoline! commands, she had stopped to unscrew the lid off a jar of peanut butter and scoop out a handful before bounding from the counter back to Duncan with his glasses while greedily chomping down the treat she had awarded herself.

Now as he rolled his chair back from the table and toggled the control to turn around so he could face Laura squarely, he repeated, "What's dangerous?"

"These!"

"I don't know what 'these' are," Duncan said irritably as he swiveled. Ottoline hopped from the table as he turned, gathering with her tail the slack leash that tethered her to his chair as she landed on the head support. She snuggled down to her favorite spot by his left ear.

"Nothing. The chocolate smell billowing out of Zip's, that's all I meant," Laura said, holding up a bag of miniature

Say Howdy! candies. "It inspired me to stop at the market for these on the way back from your office, after breathing those chocolate vapors, and look, way marked down Halloween candy."

"My mother used to buy Halloween candy for next year right about now, just before Christmas, when it was cheap. Gordy and I used to know all her hiding places. We would devour those little Baby Ruths and Butterfingers, and then Halloween would roll around and she would go nuts trying to remember where she had stashed that cheap candy we had eaten months before."

"Look, miniature fun bars, or whatever they call them." Laura rummaged in the bag. "I think they were new this year for Halloween. I ate three in the car. They're just smaller versions of the regular big ones—they come in adorable little dark and white chocolate pairs the size of a gummy bear."

"So you're saying you ate six."

"I don't agree! A single Say Howdy! *is* a pair. They're like little black and white twins. I had three pairs."

"Whatever. Just make sure you put those where she can't get them this time, please," Duncan said. Ottoline was crouching on his shoulder, with both hands in his hair, which she had been busily grooming, but now she tilted inquisitively toward the bag of candy in Laura's hand. "They are tempting," Duncan added, hearing his own dismissive tone. "You should probably put them where I can't get them, either." As if she didn't put things out of his reach every day.

"Want one?" Laura held out the bag, and Ottoline hooted and clambered down from his shoulder, drawn warily by the sweets but also ready to defend him from his wife's ordinary gesture. When Laura lowered her arm, Ottoline hopped back up to her perch on Duncan's shoulder again, wrapping her arms around his neck. She clung to him, cheeping anxiously, as was her disconcerting habit whenever Laura came close or moved too abruptly near Duncan. Laura stood still, not meeting Ottoline's gaze, and tilted her head in friendly submission the way Martha had shown her.

"Not now. No thanks." He couldn't help his impatience. "Ottoline didn't like that. So were all the latest revised Steiner schematics ready?"

"I don't know, Dunc. Whatever they gave me is all in there," Laura said, gesturing furtively, with her arm close in by her body so as not to re-upset the monkey, in the direction of the big thick envelopes sticking out of the grubby canvas beach tote she had left at the foot of the stairs. He had to turn his chair a few degrees so his gaze could follow her pointing finger. Laura crossed the room and dropped down onto the sofa, put her feet up on the coffee table, and hugged a throw pillow in her lap. "Just give me a moment. I'll start dinner in a minute."

Duncan swiveled back to face her. Was she going to wait for him to ask her specifically to put the envelopes on the rolling adjustable table and bend open the brass clasps? While nobody could forget for a moment that Duncan had lost his mobility, his loss of hand function was subtler. He hated having to ask for help. Each of them so polite with the other. The envelopes were too heavy and bulky for Ottoline to fetch them. Once they were on the table, Ottoline could no doubt pry the clasps up together, but he wasn't sure how to ask her to do it without being able to demonstrate the task so she could copy it. It wasn't like pointing at a Fetch! Ottoline! Fetch! object with the red laser dot pointer that clipped to the brace on the back of his left hand. Maybe she could learn how to open and close the clasps from watching Laura, though she might be too distracted by Laura as a potential invader of her space. Everything was a negotiation, and he just wanted to open the damned envelopes.

Brass clasp, brass clasp, exactly the sort of consonant cluster poor Gordy had spent his Wednesday afternoons attempting to master. Duncan often imagined Gordy trying to pronounce words with sibilant alliterations. He made a mental note (the only kind of note he could easily make) to ask Martha at the next check-in how to go about introducing new tasks like this to Ottoline. In addition to the brass clasps there were some other activities beyond his compromised reach and dexterity that Duncan hoped to add to her repertoire.

"I'd like to take a look, now, while you're making dinner," Duncan said after a long moment. He waited. Laura was slumped in a posture of exhaustion. When she dropped her relentless attempts to engage him in trivial chat, when he caught her staring into the middle distance this way, with a slack, vacant gaze, Duncan felt that he was glimpsing her otherwise well-hidden despair about him. About his despair. After another moment, Laura set the throw pillow aside, combed her hair back out of her face with her fingers, and got up to fetch the tote full of this week's Corrigan & Wheeler materials for him. She laid the bag on the table and drew out the big, heavy, stuffed envelopes.

When she was at the office picking up these documents to deliver to Duncan, something she did at least once each week in their new routine, Laura had wondered if his colleagues actually genuinely needed his response to anything, or if they had assembled this bundle of bid documents and reports and drawings simply out of respect for Duncan. Or maybe they were testing him.

Dave Halloran, the oldest of the partners, had assured her they were ticking along and didn't want to put any pressure on Duncan, but of course they would welcome and value his feedback, and they wanted to keep him informed about all bids, project reports, change orders, and of course any news about new clients, or old clients, and of course they would all be thrilled to see him again whenever he wanted to come in, or if he wanted to have any meetings at the house, and they would give him whatever amount of work he could handle in the future, of course, but right now but there was no reason for him to take on anything he wasn't ready for yet. The accident was only what, a little more than four months ago? Duncan should take all the time he needed.

He and Jack Simon and Austin Bartlett had divided up the major projects, and assigned the rest to the associates, with their close supervision, of course. It was important that the clients felt taken care of, Halloran told Laura, not for the first time, with perhaps a hint of condescension, as if she didn't understand such things. The firm had lost two jobs that were Duncan's projects since his accident, perhaps three if one of the farthest out in the pipeline, a pavilion behind an early Corrigan house on Monhegan Island, ended up going to one of Billy Corrigan's former partners, Arthur Hughes. Hughes, who was based in Boston, was not the only architect actively trying to poach Corrigan & Wheeler clients since Duncan's accident, only the most blatant.

The Steiner House was on schedule, Halloran assured her, changing the subject abruptly. Duncan should be glad to know this. If the weather held, now that they had moved inside, they should be able to get the last of the HVAC, plumbing, and electrical done well before spring, and move on to sheetrock and tape, and all the elaborate tile work, that is, if the subs were cooperative about making themselves available to get out there on the days the winter tides allowed them to dock on Biscuit Island. Too bad a site visit was out of the question for Duncan, of course.

In her half hour there, Laura just couldn't parse what was really going on at Corrigan & Wheeler. She knew most of the players, but few of them very well. Jack Simon was very corporate and always seemed to her more like a lawyer or banker than an architect, but he was apparently a brilliant managing partner. Austin Bartlett was well-liked by the associates, and she had never heard Duncan say anything negative about him. He and Simon had been partners in a small firm without enough work to keep going before they joined Corrigan & Wheeler.

Laura had never liked Halloran. Everything she knew and felt about him added to her mistrust of the man. He was always very friendly and deferential toward her, in an irritating courtly way, but he was much too handsomely craggy and outdoorsy. Whenever she was with him, Laura got the feeling that he was secretly convinced of his own superiority to her, to most people, certainly to all women. His shock of unruly white hair gave him a boyish yet distinguished air. He always looked as if he had just returned from a safari or an ice-climbing expedition.

Halloran had left his devoted wife for a graduate student only a few years older than his two angry teenaged daughters. This had all happened quite a few years ago, but ever since then, any time Laura crossed paths with Dave Halloran or even if Duncan just mentioned his name in passing, that betrayal was the first thing that came to her mind. Wendy Halloran now lived in Brooklyn Heights, where she taught improvisational musical theater. The daughters, who both lived somewhere in California, were not in touch with their father, who had married the graduate student. That's how Laura thought of her, "the graduate student," though Lisa Halloran had never finished her dissertation, something to do with Romanesque architecture, and was now the stay-at-home mother of two little boys, Dave Halloran's do-over family. So Laura held that against him too, the way he had derailed his pretty young wife's scholarly career (her husband-stealing notwithstanding).

Duncan liked Halloran's work. He brought some valuable institutional clients in the door, and headed the commercial side, working primarily on projects for several New England schools and other institutional facilities. But Duncan also had some serious misgivings about Halloran that he had confided to Laura, starting with questions about the way he had finessed some contractual payment agreements with a lucrative country club project in Greenwich. Then there had been something just last year about a possible outright kick-back—an elegant standing seam copper roof that appeared on Halloran's colonial revival house in Guilford, supplied by the same roofing company that won the bid on the new library and classroom quad at Choate.

When Halloran asked solicitously for Duncan, for how he was *really* doing, Laura gave him vague, peppy, upbeat answers. Of course the partners would have to take care of business, she didn't have to be told that. Since the accident she could well imagine all the scrambling, all the anxious client main-tenance lunches and dinners. No doubt there had been lots of frantic partner meetings among Dave Halloran, Jack Simon, and Austin Bartlett to discuss all the contingencies, all the possible scenarios depending on whether Duncan would or could ever return to the office.

While she was talking with Halloran, she had looked for Owen Whitlock, the nearly elderly associate (and her favorite person in the office) who had for decades crafted Billy Corri-gan's striking and elaborate architectural models that beguiled clients and helped win projects. His work area was bare and neat, and his drafting lamp was off. He was part-time these days, in a phased retirement, and when he did come in to the office, his role was to mentor and instruct the couple of eager young kids on staff who now did most of the model work, the plans for which were now almost entirely computer-gener-ated. But Owen had gone to the Cape with his family over Thanksgiving and had stayed up there to spend time with the grandchildren who lived in Boston, Halloran told her. He wouldn't be back in the office until the start of the new year. Owen Whitlock was the Corrigan & Wheeler employee she trusted the most, and if he had been the one asking her how Duncan was really doing, she would probably have given him a less sanguine reply.

Also missing from the office these days was Wendy Lewis, the recently-retired office manager who had kept Billy Corrigan's offices under efficient control for decades. Nobody knew how old she was, and there were rumors that she was Billy Corrigan's aunt, or cousin, but nobody was sure where she came from or what her connection was. Lewis, as everyone called her, knew everything about everyone. Though she frightened the interns, she was fantastically diplomatic with cranky, demanding clients, most of whom confided usefully to her about their concerns, which she could then relay to the architects before small problems blossomed into larger issues. Since Billy's death she had been openly mother-hennish about Duncan while cold-shouldering the other partners; Duncan was the only partner who was sorry when she retired. She had been replaced by Jeffrey Marks, a young and obsequious bow-tied modern design monster who, even after six months, persisted in asking Laura if he could inform Duncan what her call was in reference to before he would put her through. Did he really not recognize her name, if not her voice, after all this time? Or did he just hate her for his own reasons?

"It's about shipping the dozen giraffe saddles," Laura would reply. Or, "There's an urgent matter concerning Mr. Wheeler's toaster warranty. Is he there?"

"Please undo all the brass clasps on the envelopes," Duncan said. "Slow, please, do you mind doing that more slowly, so Ottoline can watch how those work? Wait, also would you unroll those roughs—don't tear them! And stick them down with drafting dots, or weight them at the corners with something? Carefully, please."

"Don't be so irritable! Is everything okay, Duncan?"

"Everything is perfect. Beyond perfect. Life is beautiful. Never better. "

As she slid the thick bundled documents from the first big envelope, being careful to make no sudden movements that might stir up Miss FussyMonkey, Laura tried again. "No, really, Dunc, how are you? Seriously. How was your day?"

"The sun shone, having no alternative, on the nothing new."

"Thank you, Mr. Beckett. Okay, don't talk to me. Dinner will be in about half an hour. Do you mean to let her scribble all over the Steiner electricals?"

Did some of Duncan's remoteness begin before the accident? Was it entirely about his paralysis? There had certainly been a subtle shift, a distancing, since the spring, something that had gone unacknowledged between them. They still laughed together at the absurdities of the world, they were friendly and supportive of each other, they each had interesting work they cared about, they were both serious readers with over-lapping preferences, they enjoyed watching some television shows together, they shared a taste for certain old movies, they both loved the choices they had made in their house, they collaborated on elaborate dinners from time to time, with Duncan doing most of the cooking and Laura prepping and cleaning up. Duncan loved to work in the garden, some-thing that originated with a powerful recollection of help-ing his father prune an arbor laden with fragrant, climbing old roses. Laura really didn't love the toil of gardening, but she admired Duncan's fantastically composed flowerbeds. It was another piece of their shared identity; their garden was famous in the neighborhood, and they both took pleasure in the details of their house on Lawrence Street.

Above all, until now, they had shared the hovering pos-sibility of a baby. Each of them had been secretly optimistic and then secretly pessimistic at different moments. Laura re-minded herself when Duncan seemed disconcertingly distant in some unquantifiable way that he might have been anxious about the possibility they would never conceive. The enervat-ing urgency of fruitless procreative sex had made Laura and Duncan's love life increasingly less romantic in recent months.

Sometimes it had felt like an obligation, a chore like any other necessary calisthenic that must be performed in order to achieve a goal. Had all the "trying," how Laura hated that word, "trying," had all that effort to conceive actually pushed them farther apart? Sometimes in recent months they still had that erotic purposeful charge, but not always. And now all that was in the past. What would their marriage be like, without their lovemaking to keep them close, like a re-set on the entropy and drift of each day? It would have happened sooner or later anyway. Maybe. They were older now. Laura wondered if this coolness was simply where everyone ended up sooner or later. After all, her breasts sagged a bit, they had both developed crows' feet, Duncan's hairline was receding, and he had a definite bald spot. Why would their sex life not also start to sag over time? Change was inevitable, even if it wasn't desirable.

But Laura was bothered by those muted moments of lying under Duncan while he charged over her energetically and intently with a disconcerting detachment that had become increasingly evident to her in recent months. Though they were trying to conceive a baby, something they both wanted, she had begun to feel at times as if Duncan had little idea that she was there with him. She had just about decided to call a marriage counselor in the fall, if things hadn't improved between them by the end of the summer.

Laura had witnessed some of their long-married friends go through these flat spells and then come back together stronger than ever, better than ever. She had made a note a while ago of someone who sounded good, and she had even looked up her phone number and address (it was one of several Victorian houses on Bradley Street that now contained therapist offices in what had once been bedrooms and parlors and dining rooms).

Laura was full of resolve and intention about keeping the long view in their marriage. She read every magazine article and advice website she could find about couples and relationships, and was reassured by all the recapitulation that no matter how faithful and devoted a couple might be to one another, every marriage went through these low periods, these rough patches. Especially when the question started to feel as if it was changing from when they would have their first baby to if they would have a baby at all, life in the present moment had started to feel like a holding pattern, a long pause when fate was going to take them in one direction or the other. Surely this should have made them feel closer than ever, in it together. But it didn't.

One article made the point that partners sometimes took turns carrying the marriage along—you carry, I'll rest; you rest, I'll carry. This was comforting, yet at the same time, considering this model made Laura realize that she had been the one carrying them for a while. That was okay, an investment in their future. It felt right. The long view was what had always mattered. Everything they had and everything they hoped for, this life of theirs, Laura reassured herself, was itself enough to keep them going with sheer momentum through the uncertain times.

Laura and Duncan were well-matched, in their way. She had married him because he was a little cold and distant, and she knew he wouldn't notice or mind her own deficiencies. Duncan had married her, she knew, in her heart, because he recognized in her a kindred spirit, someone who burned on an equally low flame. She had once read (in a mildewed English novel she had found on a shelf at a B&B one rainy weekend in Maine), and never forgot, a theory that men with "something wrong" tend to marry foreign women "because they can't tell." Whatever is missing or inadequate will get lost in translation and won't be missed. The title, author, and plot of the novel were long gone from her memory, but this one wise epigrammatic remark surfaced in Laura's thoughts from time to time.

She had always imagined that when they had children they would grow closer, the gap between them closing inevitably once they shared a genetic throw of the dice. Instead, the children they didn't have had not only led to a subtle tension and wary space between them, but had also led to the diminution of most of their local friendships, as one by one all the young couples they knew from work or through one of the many other webs of connections that linked people in New Haven—Yale events, museum openings, concerts, theater, tennis—started to have babies and became families. Most of their friends were young married couples their own age, so this progressive shift had left them weirdly nearly friendless.

Even faraway friends, like Laura's University of Connecticut college roommate Ann, who had been a real confidante for years (and had essentially masterminded their wedding party at the New Haven Lawn Club), had become remote. After a few years working in New York at a brokerage firm, Ann met and quickly married a prosperous English banker and moved to Tokyo, then Geneva; they had two adorable children who called her Mummy and a nanny who called her Mrs. Blackstone. The annual Blackstone family Christmas card and newsletter was the only communication from Ann at this point, and the confiding, stay-up-all-night-with-their-wine-and-coffee-and-wine conversations of years past were long gone.

Laura not only missed Ann Conklin, she missed Ann's mother, Louise, who had been a funny, caring woman who would often chat with Laura if Ann wasn't there when she phoned. Her obituary had caught Laura's eye a couple of years back, and reading the details of the private funeral for Mrs. Conklin made Laura realize that Ann, her only child, must have traveled to Greenwich, must be there right now, but she hesitated to call her, after all this time. When a week had passed, and Laura had not heard from Ann, she looked on Facebook (where she had an account that she rarely checked), and easily found Ann's page, which had pictures posted the day before of her children sitting on the Torosaurus sculpture in front of the Peabody Museum, not four blocks from her house, an apparent part of a day trip to see the sights of New Haven that also included a stop at Pepe's for pizza. That was some four years ago, and there had been no communication between them since.

When they were at a dinner party with people they had known for years, and Laura was invariably nominated to go read a bedtime story to someone else's toddler, she experienced a raw grief. She was a terrific reader-aloud, but kissing other people's babies goodnight on the tops of their downy heads, tucking them with the requisite special stuffed animal under the covers of their cozy little beds, leaving the door to the room open just the right negotiated amount, with a jolly twirling nightlight lamp casting a pretty parade of pastel shadows across the ceiling and walls, saying goodnight, sleep tight, one last time, and then another last time, and then a final last time, good night, sleep tight! she felt such sorrow and anguish that she could hardly gather herself back together to return to the grown-up company at the table, knowing she wouldn't be able to bear seeing these people again.

She missed some of them now. Once genuinely close, these friends with whom Laura had shared the smallest details of her family history and her daily life were now preoccupied with their hectic families, and they had all easily filled in the friend spot formerly occupied by Laura and Duncan with other couples who had children and shared all the myriad daily joys and stresses of family life. Added to this was what Duncan dubbed "the New Haven problem," which was the reality that a college town packed with people who had come for medical or architecture or law schools and then ended up staying and putting down roots, was a town full of mid-career professionals who weren't all going to make partner or get tenure.

They lost a number of good friends over the years, and potential good friends, too, all the doctors and lawyers and professors of economics, who took offers in Denver and Seattle and Chicago. All the promises about keeping in touch had been sincere, but email and a phone call every few months dwindled inevitably over time, especially once those friends found new sustaining connections and started to develop friendships with other families with children. The friends with children who hadn't left New Haven hardly noticed that Laura and Duncan hadn't been free for dinner, didn't call them back quickly, and gradually stopped asking them over. Without schism or rupture, those relationships had all been gently set down.

None of their friends had noticed this deliberate withdrawal, it seemed to Laura, who had done too good a job offering plausible excuses to avoid making plans with any of them. She had promised herself that if she and Duncan had a baby—when they had a baby—those friendships would be easily revived.

The New Haven people in their life with whom Laura still remained in touch had become friendly acquaintances who had each made a single visit to the hospital after the accident. Duncan's grim mood had not rewarded them for their efforts, and even the parking at Yale-New Haven Hospital was an arduous, time-consuming pursuit for busy young parents. None of them had tried to renew the friendship or make a plan to get together with Laura on her own. Duncan's accident was like cancer—everyone they knew was grateful and relieved it had not happened to them. It's a universal response to accidents, to cancer, to all calamity and misfortune. Each of these acquaintances had made their dutiful visits and had then moved on. Some had brought small gifts: books Dun-

can couldn't hold to read and CDs he had no means of playing. (And when would he ever have wanted to listen to and
benefit from the alleged healing properties of an Echinacea
Serenade, for god's sake?) It wasn't deliberate callousness or
cruelty when anyone failed to keep in touch, it was just the
way life aims people in different directions.

In the first weeks of their life with a monkey, Laura had
learned the hard way that when Ottoline was perched on
Duncan it wasn't a good idea to reach out to touch him, or
extend a hand in his direction to give him something, let
alone try to kiss him or hug him, when coming or going.
Ottoline had lunged at her a couple of times while scolding her shrilly, and once had snatched her glasses off her face,
scratching Laura's nose with a sharp fingernail. The Institute
people had walked them through (an unfortunate choice of
terms, but those were, in fact, Martha's exact words) these
early stages of settling in with Ottoline. Laura understood all
the reasons why Ottoline's primary bond was with Duncan,
her alpha. It was all hierarchical, and she was at the bottom,
the odd man out in this little tribal triangle. It made sense,
but she hadn't anticipated what it would feel like.
    Laura had carefully studied all the Institute materials before
they met Ottoline. Sometimes, despite her thorough understanding of the principles of bonding and hierarchy that made
the relationship succeed, she really felt left out. Whenever
Laura walked into the room where they were, or even passed
by in the hallway on her way from the kitchen to the stairs,
there was a chance Ottoline would react by changing her
position and chattering at Laura to stay away, stay away, stay
away or else! If Laura moved toward Duncan too abruptly,
even now, Ottoline would start shrieking at her with anxious
open-mouthed squeals, He's mine! He's mine! He's mine!
while bobbing up and down aggressively. It was unnerving.
When Laura backed away, Ottoline would pull herself up tall

in his lap, holding Duncan's chest strap with one hand, as if claiming ownership, scolding her and repeatedly wiping the back of the other hand down her fuzzy front in a dismissive, brushing-off gesture. Away with you, begone! Are you still here? Take a hint! Take a hike! We don't need you! I brush you off!

Laura could feel that Duncan enjoyed these moments. He smiled and petted her reassuringly. Talk about being in ecstatic cahoots! Each time Ottoline bristled at her defensively and clung to him, and Laura retreated, Duncan seemed both amused and also more concerned about Ottoline's delicate feelings than about Laura's reaction to the insulting scolding by the zealous guardian on his shoulder. His acceptance of this pattern could be reinforcing it, Martha had told her, and she promised she would work with Duncan to encourage him to be the one to make the disapproving Uh-Uh correction to remind her that this was rude.

Despite this behavior, Ottoline clearly felt settled and more confident, and had begun to trust Laura. Away from Duncan, she changed her tune, and had become increasingly playful and affectionate with Laura. Sometimes, while Duncan was in his room being put through all the laborious steps in his daily care routine by one of the personal care assistants who came to the house each day, Laura took Ottoline upstairs to the bedroom, where they played and cuddled on the bed.

The first week of Ottoline's placement with them, a team of Institute trainers had occupied the house for several long hours of each day, helping them all find their way. The diaper lessons had been strenuous for Laura and for Ottoline. Step One: Cut hole in center of diaper for the tail. Step Two: Thread diaper all the way down the tail. Step Three: Win argument with Ottoline about the whole enterprise and immobilize her on her back with a bribe (a blueberry) long enough to tape diaper in place, with tapes in the back where they would be less tempting to remove.

The second week, they were on their own, with phone support. Laura had observed a monkey bath at the Institute, and had studied all the steps in her handbook, but since Ottoline's placement, the team had suggested not even attempting a bath in those first days on their own, simply to avoid stressing Ottoline. Giving her the first overdue bath at the end of that second week had been a small crisis for Laura, who had phoned the Institute in tears to ask for emergency trainer support when it was over, after she and Ottoline had exhausted each other in a battle of wills, and a wet, soapy, shivering monkey had retreated to her cage, pulling the cage door shut behind her with something like a slam even before Laura could say Door!

Martha (what would they do without Martha?) had come over that night after dinner to soothe both of them and work out a solution for Ottoline's objection to being immersed, which was to start in an empty, towel-lined sink rather than try to plunge Ottoline into a full sink of warm soapy water, and to use the sprayer attachment rather than the faucet for a gentle rain of water that would be less upsetting than the noisy gushing column of water that Ottoline disliked.

Laura looked forward to bath times now that she and Ottoline were over the crisis. Ottoline had begun to take pleasure in her kitchen sink shower baths, cooperating like a lamb, as if it were some other monkey altogether who had been so difficult. When she went too many days between baths, Ottoline developed a ripe, pungent, oily aroma, but when she had been gently lathered with baby shampoo and rinsed (while she cheeped happily and tried to scoop the soap-suds into her mouth as if they were cotton candy), as she air-dried, and her soft fur fluffed out again, she had an appealing spicy fragrance that reminded Laura of the sweet burlap taste of the sorghum syrup her mother had poured on her pancakes when she was little. One of Laura's few memories of Ohio was sitting in a booster seat at their blue and white enamel-topped kitchen table eating those pancakes with that strange brown syrup. She and her mother had moved to Connecticut when she was six.

Laura had never given anyone or anything a bath before Ottoline. She grew up without pets, because of her allergies, and she and her mother had lived in a series of rented apartments where pets were discouraged. Her few babysitting experience in her teenaged years had consisted of watching television while doing her homework, eating snacks, and snooping in the desk drawers of the neighbors who employed her to sit around this way so they could go out to dinner while the babysat child slept. She couldn't recall ever having to deal with a child waking up and needing one thing from her.

After the first successful monkey ablution, Laura kept replaying the kitchen sink moments in her mind with a certain kind of joy she had never really known before. The long, wiry, dignified body, one moment like that of an agreeable toddler, with that soft, round belly, but in the next instant like a diminutive, plucky little old lady. The way Ottoline had sat still and let her squeeze a sponge over her to rinse the soapy water off her head, her tongue sticking out to catch the stream of water that ran down her face. The way Ottoline had let herself be bundled up in a towel and gently dried all over. Ottoline had quietly gazed up into her face the whole time Laura rubbed her down.

Whenever a personal care assistant was in the house, Ottoline was locked in one of her two big, roomy cages, usually the one in the kitchen, where she couldn't see the various ministrations performed by the PCAs on Duncan, either in his room or in the bathroom, from bathing to managing his bowel program and catheter maintenance, to dressing and undressing, the transfers achieved with the brilliantly designed Hoyer lift—a rolling single boom lifter equipped with step-on, lockable brakes. Laura was learning how to do a transfer on her own, from bed to wheelchair and back again, but so far, not that they admitted this to each other, neither Duncan nor Laura felt completely safe when she executed one of these maneuvers without a PCA present.

Seeing any handling of Duncan made Ottoline go berserk. The quad cough technique, a vital part of Duncan's routine to keep his compromised lungs clear, was especially upsetting. Every day, usually in the morning when he had the most energy, Duncan would be placed flat on his back on his bed while his PCA performed the rhythmic compressions on his abdomen that helped him to cough more productively. It was a collaborative effort, as he tried to cough on the beat of the compressions. The first few times she watched this being performed, observing helplessly from the doorway, Laura thought it seemed like an attempt by two people to approximate the act of sexual intercourse, which they had only ever overheard. Ottoline was kept well away from these treatments, given how, if from her cage she saw a PCA putting a dressing on Duncan's perpetual, raw pressure sore at the base of his left hamstring insertion, or simply rubbing moisturizer on Duncan's increasingly spindly legs, she might shrill and shriek and rattle the door to her cage in an elaborate show of frustration at being thwarted from claiming him, taking care of him, defending him, doing her job.

Ottoline had no front teeth, only her back molars. This was a necessity the Institute called her life insurance policy, because if one of their helper monkeys were to bite someone who had made a startling arm movement or laughed loudly, or if a person simply seemed too close to the monkey's alpha person, no matter how understanding the bite recipient might be, no matter how justified the defensive aggression might have felt from the monkey's point of view, then despite all the years spent on socializing and training, despite the Primate Institute's significant investment in this monkey, it could all be over. There would be a very real possibility that the monkey could be taken away, treated as just another out-of-control exotic pet that people should know better than to have in the house.

Laura was taken aback when this was first explained to her. It felt wrong. Pulling the front teeth of a creature designed by nature to forage for her food in the wild seemed unbearably cruel. But it wasn't up for discussion or debate, and the truth was that countless tense moments had already occurred when Ottoline's angry, open-mouthed grimacing and chattering had unnerved Laura. It was so clearly in her wiring to display the four large, sharp canine teeth she would have possessed in the wild.

At those moments, when Laura glimpsed a vestige of the wild animal who ought to be living in the tree canopy of Costa Rica in a merry tribe of tufted capuchins, she was grateful (despite her guilt about it) that Ottoline didn't have those front teeth. In her natural habitat, Ottoline would have had mates, and babies. She would not have survived twenty-five years. If she lived among her kind in a tribe in a cloud forest, she would hunt insects and grubs and worms all day long, but she would not have a passion for peanut butter, and she would not know about how many good things there are in a refrigerator, the door to which she would surely not know how to open. She would not know that when someone said Sun! this meant it was time to switch on or off an electric light. She would not know how, in response to Foot!, to safely lift and replace a lifeless foot that had slipped off its footrest and was now dangling precariously. She would not know exactly what to do whenever asked for Fetch! Page! Bucket! Turn! Change! Push! Itch! Open! Close! Slide! Straw! Living her natural, violent, giddy, tribal life among her own kind, roaming kilometers each day, swinging from tree to tree, resting, playing, sleeping as she pleased—living her life as it was meant to be lived—this had not been her fate.

Knowing that Ottoline had no bite power made it easier to dismiss the terrible stories in the news about chimpanzee violence that were so upsetting and confusing to many people. It was startling to Laura when she discovered in their first weeks with Ottoline how many otherwise intelligent and informed people apparently didn't understand the difference between New World monkeys and Old World apes. Some of Duncan's doctors and their staff had actually rolled their eyes when she first brought up the possibility of a monkey helper for Duncan, as if she were out of her mind.

Laura had never heard of monkey helpers until she picked up a Primate Institute brochure in a waiting area at the hospital, on a day when Duncan was being evaluated in order to develop a physical therapy and health maintenance plan. She had nothing to read and her phone got no signal in this part of the hospital, so she had started rummaging through the pamphlets in a rack on the wall, passing over brochures for hospital bed rentals, rehabilitation facilities, and custom orthotics. The single copy of a Primate Institute brochure was, compared to the other options, intoxicating reading, and the notion of helper monkeys for the disabled was intriguing. Could this really work for Duncan? He met the criteria for being a recipient. He was in a wheelchair, he was mostly at home, he was capable of communicating directly with a monkey helper, and there was someone else in the household—Laura realized this would be her role—to be the monkey's caretaker. Nobody she spoke with at the hospital that day knew anything about the Institute, which, she discovered when she mapped the address on the brochure, was surprisingly located in an imposing castle-like house on Forest Road.

Hundreds of people passed by the Institute every day on busy Forest Road. Laura had taken this route from Whalley Avenue to get to Route 34 on countless occasions, and had never particularly noticed or thought about this grand exemplar of Tudor Revival excess at the corner where Chapel Street ended. There was no sign, and other than a paved parking area that would ordinarily have been grassed on which were parked five or six cars, nothing distinguished the house from the other imposing brick and stone residences that lined the south side of the busy street, facing a steep wooded area that belonged to a nearby private school. There was no giveaway out front that under this slate gambrel roof dwelled some fifty capuchin monkeys at various stages of training as assistance animals to help people confined to wheelchairs by injury or illness with activities of daily living.

The idea of all those monkeys in there being trained to work as monkey helpers seemed fanciful and unreal, like something you would see on the internet after you had watched the Japanese cat jumping out of the cardboard box. Laura kept the Primate Institute brochure by the bed, and sometimes in the middle of the night during those early days she would read it aloud to herself, the way she might, in another life, have read a fairy tale to a restless child who couldn't sleep.

When Duncan was released from the hospital, Laura had hoped his despair would dissipate and he would abandon his certainty that he didn't want to live like this. Walt, a wheelchair-bound hospital social worker, had met with her privately. He encouraged her to count on Duncan's adjusting to his new limitations. He assured her that most people struggle with depression at the start of their adjustment to life as a quadriplegic. It was, after all, profoundly life-altering. He would come around; he would learn how to make the most of his new, post-accident way of life. Many people led happy, fulfilling, productive lives after this kind of catastrophic accident. There were many people living their lives with C6 injuries. The hospital had a program. Duncan could meet some of these inspiring individuals. He could find a role model, a mentor who would help him discover all the ways that his life could continue.

But this is not what happened. In the weeks after the accident, in the hospital and then at home, Duncan had only retreated further into himself. He refused to see most people, starting with these inspiring paragons of quadriplegic life on wheels. He said he really didn't think he could live this life.

Laura went to the hospital one morning on the sly, to meet with Walt again to talk about this lack of progress. What was she supposed to say or do when Duncan spoke about not wanting to live? He advised her to use an animal training technique developed by people working with orca whales called "least reinforcing scenario," or LRS. The theory of LRS, Walt explained, is that any reaction to the unwanted behavior is more interesting to the creature in question than no reaction. So if your response to the unwanted behavior is absolutely nothing, the behavior will fade away. Duncan was using the energy of her response to fuel his morbid remarks. Take away that energy and he won't be able to use it.

This didn't sound useful to Laura. Wouldn't that be like the deliberately provocative and frustrating silence of a Freudian analyst, and meanwhile, didn't some of those orca whales kill their trainers? Maybe the trainers should have been a lot more responsive to the unwanted behaviors, not less. She tried it anyway, going poker-faced and silent whenever Duncan mentioned his wish to end his life, but it didn't seem to have any effect. How could her stony silence change his feelings about wanting to end his life? He wasn't saying these things in order to get a rise out of her. It was simply how he felt.

Duncan didn't respond to calls or emails from friends who were eager to visit or at least hear his voice, and for the first time since childhood he started spending hours in front of the television, a habit he had developed in the hospital. He could stare bleakly at mindless daytime programs without apparent preference for Fox News, Days of Our Lives, Judge Judy, Animal Planet, or Everybody Loves Raymond. He gazed with equal inattention at commercials for drugs with names suited to distant planets in science fiction, like Pradaxa, Viagra, Crestor, Cymbalta, Xarelto, and at the ominous, fast-talking advertisements for law firms inviting viewers to sue drug companies for injuries or deaths caused by the same medications.

He would allow only his brother Gordon to visit with any frequency. Gordon didn't ask stupid questions or try to cheer him up. Sometimes when Gordon came to keep him company, the two of them simply sat together like a matched pair of mute children, Duncan in his wheelchair and Gordon beside him in a ladder-back chair brought in from the kitchen, watching television, with no words between them from one hour to the next.

When Laura insisted on turning the television off, Duncan would sit in his chair in front of the big front windows in their living room, gazing out at the daily life of Lawrence Street with at least a flicker of interest, which was better than the zombie television stare. Laura had no idea what could possibly hold his attention for so many hours. Their neighbors' activities had never before fascinated Duncan in the nine years they had lived on this block. The comings and goings of the children across the street, almost always herded by their au pair and not their parents, held his attention for a few moments, but sometimes, when Duncan had stared out the window all afternoon, barely answering any of her attempts at conversation with more than a syllable or two, Laura felt herself on the edge of panic. How could this go on? His point exactly. She had bought him a pair of lightweight binoculars that he seemed willing to wear around his neck, and she saw him gazing through them quite a bit, though there really wasn't much to look at out there, not for someone who had never before seemed constitutionally capable of just sitting blankly from one day to the next.

Desperate to do something, anything, Laura had made an appointment at the Primate Institute. The people there were kind, and they understood her situation. They helped her begin to believe, in a series of conversations, both at the Institute and on the phone, that a monkey helper really might make the difference for Duncan. Though there was usually a requirement that the recipient be at least a year into life in a wheelchair, this might be a case for an exception. They assured her that they would provide ongoing support. If it took days, if it took weeks, they would be there to make the adjustment work for Duncan, for Laura, and for the monkey. They would select just the right monkey for Duncan, matching their temperaments and personalities (this made Laura laugh out loud when Martha said it to her in all seriousness). The Institute always not only carried all costs of training their helper monkeys over several years, but also would provide all food, cages, and other equipment for the duration of the placement (Laura hated to think about the implications of that phrase), and they would also take care of any health concerns or treatment, with a specialized veterinarian always on call.

One afternoon during these interviews (as Laura came to recognize them for what they were, a two-way assessment process), Laura was invited to take a little tour of the monkey training area. At that point she had not yet been in a room with a monkey, because they were very excitable, she had been warned, and interacting with one of these capuchins was not a casual thing like meeting a dog or a cat. They would regard her as a potential threat. When she did see any monkeys, before a monkey was selected for Duncan, it was going to be at a distance.

As she followed Zoe (a junior trainer who dressed, like all the trainers, in nursing scrubs) down the hall to the Household Classroom where the monkeys learned to integrate in a realistic setting the tasks they had mastered, a door opened and a trainer came out of a room with three leashed and diapered monkeys clinging to her shoulders, two on one side and

one on the other. Instantly all three monkeys began screeching and bobbing up and down urgently while clinging to the
trainer, making a deafening ruckus in the narrow hallway.
Stranger! Stranger! Danger! Stranger! Who? Who? Who?
Laura remained motionless. The trainer mouthed "sorry" and
took a step back into the room from which they had come, to
let them pass. The monkey scolding continued to reverberate
down the hallway until Zoe and Laura had passed through a
heavy door that muffled the sound.

"Was that upsetting to you?" Zoe asked Laura as she held
a door open that led to the Household Classroom, which she
had first made sure was unoccupied.

"No, it was fascinating!" Laura said. "I kind of loved it!"

"Good," said Zoe, and the way she grinned when she said
it made Laura wonder if it had been a planned test. "Those
smaller two are a pair of white-faced capuchin girls who are
new to us. They're young, but I'm going to see if I can do
some training for a few months before they go out for fostering and socializing. They're such cooperative creatures by
nature, as well as hierarchical. We know that in the wild they
can learn from each other, and they can work together. So I
want to see if some of our training is more effective if they're
taught the tasks and rewarded for reaching goals in front of
each other."

"Monkey see, monkey do?" asked Laura

"Exactly!"

The fleeting burst of happiness Laura felt just then was like
a gift. She could stay here at the Primate Institute of New
England all day. She wanted a job here! Laura realized how
much she had invested in wanting the monkey helper to work
out for Duncan, for all the manifest reasons, but also simply
because with the monkey helper, she would have a team and
would not be in this alone. What a relief it had already been
to be able to speak frankly with Lynette, the placement coor-
dinator, about Duncan's lack of will to live, his talk of sui-

cide. Now Laura began to worry that Duncan would reject the monkey and she would lose all these terrific new people in her life, having just discovered them in this big house on Forest Road that was secretly full of monkeys.

And then came this particular monkey. Since Ottoline's arrival, a well-meaning acquaintance had sent them an envelope full of photocopied newspaper articles about the chimpanzee that chewed off a woman's face. Two of Laura's senior colleagues in the painting conservation lab at the Yale Art Gallery had been frankly and vocally horrified at the news that a potentially violent, potentially disease-carrying primate had come to live with Duncan and Laura, and one of them begged Laura to wear protective gear at all times whenever Ottoline was out of her cage. A friendly graduate student in Art History who overheard this contentious conversation had the next day left in her mailbox a postcard from the Uffizi of a painting by Annebale Caracci of a young man holding a monkey.

Was it so hard to comprehend the difference between a large and powerful ape with uncontrollable aggression and a thoroughly trained seven-pound capuchin monkey, smaller than most dogs or cats, who can understand dozens of commands and perform all sorts of complex tasks to assist the disabled? Laura felt that she had this conversation over and over with friends and colleagues, and with so many of Duncan's medical team, too.

Laws about "exotic pets" (a vast category in most states that included boa constrictors and tigers) meant that any monkey who bites anyone under any circumstance, service animal or not, is a monkey who could be seized by animal control and caged indefinitely, until it sickens and dies, is euthanized, or, occasionally, is placed in a primate sanctuary of one kind or another. Some so-called sanctuaries that gladly took in discarded monkeys and allowed people to believe their unmanageable, cast-off "monkids" were living happy, contented lives in a suitable environment were really fronts for drug- and cosmetic-testing laboratories. For all these risks, espe- cially given the investment and value of years of training, the Institute retained ownership of Ottoline. She had an Institute identification number tattooed on the inside of one of her sinewy, hairy thighs, and she was also micro-chipped.

From the start, Ottoline demonstrated very clear preferences for some people in the Wheeler household, with cheeping and coy head tilts for two of the PCAs, who soon developed their own vocabulary of gestures with her, and a dislike of a couple of others, which she expressed with open-mouthed scolding and rude shrieking. Her scorn and dismissal were as insulting as her affection was flattering. There was no way to predict whom she would favor, and there was no way to win her favor if she didn't like someone.

She had a thing for the UPS man. Ottoline had never even met him face to face, but by the third time he made a deliv- ery in her presence, she alerted with interest at the sound of his truck stopping in front of their house. At the squealing of the brakes, followed by the ticking of the safety blinker lights, and then the metal rasp of the sliding door panel on the truck, she would chatter happily, watching as he emerged from inside his truck with their parcel and hopped down to the pavement. Ottoline would start tilting her head and cheep- ing and make big smacking air kisses as he walked up their front steps, and she didn't stop until he had retraced his foot- steps, swung himself back up into the truck, and driven away. Laura wondered if this was some atavistic association that had to do with Ottoline's previous placement. Did the UPS man on that route give her treats? Or maybe there was sim- ply something pleasing about the brown uniform. Ottoline was also endlessly fascinated by Frank and Jesse's big orange cat, Buster, whom she would observe avidly from the kitchen windowsill when he stalked blue jays in their yard. Frank and Jesse discouraged Buster from killing birds, but they were on sabbatical in Rome for a year. Their housesitter, a graduate student, often left their old yellow Subaru in the shared driveway, blocking Laura, who would then have to knock on the door to ask him to move it, apparently always waking him, no matter the time of day. The graduate student presumably kept the cat food bowl full, but he was indifferent to Buster's murderous agenda.

Two of Duncan's personal care assistants who had recently started working with him had simply quit when Ottoline arrived. The agency found replacements for their shifts, two women in their forties who were eager to take care of a quadriplegic man with a monkey. Darlene and Cathy were cousins who shared a house near the shoreline in West Haven, and they were both relentlessly cheerful and patient. Darlene, who wore pastel scrubs festooned with teddy bears because she worked for a pediatric practice most afternoons, often trailed a faint sillage of cigarette smoke when she came into the house, but she promised she was trying to quit. Smoking was a violation of agency rules, but Laura told her they wouldn't say anything about it if she really was trying to quit. Cathy had worked in a wound care clinic at Waterbury Hospital, which was particularly useful, given Duncan's already chronic pressure sores.

Ida Mae was a massage therapist with crazy red hair and tattooed eyebrows who had moved back to New Haven, after twenty years in Florida, to take care of her father, now that he couldn't manage on his own. She was full of stories about her hapless ex-boyfriend Floyd, the man of a thousand schemes whom she had left behind in his RV in Pahokee. Before long, Laura and Duncan had a vivid sense of Floyd's crafty ways and poor judgment, and they often spoke about him familiarly, as if he were a regrettable though colorful relative of their own.

Floyd was a ticket-taker for boat tours in the Everglades National Park. He had dabbled in breeding exotic pets, and at one time had operated a petting zoo menagerie, which had been closed down after a child was bitten badly by one of his ill-treated, malnourished, captive creatures. He was also a bottom-dealing, hand-mucking poker player who fleeced the bass-fishing anglers in local bars, which is to say every so often he got beaten up pretty badly and was often "laying low." Ida Mae was already on her last nerve with him when he persuaded her to cash out her modest retirement account so they could invest her money in a chinchilla farm, with a plan to breed chinchillas and harvest the valuable pelts.

The humid heat on Lake Okeechobee was not very much like the dry, cool air of the Andes, and all 300 sweltering chinchillas stacked in their cages in the repair bays of a vacant muffler shop down at the end of Lemon Street soon developed a condition called "furslip." (You couldn't even stuff a little pillow with the fur they let loose, it was so nasty, according to Ida Mae, who had tried.) There was no fortune to be made with naked, listless chinchillas, and it was the end of Ida Mae's bank account along with her romance, though it wasn't the last straw, the way Ida Mae told it. (It was the pen-ultimate straw, Duncan suggested, and she latched right onto that word very happily for future tellings.) When Floyd had attempted to pass off stringy chunks of gamey chinchilla meat as nutria in the spicy gumbo he brought to a swap meet to sell by the Styrofoam cup out of his big crockpot, *that* had been the very last straw for Ida Mae.

During her first visit to their house to discuss her duties, among the many issues of Duncan's care was the perpetual risk of his having an autonomic dysreflexia response to a long checklist of potential triggers. Because his body's thermo-stat was essentially paralyzed, and he didn't sweat below his level of injury, one significant worry, once warmer weather arrived, was going to be keeping him indoors and cool on any day air temperatures ever rose above ninety degrees. "Trust me, I'm an expert on the signs of sensitivity to heat and humidity," Ida Mae assured them unreassuringly.

Wendell, a confident coffee-colored man who told them he was taking classes to become a Physician's Assistant, made all the transfers and lifting seem effortless. (Laura and Duncan were curious about his ethnic background but were too polite to come straight out and ask; they would never know that he was from Mauritius, though it was one of Duncan's guesses.) Laura was always happy to see him, knowing how competently and respectfully he handled Duncan, from the intimacies of his bowel program to bathing to dressing. There was something reassuring about his presence, and she imagined that for Duncan it was nice that at least one of his PCAs was a man.

Mounika, a small but impressively strong and capable Indian woman with a bindi, told Laura and Duncan on her first shift a few days after Ottoline's arrival that she was honored to be in a house with a monkey. She spoke respectfully in a soft voice to Ottoline whenever she passed by the cage in the kitchen. Ottoline might be playing with her plastic stacking rings and bucket, but when Mounika told her in Hindi each time she greeted Ottoline at the start of her shift that she was fortunate to be fed every day, because there is a Hindu belief that monkeys should be fed only on Tuesdays and Saturdays, which would probably not do at all for Ottoline, the busy monkey would drop her toys and sit up, quiet and alert, tilting her head and gazing at Mounika pensively.

A total of five personal care assistants did everything for Duncan, with rotating daily morning shifts, which often included giving him breakfast, which he was only ready for after ten in the morning, because his care routine took a minimum of two hours, and end-of-the-day shifts which concluded with his being transferred into his bed for the night. There were sometimes additional shifts at other hours depending on Duncan's needs and Laura's work schedule at the art gallery. Now Duncan could spend most afternoons on his own, thanks to Ottoline.

The annual cost of the PCAs would run beyond $40,000, but Laura and Duncan were better off than most people in their situation, and never had to give a moment's thought to the hourly cost of scheduling the PCA hours Duncan needed. Not only were they what Duncan's relatives liked to call "very comfortable," but also Duncan continued to draw a partner's salary at Corrigan & Wheeler, though sooner or later there would have to be some negotiations about his future role, and if he was ever going to return to work.

The combination of a lump sum payment from worker's compensation, his monthly Social Security disability payment, and a single large payout from a long-term disability insurance policy that Corrigan & Wheeler carried for all the vested employees (Duncan being the prudent son of an insurance man who died young) more than covered the cost of the PCAs. The single large discounted payout on the long-term disability policy was an unusual choice, and all actuarial tables made evident the fact that the better and more prudent option would have been the ten-year payout plan, but as with workers comp, Duncan had been adamant that he wanted the lump sum payment now, instead.

Laura, Duncan, and Ottoline were in fact adjusting to each other a little more every day as they began to settle into routines. In the time when Duncan was home from the hospital, but before Ottoline, on the afternoons when Laura worked in the conservation lab at the Yale Art Gallery, when she came home at the end of the day, Duncan would be alone in the dim living room, either watching television or staring out the window, the apologetic PCA having been banished to the kitchen, where Laura would find her at the table, leafing through a magazine. Now, with Ottoline, Duncan was able to spend hours without a PCA in the house, from just after lunch until Laura came home between five-thirty and six. He agreed to wear the Able-phone headset whenever he was alone for this much time, so that he could, in an emergency, whistle to initiate a call. His phone was programmed with voice recognition for "call Laura" or "call 911" or "call the Primate Institute." The evening PCA who managed all the bedtime care usually arrived just as Laura was clearing the table after dinner.

Duncan didn't want to give Laura the satisfaction of knowing that he had gotten back in the habit of reading email from the office every afternoon during his solo hours. He used voice recognition software to dictate replies and comments, which kept him more connected with work than he had imagined would be possible. Duncan had been back in the loop for several weeks before Laura caught him one afternoon when she came into the house and heard his voice coming from his room. At first she had thought he was speaking to Ottoline, then she heard him say something about the planning and zoning permits and she thought he was on the phone, which was surprising enough.

The voice recognition software had been Laura's idea, years ago, when she got it for him after he broke his wrist skiing a rocky double black diamond run that was well above his level of ability (though Laura had begged him to skip this last reckless run of the day). Duncan had resisted using it, because, he had felt at the time, childishly, that doing so would be a concession to her unspoken told-you-so. Now he was sheepish when she caught him in the act of dictating emails.

Duncan loved the solitude of those precious afternoon hours, and was disappointed on the days Laura didn't go to work or arrived home early. He had, at first, been challenged by Ottoline's cage doors, which fastened with a spring clip barely soft enough for him to operate with his weak grip, but after a struggle, he mastered it, along with managing to clip the leash lead onto the ring on her harness, the other end of which he fastened to the ring loop on his chair. These were necessary tasks to master if he was going to be able to handle Ottoline's comings and goings from the cage to his chair and back again. He could only manage to do this if he wore the tenodesis splint on his left hand, something he had resisted before. He had felt sorry for himself. It was enough trouble, trying to feed himself with the utensil cuff Velcroed in place on his feeble wrist with its slot to hold a fork or spoon, the only way he could now lift the smallest morsel of food to his own mouth.

The occupational therapist had come to the house several times to fit the custom-made tenodesis splint and teach him how to adjust it himself with the Velcro straps. He had relatively good wrist flexion and extension, she explained on each occasion. Duncan wasn't sure if she didn't remember that she had already told him these things the first time, during the initial evaluation just before he came home, when he had been moved to the rehab wing of the hospital, or if she thought he couldn't retain the information. His spinal cord injury had left him with a very weak pinch grip.

Before Ottoline, Duncan had been pessimistic about physical therapy and the concept of making the most of whatever he could do with his left hand. But the practical necessity of being able to get her in and out of the cage and tethered or untethered to his chair without assistance had motivated him. Clipping and unclipping Ottoline's leash fasteners, opening her cage door fastener and re-latching it—these were the first difficult tasks he had been willing to work for since the accident.

Increased grip strength and dexterity did make lots of small differences for Duncan, among them an improved ability to hold his binoculars steady. Ottoline loved the binoculars, and he let her look through them, at her insistence, though it wasn't apparent that she could really see anything at all, and it was unlikely that she understood that she was seeing distant things as if they were much nearer. Ottoline liked to duck under the binocular strap around his neck to tuck herself into a leisurely position on her back. She would lie there against his chest, holding the binoculars in front of her face with her hands and feet, aiming them this way and that. Monkey see, monkey do. She often smeared up the lenses. She liked best to flex the rubber eyecups, and she could happily recline on Duncan as if he were a lounge chair, one leg cocked over the other, flipping the pliable rubber eyecups in and out, in and out, over and over, *plip-plap, plip-plap*, for very long intervals, if nothing distracted her. At other moments, she had taken to folding down his ears similarly, over and over, as if she was hoping to achieve the same effect.

"What's going on with the McCarthy kids, Ottoline?" Laura overheard Duncan murmuring in a confiding tone to the monkey in his lap. It was mid-afternoon, on a day she had finally concluded a painstaking cleaning of one of the Gallery's treasures (for the two weeks she worked on "Hercules and Deianira" she had perseverated the artist's name, *Pollaiuolo, Pollaiuolo*) and headed home from work earlier than usual. The streets in their neighborhood came alive with children each day when all the neighborhood schools let out. Duncan was using a gentle, lilting voice she had only ever before heard from him when he encountered someone's cat or dog.

"What do you think, missy? Let's take a look. No, now it's my turn. Wait! You had your turn. Thank you, good girl! Now they're getting out of the car. There's the older brother, and look, he has a toy helicopter. Here comes the little sister. Ingie sets her down on the sidewalk and she goes for it! Is she going to get her hands on his helicopter? No, she is not! Is her brother going to put out her eye with the helicopter before Ingie notices? There's Ingie going for the trash can next door. Wait for it! Here comes the McDonald's drop, in three . . . two . . . one. Okay, *now* it's your turn."

# FIVE

*Lately, after Duncan and Ottoline*
*had each been tucked in for the night*

LATELY, AFTER DUNCAN AND OTTOLINE HAD EACH
been tucked in for the night and the evening shift PCA had
gone home, when Laura went to bed, upstairs, alone in the
room she had shared with Duncan, the room he would never
see again, she found herself putting aside her disappointing new novel of the moment (ever since Henry's Bookshop
closed, her reading choices had been hit and miss unless she
picked an old favorite off a bookshelf for re-reading), or tried
to absorb one of the growing stack of unread issues of the
*New Yorker*, and instead reaching for the dog-eared folder of
Primate Institute material and advice. She still slept on her
side of the bed, out of habit. She had all the pillows to herself
now, and she arranged them just so for reading in bed, with
the two that used to be Duncan's appropriated the way she
used to deploy them only when he was away for a night or
two on a work trip—one to prop her elbow to facilitate holding her reading material, and the other folded in half under
her knees. Capuchin monkeys will respect men before trust-

ing them. They will trust women before respecting them; respect has to be earned.

There was nobody to tell her how late it was, stop reading about monkey hierarchies, turn off the light, cuddle me. She often stayed up until two or three in the morning reading about the proclivities and training of capuchin monkeys. Tonight as she paged through the familiar advice, she had for company a generous glass of Italian pinot noir, from the last bottle of the last case Duncan had brought home from an office party, and the bowl of leftover Halloween candy (it had dwindled down to a few sad Milky Ways and Butterfingers, but was brimming again, supplemented with the new Say Howdy! miniatures).

Across the hall was the small room the glib and persuasive realtor who sold them the house had called the baby's room, which they had never once called the baby's room, not wanting to jinx their luck. The box room, they called it, with ironic awareness of the pretentious Bertie Wooster tone of that term, rather than settle for the dull respectability of guest room or the tidy-as-a-pin spare room of Virginia Woolf's Lucy Swithin, though it was tidy as a pin, with a day bed, a scarred maple chest of drawers Duncan grew up with, and a closet holding Duncan's old ski clothing and Laura's abandoned Pilates equipment. A single black and white photograph of Frank Lloyd Wright's Fallingwater house was all that hung on the walls. It was the plainest and least personal room in their house, and it would never be anything but the box room.

Laura sipped her wine, mindful of not dribbling on her favorite soft blue-and-white-striped sheets they had brought back from their romantic Christmas trip to Milan last year. They had hoped the trip to Italy would change the frequency after those eighteen months of trying unsuccessfully for a baby. Laura had been particularly optimistic about conceiving on that trip, and had even allowed herself to imagine the future, eighteen or twenty years hence, when she would have the disclosing conversation with that child, during which she would reveal, tastefully and appropriately, without too much detail, the fact of that tender Italian beginning. You were just the tiniest *zigote*, she would tell their firstborn, perhaps to mark the occasion of Clementine or August leaving for a junior year abroad, in Italy or France.

Medical tests showed nothing wrong with either of them. She was ovulating on schedule. Her fallopian tubes were clear. Her hormone levels were normal. She did not have cervical mucus hostility. (Thanks a lot for that mental picture, thought Laura when she read the lab report.) Duncan's sperm was motile. (I contain multitudes, he had declared with pride when they received his highly adequate sperm count, upwards of two hundred million, which took the edge off the warm plastic cup embarrassment.)

How many times had they been hopeful? How many times had Laura carried herself with extra care, feeling with certainty that tiny spark of life taking root deep inside her? How had they ever been so cocky as to joke about the possibility of twins running in the family? Month after month, she welcomed the sperm, offered her egg, coaxed and willed each zygote into being, into becoming an embryo, into staying and making itself at home.

How many mornings had she been woken by the disheartening ooze of blood trickling between her legs? How many times had she realized that her tender breasts only heralded that familiar shift in her belly signifying the shedding of another uterine lining? Now it was two years of the dreaded trickle in the middle of dinner with friends, at the movies, at work, at the grocery store. Two years of farewells to what might have been, each month bringing a fresh grief of goodbye, baby who never was, goodbye, this month's uncleaved zygote, goodbye, little not-an-embryo, goodbye, little laughing boy who might have been, goodbye, sweet napping girl in my arms who wasn't meant to be. You are not meant to be this month, my future baby. Maybe you are meant to be next month.

The day before Duncan's accident, Laura was five or perhaps six days late. Her cycle was fairly regular, so this lateness had once again lit a tiny flicker of hope. She had planned to wait a full week, hoping, hoping, hoping, before telling Duncan. But at dinner, seared scallops and a big slightly sandy salad (because Laura was inattentive to her one kitchen assignment, washing lettuce, a tedious task she disliked and did badly), as Duncan reached over and speared one of her untouched scallops, he caught her eye and after a long moment, it registered.

"Are you? You really think?" She had nodded without answering, not even wanting to say anything aloud this time. They didn't speak of it again, but lay in bed that night in a tight spoon, neither of them able to go to sleep. "I want embryo to take piano lessons," Duncan whispered against the back of her neck in the middle of the night. They had not spoken of it the next morning, though it was in the air as they had their usual companionable granola and yogurt together while listening to public radio, before Duncan walked out the door for the last time to go to work.

Laura had taken to laundering these blue-and-white-striped sheets and putting them right back on the bed still warm from the dryer, preferring the soft Italian cotton to all the other sets of bed linen on the hallway closet shelf. There was nobody in the world who cared what sheets were on her bed or how often they were changed. Upstairs, alone. Alone upstairs. The solitude of this time of day was something she looked forward to but also dreaded.

It still felt unreal to lie in their bed, her bed, after she had turned out the light, staring at the dark, realizing all over again with fresh grief that she would never hear Duncan's familiar footsteps as he bounded up the stairs, that she would never hear the sound of his pocket change going into the silver dish on his bureau, that she would never again be annoyed by his whiskers and toothpaste left in the un-rinsed sink, or his discarded socks and underwear dropped and forgotten on the bedroom floor the moment he stepped out of them, or his damp bath towel left on the bed after a shower instead of hung up to dry. Such clichéd, ordinary male behavior for someone who prided himself on his originality and attention to detail.

Laura missed the easy intimacy of those thousands of ordinary frictions. Of course, the loss of those particular little nuisances of their life together—the toothpaste, the socks, the forgotten damp towels, not to mention the messes Duncan left in the kitchen whenever he cooked a meal—none of it mattered in the larger scheme of things, but quotidian (a favorite word of Duncan's) encounters in their domestic life together were the incandescent particles that sparked the vitality of their marriage, he had written in uncharacteristically flowery language on the card that accompanied a fifth-anniversary gift of beautifully incandescent sapphire earrings.

There was an almost formal distance between them now, and it wasn't just the literal physical space that Ottoline so often demanded, or the separation created by the impossibility of ever sleeping together as they had all their married life until now. Laura missed the sweet intimacy of spooning more than she missed sex. Nor was it simply the loss of spontaneity between them, now that the most ordinary moments of daily living required strategies and preparation and the negotiation of constant accommodation. Though that was indeed a loss. Of course she could lie down on his bed and cuddle with Duncan, and they did this nearly every day, but it could be awkward and complicated to arrange herself against Duncan, and Laura could hardly bear the realization each time that he didn't feel her hip against him, or her hand on his waist.

There were options, suggested the female hospital social worker who called her to discuss how Laura and Duncan were doing, attempting to open a door on a frank discussion of the creative strategies a couple had for maintaining a lively and intimate sexual connection when one partner was paralyzed. There were things they could do. Laura was sure that this was true for lots of couples. She could imagine very different people finding their way somewhere new, collaborating, being really in it together on this weird adventure that would be intimate and profound in its way. But Duncan had become so remote. How could you get there from here?

At moments, even the most ordinary and natural gesture of affection felt like a procedure she was administrating and Duncan was receiving. Lying in his hospital bed, barely able to turn his head, with only limited possible movement of one arm, he seemed so helpless and incapacitated compared to the sturdy man who used to live in that body. How could Laura gaze at Duncan without feeling that she was entirely responsible for him? This was a disconcertingly unromantic thought. When she kissed him, he was often minimally responsive, though polite. Nothing felt reciprocal. Touching Duncan, no matter how lightly she stroked him, no matter how delicately she walked her hand across his upper torso with delicate, brushing fingertips (something he used to love so much it made him groan with pleasure), Laura would watch him just lie there silently, perhaps waiting for her to stop. His passive politeness made her feel nurse-like, as if he accepted that her every touch was just one more thing she was doing to him.

She was in a kind of phantom mourning, longing for these lost aspects of daily life with Duncan. Meanwhile, Duncan wasn't the dearly departed, he was the dearly downstairs. As she lay there awake, Duncan was deep in a drugged sleep with the swish-swish-swish CPAP machine running, the mask snugged on his face reminding Laura at different moments of

elephants, divers, welders, soldiers, protesters, HazMat workers, exterminators. He only needed breathing assistance while
he slept. The trauma surgeons had said Duncan was lucky
(that word again!), that he was just millimeters away from a
C4 or C3 spinal cord injury, which would have left him forever dependent on a respirator to do all his breathing for him,
never mind that Christopher Reeve had managed to breathe
on his own for fifteen minutes at a time after undergoing surgery to implant electrodes in his diaphragm.

Never mind Christopher Reeve altogether, though Duncan and Laura were constantly reminded by well-meaning
friends and helpers about how impressive and dignified and
determined he was, how he had managed to do so much after
his accident, not to mention his wonderful contributions to
research. Yes, Christopher Reeve was everybody's favorite
poster child for life with quadriplegia, but let's not forget that
the poor man's death, after all that valiant effort, was a consequence of pressure sores.

While Laura lay alone and awake ruminating in the dark
upstairs, Duncan lay directly beneath her, sleeping in his
hospital bed in the room that used to be his spacious home
office (which had each year made fourteen percent of certain
household expenses tax deductible), now set up like a hospital room. He was not alone. Across from the rolling lift was
the large cage which held a sleeping tufted capuchin monkey,
snoring faintly under her faded flannel baby blanket where
she lay peacefully beside her favorite little red teddy bear.

# SIX

*Laura missed her mother
in a new way since the accident*

LAURA MISSED HER MOTHER IN A NEW WAY SINCE THE accident, even while imagining how useless and irritating she would have been in this situation, in between occasional moments of being kind and helpful. Marion Keller's excision from Laura's story had not been a sudden picnic, lightning sort of event, but a gradual effacement caused by early-onset dementia, to the point of near-extinction of the part of her mind where Marion dwelled. The lively, sharp-tongued retired dental office receptionist from Ohio who had raised Laura on her own had simply gradually ceased to exist. She lived on, however, in a nursing home called The Willows, on the other side of New Haven. There was a wing devoted to residents who shared Laura's mother's "exit-seeking behavior."

When Laura cleaned out her mother's apartment on Whitney Avenue the week of her precipitous move to The Willows, when it had quite suddenly become apparent that the support of daily visiting nurses and Meals on Wheels were no longer enough to keep Marion going and there had been a fortuitously available room, she had found a heartbreaking mess. A flannel nightgown was wadded up in the crisper drawer in the refrigerator, while spoiled boxes of frozen vegetables were stacked in the linen closet. Thick rubber-banded bundles of unopened mail were wedged under the sofa cushions. On a notepad beside her mother's bed, in a wobbly version of her mother's familiar handwriting, Laura spotted these urgently underlined reminders: TOMORROW WILL BE TODAY. IT IS STILL TODAY RIGHT NOW.

Marion hadn't shown more than a flicker of recognition of Laura for nearly two years, and the last time she had spoken to Laura at all, after months of silent staring, which the doctors called elective mutism, she had declared, inexplicably and unexpectedly, at the end of a visit on her fifty-fifth birthday that had consisted of Laura nattering (while Marion gazed at her, expressionless as always) about the chocolate birthday cupcake, the rainy weather, and Duncan says hello and how nice her mother's hair looked that day, "You're just like me! We're loners! I never thought in a million years that anyone would love you enough to marry you! Bet you didn't think so either!"

A nursing aide assured Laura that demented people say strange things when they are no longer really themselves, for example Sylvia, the sweet old lady across the hall who played the organ for the Methodist church in Hamden every Sunday for forty-three years, these days she swears like a sailor whenever anyone tries to comb the tangles out of that wispy little head of hair she's still got.

"She didn't mean nothing by that, sweetheart," the kindly aide had said to her as she walked Laura out through the double set of locked doors. "Your mama loves you. I can see it in her eyes." Laura had parsed this double negative on the way to her car. If she didn't mean nothing, then surely she did mean something.

———

Marion Keller did indeed love her daughter, though she had always been a brisk and unsentimental mother. Marion herself was an only child. Her mother had died when she was in eighth grade, and for reasons she never spoke about, she wasn't close to her father. There was a lot she didn't speak about. Having grown up on a hardscrabble farm on the outskirts of Centerburg, Ohio, a small, plain town in the center of the state (thus the name), Marion had left home the day after her high school graduation.

Though she claimed to have never wanted to return to the farm, Marion only moved as far as Westerville, twenty miles down Route Three, where she got a job at a dry-cleaning shop and lived in a small apartment over a travel agency on West Main Street. Laura lived in this apartment with her mother for the first six years of her life, until they moved to Connecticut.

Marion was as vague about the identity of Laura's father as she was inconsistent about the circumstances of their brief marriage. As Laura grew up, she heard a variety of her mother's accounts of her life between leaving home and having Laura. Marion had left home to share the Westerville apartment with her best friend from high school. Marion eloped with her high school sweetheart (whose name was too painful to say) right after graduation, but he was drafted and was shipped off to Vietnam, while she stayed in Westerville with her best friend from high school to await his return. But she got word that he was lost in action right away, and after a while he was declared MIA. By then, Marion, only eighteen at the time, was quite pregnant with Laura.

Marion was never able to qualify for benefits, she explained to Laura when Laura was old enough to inquire about such things (and Laura was very much the sort of child who concerned herself at a young age with insurance forms and knowing if the utility bills had been paid and if the car registration was up to date), because when they eloped, it turned out their marriage was never properly registered, because of a technicality. Because someone forgot to sign a form. Because they didn't know they had to pay for something to be registered at some town hall somewhere. They were kids! Because some town hall office somewhere was closed on the afternoon they went there. But someone performed the ceremony anyway, without the paperwork. Because some town hall office lost the papers, or filed them incorrectly, or spelled a name wrong. Who can remember the name of a little town in the middle of nowhere? Did they even know the name of the town where they got married that day? They were so young! The way Marion told it, they just drove and drove until they got to a town where they could get married and that's what they did.

The creased snapshot Marion carried in her wallet, the one photograph of Laura's father in her possession, had been taken, according to Marion, by the waitress at the diner in Butler on their way back from the courthouse or the town hall or the whatever, wherever they had gotten married. All versions of the story landed at the same conclusion, like a folk song with many verses and one familiar refrain: he was a war hero and Laura should feel proud of the man who was her father, and let's leave it there. "Never look back unless you're planning to go that way," Marion liked to say.

When Laura was in fourth grade, a Vietnam veteran gave an assembly presentation at her school, and as she shifted in her folding chair with rubber-tipped feet that squeaked on the linoleum floor of the "cafetorium," it dawned on her that the war in Vietnam had ended four years before she was born, as had the draft. But she knew by then that this was not information with which to challenge her mother. By high school, she figured that her mother and father had probably not been married.

———

Was the nameless man in the photo actually even her father? She would slip the photograph from her mother's wallet, where she knew to find it in the slot behind the Stop & Shop loyalty card, and study his features. Did Laura resemble him? Sometimes she thought she did. But then at times when she looked at the teenaged version of Marion, on whose shoulder his leather-jacketed arm was draped, Laura could barely find anything of her own features in her mother's young face.

In more recent years Laura had been frustrated all over again by her mother's fluctuating versions of history, which were utterly useless as she attempted to gather more complete medical background information as she began to worry about her fertility. By then Marion's recollections of personal history were beginning to get looser and vaguer, a mental state that seemed to match her temperament. She retired from her last job at the front desk of a downtown New Haven dental practice, where she had worked for nearly twenty years.

Armed with a few dubious facts extracted from her mother, Laura spent many hours on the internet tracking down some dead ends, and she also called various town clerks all over Butler County, with fruitless results. Laura even telephoned two diners in Butler, Ohio, hoping absurdly to find the salty waitress with a heart of gold who had worked there for a little more than Laura's lifetime, someone who would remember the newlywed couple ("Sure, sure honey, of course I remember them! They had just gotten married that day! They asked me to take their picture. It was my first week on the job. Cute couple, so in love. He had a farmer's breakfast and she had a short stack. How about that, after all these years!") But it was another double negative, proving only that there was no evidence for a marriage that did not exist.

Who was the guy in the photo? (Laura now kept her mother's wallet in her desk drawer.) Was he a one-night stand? A date rape, or worse? Laura's college roommate Ann had suggested, imaginatively, that if her mother had worked not at a dry cleaner's but at a VA hospital, on the night shift, where she met Laura's Vietnam war hero father, who was in reality a fatally wounded and hideously disfigured patient there, then perhaps her conception had been like Garp's. They had both laughed hysterically at the image, feeling wildly intellectual and sophisticated while yelping Garp! Garp! Garp!

Indulging this fantasy, Laura once looked up VA hospitals in Ohio, but the nearest one to Westerville was more than sixty miles away, an unlikely commute, and in any case it had not occurred to her before then to doubt the part of her mother's story about her job at the dry cleaner's, though in later years, during the slide into dementia, her mother more than once claimed to have worked at a travel agency while living over a dry cleaning shop. The last time Laura tried to pin her down about these details her mother had barked at her Fine! Maybe it wasn't Ohio at all, how about that, sister, maybe it was Iowa or Idaho, who can say? Want to put that in your pipe and smoke it? Since when is my life your fucking business?

Laura envied Duncan his compact and complete dead father story, over and done in a sentence or two: John Wheeler was a very successful life insurance executive who died of a massive heart attack at the age of forty-two (a terrible irony, given his profession), leaving a young wife and twin eleven-year-old sons. Duncan knew exactly who his father had been and he knew precisely where his father was now.

Laura had just a single memory of visiting her grandfather on his farm, because she had only met him the one time, when she was six, that same summer they moved to Connecticut. Her mother said they were going to the farm so Laura could meet her grandfather and also say goodbye to him before they left, a hello goodbye, which sounded to Laura like some kind of game, and she waited for her mother to explain the rules.

The goats and their crazy eyes disturbed her, and their rank smell made Laura spend that afternoon breathing through her mouth, which caused her mother to ask her repeatedly if she needed to blow her nose. There were kittens among the hay bales in the barn. These were Laura's first kittens and she loved them. She tried to contain three of them in her lap while they squirmed away, over and over, until her nose really did stuff up with her first allergic reaction to cats.

When it was time to go in the house for a snack before they went home, Laura tried to be on her best behavior, as her mother had requested. Her grandfather moved slowly around his kitchen, as if it pained him. He was tall and thin, and a little bent over, and he looked down at the floor all the time, as if he was always expecting something underfoot. Laura's mother knew where things were kept in the pale blue kitchen cupboards. She shut them with a bang.

Instead of saying her name he called Laura "Sister," which was strange, because she was an only child, and he didn't say it in a particularly friendly way. She sat with her feet swinging under his white enamel-top kitchen table, nibbling tiny mouse bites from the stale end piece of pound cake he had tipped onto her plate from its Sara Lee foil loaf pan. Her mother never gave her bread heels and always put them on her own plate, turning them to the inside of her tuna sandwiches to fool herself into not noticing.

"You fussy like your mama, Sister?" he asked Laura suddenly.

"She's entitled to her likes and dislikes, Pops," her mother answered for her.

"I don't expect a fig from a thistle. You weren't any kind of fig either, that's for damned sure, not from your mama. Anyways, those kittens might could have fleas. Probably do. And ringworm. Real easy to catch that."

"Don't worry about it, Pops."

"You had the ringworm more than once. You were always a dirty little girl."

"Here we go. Come on Laura, finish up your cake. Or leave it."

"I meant to drown them before now. One thing I don't need is a barn full of damn kittens turning into cats."

"Nice. Really nice, Pops. Wonderful having this visit with you."

"You hear on the news about that carnival ride, what happened there on the weekend? That's what people get when their brats run wild all over the damned place."

"Good evening, Mr. and Mrs. America, and all the ships at sea," Laura's mother said, though it was still afternoon.

Laura chewed the dry cake into a paste in her mouth and swung her feet faster under the table. Her nose was completely stuffed. Her grandfather hadn't given her a napkin and she didn't know what to call him and she didn't dare say anything. She couldn't wipe her nose on her sleeve because she was wearing a short-sleeved shirt, and her mother was standing by the window lifting the limp curtain and looking out, with the car keys jingling in her hand, so Laura snuffled in, which made her mother turn around and pull out a crumpled tissue from her pocket and reach across the table and wipe it across Laura's nose as if she were a little baby. How could she?

"Now you can't say you never met your grandfather," her mother said over her shoulder on the drive home. When, in the years that followed, Laura would from time to time ask her mother about why they moved east that summer, her mother would always say something about it having been time for a change, or she would remind her about how much she hated the smell of those goats.

On just one occasion, when Laura was ten, when she was up in the middle of the night with a fever and a miserable, croupy cough, and her mother had lain down beside her on her narrow bed to soothe her back to sleep, Laura dared to bring up her memory of a day at some fair or amusement park.

As the steamer hissed and tendrils of cold steam drifted and unfurled across the room, the dim light from the hall-way illuminated the mirror on her closet door misting into a cloud until her reflected room faded and then disappeared. Laura asked her mother, did she witness an accident on a car-nival ride when she was really little? That summer before they moved out east? Was she on a ride when someone fell out? Laura was sure she remembered people screaming. Was everyone running from a fire?

Nobody died, her mother told her. Now hush. It had noth-ing to do with you. It was a long time ago. You're probably remembering hearing your grandfather talk about it that time we visited. Remember those stinky goats?

Her mother held her close. It was nice. Laura fell into a fever sleep.

The red button so appealing, like a clown's nose waiting to be honked. The wooden steps so inviting, like a ladder waiting to be climbed. The exciting music, frantic and falsely cheer-ful, but with that hysterical pitch which on television always signifies something about to go wrong.

The red button so intriguing.

Laura hated the man in the dirty green T-shirt who ran the Twister. He got to push the red button each time the ride stopped and started. That was his whole job, and it should be fun, but he was so bored and indifferent, like the unsmiling school bus driver whose bus passed her house every morning, the one who never, ever waved back.

The red button was so big and smooth-looking under the fingers of the bad green T-shirt man. His cigarette dangled between his lips and a curl of greasy smoke hung in the air in front of his scowly face. He smelled.

She knew he smelled because this was the second time she had ridden the Twister, all alone because she was a big girl of six and her mother didn't like rides much anyway, but after all, she said to Laura, it's the Ohio State Fair, so let's go, so she let her go on the rides while she waited and watched the crowds. The first time he had bent over Laura to adjust the safety bar she had accidentally breathed in a nasty whiff of armpit. Now, after some obligatory rides on the boring junior roller coaster and the babyish merry-go-round, she was back on the Twister, an experienced adventurer adjusting the safety bar all by herself to pre-empt further assistance from bad smelly green T-shirt man.

As she had earlier, Laura's mother waited under a tree where it was shady and she could hold her daughter's blue balloon and watch her going around and around and around. It was beginning. Slowly at first, a teasing lazy few turns around. A mild little ride, nothing at all to be afraid of. But then more and more speed, more and more spinning as the Twister uncoiled and recoiled its armloads of frenzied, screaming passengers. Around and around, each time they passed the big tree Laura turned her head against the force to look for her waving mother, until the Twister whirled too fast and her mother became an indistinguishable element of the motion-striped blur.

Each time she spun past the control platform, green T-shirt man was there leaning on the railing staring at nothing. As the coiled arm of the Twister flung each car out and then gathered it back in, Laura was suspended for a motionless moment directly over him. She could see the red button next to his bored hand.

Green T-shirt man was dirty, but his red button was clean and smooth and she really wanted to touch it.

The ride slowed disappointingly and then came to a stop, the way it always did, some cars continuing to swing around. She tried to predict where her car would stop and was almost right. The music insisted that everything was thrilling and wonderful but just wait. Green T-shirt man walked around popping open safety bars. In his wake, kids erupted out of the seats and scampered towards the exit steps, sneakered feet squeaking and thundering on the painted plywood platform. Grownups didn't usually need his help, but a fat lady over on the other side seemed unable to raise her safety bar and he ambled over to help her.

The red button was all alone and Laura was standing on the top step for the exit, right next to it, only a thin drooping plastic chain between them. Just a touch. Just to feel for a moment if it was as smooth as it looked.

Ducking under the chain, she found herself standing directly in front of the red button. It glowed beautifully, like a sucked cough lozenge.

Green T-shirt man was now standing beside her but he had his back to her as he lifted open the gate on the entrance ramp. Kids stampeded onto the platform, racing to claim seats.

Sweetheart! Her mother's voice was far away, all the way on the other side of the Twister. Green T-shirt man would turn around any moment.

She reached up and touched the red button. With just her fingertips. It was warm from the sun. It felt smooth and nice, the way her mother's pearls felt, neck-warmed, when she was allowed to play with them for a few minutes at bedtime.

Hey! Kid! Don't touch that!

Green T-shirt man's unexpected crawly touch on the back of her neck made her jump.

Her hand splayed on the red button, pressing down for just an instant.

The Twister came to life, turning, twisting, grinding.

Screams and screams and screams.

Green T-shirt man smashed his fist down on the red button just as her mother grabbed her under both arms and dragged her roughly down the wooden steps, away from the platform.

Slung over one of her mother's shoulders, Laura was bouncing too hard to focus. Everyone was yelling, and there were people running in all directions. She shut her eyes, feeling all through her the jolt of the pounding feet, the pounding heart, the relentless sour music from the rides.

Her lower lip was cut by her own front teeth as her mother ran. She felt the blood pooling under her tongue and she opened her mouth to let it escape. Like Hansel and Gretel in the forest, they left a trail behind them. Would the green T-shirt man follow the blood drops and catch them? She was afraid. She began to cry.

At the car, her mother deposited Laura in the back seat. Was she crying too? Her breath sobbed in and out of her as she bent over to lower Laura onto the seat, with extra gentleness. Her mother's blouse was wet with sweat. Laura didn't like it that her mother smelled different than she ever had before. It seemed bad, like a rule that should never be broken.

The music, grinning and mean, seemed to follow them down the road. As they turned onto the highway towards home, an ambulance going at top speed in the opposite direction passed them blaring Dir-ty! Dir-ty! Dir-ty!

Hungry, sweetheart? Laura's mother was looking at her in the rearview mirror as she drove. There had been a plan to have hot dogs at the amusement park.

Laura shook her head no. Her tears had dried on her face with the blood from her bottom lip, and there was a bad metal taste in her mouth. She was suddenly very tired. Her balloon was gone.

Me neither, her mother said softly. They drove in silence and after a while Laura fell asleep. When they got home, Laura was hungry after all, and Laura's mother made breakfast for dinner, as a treat to make up for missing the hot dogs— pancakes with sorghum syrup. When Laura got into bed, she waited for her mother to tuck her in, but she didn't come for a long time, and Laura fell asleep.

She woke up in the middle of the night, uncertain where she was, afraid of the green T-shirt man, but she was safe in her own bed, in her dark room, and her mother was sitting up beside her on the bed, her familiar form barely visible in the dim misted light from the hallway.

Is it now, or are we still in Ohio? Laura whispered.

Of course it's now, her mother said, placing a cool palm on her forehead and then smoothing Laura's damp hair back from her face. It's always now. You're still burning up. The steamer mist had left a silvery web of tiny droplets on Laura's quilt, like dew. I just told you, nothing bad happened to anyone. Forget about it. Have a sip of water now and try to go back to sleep. She lay back down on top of the covers beside Laura and nestled up against her again in a reassuring spoon.

Laura burrowed back into her fever sleep and there was the green T-shirt man. He was tall and thin, and he looked down at her with crazy sideways eyes. The red button was on his belt buckle, and he held her wrist tightly and forced her to touch it, over and over, while it glowed hotter and hotter until her fingers were burning, but she couldn't pull her hand away. He laughed at her and called her Sister, and said she was dirty just like her mama, and she ought to be drowned along with the kittens that were running all around. Her nose was stuffed up from the kittens and she couldn't breathe and her throat was tight and then a barking barking barking dog came running in and frightened the kittens away and woke her up and she was cough cough coughing her croup croup croup cough and her mother was still lying right beside her, one arm over Laura's waist holding her close, and it was still now.

# SEVEN

## *Every day at the hospital Laura had updated Duncan*

EVERY DAY AT THE HOSPITAL LAURA HAD UPDATED
Duncan with all the details of the necessary changes in the
house, starting with the construction of a wooden ramp that
zig-zagged up the entire left side of their front lawn to the
front porch. The builders had been sent over by Dave Halloran with materials and a sketch in hand, and the firm had
paid for everything. But, sedated and drifting, Duncan had
not taken anything in.

"Isn't that Ipe? What was the materials cost?" he asked,
as he was rolled up the ramp for the first time on that September day when he came home from the hospital. "Cedar
would have been adequate. This ramp's going to last fifty
years. Nobody's going to need this ramp in fifty years. Or in
five years."

"Don't talk that way, Dunc! You're home! I have no idea.
The office just made it all happen. They never sent a bill. The
builder called it something else." Laura was walking backwards up the ramp in front of him so she could see his face.
The two medical transport techs would settle him, and the

first PCA was already a few minutes into his shift. Laura had longed for this moment.

"Ipe as in tripe, maybe?" Duncan eyed the smooth planks as best he could while barely moving his head, and then they bumped over the threshold and were in the front door, and then they were rolling through the foyer, home, home, home, and then came the shock of seeing his former office, now set up for him with his beloved red and blue dhurrie rolled up and stored under his desk, which had been pushed against the floor-to-ceiling bookcases on the far wall.

An ugly hospital bed dominated the center of the room, made up and ready, as if on display, the side rails down, awaiting the patient. The hideous commode was positioned in the corner. The rolling Hoyer lift dangled at the ready like some mechanism you would expect to see used on an automobile assembly line.

Now Duncan saw with startling realization all the dismantling and disorder that had been imposed on his beautiful room, the room where he had made everything exactly the way he wanted it, the room where he loved to work in solitary reverie, a quiet sanctuary that was the antidote to the collaborative hive of activity that surrounded him at Corrigan & Wheeler. Duncan had a private aversion to open-plan offices but had never felt entitled to contravene Billy Corrigan's original layout design that dated from the occasion six years ago when Corrigan & Associates moved from their Chapel Street office overlooking the New Haven Green to the old brick ladder factory building in Fair Haven, once the heart of nineteenth-century New Haven industry. That was when the firm became Corrigan & Wheeler. Duncan conducted all of his business at the office, but when he was drawing new projects or brainstorming challenging design problems, he went home to his sanctuary to concentrate, if only for an hour, away from the lively and endlessly distracting atmosphere of Corrigan & Wheeler's resonant expanse.

On that September afternoon, after he had done all the healing he was going to do in the hospital, Duncan was rolled up the ramp and into his house, and he understood in a grim new way just how much his life had changed. He had longed to leave the hospital and had counted the days until he could go home. Home. He thought he wanted to go home, but what was home? He hadn't simply wanted to go home, he had wanted to go back in time. How could he live here, or anywhere? Not only was he transformed, but now his beautiful room was filled with mis-proportioned metal and plastic necessities in egregious colors and finishes that were already horribly familiar aspects of his life after two months in the hospital.

A steel, tiered trolley (better suited to the icy, soulless gleam of a Richard Meier interior) was stacked with the ubiquitous folded blue disposable underpads and stocked with catheter tubing, irrigation trays, syringes, drainage bags, boxes of disposable gloves, basins filled with bowel care items (do you laugh or cry when you depend on something in your daily life called Enemeez?), a stack of blue plastic kidney dishes, tubes of lubricant, a blood pressure kit, Nitro paste, swabs, alcohol wipes, gauze, tape, and all the other paraphernalia required for the new regimen of maintaining the functional workings of Duncan's inert yet all too organic body. The worst of it for Duncan was the sight of the commode squatting on its rubber-tipped feet on the lovely spalted maple floorboards (he had refinished them himself over a long weekend), which glowed like honey in the late summer sunlight filtering through branches of the overgrown rhododendron outside.

His blood pressure had soared within minutes after he rolled in the door. A headache suddenly pinballed from temple to temple as he looked around his reorganized study. He felt the room growing dark. "They must work hard to make all this shit as ugly as possible!" Duncan exclaimed.

One of the transport techs hovered over Duncan with the Nitro paste, ready to open his shirt and smear the paste on his bare skin to bring him out of dysreflexia, but his blood pressure subsided and it wasn't necessary. After the moment passed, Duncan was transferred into the bed from the transport wheelchair by the techs and Oliver, the very agreeable and competent PCA on this inaugural shift. Oliver was a medical student from Taiwan. (He was one of the two PCAs who would soon quit over the arrival of a monkey. Duncan was very sorry to see him go. The other PCA who would leave because of Ottoline was the sweet and devout Natalie, whose relentless chitchat about the Holy Spirit and His plans for Duncan in those early weeks at home made her departure a relief.)

Duncan was anguished over the reality of his new living arrangements. But where the hell had he thought he would sleep? How the hell had he thought he would live? Did he expect that as soon as he was in his house he would jump up out of the chair, race upstairs, empty his pockets into the dish on his dresser, change out of his work clothes into a comfortable sweater, and then go down to the kitchen to make himself a gin and tonic before starting to prepare dinner just as he used to do? He simply hadn't allowed himself to understand that daily life as he had known it was over. He simply had not begun to imagine what it was really going to be like to live this new, constricted life in his own house. And now here he was. How could anyone live this way?

"Maybe this is my chance to one-up Michael Graves in the category of over-designed objects for the home—the Duncan Wheeler Home Hospital Furniture System," Duncan proclaimed with the counterfeit enthusiasm of a radio announcer. "The ultimate in modular modern classics, designed for the home-bound cripple."

"So why don't you do it?" Laura asked.

"I'm joking."

"But why not?" she persisted. "It's a good idea! You could design a line of household objects for—"

"For rich cripples? For prosperous, tasteful gimps and quads?"

"Yes! Damn it, yes! Duncan, you know you could actually do it if you wanted to."

Why was she arguing with him? Laura couldn't stop herself, though she knew it was futile trying to persuade him about anything these days. In the hospital, every optimistic thought or hope she had launched was just something for him to shoot down, with deadly aim, another clay pigeon arcing across the sky for him, a target he could blow to smithereens in an instant. Now that he was home he was even more obdurate.

Laura had not been careless or hasty as she had gone about setting up Duncan's room. It was the only reasonable arrangement if he was going to live in this house. The downstairs bathroom was too small to accommodate a commode and still allow an adequate angle for the Hoyer lift. As it was, the lift just fit, barely, with careful maneuvers, to position him for bathing in the shower stall on a high-backed plastic chair fitted with a webbed chest restraint.

It took skill to roll Duncan's inert body this way and that, in order to situate him in the center of the sling where it lay opened flat on his bed, then hook him in, and then lift him and move him into the bathroom as he dangled like a prize grabbed up from the pile in an arcade claw machine. Duncan was nearly six feet tall, and even though his body had dwindled considerably since the accident, lost muscle mass he would never get back, he was still a large, solid dead weight. It would take weeks before Laura felt confident making a transfer without one of the PCAs talking her through each step. As she grew more dexterous at operating the lift, it never stopped feeling to her that every moment of the maneuver, from bed to bathroom for showering and then back again for dressing, was a potential humiliation for Duncan.

Who would want to be handled this way by his wife, like cargo, like a permanent giant damaged baby, like the dependent, diminished quadriplegic husband he had become?

A small painted chest of drawers moved down from the attic (it had been there when they bought the house, filled with somebody's dead grandmother's moldy dinner napkins and tablecloths) held the limited selection of his clothes in which he could be most easily dressed. Laura had simply left everything else upstairs in Duncan's bureau drawers and closet. His new room was set up, she assured him, with enough clearance so that he could maneuver his wheelchair to sit at his desk to work.

Duncan had built the desk himself, before he met Laura, out of layered wafers of Baltic birch plywood salvaged from a kitchen renovation he helped a classmate build one summer during college. He was particularly proud of the pin and cove dovetailing in the three drawers. Laura had pushed it back against the wall of bookshelves but had not otherwise touched anything on or in the desk, and it was just the way Duncan had left it in July.

A flimsy cardboard tube of architectural drawings had fallen onto the floor from a lower shelf, out of sight behind the desk. Duncan had shoved it there carelessly a long while ago, when he had brought home several boxes of books and papers from his mother's attic after she died. When Laura nudged the desk right against the bookshelves, she had accidentally squashed the tube, and it was with trepidation that she tugged out the flattened roll of papers inside to see if she had damaged something precious.

The faintly pleated architectural drawings she unfurled on the floor of Duncan's study were puzzling to Laura. She had never seen anything in Duncan's work remotely like these elevations and plans for an utterly charming house. Was it some architectural curiosity he had found somewhere? Was she failing to recognize a famous house by Frank Lloyd Wright? But if Duncan possessed original Wright drawings they would be a proud possession, not hidden away out of sight. Laura knew to look for Wright's little red chop mark. None of the drawings had any kind of signature.

For a minute Laura wondered if these were the plans for the house Duncan grew up in, which made sense if they came out of that attic. But when Laura studied the details of the front elevation she could see that the windows on the center dormer were entirely different, and there were rounded columns running along the front porch that weren't a match for the square columns on the house on Broadfield Road. This house seemed more expansive, somehow a little grander in proportion. She could easily picture Duncan's old front porch not only because she had been in that house countless times when Helen and Gordon lived there, but also because on a May evening just a few months ago when she and Duncan were a little early on their way to a nearby dinner for some new associates, hosted by one of the partners who lived on Underhill Road, they had detoured a couple of blocks in order to drive slowly past his childhood home. It had been a mistake. Duncan was not only appalled that all the rhododendron bushes were gone, but also by the discovery that the original wooden front steps had been replaced by a mean little set of concrete steps in front of the generous porch that spanned the front of the house, flanked by cheap readymade steel handrails made to look like wrought iron. This change to the Broadfield Road house had really bothered him. Later that night, Duncan had fretted over telling Gordon about this act of desecration and had decided to keep it from him.

Gazing at the mysterious drawings, Laura realized that the blocky architect's lettering on the plans with the words "Explicated Four-Square House" was Duncan's handwriting. These were his drawings. This winsome house was his design. The front elevation with its deep inviting porch was particularly appealing. She smoothed it out. The creases in the architectural vellum weren't too bad. All of these drawings could be flattened in the paper conservation lab. She flattened out another sheet, this one showing the house with a strange perspective. She recognized it as an axonometric rendering.

Duncan had once tried to explain the principles of axonometric rendering to her, but she had gotten lost somewhere between the x and y axis set at 45 degrees to the picture plane and the reason they are orthogonal to each other. Why not just say ninety degrees? Laura thought orthogonal sounded contraceptive. Duncan had tried to explain the lack of vanishing point, but she had only grasped the sense of what he was telling her for a fleeting moment.

Laura studied the drawings some more. She loved this house. Why had Duncan kept it a secret? Was it very early work, some failed project before they met? She wished he designed more houses like this, so different from the usual Corrigan & Wheeler domestic confections for the rich. He must have done it when he was a student. Though the firm designed houses for clients who came to them for the Billy Corrigan style, surely there were other sorts of people in the world who would choose to build Duncan Wheeler's Explicated Four-Square House if given the opportunity to know that such a thing was possible. Laura rolled the vellum sheets carefully and reinserted them into the tube. She would take them to the conservation lab and flatten them. She would surprise Duncan by matting them, and maybe framing the front elevation, too. It could go in the dining room on the wall now occupied by a large poster for an Italian cherry festival that was a wedding present from an architecture school friend of Duncan's who had taken it off a wall in a small village near a Palladian villa to which he had made a pilgrimage.

Though Duncan recognized how thoughtfully Laura had set up his room, on that first afternoon at home he felt himself plummeting into despair over his hideous surroundings. The commode especially was a chronic reminder of the way he would be forever dependent on another human being to assist him with a basic biological function that should be a man's most private and independent act—taking a shit. By God, he missed the simple pleasure of having a good, leisurely bowel movement first thing in the morning, *alone*, comfortably ensconced in the downstairs bathroom, with a cup of coffee and good reading material for company.

"It's not *Ipe*," said Duncan vehemently.

"What?"

"The ramp out front, the wood."

"We're still talking about that?"

"Learn how to pronounce it, for Christ's sake, now that the curb view of our house looks like I'm trying to compete with Tom Luckey—poor bastard may have broken his neck and ended up a quad, but by God he designed the most wonderful climbers! The late, great Tom Luckey is my new role model, right? Anyway, it's a fucking expensive, dense timber from South America, and it's pronounced Ee-pay."

"Okey-dokey. Like pig Latin?"

"No, like the right way to pronounce it."

"With humor, my dear Zilkov, always with a little humor."

"Not today."

Duncan's routine required him to endure daily procedures involving the use of enemas and suppositories that took at least half an hour on each occasion. The alternative to being hoisted onto the commode and parked there (with neither his reading glasses nor an ability to hold anything, and so nothing to read!) was the even more un-private and mortifying experience of lying flat on his bed, on his side, on a waterproof pad, while one of the PCAs inserted a gloved finger in his rectum for stimulation, in order to induce what was so politely called evacuation. At times, when things weren't optimal, the PCA would have to perform manual extraction to avoid, or solve, fecal impaction. At these moments Duncan would remind himself that he could be dignified in undignified circumstances, something his mother used to say to Gordy when he had been teased and shamed at school. But this whole process was humiliating, and there was no dignified way around it. You lose mobility, and you give up privacy and dignity because your body keeps living. There was no dignified or undignified way around any of this.

Each morning as Duncan lay in the hospital bed (its only saving grace being that this unaesthetic object wasn't in his view, as Billy Corrigan often remarked about the best reason to rent space in the MetLife Building), trapped in his CPAP mask until someone came in with a lot of cheery morning chat and took it off, he was infuriated and devastated that this was his life now. True, once she arrived, Ottoline's sturdy little presence, tucked under her blanket in her cage by the window, gave him some small pleasure when he awoke. But the first thing that met his gaze each morning was his $9,000 motorized wheelchair, a model pathetically called "The Gladiator," as if enough robust, combative nomenclature could somehow empower the enfeebled occupant. It was parked each night with its back to his desk, cocked like a dentist's chair for easy transfers in and out, his padded harness and chest strap dangling, another day done, another day ahead.

# EIGHT

## *In those first blurry days at the hospital*

IN THOSE FIRST BLURRY DAYS AT THE HOSPITAL FOL-
lowing the accident, once Duncan was no longer "critical and
unstable," Laura alternated nights when she slept on a cot
beside him and nights when she went home for a few hours.
She had almost forgotten that she might be pregnant, but she
knew she needed to take care of herself, and that meant eating
and sleeping, even when she could barely manage either. He
was still heavily sedated and drifting, with very few moments
of clarity. Even when he appeared to be conscious, he was
unable to speak that first week because he was on a ventilator.
His bed was positioned so that he was hinged at the hips and
tilted back in a semi-upright slant, while the lower portion of
the hospital bed was tented in a hump under his knees.

In all the movie and television shows she had ever seen,
when someone has survived a bad accident and is in a hospital bed on life support, there is always a tranquility and
peacefulness to the patient's supine repose, like a figure on a
sarcophagus. But there was nothing tranquil about the array
of clacking and humming and beeping machines clustered
on either side of Duncan's bed. Every so often, pneumatic
compression leg wraps filled with air and tightened around

his legs to prevent blood clots, as if there were small restive animals under the covers resettling themselves. There was nothing peaceful about the constant background sounds of footsteps, wheeled carts clanking in the hall, loose threads of conversations passing by, constant announcements and pages, all punctuated by the scarred swinging door at the near end of the hall banging open repeatedly by gurneys or equipment coming into and going out of the Critical Care unit.

Laura worried that Duncan's canted physical position seemed weirdly haphazard and precarious, though none of the hospital staff who swarmed his bedside seemed concerned. He didn't look remotely comfortable to her. When she asked a nurse if there was any risk that Duncan would slump further sideways, and what if he slid any further down in the bed, and shouldn't they do something to straighten him up more, the nurse answered without looking up from the chart she was notating to reassure her, honey, we're doing our best—believe me, we don't like to lose them.

In the middle of one of those first nights, momentarily alone with Duncan in his deep, drugged state amid all the chugging, clicking, beeping machinery, Laura pulled down the sheet and cotton blanket that covered him and touched his chest lightly, rotating her fingertip in a tiny circle, gently centering over his heart, moving outward while avoiding the sticky heart monitor electrodes, tracing the cool surface of his body, skimming all five fingers of her hand across his rib cage and sternum the way he always loved, mapping the equator of his sensory level, delineating what she had been told by one of the nurses was the edge of his feeling and not feeling. She had secretly hoped he would wake at her touch, but he did not. The edge of feeling and not feeling—that was her own address these days.

Gordon was at the hospital nearly every day from the start. Usually, he took the Shoreline commuter train into New

Haven with his bicycle, and then rode over to the hospital from Union Station. Somehow he was able to linger in Duncan's vicinity on the Critical Care floor before and after visiting hours, and nobody objected to his quiet presence. He had offered to give blood, but a directed donation wasn't necessary, the doctors told him, though a blood donation was always welcome. Gordon was disappointed. They had the same blood type, and he didn't understand why his blood wouldn't be better for Duncan than any other blood if his twin needed a transfusion. Fortunately, other than two units in the first hour when Duncan arrived at the hospital in the Lifestar helicopter, he had not suffered significant blood loss. His spleen had not ruptured. But wouldn't giving Duncan some of Gordon's blood be a good thing anyway? Apparently not.

On the fifth morning after the accident, when Laura had gone home very late, finally exhausted enough for a few hours of fitful sleep and a shower and change of clothes, she returned to Duncan's curtained corner of the unit, just as the sun was rising, to find Gordon there, asleep on the single visitor's chair allotted to the cubicle, which he had pulled up to the side of the bed, his woolly head on his arms beside Duncan's inanimate legs. His snore rose above the beeping and clicking machines that sustained Duncan. It was a soothingly familiar sound to Laura's ears. Finding him there, Laura felt something almost maternal as she gazed at the Wheeler twins, the pair of them, sleeping contiguously as they had all through their childhood.

Whenever they were together, Laura could see something of the boys they once were. After their mother's death, once he had settled Gordy in an apartment on Whitney Avenue and closed up her house, Duncan filled a shelf in his study with the family photo albums. Laura had pored over snapshots of the Wheeler boys as they grew up. As babies they really were truly identical. But soon enough, by toddlerhood, confident, straightforward Duncan seemed easy to identify, to Laura's eye, even though they were towheads dressed alike, with identically regrettable pudding-bowl haircuts. In her painting conservation studies she had learned ways of spotting the discrepancies that revealed the forger's hand rather than the hand of the original artist; making the distinction between the Wheeler brothers required the same eye. Duncan had the aura of the authentic, the original.

In recent years, though, the casual observer would have hardly noticed their twin-ness. Grown-up Duncan was always clean-shaven and wore his hair trimmed very close, while Gordon had his unruly beard and only got a haircut when he thought about it, which was only a couple of times a year; he alternated between looking like a mountain man and a monk. Whenever Gordon came to the house for dinner, Laura was always freshly surprised, observing the two of them together, how despite the way time had effaced some of their identicalness, despite how different they were in countless ways, they did still share most features.

An English teacher in junior high school once gave her a memorable homework assignment requiring sentences illustrating the distinctions among the words "same," "identical," and "similar." When the brothers sat hunched intently over their after-dinner card games in matching poses, like bookends, they were similar. Gordon and Duncan had touchingly identical bald spots and receding hairlines. They walked with the same loose gait. There was a remarkably similar timbre in their voices, but they were never, to Laura, identical. One June night, the last time they played Hearts while she did the dinner dishes, hearing them quibble over the rank of suits as they cut the deck, Laura had realized that she thought of Gordon as the lowly Jack of Clubs, while Duncan was the powerful Jack of Spades. Similar, but not identical, and not the same. Nevertheless, in high-stakes poker, you need a pair of Jacks to stay in the game.

Standing at the foot of Duncan's awkwardly-angled bed on this fifth morning after the accident, looking at the Wheeler brothers as they slept, seeing Gordon's face jammed up against Duncan's inert, sheeted thigh on the tilted mattress, Laura had a tiny pang of envy for their twin-ness. Neither of them had ever known what it was to be alone in the world, truly alone, a lonely only whom nobody matched. Even here in this circumstance, the two of them together made her feel like the outsider. Laura could imagine them as twin fetuses, clinging to each other in their watery dark, their umbilical cords tangled through their entwined limbs.

"Hey Gordy," she whispered, touching his shoulder lightly. He stirred, and then sat up, realizing where he was. He scrubbed his knuckles into his face.

"Dunc okay?" he asked anxiously, looking around. A nurse swooped back the slithery curtain and scowled at them, not expecting visitors at this early hour.

"Family, family," Laura declared, pointing first to herself and then to Gordon. The nurse shrugged and carried on monitoring and adjusting Duncan's various clicking and beeping machines and monitors. When she bent to check the fluid level of the catheter bag hanging at the side of the bed, Laura followed her gaze and could see that the contents were still a murky dark red. She put her hand on Duncan's leg, knowing but not yet really accepting that he couldn't feel her comforting touch. It made her more aware of how instantaneously Gordy had responded to her soft tap on his shoulder.

Gordon had arrived at the hospital a little after two, he said, which meant he must have been chaining his bike at the front entrance only minutes after she had gone home so reluctantly. Laura was glad to know that Duncan, though unconscious and oblivious, hadn't been alone after all while she was at the house. It hadn't occurred to her to ask him to spell her at that hour. What a strange yet Gordy-like thing to do.

"You biked all the way to downtown from Madison at two in the morning?"

"The Shoreline train wasn't running. There's not much traffic on the back roads."

They talked about nothings for a few moments: weather (such a hot and beautiful summer after the cold wet spring), Ferga (a neighbor boy whose company she enjoyed was going to be walking and feeding her today), the bookstore (he had asked for some days off). Gordy looked seedier than usual. He was grimy and a bit ripe.

"Gordy, hey, here's my key—why don't you go to the house and take a shower," Laura said, rummaging in her bag after they had lapsed into a long silence. "You could take my car, oh, right, well, you'll bike, it's not too far." That was brilliant, offering her car to the oddball who can't or won't drive. "The alarm's not set. You can find all clean stuff of Duncan's, and then just leave everything you're wearing on top of the washer and I'll run your stuff with our wash, my wash. You know what I mean. Okay?"

Laura didn't want to hurt his feelings, but he really was pungent in this small space. His hands didn't look particularly clean where they lay on Duncan's bleached white covers. Did he pare his nails with a pocket knife? Though the invisible germs in hospitals were the ones to worry about, not honest, ordinary, Gordy-type grubbiness. Probably. He nodded in agreement, in any case. Duncan's pneumatic compression leg wraps under the sheet suddenly inflated with a sibilant swish and they both reacted with a start, because, not for the first time, it had seemed for a brief misleading instant as if Duncan had moved his legs.

"I'll be right here with him, so he won't be alone if he wakes up," Laura said as Gordy bent over his scuffed work boots and re-tied a floppy lace in preparation for getting on his bicycle. "Take as much time as you want. There's shampoo in the shower in our room, and also in the hallway bathroom you use when you stay over, so feel free to use either. Okay, sweetie? Gordy?" She was talking too much. She hoped she wasn't insulting him.

"Then when you come back, we'll go for lunch," she continued in too loud and bright a voice, as if speaking to a special needs child, but somehow she couldn't shut herself up. "Maybe just down in the coffee shop or something." Gordy stayed bent over, not moving, just gazing down at his shoes, clearly waiting for her to finish what she was saying. "Or we could get something from the food trucks. Do you want to do that? Everyone says they're terrific, but I'm never over here by the hospital, and the parking is such a drag, but here we are. Maybe we can find a bench outside in the shade." Now she was just babbling.

Gordy straightened up in the chair and then rose to his feet, looking down at her across his unconscious brother, their eyes meeting for a long moment. "I know," he said softly, his lisp clinging to his sibilants the way crumbs often stuck in his beard. "How hard this is. But please don't talk to me so much."

When Gordon returned a couple of hours later, Laura was the one dozing in the chair with her head in her arms on the tilted mattress beside Duncan's leg. (The cot they brought out for her at night was always folded up and rolled away in the daytime.) Somehow she had been able to drop into a deeper sleep here, next to Duncan, despite her awkward position, the blare of incessant pages and codes, the rising and falling voices of passing nurses, the squeaking of equipment and food carts, and the frequent bedside check-ins by a variety of nurses and residents and technicians whose duties Laura couldn't identify before they had concluded their business with Duncan and flitted out past the curtain on their rounds. The whooshing, beeping monitors and other devices that had at first seemed so nettlesome had become, at moments, a comfort to her, each beep, beep, beep, beep heartbeat signifying that he was alive, alive, alive, alive.

Laura was asleep with her head in her arms and then she woke at the sound of his accustomed footfalls coming near, and then for a moment it was Duncan sliding back the cubicle curtain and walking toward her, here he came at last (how long had she been waiting?), the familiar mass of him, wearing his favorite tattersall-checked blue and white shirt, the one with the subtle red stripe, the shirt he had left draped over the back of the chair in their bedroom only a few days ago so she would remember to sew on a new button to replace one that had been cracked in half by the shirt laundry. She had not yet sewed the button. But this was not Duncan, of course not, here was bearded Gordy in Duncan's clothing, Gordy with his hair still wet, Gordy wearing Duncan's blue-checked shirt and a pair of his khakis, without a belt, and as he came closer and Laura sat up and tried to clear her head, she could see, just above his bellybutton, a gap in the shirt placket where the cracked half button had not stayed buttoned. A glimpse of his bare stomach. A little whorl of crinkly hair exactly, unbearably like Duncan's.

Every molecule of air in the room hurtled away from her and nothing was left around her but nothingness as she re-felt and re-knew everything all over again and all that had happened slammed back into her consciousness with full force. She gazed at Gordy as he stood there unhappily at Duncan's bedside, seeing him with a new, sharp clarity, that sudden kind of seeing that is the opposite of blindness.

Gordon carried in a chair from an unoccupied cubicle and parked himself in the corner beside the crash cart. They sat without talking, just keeping each other and Duncan company. The medical personnel came and went. The sun kept shining on the nothing new. Laura closed her eyes and put her head down on her arms, but it was impossible to re-enter the dream. Without opening her eyes, she reached out and tried to put her hand into Duncan's hand, but it was taped into a padded splint to prevent it curling into a claw. She settled for just holding his wrist awkwardly and tried again to let herself slip back into that dream state, but she just couldn't find the way. She tried to match her breathing to the slow, steady rhythm of Duncan's ventilator, but she couldn't do it without needing to draw extra shallow breaths.

She sat up and looked over at Gordy, who was dozing in his chair, his chin on his Duncan-shirted chest. She noticed then that she had been almost panting with the exertion of trying through sheer force of will to hold back the inevitability of what was coming next. She tried to rearrange the immediate future with all her heart, even as she surrendered to the awareness that for a couple of hours now she had been feeling that familiar ache, that approaching cramp, that familiar blood-dimmed tidal shift of something loosed once again.

No, no, no, no. Please, no. Now she felt the trickle, the need for a pad. She put her head down on the bed beside Duncan's leg and refused to open her eyes for just a little while longer. No, no, not this lucky baby, this magical last-chance baby, conceived just in time. Can't we at least have that? She listened to the beeps and whooshes of the ventilator pushing air and oxygen into Duncan's lungs through his endotracheal tube, followed by the whoosh of carbon dioxide leaving his lungs, and finally she was able to relax into the rhythm and match her breathing to the steady rise and fall of his chest. Goodbye, goodbye, goodbye, goodbye.

On day eight, the State Police accident investigator was eager to question Duncan about the accident, and there was some urgency about it because a death had occurred. This was the same day the ventilator had been removed and Duncan was successfully breathing on his own, and the investigator arrived on the ward during rounds, while the team of doctors was still telling Duncan about his complete C6 spinal cord injury and what this meant for him.

He would never walk again. He would never feel anything below his level of injury. He would require perpetual bowel care. He would need to undergo a surgical procedure to install an indwelling catheter. He would need to avoid extreme temperatures, heat especially, or his blood pressure could rocket and he could all too easily slip into a dangerous state of dysreflexia. Personal care assistants would have to assist him with nearly all activities of daily living. His caregivers would need to be vigilant about pressure sores. They enumerated this horrific catalogue in a practiced chorus until one of them, a haggard neurology fellow, the only woman in the quintet of doctors surrounding the foot of Duncan's bed, interrupted the litany to say that life could be lived this way.

As the rest of the team closed their files and clicked their pens, she spoke about the range of wonderful assistive devices, the variety of ways of adapting. The others didn't wait for her to finish, three of them using the moment to check their phones as they headed for the door. As a matter of fact, she added, her hand on the door lever, the last of the procession to file out of Duncan's room, he might well live out his full ordinary lifespan with this complete C6 injury, if he followed medical advice and had good support.

Duncan had just lain there blinking, making no eye contact, staring straight up from some depth Laura felt that only she could see. He was like an underwater floating corpse, his face just barely breaking the surface. His head was completely immobilized by a cervical collar and a halo crown. A neurology resident had told Laura the day before that he would probably have very little neck mobility from now on, and would probably only ever be able to turn his head a few degrees.

As the doctors had rattled off the news, as she held Duncan's rigid clammy hand, still encased in the padded splint, Laura wondered if he was really taking in all the devastating information being dumped on him, or if he was only semi-conscious. Maybe what filtered through felt like a bad dream. She wished she could let him drift away. Why today, why right now? Just because the respirator was gone and the room was quiet and technically Duncan could now speak? She had only heard him croak a few syllables at their request. Did this team of doctors simply need a data purge so they could re-set for the next unfortunate soul with a devastating spinal cord injury? Surely, there was no big rush. He had the rest of his life to know about everything he had lost.

And she couldn't let him float away right then. It wasn't clear what, if anything, Duncan remembered about the accident. Presumably he didn't know that Todd Walker had died. Conor Flahavan was a former state trooper who had made sergeant before he transferred to accident investigation (a credential he emphasized to Laura for no obvious reason when he introduced himself, but once he said it she could picture him in the snappy Connecticut state trooper's uniform instead of his khaki pants and synthetic-looking, short-sleeved white office shirt, and wondered if he missed wearing it). Sergeant Flahavan insisted that he needed this brief interview now, today, having been informed by the hospital that Mr. Wheeler was able to speak.

There were questions for Duncan about the accident, questions the driver was legally required to answer, given that there had been a fatality, and it was imperative that the report be completed so the file could be closed. Sergeant Flahavan wouldn't agree to come back another day, as this interview was already one day later than the timetable of ordinary protocols, but he was sympathetic, and said he would wait out in the hallway with Gordon, who had just arrived (a little breathless and very sweaty as usual), so Laura could first break the news about Todd's death to Duncan, alone, just the two of them, so that Duncan wouldn't be learning about it for the first time in the course of the interview.

Laura had met Todd a few times, but only in passing. She gathered from various remarks Duncan had made in recent months that Todd was a particularly appealing and inventive young architect who had been very helpful on a number of projects, most recently the Steiner house. Duncan *always* had a Todd, a favorite apprentice. They came and they went. Laura thought there was something marvelously generous about the way Duncan gave so much time and attention to cultivating the talents of these young men, granting each of them the valuable experience of working closely with him. After a year or two developing their abilities and gaining experience under Duncan's avuncular guidance, each of them would be well prepared to take the next step in a bright career, with offers in New York, or from one of the bigger firms in town with more opportunities for advancement, like Pelli Clarke Pelli or Roche-Dinkeloo. One by one, Duncan's young men of the moment moved on after a year or two, to be replaced by the next protégé, the next Todd.

When she told him, very simply, very gently, that Todd had died in the crash, Duncan, still staring vacantly at the ceiling as he had during the visit from the cluster of doctors, had closed his eyes for a long moment. Then he opened them and whispered his first words to Laura since the accident, a hoarse, rasping, "I missed the funeral?"

There had been a memorial service in New York five days after the accident, Laura told him, in the Great Hall at Cooper Union. A lot of the Corrigan & Wheeler staff had attended. She heard that Dave Halloran had given one of the eulogies, along with Todd's brother who lived in New Hampshire, who was so undone by grief that his voice kept breaking and he had been unable to finish his remarks. Two of Todd's teachers—Ricardo Scofidio from Cooper Union and Peter Farbrecher from Yale—also spoke. Todd's friends had been galled by Farbrecher's fulsome remarks about the tragic loss to the world of Todd's remarkable talents as an architect. It was known that Farbrecher had been so dismissive of Todd's sectional elevation drawings for the class project, a Habitat house, that Todd had cried during the crit.

Duncan remained silent, only blinking occasionally as Laura held his splinted hand and described what she knew of Todd's memorial service. She couldn't tell if he was still listening, but she didn't know what else he would want to know, so she began to enumerate the specifics of Farbrecher's self-serving eulogy that had outraged various people who were there, until he interrupted her in a barely audible whisper to say, "Stop, what about our baby? Are you okay?"

Laura had not planned on lying to Duncan, but he misunderstood her hesitation and fleeting attempt at a smile as she tried to find the words to tell him that the baby, if there had ever been a baby, was gone.

"Okay, fine, that's still what you want, don't worry, we can, even so," he mumbled, before he closed his eyes and dozed off.

She couldn't tell him then. There was no point in forcing him to know the truth right now. What difference would another day or two make? He had lost enough this afternoon.

While Duncan was questioned, Laura hovered. She had promised Sergeant Flahavan that she wouldn't speak at all, as the interview had to consist entirely of Duncan's unprompted answers. A lot of the questions were simple reiteration of facts on record, such as his date of birth, and who owned the car, and where his license had been issued, his driving history, and so on.

Duncan had little to contribute once they got to the actual accident. Did Duncan have any recollection of a bee or wasp in his car just before the crash? Bees in cars were thought to be the number one cause of single-car loss of control fatal accidents in daylight on dry roads, the sergeant told them both. Laura thought this seemed a lot like prompting. Did he remember being stung? Sergeant Flahavan nodded encouragingly as he asked this again, his pen poised over the form on his clipboard. Yes? On his neck?

"I don't remember," whispered Duncan, in response to question after question. He kept drifting off. Months from now, he would have no memory of this interview.

Sergeant Flahavan and Laura walked out of Duncan's room together, and Gordon, who had been hovering by the door, went in, heading for his usual corner, where he would settle in to spend the next few hours simply watching over his brother. The sergeant confirmed to Laura, as she walked him to the elevator, that the investigation had found nothing wrong with the brakes or tires on Duncan's Volvo. Though her old Saab was far tidier than the Volvo, it was actually in less optimal condition, being overdue for an oil change and new rear brake pads. It had balding tires. One headlamp had been out for weeks, and Laura had reminded herself to get it replaced only two days before the accident, with a Post-It note on the bathroom mirror marked PADIDDLE, but she had still not gotten around to it. When Duncan and Gordy were children, they called one-eyed cars padiddles. In fact, they still did this whenever they were in a car together after dark; whoever was first to spot a padiddle on the road scored a point in their never-ending competition that somehow also involved cumulative points in an ongoing game of Hearts.

Laura had promised herself to get all these things dealt with before winter, but she was as reluctant to put money into a fifteen-year-old car as she was to buy a new one. Now this frugality seemed insane. But it didn't signify—Duncan had been driving the newer and safer of their two cars, and the hot summer day had been dry and clear. Of course it had not been her fault, but since the accident Laura had repeatedly scrolled through the possible ways that she had played a contributing part, by commission or omission. She had not delayed Duncan's return drive by phoning him with a reminder about picking up corn at that excellent Branford farm stand after the Steiner site visit. She and Duncan had not argued that morning. There had been nothing like that. But if she *had* delayed him in those ways, maybe that would have saved him.

In fact, it had been a particularly nice start to the day. How many times had she gone over that last morning? Together, they had been brimming with the possibility of her pregnancy, which they did not speak about, though it was a presence that floated with them in the room. They had eaten their granola and yogurt and blueberries in companionable silence (except for the crunching), while listening to a podcast of a public radio broadcast from some other moment, an interview with a dead poet laureate on the anniversary of something or other, one of those public radio significances. The interview concluded with his reading in his old man voice. *The heart breaks and breaks and lives by breaking.*

Laura wasn't responsible for the accident. Of course she wasn't. She knew that, rationally. There was no sane thread of connection, as many times as she talked herself in and out of this feeling, but it kept coming back. She stood in the hospital corridor, watching the elevator door close, feeling guilty about something, but what? About not having been in the accident herself? About wondering what it would be like if Duncan had died in the accident? About wondering if he would have been better off if he had died, like Todd? About dreading what their life together could possibly be like?

She felt guilty that she had misled him about still being pregnant. In another moment she knew she would have to go back into that room to poor, marooned Duncan, to tuck him in for the night, and then after that take Gordy somewhere low-key for dinner on this hot awful night, though she couldn't imagine ever being hungry again. But Laura stood paralyzed against the scuffed hospital corridor wall, just barely holding herself together, wishing for a moment that she had a mother who would just sweep her up in her arms and hold her tight and carry her to safety, away from the nightmare of this accident that was not her fault.

It began to rain while Laura and Gordon nibbled their dinner in the tapas place a block from the hospital. It had been a brutally hot day, so the rain was a welcome change; everything had been dulled and clotted with humidity on the short walk over. Laura had been here once before, with Duncan, late one night after a movie. Gordon rarely ate in restaurants.

Their conversation was awkward and kept dwindling to silence. Gordon asked no questions and was perfectly content to sit at the table with Laura listening to the loud Spanish music, which had an insistent beat he liked, with no obligation to do more than choose his next bite of nice interesting food from an array of little plates in front of him. Laura had ordered their meal, along with a bottle of Spanish Rioja, which the waiter had poured into their two glasses, though Gordon didn't really like wine and had a plan to bicycle home to Madison after dinner. He had certainly never eaten a restaurant meal like this one, composed entirely of snacks, and he liked it, though he was wary of attempting to utter the word "tapas," which he mouthed silently to himself, experimentally, while Laura was reading the menu.

But Laura kept trying to propel the dinner chat, like a good hostess, which meant that in between close analysis of each dish (the sardines and tomatoes on grilled bread with aioli were wonderful, it was true, but this was the first of many items Gordon preferred eating to discussing), she asked him questions about the bookstore (what were his responsibilities, his hours, did he like the work), about Ferga (what did she eat, how did he train her, what did she do all day, where did she sleep), about any good books he had read lately (she misunderstood his silence—he was thinking—for a non-answer, and urged him to read an Iris Murdoch novel, either *Bruno's Dream* or *The Sea, The Sea*, two novels he knew well, though he remained silent), and about when to change gears on a bicycle (she always found hills very challenging).

Gordon's answers were brief and did little to sustain this colloquy satisfactorily. Gordon was always happy to do just one thing at a time, and he would have been content to eat this dinner with Laura without any talking. They had never before had dinner alone together in a restaurant. Laura found herself recalling that Duncan once told her, after driving his brother home on a cold winter night after dinner, that their mother had said more than once that Gordon was someone who tended to catch the conversational ball and put it in his pocket.

The waiter kept refilling her wine glass until the bottle was empty. By the time they were having their flan and cookies, though she didn't notice when, Laura realized she must have also finished Gordon's untouched glass of wine. She had gone months without a drink, without missing it, but now that it didn't matter any more, she had been greedy for the wine. She had also ordered ceviche. Laura had followed all those rules and restrictions so diligently, for nothing. As she finished signing the credit card slip, a white-haired couple who had been staring at them from across the restaurant for a while approached their table with huge grins and semaphored waves.

"Duncan! How wonderful to see you!" the woman cried out, as they neared. "We had heard your accident was serious, but look at you, already out to dinner! Does this mean you can still come up to the Vineyard sometime this fall, maybe for a weekend—"

"You should both come!" Her husband interrupted. He held out his hand to Laura. "Stew Henley, Stew and Millie. Very happy to meet you, Laura, at long last, and to see you both here! That beard looks sharp on you, Duncan! Been rusticating since the winter, I see! Gives you a sagacious look. This is one of our favorite spots in New Haven.

Whenever we visit our grandson at Yale we try to get in here, and they always find us a table, don't they, Millie? We should make a plan to have dinner here together next time we're in town. Don't you love the brave potato things, what do they call 'em?"

"So we really can count on you for our pavilion after all?" Millie persisted. "You still have us on your list? This is wonderful news!"

By the time Laura had introduced Gordon to the Henleys, explained that he was Duncan's twin brother, and told them in vague, upbeat terms that Duncan's prognosis was still uncertain but everyone certainly hoped for the best, and by the time the Henleys had chimed, oh of course, now they could see it, and yes, they knew Duncan was a fighter, he would beat this thing, give him our regards—their dismay and disappointment barely concealed—the temperature outside had dropped twenty degrees, a gusty wind was blowing in several directions, and the rain was falling in enormous, heavy drops. The sky flickered continuously, and thunder rumbled somewhere on the horizon.

"Gordon Wheeler, you cannot bike home all the way to Madison in this! That's crazy, and with the lightning, it's not even safe," Laura said, after they had stood together in the restaurant entrance for several minutes hoping the rain would ease, though it had actually intensified. There was an enormous simultaneous crack and flash and now the rain was pouring out of the sky, rushing rivers forming in the street against the curbs.

"Come to the house," Laura yelled at him over the noise of the rain crashing down. "You can ride home later, after it clears. We can put your bike in the back of my car—it will fit, I've got the back seat down flat." Gordon hesitated. Even in the protected doorway of the restaurant, they were getting soaked by the rain bouncing up from the pavement in front of them.

The relentless din of the rain was disorienting. It transformed College Street into an alien drumming surface. Whenever a car went by, slowly, windshield wipers dragging uselessly back and forth, it would throw up a furled sheet from the pool that had collected in a declivity of the street surface.

"Come on, Gordy! Let's go! We can't just stand here!" Laura shouted, putting her hand on his sturdy, familiar arm to steady herself, suddenly feeling exhausted and desperate to get home. The encounter with the Henleys had been disconcerting, and she didn't really know to whom, if anyone, she ought to report that Corrigan & Wheeler could lose these clients if they weren't courted. But maybe it didn't matter. She remembered now how much Duncan had been irked by their self-important demands, though they were no different from most of his rich, spoiled clients. She remembered reading a profile of the Henleys that quoted Stew saying he had changed his name from Horchatzsky to Henley because of the regatta.

But she couldn't just let Gordy pedal off in this deluge. Another theatrical crack of thunder and lightning together helped her to emphasize her point. "Just go right now and get your bike and walk it to the north parking garage exit!" she shouted over the fresh torrents of rain hitting the pavement. "I'll go get my car up on three and meet you there at the bottom of the ramp—wait for me by the pay station, where it's dry."

At the house, with Gordon's bicycle dripping in the front hall, they settled in the living room with mugs of Oolong tea (Duncan and Laura had no idea how rare this particular tin of tea actually was; a very generous Christmas gift from a grateful client of Duncan's, it had been sitting on a shelf in their pantry for a couple of years). While she made the tea, Laura directed Gordon upstairs to Duncan's bureau for a change of clothes, as he was so completely soaked that there had been steam coming off him in the front hall. Now he wore Duncan's jeans and an old blue work shirt that was soft and frayed at the collar and cuffs. It was perfect that Gordon had chosen this one threadbare shirt among all of Duncan's crisp oxford cloth and tattersall shirts that he kept filed by color in wide drawers.

Gordon sat in the big red armchair, which was Duncan's usual spot because it had the best reading light. He held the damp towel he had used to dry his dripping hair and beard (at Laura's instruction) in an awkward bundle in his lap until Laura told him he could just drop it on the rug. Laura had changed from her wet clothes into old yoga pants and a T-shirt. As she settled back into the sofa cushions with her legs stretched out on the coffee table, cradling her mug of tea, Laura gazed at Gordon. God, he looked like Duncan when he sat in Duncan's chair and wore Duncan's clothes, even with the beard and wild hair. Clothes do make the man. Gordon stared down morosely into his mug of tea.

"Are you okay to be drinking wine with dinner like that?" he asked Laura suddenly, after a long silence. She had nearly dozed off, and his voice startled her.

"Why? Did my driving alarm you? Am I slurring my words?" Why am I being so unpleasant to poor Gordy, Laura wondered without being able to stop herself. Nothing more about slurring words, for Christ's sake. "Can't a person unwind?"

"No, no, sorry, I don't mean to be a jerk, you're fine, I'm not judging, it's just that Dunc told me today, when you went out of the room with that accident guy . . ." Gordon hesitated and then plunged in. "It's none of my business, but he said you guys were going to have a baby. And so I thought you weren't supposed to drink. That's all. I wanted to say something at the restaurant, but I didn't know how to bring it up."

"Oh, Gordy." Laura put her tea down and flopped back in

the sofa cushions with her eyes closed, heaving a huge sigh. "No. I'm sorry, I didn't mean to snap at you. I did think I was pregnant, we thought, but either I was wrong, or I was only pregnant for a little while. Either way, there isn't a baby now. Duncan doesn't know yet. I was going to tell him today, but then I just couldn't. I was going to. I meant to." Laura looked over at Gordon's dear, kind face. Was he going to cry?

"Can you try again, I mean, do you have, you know, like frozen embryos and sperm and eggs and things? I understand if it's none of my business," Gordon added, looking around for somewhere to set his mug down, but then once he had put it on the table next to him, he picked it up again and took another sip of his tea, and another, practically hiding behind his mug.

"No, Gordy, nothing like that, we were just starting up that path, actually. We haven't frozen anything. We had appointments—we have appointments—I don't know how much Duncan ever talked to you about any of this." Laura tried to hold eye contact with Gordon, but he kept looking away from her, casting his gaze all over the room, down at the rug, anywhere but back at her face.

"But can't you still, you know, do something, so Duncan can still be the father . . . you know?" Gordy trailed off.

"Actually, there is something for men with spinal cord injuries called sperm extraction—I've read about it, but we could only try that if Duncan agrees, at some point in the future, and it's way too soon even to bring it up, with everything else going on for him right now. I have no idea if it's even an option for us."

"I hope you can do that," Gordon said in a near whisper. "Whenever."

Laura got up and went over to the bar cart (which had been a prized possession of the late Helen Wheeler—Gordon had no use for it and Duncan loved it, though it was incongruous in their living room) and poured herself a cognac, which she carried back to the sofa. When she wasn't trying to get pregnant, Laura had never really been a drinker of anything but wine, and she rarely liked the strong taste of spirits such as cognac. On the rare occasions when she wanted a brandy or an eau de vie, it was on cold winter nights, but this bottle of cognac across the room had suddenly looked very desirable.

She cradled the heavy crystal snifter, one of a pair Duncan liked much more than she did because it was a little too big and heavy in her small hands. Would he ever lift one of these glasses to his mouth again? She took a generous sip, settling back on the sofa and feeling the sweet heat all the way down her throat to her stomach. What time was it? The rain was still boiling outside, a real summer storm. This was a wild conversation to be having with Gordy. Laura felt a weird mix of anger and longing welling up each time she looked over at him sitting there in Duncan's clothes, in Duncan's chair, not being Duncan.

"I wish there was something I could do," Gordon said sadly. "I feel so useless. They didn't want my blood for Duncan, even though it's a perfect match."

Laura regarded him over the rim of her glass. "I know, you keep saying. So how serious are you?" She tipped the glass back to spill a little more of the cognac onto her tongue, and as it slid down her throat, it was burning and cloying and heady in that confusing way that reminded Laura that she was never certain that she actually liked cognac, although this was a really good bottle of VSOP which had impressed Jesse and Frank last summer. If only this wasn't their sabbatical year away. "Give me an example of what you would do for Duncan." Such an obvious remedy, but was she really going to ask him for this? Tonight she felt just hopeless and reckless enough to go for broke. Laura went over to pick up the cognac bottle so she could read the label, trying to remember what VSOP stood for. Very Special Something Something.

Ah, Old Pale. She brought it back to the couch, where she poured herself a new splash.

"What are you asking me?" Gordon said, rubbing his hands nervously back and forth on his thighs. Which looked like Duncan's thighs in those jeans. "I think the rain is letting up. I can go now."

"Don't be crazy, Gordy, the rain is not letting up, can't you hear that noise? It's the rain beating on the roof and gurgling in the downspouts. Noah started making plans when it rained like this."

"Okay, it's still raining a little. That's okay. I don't mind it."

"Well I do mind it! Sit down! You're not leaving now! I don't need both of you in the hospital! Don't be an idiot!"

"Please don't yell at me, Laura." Gordon had begun to stand up but now he dropped back into the armchair. "What's wrong?"

"You're running away instead of answering me when I'm asking what you would do for Duncan."

"I would do whatever I can. I'm not running away. I need to take care of Ferga. It's late."

"You would give Duncan your blood."

"Yes, I told you, but I guess Dunc didn't need it. They said I could donate at the Red Cross in his honor, but it's not the same thing."

"I understand that. But would you give him one of your kidneys?"

"Is there something wrong with his kidneys?" Gordon asked anxiously.

"No, no, I'm not saying that, but if there was?"

"I don't get your questions, then, but of course, yes, I would give him a kidney."

"Would you give him part of your liver?"

"Are you going to name a lot of body parts? Can I just stipulate to all organs?"

"Would you cut off a finger for him?"

"I don't understand what you're asking me, Laura. A finger isn't an organ, but sure, whatever Duncan needs! Do you think I don't love my brother enough?"

"I'm just trying to understand what you really mean when you say you would do anything for Duncan. Would you cut off a finger?"

"Yes, okay, I guess I would, if it would help him. He could have a whole hand."

"So you would cut off your hand for him?"

"I'd rather not, but, okay." What the hell. Gordon could usually count on Laura to be kind.

"Would you cut off your arm? Would you cut off your leg for him too? What else? Would you give him one of your eyes?"

"Yes, yes, yes! I would give Duncan anything! This is getting biblical! Why do you keep asking? I feel like you're attacking me." Gordon could hardly bear even the most ordinary sort of confrontation. She *knew* this about him.

"I don't mean to be attacking you, Gordy. I'm just trying to figure out if you really mean it, when you say you wish you could do something for Duncan."

"I don't understand what you're asking. And even if you're not pregnant and you're upset and it's none of my business, maybe you shouldn't drink any more of that paint thinner."

Laura took an exaggerated sip from her snifter. "Maybe you should try having a drink, Gordo. You're an adult. You can do adult things. Have you ever even tasted cognac? Have a sip of mine." Laura held out the snifter for a moment as if she seriously thought he would take it from her, before putting it down.

"Did I do something wrong, Laura? I just want to go home now."

"Little Gordy needs to avoid grownup things? Fine, run home to your dog." Laura was horrified by the words coming out of her mouth but she couldn't stop.

"Just tell me what you want from me," whispered miserable Gordon. "What do you want me to say? Just tell me the right words, please."

"What else would you give for Duncan? What else would you do for him, damn it?"

"Why are you yelling at me? Just tell me the right answer, and I'll say it, okay?" One of Gordon's legs was jiggling up and down. He watched it for a moment, before putting both hands on his knee to hold it still. "What do you want me to say?"

"What I want you to *thay*? Do you have any interest at all in women, Gordy?" Jesus, Laura couldn't believe she was asking him this. Duncan had only shrugged when she asked him once, long ago, if he thought his brother was a virgin.

"I'm leaving now." Gordon scrambled to his feet.

"I am so sorry, Gordy, that was way over the line. Stay, stay. Please? You just can't bike on a night like this. It's not safe. If you have to go home tonight, let me drive you."

"Um, no thanks. You've been drinking. Speaking of not safe. And no thanks, anyway."

"Oh Gordy, let's start over. Don't you get it? I'm just trying to fix something that might be fixable. Please hear me out."

He stood in the doorway, waiting, looking down at his shabby work boots.

"I apologize for not being clearer. I'm asking if you would be a sperm donor. For us, for the baby we want to have. For all of us. If we caught the next cycle and it was successful, Duncan wouldn't even need to know."

Gordon sat back down slowly, still looking down, not meeting her gaze. Minutes passed. Laura sat forward to take an astringent sip of the dregs of her now stone-cold tea instead of the cognac.

"That's just crazy, Laura," Gordy whispered finally, looking up now and fixing her with his sad gaze. "You've had too much to drink."

"I know what I'm saying! Why is it crazy? Being a sperm donor is less invasive than giving blood! Just a few minutes of your time, and I would take care of the rest. Don't worry, I'm not asking you to have sex with me!"

"No."

"No to what?"

"No, I can't do that."

"You can't, or you won't, Gordo? Don't you even have a wank from time to time? Am I embarrassing you? Don't worry, you wouldn't have to touch another human being. We could get you a Dog Fancy magazine, or whatever floats your boat." Laura was shocked by her own viciousness.

"You said you were sorry a moment ago when you were so nasty, and now you're asking me for this, but you're being cruel. Please stop. I'm saying I won't do that because I won't trick Duncan. I just can't do that."

"Oh, Gordy, you're right, you're right, I am so sorry. I love you, and I don't mean to be hurtful. I'm just so frustrated trying to understand how you could say you would do anything for Duncan when that's not true and you don't mean it."

"I just can't do that to Duncan. Maybe if you hadn't been drinking you would understand what I'm saying."

"But you would be doing it *for* Duncan."

"Behind his back."

"For now, anyway. But maybe he would never need to know. Would it really matter that much? You were so keen to give him your perfectly matching blood. Explain to me why this is so different, really."

"Laura, I just can't have this conversation with you. This is just crazy talk. What happened to the Chinese baby idea? You guys were doing that, weren't you? Duncan told me a while ago. I thought you guys were on some waiting list."

"We've lost that chance. They have a long list of rules and a parent in a wheelchair is a deal breaker."

"How would they find out about the accident?"

"Oh Gordy, I don't know how you imagine it works, but you don't just fill out a form and then they send you the baby. They require both parents to go to China. It's a long, complicated process that takes weeks once you're there. There's no way we could lie or conceal something like this. Unless you want to go with me to China and be Duncan?"

"Now you're just saying more crazy things."

"I hadn't thought of it until just now, but seriously, why not? You could be Duncan for a few weeks. You could travel on his passport. Surely you and I could figure out how to share a hotel room."

"I think that's a federal crime, Laura. Probably some kind of international crime. I could end up in some Chinese dungeon. Not that I would do it in the first place. You're not serious about any of this."

"I'm just trying to fix this, Gordy. I can't believe you won't help me fix this."

"Not everything can be fixed."

"Don't you want to give Duncan one good thing to look forward to in his life right now?"

"Now we're going in a circle again. I just can't do this for you. I can't. I can't be Duncan! Don't ask me to be Duncan!"

"Can't or won't?"

"What's the difference, Laura? I can't! I'm not Duncan! I'm Gordy! Please, stop asking me about any of this!"

"It matters to me. Can't or won't?"

"Please, Laura. It's a distinction without a difference."

"Duncan says that all the time. Is it some kind of fucking Wheeler family saying? What the hell does it actually mean?"

Gordon stood up again, shaking his head as if to dislodge something. He stood there, just looking at her.

"What?" Laura felt a pang of guilt for how sad he looked just then.

"You and I can't be fighting, Laura. Let's just forget this whole discussion, okay? I know how hard this must be for you, not just the accident, but what you just told me about, you know, not having a baby. I'm really sorry."

"But we *have* had this conversation. What's done cannot be undone."

"We haven't done anything but talk, Laura. Don't be so dramatic. What's done cannot be undone? Seriously? You're not Lady Macbeth. If I can forget it, you can forget it."

"Gordy, I admire you. I do. You're a very big person. There's a lot more to you than meets the eye."

"I'll take that as a compliment and not an inebriated insult, and you're my only sister-in-law and I care about you, but I think you really need to go up to bed now before you say anything else." Gordon edged toward the door as he spoke, and opened it. "And I am really going."

"I mean it, Gordy. You have a lot of dignity, for a—"

"Listen, do you hear that?" Gordon interrupted.

"What? I don't hear anything."

"Exactly. That's the sound of it stopped raining a while ago." Gordon wheeled his bicycle out the front door and propped it on the porch railing. The wet street glittered. He bent down to tuck his jeans inside his work boots. "Goodnight, Laura. Hey, you're going to need to build a ramp, you know that, right?"

When Duncan had been stable for twelve days, Laura stopped feeling obligated to doze fitfully beside him every other night. He still wore the intermittent pneumatic compression leg wraps that prevented blood clots. Even when there was the quiet between nurses barging in to check Duncan's vitals, each time Laura had dropped into sleep, only moments later the pneumatic compression leg wraps would come to life and inflate, and the whooshing sound would nudge her back up into consciousness each time.

The morning after the humiliating conversation with Gordon, Laura told Duncan that she wasn't pregnant, and maybe hadn't been. She didn't tell him how long she had known, and he didn't ask. After whispering how sorry he was, Duncan simply closed his eyes, his only option, given his inability to turn his head, and said nothing more.

He often spent hours lying so still with his eyes closed that it was hard to tell if he was awake or asleep. After spending most of each day sitting beside Duncan trying not to be panicked by his increasing silence and withdrawal, or talking with doctors and trying not to be discouraged by their irrefutable prognosis, Laura felt guilty about her relief at being able to escape.

She ate dinner on her lap in front of the television most of these nights, zoning out on mindless microwave comforts and old sitcom re-runs (two things Duncan deplored) before going upstairs where, after she turned out the light, she lay still and wide awake under the covers, thinking of Duncan's position in his hospital bed as she left him for the night a few hours earlier. Laura developed a habit of deliberately positioning herself exactly as she knew Duncan was still lying, just as she had left him, pegged in place like Gulliver by monitors and catheters and intravenous lines, braced by a padded halo vest that kept him stable.

She would lie there replicating Duncan's position: supine, legs straight, arms straight at her sides, palms up. She would try to imagine her way inside his body, what it felt like to be Duncan, what it felt like not to feel. Lying there that way, feeling profoundly grateful that she was not paralyzed in the least, Laura had to fight her obsessive return to the crazy belief that she was somehow responsible, that something she could have controlled had led to the accident. She couldn't keep herself from ruminating that she should have called Duncan to ask him to pick up corn from one of those farm stands on the way back from Stony Creek, thus delaying his drive back into town, which surely would have changed everything that happened that afternoon. Or she shouldn't have kept him those extra minutes at breakfast, listening to public radio poetry when his mind was probably already focused on the work of the day that lay ahead.

The first rule of art conservation, as Laura knew very well (antithetical as it was to Lady Macbeth's lament), is "Do nothing that cannot be undone." The second rule of art conservation, as Laura also knew very well, was that nobody, even conservators, could always follow the first rule.

# NINE

## *Laura enjoyed her work in the conservation lab*

LAURA ENJOYED HER WORK IN THE CONSERVATION LAB at the Yale Art Gallery. She was very good at her job. She had apprenticed in both painting and object conservation, and was technically proficient in skills that were in incessant demand for the maintenance of paintings and objects, such as Chinese porcelains, in the Gallery collections. Her work was usually devoted to analyzing and assessing condition and damage, after which, with supervision, she conducted certain basic treatments for cleaning and stabilization.

She was occasionally given some restoration assignments for straightforward repairs of damage to paintings in the collection, which often meant the painstaking removal of the problematic older varnishes of the past and the application of new varnish that met contemporary standards. She had a reputation for a very steady hand and good, careful work. She was a generalist, but she had a special knowledge of the issues and materials of seventeenth-century paintings. While getting her undergraduate degree in art history at the University of Connecticut, Laura had thought her devotion to works on paper was immutable, particularly Renaissance prints and drawings, and she had planned to pursue a graduate degree to become a paper conservator. But after a two-month postgraduate internship in the Philadelphia laboratory of Renaissance specialist Carolyn Maybank (who was as overweening as she was legendary in paper conservation circles), Laura never again had the nerve to work with paper.

Exactly what had gone wrong and why, and who was responsible for the fate of the precious Dürer woodcut (St. George and the Dragon) that was accidentally bleached out of existence before Laura's eyes?

The annoyingly prim Jill Feldman, the other intern (as she and Laura each thought of the other), had been assigned the basic task of creating a simple weak paper wash cleansing solution for the woodcut. She had misread the written instructions in the Maybank Conservation Laboratory Manual of Practices and had added ten full syringes, a total of one hundred cc's, of ammonium hydroxide to the gallon of water in the tray, rather than ten drops. (To be fair, the instructions were penned in highly ornamented fountain pen script, and the heavy, leather-bound Manual was more like a sacred volume of recipes for Merlin's spells than it was like a compendium of modern scientific laboratory standards of practice.) Jill had asked Laura if she agreed that this was the correct proportion, but Laura had neither agreed nor disagreed, because she wasn't listening to Jill Feldman, though this was a matter of dispute later that day.

Laura was engrossed in making diligent notes in her Moleskine notebook about the science of this task, committing to her little gridded pages as much as she could quickly copy from the precious, leather-bound Manual of Practices as soon as Jill had let her take full possession of the volume: Water can cleanse acidity, discoloration, and degradation from paper. Wetting a work on certain kinds of paper can strengthen its structure by re-establishing the bonding of the fibers. Ammonium hydroxide is a weak, volatile alkali, and its salts are soluble in water. This sort of solution was favored, in the Maybank approach to paper conservation, as superior for brightening when compared to other diluted de-acidification solutions.

The titular (in every sense) Carolyn Maybank (who rarely let a day pass that didn't include mention of her Wellesley Method art history training) had imperiously donned cotton gloves to demonstrate to her two interns (would she ever be able to shape these two imprecise and easily distracted girls into capable, competent paper conservators?) the best practice for slipping the precious, fragile Dürer woodcut gently into the tray of solution—the gallon of deionized water treated with what should have been the merest tincture of ammonium hydroxide.

Laura was then assigned the tedious (and to her mind utterly pointless) task of twirling tiny tufts of pulled cotton fibers onto the ends of bamboo skewers in order to make perfect fine-pointed cotton swabs. In the Maybank Laboratory, stray fibers from commercially manufactured cotton swabs were not tolerated. When she had done fifty of these (she was supposed to complete a hundred), she took a break and walked across the lab to take a look at the Dürer woodcut floating in its bath. The picture was nearly gone, almost entirely effaced, with only the faintest image of the vertical line of St. George's lance penetrating the dragon's mouth, along with a trace outline of his rearing horse's forelegs.

Two postdoctoral apprentices nearly knocked Laura to the ground, pushing past her when her squeak of dismay attracted their attention. Jill Feldman, who was organizing supplies in flat files on the other side of the laboratory, stood up, and when she saw all their shocked expressions she burst into tears. Carolyn Maybank shoved everyone aside ("Stand back!") to administer the emergency treatment, first flooding the tray with deionized water over and over to rinse away the toxic solution, then lifting the dying woodcut onto blotting paper, and then, finally, placing it on the vacuum suction table in a last attempt at resuscitation. The work of art had disappeared.

The bright, stabilized woodcut of St. George and the Dragon sent back to the collector by the Maybank Paper Conservation Laboratory a few months later, in its original triple-matted gold leaf cabinetmaker's frame, was in fact another example of the work in a similar state that Carolyn Maybank had quietly obtained from a dealer in London. She had, working alone after hours, treated it very carefully to approximate the conditions of the destroyed woodcut, which she had documented with digital images before treatment, as was her prudent practice. This substitution of an imposter woodcut included the painstaking addition of minute, stabilized foxing marks along the top edge, though they were concealed under the inner mat, in addition to the creation of a tiny repaired tear in the lower left corner. Nobody in the Maybank Paper Conservation Laboratory knew about this subterfuge. The truth about the destruction of the Dürer print at the hands of an intern in her laboratory, where she famously performed all conservation treatments herself, was the last thing Carolyn Maybank would have ever wanted revealed to the world of paper conservation.

Jill Feldman never returned to the laboratory after that day. Laura completed her internship in the chilly Maybank atmosphere (not only was there a Maybankian froideur, but also there was a strict rule that the ambient room temperatures were never to go above fifty-eight degrees Fahrenheit), but decided to pursue painting and object conservation after that. Paper was just too fragile, too ephemeral. She wanted to work with more substantial objects and sturdier surfaces that she thought would surely be more forgiving of error. She had a series of good placements and apprenticeships for the next couple of years. She never crossed paths with Jill Feldman, who left conservation studies. (She ended up managing a storefront franchise of a paint-your-own-pottery business in Scranton, Laura learned many years later when she was idly Googling lost people the way one does.) The effaced Dürer woodcut was a secret. Carolyn Maybank had brought confidentiality agreements to the laboratory the next day, and everyone on the premises had been required to sign one.

Though she wasn't specifically intimidated by the confidentiality agreement, Laura never told anyone what she had seen that day, not even Duncan. She felt as if she had witnessed a violent crime. She felt guilty and complicit, even though whenever it came out that Laura had an internship with Carolyn Maybank, people were impressed. It opened doors for her professionally. She dined out on stories about twirling those damned cotton swabs, and she did a perfect impression of the Maybankian lockjawed pronouncement on the superiority of the "Wellesley Method of art history training." Her Maybank credential surely helped her win the Yale job; the other two final candidates (Laura found out who they were after she was hired) had superior academic credentials. But when she read Carolyn Maybank's obituary in a back issue of the *Paper Conservator*, while sitting one morning in a fertility doctor's waiting room, Laura had felt an unexpected relief.

Laura didn't really keep in touch with anyone from her Maybank days, even though she had enjoyed the company of some of the other interns, especially Dan Smith, a soft-spoken illuminated manuscript specialist from Oregon who always pronounced *die Buchmalerei* with an exaggerated German accent. Once when they were alone in the freezing Maybank document storage area he had shown her his trick of photocopying needless duplicates of conservation reports in order to warm up his hands on the hot pages that emerged from the printer. After that they would often sneak down there together. On one particularly chilly and unsupervised afternoon, Laura lifted her shirt and inserted a nice thick and warm condition report under the waistband of her pants, where it was as comforting against her skin as a hot water bottle, though she rustled when she moved, and the warmth was fleeting. Were they a couple? They went out together a few times, but went to bed just once, an unsuccessful experience that proved to them both that it had been a mistake to go beyond friendship, and they never attempted to do so again. Dan found work in a university library in Germany, and they exchanged a few emails for a while before falling, inevitably, out of touch.

Once, when a friendly visiting conservator who was invited to Yale from the Opificio delle Pietre Dure in Florence to work on a surface problem with the Gallery's Ghirlandaio told her over coffee about the nightmarish occasion (*un incubo*, she called it) when she had accidentally punctured a Rubens canvas that was being relined, when she was a young intern at the Uffizi, Laura remained silent about the effaced Dürer. "It happens all the time, at least once, to everyone," the Italian conservator had said with a shrug and a laugh. "And then everyone tells me it is just like doctors when they have their medical training. Every conservator has murdered at least one patient."

Duncan's nicely flattened and matted drawings of the Explicated Four-Square house were waiting for Laura on her worktable when she got to work, courtesy of a generous and shy colleague in paper conservation who had wanted to do something for her. She left them there for the time being; it was a drizzly day, and there was no rush, no reason to risk carrying something up the street to the framer in the rain.

Her current projects were nearly complete, the writing of two condition reports. The first was a detailed preliminary assessment on a William Merritt Chase painting in the collection that had a serious condition problem. She had never seen this painting before, as it had been in storage, hanging on one of the sliding racks in the Gallery basement until Laura was assigned to review it as part of a routine sweep through the collection, when it was brought to the conservation lab. She had done the work, following a checklist, and was now simply revising her language to make the report concise and clear so the senior conservators would have a sense of the scale of conservation work it required.

"Monkeying with Literature," painted circa 1877–1878 when the painter lived in Venice, is an oil on canvas depicting Chase's pet monkey Jocko rummaging through a pile of books, some of them cascading and splayed open on the floor. Examination reveals that large sections of the canvas are affected with a fine crack pattern, lifting and cupping paint, and paint loss due to insufficient adhesion between the top layers. The overall surface gloss of the varnish appears uneven and patchy. Fibers in the surface and examination under UV light indicate numerous prior conservation treatments where the old varnish was reduced inconsistently. There are traces of fiber from cotton swabs. [This would never have happened in the Maybank Laboratory, Laura thought, as she noted this observation with obscure satisfaction.] The probable course of treatment for the painting, given that the original paint layers may be potentially sensitive to most solvents, should be quite conservative. Securing of the flaking paint is the priority. All lifting paint should be consolidated locally, presumably with four percent sturgeon glue and a hot spatula. After consolidation of the paint layer eventual remaining matte areas should be locally treated with an appropriate varnish to improve the surface gloss.

Laura's remaining task of the day was the final report on the repair done by the senior object specialist on a Song Dynasty qingbai bowl that was on loan from Dud and Jinxy Cavendish, the demanding collectors who had verbally promised it to the Gallery as part of their hoped-for bequest. There had been a lunch with the college president and the Yale Art Gallery's director, concluding with a walk-through of the potential Gallery space on the third floor that might house a future Cavendish Collection. All sorts of privately held, valuable works of art pass through conservation departments in museums around the world for this reason, though museums making this investment can be disappointed to learn that a competing institution, or a family member, has, in the end, scooped the pool.

The loan and conservation of the Song Dynasty qingbai bowl, which had set a record price for a Song Dynasty piece at auction in Hong Kong when they bought it, was a test of the relationship, Laura knew. The self-important Cavendishes would scrutinize her condition report, looking for errors and omissions. She had been encouraged to write her report in the most positive (i.e., flattering) language possible, while also, if possible, making the case for Yale's conservation virtuosity. The Cavendishes were in the habit of using museums this way, collecting one restored object while delivering the next exquisite object in their collection with conservation issues. They made it clear that they fully expected the museum's conservation resources to be at their disposal. Suggesting otherwise, or charging them for these services, would have been impolitic for an institution hoping to acquire the Cavendish collection.

They had played this game for ten years at the Fogg before claiming back their long-term loans and reneging on their promises in order to follow the Asian Arts curator with whom they had a relationship when he departed Harvard for Yale. (Dud and Jinxy, whose money came from woolen mills in her family, had no idea that his promise to bring the extraordinary Cavendish Song dynasty porcelains and Ru ware—conservatively estimated to be worth triple-digit millions—to Yale had helped him win the appointment.) The Cavendishes, who raised a rare breed of sheep in Hallowell, Maine, were both in their early seventies, which meant that they could easily outlive their current fondness for Yale and move on to yet another courtship with an institution eager to acquire their vast, lovely, and exceedingly valuable collection.

Yale had an additional advantage, according to the department memo, because a Cavendish granddaughter was in the sophomore class, a first for the Cavendish family. (Dudley Cavendish was a West Point man; the former Josephine Callaghan attended Sweet Briar. They had met at a poker game the night before a wedding in Newport News; he was the best man, and she was her roommate's maid of honor.) They would travel down to New Haven to visit their granddaughter sooner or later, if not this semester then in January after the Christmas break, so there was an urgent need to take care of their bowl quickly. The museum director had promised them that whenever they came to New Haven, the work on their exquisite bowl would be complete. Completion of full documentation of the repair, Laura's responsibility, was a priority, so that whenever they showed up, which could be next week and could be months from now, every i would be dotted and every t would be crossed. (Laura hated that expression, which the head of her department used often.) Laura wrote:

> This extraordinary Song dynasty qingbai bowl, a fine example of Ding ware that has been repaired superbly, has incised decoration that depicts the reflection of clouds in the water. The white, translucent body has a pleasing texture of very fine sugar, having been made using crushed and refined pottery stone instead of the more usual pottery stone and kaolin.

Though standard practice required the wearing of protective cotton gloves at all times when handling objects such as this, Laura furtively removed a glove to caress the sugary texture with a fingertip, just for a moment. It felt smooth and nice. She wrote:

> This was a very successful hairline crack repair, barely visible to the naked eye. When the thousand-year-old bowl is back on display in the vitrine, nobody will be able to detect that a channel has been created across the crack using a very fine diamond rotary disk bit, in order for a hair of copper wire peg to be embedded. This exceptional repair was completed by a sequence of very intricately timed applications of warmed epoxy and delicate clamping. This remarkably imperceptible repair was finished with microscopic amounts of sanding and buffing to blend the surfaces inside and out. This is an outstanding example of the appropriate and necessary conservation work on an exquisite piece of Song dynasty qingbai that can only be executed under optimal circumstances in a museum conservation laboratory environment.

Laura carefully placed the thousand-year-old qingbai bowl in its padded box, which she positioned in the secure vitrine reserved for objects in conservation. She made copies of the conservation report and left all the paperwork in the correct files. Then she headed home to her broken husband.

# TEN

*Gordon Wheeler admired the gorgons,*
*beasts, and owls that came to his door*

GORDON WHEELER ADMIRED THE GORGONS, BEASTS, and owls that came to his door. Ferga was less appreciative, though with gentle reminding she resisted the temptation to bark at the costumed children as they straggled up and down the path. Some of them waded through the unraked leaves that covered the lawn in order to cut across in a direct approach from an adjacent neighbor's front door. Ferga was especially jumpy when they did this because of the crackling-swishing noise they made in the leaves, which was to her ears identical to the sound squirrels made as they zig-zagged across the yard before running up a tree. A squirrel can make a huge racket getting from here to there. That was why Ferga liked autumn best, when a blanket of telltale leaves on the ground gave her an even chance.

Every Halloween, Gordon spent more money than he should have on a mountain of Kit-Kats. He avoided brands of candy that he had difficulty pronouncing, which ruled out quite a few options he liked, among them Nestle's Crunch, Baby Ruth, Reese's Peanut Butter Cups, and Tootsie Rolls.

When Gordon was a child, making Halloween rounds with Duncan, he only whispered the cruelly challenging requisite phrase, while Duncan shouted it out loud enough for both of them.

Now, when the costumed children on his front step chanted dutifully through the torn screen, he opened the door and held out the bucket of Kit Kats, letting them each take one or two, rather than dropping a single candy into each of their outstretched bags. He preferred to respect their judgment and independence, though his trust was inevitably betrayed by the occasional trick-or-treater who grabbed a handful. Thank you, thank you, thank you, the princesses and ghosts and Power Rangers and Nixons (still!) mumbled as they turned away and swished off into the leaves, to the house next door (where they only gave out the smallest Snickers, bite-size, and only one of those per child). Ferga kept sitting down and sighing and standing up again as the trick-or-treaters came and went through the afternoon and evening.

It was a busy, child-filled neighborhood anyway, but their street was especially popular because the two women in the purple cottage with blue trim on the corner went all out every Halloween, planting tombstones on their lawn and lighting them dramatically, mounting a giant tarantula on their roof, and hanging ghosts and skeletons from the trees that shaded their house. They answered the door in elaborate costumes and greeted the children with disconcerting cackles of ghoulish laughter. Starting in the middle of the afternoon, they played a loop of dissonant, sinister music from speakers hidden in their shrubbery. Halloween was obviously very important to them. Year-round, every week he biked past Gretchen and Holly's house on his way to the bookstore. On recycling days Gordon had noticed in their blue bin at the curb a great number of vodka bottles along with diet soda cans and bundles of pizza boxes and newspaper. He thought it was marvelous that they had each other.

Halloween excited and exhausted Ferga. Her border collie heart's desire each year would have been instruction from Gordon to go out and round up all the children wandering through the neighborhood and herd them together into a satisfying pack, all the worrisome unruly creatures consolidated in one manageable place in their backyard. Sometimes on winter evenings after dinner, while Gordon read a book in the worn stuffed rocker that had been in his childhood living room, when Ferga lay snoozing in front of the wood stove, her paws twitching, she was dreaming of this.

Gordon couldn't stop thinking about his brother, whom he loved more than anyone else on earth. If Duncan didn't want to be alive, did anyone else have the right to insist that he keep living? He was devastated by what had happened to Duncan. Gordon was wary around Laura since that rainy night when she drank too much. Though he understood her desperation to find something that would give Duncan a different feeling about the future, he didn't think she could do anything to change what Duncan felt. Whenever they were alone together, a circumstance Gordon tried to avoid, Laura would attempt to enlist him in finding strategies to help Duncan adjust to his new life and make the most of it. She talked about Duncan's life before the accident and Duncan's life after the accident, but Gordon felt as if the accident was one continuous event that was still happening, as if Duncan had rolled down some enormous steep hill and landed disastrously at the bottom, but he was still rolling, farther and farther away.

At the bookstore, Gordon was pretty much the entire shipping and receiving department. He inventoried and shelved the books that arrived each day, and once a week he boxed up for return all the books that had been over-optimistically ordered for readings, which the store hosted twice a week. In the first month he worked at Roxy's, Gordon had made some bad mistakes, and he was profoundly grateful to Roxy for the graceful way she had handled them.

She had neither fired him nor shamed him when, the day after the shipment came in, Gordon accidentally returned all one hundred copies of a novel that had been ordered for a reading, leaving only the four copies stacked in the front window display available for sale at the very well-attended event (for which the author had traveled to Connecticut from Vermont). He had not yet developed a system, and the title on the returns box was quite similar to the title of the new novel, and the boxes had been shifted several times in the course of the morning. Though it had cost the bookstore, and the author had been pretty upset, Roxy never brought it up again after that night.

Gordon had in those same early days offended a certain local celebrity cookbook author (he didn't watch cooking shows on television and he didn't recognize her face, her name, or her signature exclamation, "Golly whillikers!" which, when shrilly deployed at high decibel, was usually a foolproof means of getting the attention she needed). He had been insufficiently obsequious and contrite when she complained that the store had only three copies of *Maggie Match's Down the Hatch* in stock, since she had dropped by to offer, magnanimously, to sign her newest cookbook for children. (No author hoping to see her recent book in a prominent spot on a front table ever wants to be reassured that the store can order that book, what's the title, and how do you spell the author's name again?) Gordon didn't recognize regular customers, either, and this was a bit of a problem, which was why he was only put on the counter when the store got really busy. Roxy figured that Gordon might have very low facial recognition skills, and he didn't disagree with her, but the truth was, Gordon didn't often look people square in the face.

Gordon's tasks of the day included packing up what Roxy called all the Halloween tchotchkes (a word Gordon wouldn't dream of attempting to utter aloud) to make room for the incoming holiday items that would be arriving in the next few days. The store made its margin on gift items, Roxy often reminded staff, even though we all love books and nobody works in a bookstore out of a love of coffee mugs and calendars, which only made Gordon glad that he didn't have the responsibility of owning a bookstore.

The frankly Halloween-themed objects were obvious, but after he had packed up the Virginia Woolf and Mark Twain masks and the Jack o' Lantern candles, along with the glow-in-the-dark pumpkin buckets and the candy corn note pads, he hesitated over the one remaining pumpkin spice gift box of the thirty-six that he had arranged in a pleasingly perfect spiral on the center table. The gift box consisted of a pumpkin spice muffin mix and two orange coffee mugs with pumpkins on them. This wasn't literally a Halloween item, but it was Halloween*ish*.

He left this one remaining gift box out on the table for the time being, and took the other items down into the basement to enter them into the system for storage or return, depending on the source. Then he either boxed them for shipping and printed out labels accordingly, or shelved them in inventory. By the time he had done this, he had changed his mind, recognizing how needlessly compulsive he was being about this one item, but it was on his mind, so he went back up the stairs and back onto the floor to get the pumpkin spice gift box, but it was gone—a customer had probably picked it up and moved it. He roamed through the store, scanning for the orange mugs with pumpkins on them. He straightened and re-shelved books in proper order as he went, tucking in the shelf talkers that had gone askew. There was the pumpkin spice gift box, at the top of a stack of books that a customer was pushing forward on the counter as her turn came in the queue at the front desk. Sold! What a relief.

Four days of the week, Gordon's shift at the bookstore ended at three. As he pedaled past the tea shop that had recently opened a few doors down, he saw a sidewalk sign advertising a tea lecture and tasting that had just begun. Today's topic was a comparison between the oolongs of Taiwan and China. Wondering how political designation affected the taste of tea, Gordon cocked his leg over his bike to dismount.

As he dropped into a folding chair in the back row, the speaker was elaborating to an audience of about thirty people the details of the ten steps required to process oolong tea. The plucking of the leaves, by machine or hand, was step one. Gordon settled in his uncomfortable seat and closed his eyes, his favorite way to attend readings in the bookstore, in a semi-dream state. He floated through the selection of the top leaves, the withering in the sun, the indoor withering and oxidation. The ratios of oxidations didn't interest him as much as did the concept of oxidation as a continuum, ranging in degrees from zero to 100%. But this was actually quite a lot like listening to paint dry. Gordon dozed some more as he half-heard about the fourth step, pan-firing the leaves, and then the oolong leaves are rolled around in a machine, and after that they are separated and dried. Wait, was that the fifth step? Or was it the second part of the fourth step? Was anyone else still awake? Gordon opened one eye and saw that there were attentive souls all around him. A woman in the row ahead of him was taking notes. He still hadn't heard anything about Taiwan versus the mainland.

Drying, rolling, baking. Gordon hadn't eaten lunch, and now the vocabulary of the processing of oolong tea in China made him think of pie and cake and cookies. His stomach rumbled. He stretched out his long legs in front of him and accidentally kicked a chair, causing its occupant to whip around and give him a hard stare. He mouthed "sorry," and hunched his shoulders in the universal gesture of contrition, and the man turned back, satisfied.

Now the speaker was talking about China and Taiwan, and Gordon wondered if Chinese people didn't think Taiwan was Chinese, if a separate political state. In China, the oolongs are oxidized more and baked longer than Taiwan oolongs. Was that the bottom line? And why was this so? He waited to hear more about the reasons for this difference, but the speaker was now describing a rare and inaccessible tea garden on a cliff in the Fujian province (had he been there himself, or was he in effect describing a description?) where an exceptionally rare tea is made from the leaves of one ancient tree. People go to such trouble!

The talk was drawing to a close. The speaker pronounced the tea they were about to taste both mellow and rich, with the aroma of orchids and an aftertaste reminiscent of peach pits. Everyone stood up and milled around, and samples of the first oolong were poured into short white paper cups.

Gordon stood with his paper cup, sipping delicately, trying not to burn his mouth. His mouth burned very easily. The tea was partly strained through his mustache, so the aftertaste was probably reminiscent not only of peach pits, which he tried to detect, but also the crumbs of the blueberry muffin Roxy had left him on the shipping and receiving desk that morning.

"What do you think?" A teenaged girl sipping from her cup was speaking to him. She was short, and Gordon was tall, and he had an uncomfortable sense of looming over her.

"Some have an almost woody flavor, while others may be slightly bitter or astringent on the first infusion," Gordon heard the man whose chair he had kicked informing the note-taking woman, who looked trapped. He was clearly one of those people—Gordon encountered them at the bookstore each time he was responsible for setting up for readings in

the upstairs space because they were usually first to arrive—
who love to show up at readings and lectures on topics about
which they feel vastly more informed than the speaker at the
front of the room.

Gordon smiled and the short girl grinned back, sharing
amusement over the adjacent expertise. "It has a note of pocket
lint and candy corn, don't you think?" Gordon said.

"But with a tobacco finish," she replied, raising her paper
cup with her pinkie lifted. They touched cups and swigged
down the remains of their tea. The expert glared at both of
them angrily. The Taiwan oolong was now being poured.
People hushed one another so the speaker could tell the
milling group that in Taiwan, the oolong leaves harvested
in spring and winter are superior to the leaves picked in the
summer and fall. Everyone was fascinated. Was this not also
true in China, Gordon wondered? Why, or why not? He
would never dream of asking a question. Anyway, he had to
pee and was tired of standing around. He didn't want more
tea. He wasn't sure if he was the kind of person who could
make the subtle distinctions. Or care about them. It was getting late and Ferga was waiting for him.

"I have to go. I hope the angry tea expert guy doesn't zap
you with his laser eye beams," he leaned over and whispered.

"Thanks," the girl whispered back. "He's my dad."

As he pedaled home, Gordon thought about how he would
describe the tea tasting to Duncan at his next visit. He would
not mention the girl because Duncan perked up too much
when he mentioned girls, or teased him, and then he would
have to explain that this one was about fifteen for god's sake
and he wasn't interested in her that way, she was just a nice
kid who was easier to talk to than anyone else there.

Gordon just wasn't very interested in girls, or boys, or in
getting close to anybody. He knew this about himself, but
Laura and Duncan never gave up, and each of them had talked

with him at different times about meeting just the right person, how it would happen if he wanted it to. Laura had always been so careful to keep the "right person" conversation in a gender-neutral zone before that night. Then came those ugly, relentless questions. It was hard for other people to understand how Gordon could be content to draw a very small circle around himself and live inside it. He was content with his life just the way it was. Ferga was good company. He didn't need more than he had.

At certain sharp and unexpected moments he did miss his mother, maybe more than most men his age ordinarily would. He knew that. He was okay with himself being one of those men whose mother remained very important in his daily thoughts. Now that she was gone, he often imagined conversations with her. He would have told her about the tea tasting. He would have bought some oolong tea for her, too, some from China and some from Taiwan, and he would have brewed two pots of tea and poured four cups, and then they would have tasted them together. For fun, he might have put a peach pit on a saucer, too, for comparison to the aftertaste of the tea he had tasted today.

Among Helen Wheeler's many habitual little expressions was that she wouldn't do something, or go somewhere, or eat something for all the tea in China. Or she would give all the tea in China if only something impossible would happen or she could find out something unknowable. As he stood on his pedals to make the one hill on his way home without slowing down, Gordon felt with all his heart that he would very much like to be biking home after speech therapy, turning down Broadfield Road on a darkening Wednesday afternoon like this, coasting the last gently sloping block, knowing that his brother would be home from his piano lesson by now and would be hitting a tennis ball over the chalked net line on the garage door, over and over and over, counting to see how many times he could do it without error, so he could be a natural who never practiced, and their father would be coming home from the office soon and Gordon would wait for him, sitting on the big wicker swing that hung on the front porch and reading, moving the swing just a little bit, back and forth, back and forth, with one foot tucked under him and the other on the gray painted boards, while he waited for his father to come home.

While his father parked the car in the driveway, Gordon would keep his head down, still reading his book and swinging back and forth just a little bit, and the car door would slam, and his father would cut across the lawn, and now Gordon would listen to the familiar thumping footsteps on the hollow wood steps to the porch, where he would pass by Gordon, bent over his book, not looking up, though not really reading either, and his father would call him Chief and grab the back of his neck in the rough but nice way nobody else ever did, before going in the front door, declaring that he was home while unbuttoning his shirt collar and loosening his necktie as he dropped his keys and change on the front hall table, and Gordon's mother would answer from the kitchen where she would be making dinner, her roast chicken with mashed potatoes or her pot roast, and Gordon knew just how the house would smell, either way, and how cozy and warm the house would feel when he got off the swing and went inside, and he would give all the tea in China to go home to that house again.

# ELEVEN

## *Primate Institute of New England*

### Progress Report

Placement Date: 10.22.14
Name: NORMA JEAN, A.K.A. OTTOLINE
Tufted capuchin # PI06131028
D.O.B.: unknown
Gender: F
Spayed/neutered: YES (date unknown)
Age: unknown, approximately 24–26 y.o.
Prior Placement: YES
Placement Trainer: Martha Peterson
Recipient: Duncan Wheeler, age 37, C6 spinal cord injury,
    complete
127 Lawrence Street, New Haven, CT 06511
60 Day Update: 12.21.14

Ottoline has settled in well with her recipient and the two
of them have already developed a wonderfully bonded
relationship. The initial need and personality assessment

of both Ottoline and Duncan Wheeler accurately predicted that this would be a very good match between monkey and recipient. The Wheelers are still struggling with some of Ottoline's quirks, and we have had frequent telephone check-ins, often several a day. Food and diaper routines have been established. Ottoline willingly goes into her cage at night and tucks herself in with fleece blankets. She sleeps until 8 a.m. without difficulty. (This was noted at her prior placement, as there is a marginal note in a Progress Report dated October 2001 that states: "Ottoline is not a morning monkey.") Ottoline's aversion to being immersed in water in a tub or sink was the most significant ongoing source of adjustment anxiety for the Wheelers. After several frantic calls about this, on our advice Laura has stopped trying to give Ottoline a bath and instead has developed the necessary bathing routine using the sprayer in their kitchen sink. This is acceptable to Ottoline, who enjoys running water but has a fear of standing water that may be a consequence of some unknown prior incident such as falling into a full bathtub or being roughly handled around water at some point in her life. As tasks have been introduced, once comfort levels were established and the tribal hierarchy seemed stable, the Wheelers have become even more aware of the ways that Ottoline is both very smart and also quite opinionated. As their Primary Advisor, I note that both Wheelers are too indulgent and lenient with Ottoline when she refuses a task or steals food. They were reminded of the need to stay within guidelines in order for Ottoline to perform her tasks as well as for the protection of her health. We will need to reinforce with them on a regular basis in order to keep the placement functioning optimally.

This is a very successful placement.    MP

# TWELVE

## *Duncan rolled out the front door*

DUNCAN ROLLED OUT THE FRONT DOOR AND PAUSED on the porch. It was well above freezing, and the accumulated snow had melted quickly, leaving the sidewalks bare. It was one of those herald-of-spring April days that had lost its place in the calendar and arrived out of sequence here at the end of January. Duncan hadn't been outside in three weeks. He waited in the watery sunlight at the top of the ramp for Ida Mae, who had sat down heavily on the bench beside their front door to finish jamming her "poor feet" into her unnecessary snow boots. The clear, wet sidewalks gave Duncan a chance to navigate around the block, if no further. Slushy puddles of uncertain depth flooded the curb ramps on the corners and made crossing the street in his motorized chair a risky endeavor.

He tried to look up to see how the porch ceiling paint was holding up. Three years ago he had caulked and repainted that ceiling a lovely pale blue with a hint of green (Benjamin Moore called it Palladian Blue). Duncan had always loved projects like this, and he particularly missed the satisfaction of methodically brushing paint onto wood, like spreading jam on toast, all the way to the edges. He had meant to hang the old porch swing from the house on Broadfield Road. It was down in the basement where he had sanded it and applied a base coat of paint, but then he had never finished the job. He wanted to replace the rusted chains, but hadn't gotten around to it.

Ida Mae had informed them during her first week on the job that Floyd would have approved of the Wheelers' haint blue front-porch ceiling color, because its resemblance to water tricks the haints, the dead, and prevents them from coming into the house. The dead can't cross water, Ida Mae explained. Floyd had told her so. (Crossing water probably wouldn't be your chief ambition if you were dead, Laura pointed out to Duncan when they discussed this revelation later.) Duncan couldn't raise his chin sufficiently to see anything directly overhead (looking up was one of many ordinary abilities he had never valued until he lost it), and had to make do with a glimpse of the haint blue-painted tongue and groove ceiling boards at either end of the porch. Would the dead really be that gullible? What about the dead already in the house, would this mean they couldn't leave?

Several times during the first weeks of this exceptionally snowy winter, their roof had been blanketed with inches of snow sandwiched by layers of the heavy ice that formed during ice storms. Before now, Duncan had always loved snow; the smooth contours of snow drifts made him crave vanilla custard ice cream. He couldn't understand why most people, Laura among them, thought ice cream was a summer treat. On hot summer nights, when they drove up Whitney Avenue to Wentworth's in Hamden for ice cream, Laura always chose the same thing, a single scoop of coffee ice cream on a sugar cone.

This icy winter, with the thermostat set a few degrees warmer than ever before because his injury made him nearly as susceptible to dangerous chills as he was at risk for overheating into dysreflexia, the warm air escaping from their inadequately-insulated attic had melted the innermost layer of snow on the roof trapped under the ice, which had led to the melt water seeping under their roof shingles. Water traveling down the rafters had caused some ominous stains to appear up near the ceiling in two corners of their upstairs front rooms, Laura had reported. The box room was one, and their bedroom was the other.

Some books on the top bookshelves in their bedroom were ruined, having sponged up the water as it seeped down the wall for quite a while before Laura heard a telltale dripping in the night. The books in their house were shelved by category in alphabetical order from one room to the next, all through the house. The drowned books were novels by Thomas Mann, J. P. Marquand, W. Somerset Maugham, William Maxwell, Carson McCullers, Alice McDermott, Herman Melville, Steven Millhauser, and Iris Murdoch.

Duncan had made Laura give him a Skype tour of the damage, using her iPad. On his desktop computer screen, the upstairs rooms looked dark and ordinary, like rooms in anyone's house, familiar but very far away. It was like seeing old snapshots taken in half-forgotten houses of distant relatives visited in childhood. The roofer Laura phoned had made the inevitable remark every roofing contractor makes about how the roof of a house is not constructed like the bottom of a swimming pool. Nothing could be done about the leaks caused by ice damming until spring.

The inimical water had also penetrated the gable roof over their front porch, thus Duncan's concern about possible damage. Icicles had formed, dripped from the cracks between the porch ceiling boards, lethal stalactites that grew heavier and longer until they fell at odd moments with a startling crash, leaving broken ice scattered across the porch like the broken glass that marks the scene of an accident. Duncan recalled ice lance jousting with Gordy, when huge icicles dripped from the clogged gutters of their house one very snowy winter. Their lances had shattered, but then Duncan stabbed Gordy with a dagger-like shard, and by dinnertime a deep red bruise had bloomed and spread across Gordy's neck. It's a wonder most children don't kill themselves or each other.

Trussed successfully into her snow boots at last, Ida Mae now stood behind Duncan, pulling his knit watch cap down to cover his ears. She moved around to the side of his chair to fuss over his scarf and cinch his chest strap more snugly over his jacket, until he simply toggled into motion and she had to step out of the way as he began to roll down the zig-zag ramp. He relished the opportunity to have a moment in the fresh air by himself, and when he reached the end of their front walk, he didn't wait for her before turning onto the sidewalk and heading up the block at a good clip.

He navigated the length of the block, turned right on Livingston Street, rolled to the end without incident, and turned right on Cottage Street. The air was very cold on his face and the exposed fingers of his left hand. He wore a mitten on his right hand, which lay in his lap like a small helpless creature. He could do this. He rolled down Cottage Street, slowing to bulldoze through a couple of empty plastic trash bins lying on their sides which blocked his path, and when he reached the next corner, he turned right on Foster Street. The houses on this block were smaller, but there was something pleasing about the rhythm of all the narrow gable ends as he sailed by. He had always aligned his Monopoly houses very precisely. Foster Street had a number of two-family houses. Low chain link fences demarcated occasional property lines, something Duncan had never noticed before. Had he ever walked all the way around his own block? He couldn't remember having done it in all the years of living in this house, when walking out the door and going for a quick turn around the block would have taken but a moment, and been so easy.

Duncan encountered only one person on foot, a woman on the other side of Cottage Street, walking a pair of briskly waddling dachshunds saddled with matching plaid coats. He came to Lawrence Street and turned right again. A barberry bush that protruded onto the sidewalk through a low chain link fence was alive with little twittering birds. Wrens? They were the same birds who nested in the dryer vent every spring. They abruptly took off as he approached, and rose in a loose skein into the overhanging maples. A chime of wrens?

It had not occurred to Duncan to go the other way around the block. Most people automatically choose a clockwise direction. That's why the queues on the left are always a better bet in places like airport security checkpoints. He passed Frank and Jesse's house. Are you pro- or anti-clockwise, he had overheard Frank ask Jesse playfully one night at dinner, when everyone was a little silly after the third bottle of Zinfandel had been poured and the cheese board was being passed, with Laura's raisin walnut bread, and a watercress salad. Next time he would go around the block anti-clockwise.

Duncan rolled along, spotting his own house up ahead. The glimpse of haint blue porch ceiling was pleasing. When he reached home, there was no sign of Ida Mae. He had assumed she would be waiting for him. Had she followed behind him? He couldn't easily turn his chair to see on this very narrow patch of sidewalk, and he wasn't in the mood to execute a three-point turn where he could get a wheel wedged over the edge of the sidewalk in the mud and snow, just to look for her. A rearview mirror would be handy.

Duncan kept going, passing his house, relishing the tiny recklessness of this unsupervised jaunt. He could feel his nose dripping. He certainly wasn't lost—he knew where he was. Ida Mae would find him. He had now circumnavigated the block. Maybe he would go all the way around again. As he rolled once more toward the corner of Livingston Street, he could see the McCarthy children bobbing along on the far side of Livingston, coming from Whitney Avenue, walking rather than being transported home from school in the old red Saab on this enjoyable afternoon, the two boys' unzipped parkas flapping like wings. They were pursued by their glamorous au pair Ingie, who herded their toddling little sister in front of her.

As they charged closer, Duncan could see that Ingie was struggling to keep up as she pranced along the sidewalk behind them in her spiked, knee-high boots. Her short white jacket with a puffy rolled collar was snugged tight on her, like a life vest. Her fine blonde hair was tucked inside a blue and yellow cap with a pom-pom that had probably been knitted by her grandmother beside the family fjord during a cold Scandinavian winter. Could she be wearing nothing else but a pair of tights? Laura had a thing about women who dressed this way, even tiny-bottomed ones like Ingie, or perhaps especially tiny-bottomed ones like Ingie, and would often mutter "tights aren't pants" under her breath when she espied offenders. Duncan was supposed to share her opprobrium, though sometimes he thought it was marvelous.

The boys galloped across the street in front of Ingie and their sister, straight toward Duncan as he motored in their direction, until they came face to face at the corner. The little girl halted in her tracks and turned toward Ingie with both arms outstretched, whimpering, "Up me! Up me!" until Ingie scooped her off the sidewalk, though she was a substantial toddler, and her muddy snow boots left streaks on Ingie's white pants or tights or whatever they were. Duncan stopped his chair, lurching a little bit and rebounding against his chest strap.

"Cool!" the older boy exclaimed, reaching for the toggle control. "How do you drive it? How fast does it go?"

"Jackson, do not be a bother to the man," Ingie said, grabbing for his shoulder to pull him back with her one free hand.

She grasped only his jacket, which slid off as he ducked out from under it and whirled around to reposition himself in front of Duncan.

"Are you the loose wreck?" the other boy demanded.

"Do not be a rude, Bailey!"

"Do not be a rude, Bailey!" the now-unjacketed child shouted.

"Woo-ood, Baa-wee!" chimed the sister.

"I am not being pleased with you children!" Ingie implored, struggling to deposit the clinging toddler back onto the sidewalk, but she retracted her little legs with each dip, keeping her boots from touching the sidewalk. "We are not at all having a polite time!"

Jackson and Bailey surged forward together, and Jackson climbed confidently halfway onto Duncan's lap while Bailey reached for the toggle control. "Can I touch it?" he asked, touching it. The chair lurched forward. Duncan's clawed left hand in its splint splayed over the small smooth child's hand as he took control, stopping the chair.

"Cool! My turn!" Jackson shouted as he slid off Duncan's lap, reaching over for the toggle while clinging to Duncan's chest strap with his other hand.

"Boys! Do not be without your control! It is imperative!"

"It is imperative!" they shouted together in remarkably accurate accented falsetto.

"Impewatif," echoed the snowsuited limpet. Ingie's command over the McCarthy children was as successful as her mastery of English.

"Careful! Careful!" Ida Mae called out breathlessly as she caught up to the contingent on the sidewalk. "Duncan, are you all right? Is something wrong with the controls? You just kept going and going and I was worried you couldn't stop!"

"I'm fine, nothing's wrong," Duncan said, a little more irritably than Ida Mae deserved. She was panting with the exertion of following him around the block.

"Oh, I was so worried," she puffed, as she reached out to adjust his knit cap. And then she dabbed at his dripping nose with a tissue. How could she?

"Lay off," he barked.

"Well, excuse me! Somebody's got on his grumpy drawers!" Ida Mae said, playing to the crowd while withdrawing the wadded tissue in an elaborate gesture of obedience. The McCarthy children shrieked with laughter.

"Grumpy drawers!" Bailey shouted.

"Bumpy bores!" the little girl enunciated with surprising clarity.

"Dumpy doors!" shouted Jackson. Duncan had hopes for what might come next.

"Humpy—"

"Bailey!" Ingie implored uselessly. "You are without order! Come here!" Both nannies had disrespectful charges on their hands.

"So are you?" Jackson demanded of Duncan.

"Am I?" Duncan answered. "I don't know. Maybe. Are you?"

"Am I what?" Jackson stared up at Duncan while Ingie stuffed his arms back into his jacket.

"I don't know. You asked me first. What did you call me?"

"Are you the loose wreck? My daddy said you don't go outside or talk to people anymore because of your accident and now you're a loose wreck."

"Well, look at me," Duncan said. "I'm outside, and I'm talking to you. How much of a loose wreck could I be?"

Jackson shrugged elaborately in a way that made Duncan wonder if it was a gesture copied from some show on television. Bailey copied him, and then their sister squirmed away from Ingie's grasp to lean out so she could shrug too, which gave Ingie the opportunity to attempt another landing. The chubby little legs folded up the first two times, and only on the third try did she allow Ingie to set her down.

"So if he's Jackson, and he's Bailey, what's your name?" Duncan asked her. She didn't answer but took a step towards him, and then another, until she was touching his knee.

Ida Mae declared that Duncan was getting too cold and needed to get back inside and warm up before he became hypothermic. All three McCarthy children were now crowding in and leaning against his legs, eager for more news from the loose wreck. "Step back!" she instructed them crossly. Duncan suddenly felt weak and exhausted. She was right.

"Watch this," he told them as they backed away, and he toggled the control to spin the chair around in a tight circle to face in the opposite direction.

"Cool!" Bailey exclaimed. They trotted after him as he motored the half-block towards home, followed by Ingie, while Ida Mae stumped along at the rear. A headache was nagging at his temples. When he turned in at his front walk and aimed for the ramp, as a dramatically huffing, puffing Ida Mae caught up with the group, Ingie told the children to say goodbye.

"See you later, alligator!" Bailey and Jackson chorused together.

"Cwocodile," their little sister echoed, as Ingie grabbed her hand to pull her away.

Duncan paused just before the bottom of the ramp and carefully executed a three-point turn as he had learned to do in the many tight corners of the house, so he could face them. "Hey!" Duncan's lung power was weak, and he had no projection. It felt like winter after all. The air was raw and the overcast sky was suddenly blunting into darkness. "Hey, you guys," he tried again, louder.

The children were now across the street in front of their own house, walking up the steps with Ingie, who was looking down at her phone, which she jabbed at intently with both thumbs as if she were wringing the neck of a small animal. The boys turned at the sound of Duncan's hoarse, raised voice.

"Do you kids want to meet my monkey helper?"

"Eeeewww," Bailey shrieked with exaggerated incredulity. "Monkey helper! Is that like Hamburger Helper?"

"See for yourself," Duncan heard himself call back. He could hardly believe it.

"Scout!" called the little girl.

"What?" Duncan was really breathless and exhausted now.

"My sister's name is Scout," Bailey shouted helpfully.

By the time Laura drove home from work, though it was only a little after six, it felt like the middle of the night. Before sunset, the skies over New Haven had darkened like a bruise, with rumblings of thunder and flashes of lightning, bizarre for January but unsurprising for the day, given the temperature, and so the warmer air masses were now colliding with the next blast of arctic air. Hailstones like gravel began to fall, clattering on the roof of her car as she drove very slowly. As she approached Lawrence Street the hailstones grew larger, and were bouncing off the street like popcorn popping in a pan, though as she was parking the car the hail stopped as abruptly as it had started.

Duncan's headache was a bad one, probably made worse by the barometric pressure, opined Ida Mae sagaciously, not that she could have explained to anyone the first thing about barometric pressure. He had been so exhausted after his excursion into the open air that he wanted to go to bed early, so Ida Mae had stayed later than usual to complete his evening routine and transfer him before leaving, though Laura had grown comfortable and adept by now with these tasks.

Laura found Duncan propped in bed, glazed by the narcotic he had been given for the now throbbing headache. Ottoline was sprawled contentedly on his shoulder, rummaging in his hair. Neither of them seemed to be watching the show on Animal Planet, though the station was clearly

Ottoline's choice (whenever she had the television remote, that was the channel on which she stopped). Duncan would have opted for one of the numerous Canadian home renovation shows on HGTV. He loved the predictability of all the open plans and kitchen islands and granite countertops and subway tile and identical finished basements and the way prosperous Canadians talked about what kind of "hauwse" they wanted.

When Ottoline saw Laura, who was still in her coat, having rushed through the house hunting for Duncan, disconcerted by the empty living room and kitchen where he would have ordinarily been waiting for her to come home and start dinner, the little monkey squealed with delight and sprang across the bed to jump up into her arms. She hugged Laura tightly around the neck, making the grunty, squeaky, hooty noises of happy welcome that she reserved for members of her inner circle.

"Do you think I'm a loose wreck?" Duncan asked Laura.

"A what? Are you feeling off? Another headache?"

"I met the McCarthy children when I went out for some air. I went around the block. They were a riot. The little girl is named Scout."

"You're kidding. *To Kill a Mockingbird* Scout?"

"Don't you think it's the perfect name for the child of the world's most modest criminal defense attorneys? At least they didn't name one of the boys Atticus. Just think how they'd feel now."

"I get Jackson, that's her maiden name, but where do you think Bailey comes from?"

"I'm guessing F. Lee."

"Oh Christ, I'm sure that's it."

"Anyway," Duncan said, his voice fading into hoarseness, "They've really got Ingie, that beautiful au pair, on the run. But the cold air triggered this nasty headache, and I probably stayed out too long. I don't think I can eat anything. Maybe soup."

"I'm sorry about your head. But that's great! You went all the way around the block with Ida Mae?"

"That's probably not how she would tell it. She followed me."

"So wait. Those kids called you a what?"

"I figured it out. Think about it. The older boy, Bailey, he said their father told them I had become a loose wreck since the accident, now that I stay home and don't see people. In other words, a wreck loose."

"Ah! Well, he's our very own wreck loose, right, Ottoline?" Laura leaned down, with Ottoline still clinging to her, and kissed Duncan on his forehead, which felt clammy to her. Ottoline rappelled down Laura's coat, using an end of Laura's scarf, and clambered back to her place beside Duncan. She grabbed Laura's hand and tugged at it impatiently until Laura sat down at the edge of the bed.

"Ottoline really likes it best when the three of us are together," Duncan said. He closed his eyes while Ottoline inventoried the cuticles on his curled right hand, carefully delving into his fisted palm and extending each finger one at a time.

Laura got up to take off her coat and then she sat down in Duncan's wheelchair, which was parked close enough for her to rest her feet on the foot of his bed. He was dozing off again. An African wildlife show began. Giraffes floated silently across a savanna. Ottoline picked up the television remote that lay beside Duncan's leg and pressed the mute/unmute button. A plummy British voice explained that although a giraffe's neck is more than a meter and a half long, it contains the same number of vertebrae as a human neck. Duncan's lips parted as he began to snore. She would have to settle him for the night with the CPAP, but he didn't need it for a nap. Laura closed her eyes too and listened to news about giraffes. Giraffes have the largest hearts of any land mammal.

A group of giraffes are called a tower. Male giraffes fight with their necks over female giraffes, and this is called necking.

Laura's afternoon in the conservation lab had been unsettling in a number of ways. Dud and Jinxy Cavendish had dropped in unexpectedly. They were dressed in jeans and flannel shirts and sneakers, and they wore matching puffy down vests. They had matching short white hair and matching pale blue eyes. Their profiles had been chiseled from the rockbound coast of Maine. The Cavendishes seemed friendly and approachable, and they immediately instructed her to call them Jinxy and Dud, but given their well-known reputation for institution-hopping, Laura knew not to be too casual with them, no matter how down-to-earth they seemed. She had given the beautiful catalogue of their Shaker furniture collection to Duncan one Christmas. Were they still committed to Winterthur, where many pieces were on extended loan? Did Yale have a chance at it, given the Garvan Collection?

Nobody senior to Laura in conservation was present at that moment, as it happened, owing to preparation for an imminent colloquium on chairs in the Furniture Study, and she knew the Director and chief curator were both in London, so she did her best to host them in a warm and gracious— but not obsequious—manner. (Obsequiousness did not come naturally to Laura, so it was a small risk.) She would handle the Cavendishes with the same delicate touch she used when deploying a three-bristle badger brush to dust the most fragile Qing dynasty red porcelain cup in the Gallery's collection.

Dud was carrying a scuffed L.L. Bean canvas tote, from which he drew out a rectangular suede box that he placed on Laura's worktable. "You are just the person we hoped to find here today! We hope you don't mind," Jinxy said, gazing at Laura, who couldn't imagine the Cavendishes having any awareness of her existence, "but we've brought along something that is rather urgently in need of a conservation report, really just for insurance purposes, so we were hoping you could actually do that for us today while we're here in New Haven visiting Paige—"

Dud undid the catch and opened the lid of the box. Nestled inside the padded satin lining was a pair of diminutive blue-green, flower-shaped bowls. "Do you know Ru ware?" Jinxy asked.

Laura gazed down at the apparently matched set. She was surprised by what she was looking at, and felt very much put on the spot by this request. "Yes, though I'm sure you both probably know a lot more than I do on this subject. Ru ware was made during the Northern Song Dynasty," she said slowly, trying to think of how to handle this potentially awkward moment. "So these are maybe a thousand years old . . . if they're genuine." There it was.

"I assure you that we have very high standards for our collection," Dud said a little frostily.

"Oh, I think they're beautiful," Laura said, backpedaling now, regretting her choice of words. Mustn't insult the Cavendishes! "Would you take them out so we can look at them together? I was just surprised to see a matching pair. I didn't think such a thing existed."

"Look at the long fractured craze lines they call cicada's wings," Jinx instructed, tracing the edge of one of the cups with her fingertip. Laura was intrigued by her ragged cuticles, which made Jinxy a little less intimidating.

"These were found four years ago at a kiln site in Henan, an excavation in the middle of what is now a wheat field," Dud said. "They were both broken and somewhat incomplete of course, but we had them beautifully restored, as you can see, at the Fogg."

Of course they had.

"These two bowls were the most intact finds on the site. The Shanghai Museum wanted dibs on that excavation, because all the shards that came out of that kiln were apparently made to an imperial standard, so it's a very important find, but it was our good fortune that we had funded an independent dig with some Henan archeologists supervised by our own people, so we had an inside track." Whatever that meant.

"It's just that I have always been taught that there was no such thing as a matched pair, only mirrored pairs," Laura said. "It's such a beautiful bluey-green glaze. Can you imagine how exquisite and magical this glaze must have seemed to people a thousand years ago?"

"Of course, we had these very thoroughly tested in a laboratory," Jinxy said, sounding a little defensive to Laura. "Both of these pieces were definitely authentic. They have the characteristics of high-alumina Ru clay found in the vicinity of that kiln. The thick Ru glaze is exactly as it should be. Look at the adorable little fully-glazed splayed feet. These are exceptionally refined."

"Aren't there only maybe seventy known Ru pieces?" Laura asked, scrambling into safer territory, glad she could remember as much as she did, which she hoped would go a long way with the Cavendishes. She had only ever seen one Ru piece up close before. "Is this the only known matched pair of intact Ru ware bowls?"

"Exactly so!" Dud said emphatically. "Frankly, strictly between us, this is why we have been very discreet about possessing them. No fanfare, though of course we have been beside ourselves with excitement about them. We didn't want trouble with the Chinese government. Nobody knows we've got them." Not exactly true—the Fogg people know, and now here they were, asking for a favor at Yale. Why, Laura wondered, did they not ask the Fogg conservator to write this report?

"They're really the heart of our collection," Jinxy added. "But they're such a secret, we haven't even dared try to insure them before now."

That didn't sound quite right. Laura turned on her table lamp and swung it over, pulled on a pair of the usual Sure-Grip cotton conservation gloves (they had non-slip vinyl nodules on the palms and fingers), and then she gingerly picked up first one and then the other bowl; each was no more than five inches in diameter. In the raking light and with magnification, she could just barely make out the repaired fractures and in-fills under the glaze, which had been very proficiently in-painted. The crazing helped to hide the repairs. She looked at one, and then the other flower-shaped bowl again. They would have been ceremonial, not for daily tea-drinking. She turned each one over and scrutinized the bottom surfaces with a loupe. Laura began to recognize that what her gut reaction had told her was probably true. Even so, she couldn't be utterly certain.

"So, do you have that laboratory report, the testing you mentioned? I could use it as the basis of a condition report," she said, head still bent over the bowls. Neither Dud nor Jinxy answered her.

"Or I could just request a copy if you want to give me your contact there," Laura said, now looking up at them after the silence had gone on a little too long.

Crickets. Or cicadas. Had they actually named this laboratory? Were they just being coy because they had probably broken several laws in more than one country obtaining the bowls? Maybe this laboratory was in China. Laura was growing more certain that the perfectly matched pair of bowls were in fact genuine shards of one Ru bowl made into two. Perhaps the Fogg had suggested this undesirable possibility. Of course, if the clay was tested in the right places on each, authenticity could easily be established for the Cavendishes' hoped-for documentation. She wondered if they knew. Had they been swindled, or were they themselves swindlers? Perhaps Dud and Jinxy really didn't know the truth, and didn't want to know.

"Do you think you can write your report this afternoon, while we wait, perhaps while we take a walk around the Gallery and see the permanent collection? We were so rushed when we were given a tour the last time we were here. You probably heard about that?" Jinxy fixed her with a shrewd gaze. She was probably a killer at the poker table. Laura recalled overhearing something about the director being furious with a clueless junior curator who had been insufficiently deferential to them that day. The junior curator did not know who they were, and had erroneously assumed Dud was just another patrician Old Blue. When she asked Dud which Yale college was his—a question Old Blues loved to answer—the Cavendishes had departed abruptly.

"Why don't I go get your bowl and let you see that condition report first, okay? Laura said, stalling a commitment to write their damned report. Why was this her responsibility? She left Jinxy and Dud at her worktable for a moment while she went to unlock the secure vitrine and fetch their qingbai bowl in its square padded box (which she realized matched the one they had brought with them today), along with her reports. She wheeled the box across the conservation lab on a cart, the standard procedure for moving precious and fragile objects (though Laura probably would have carried the box in her hands, a violation of protocols, had she been alone and unobserved).

As she returned, she discovered the Cavendishes looking at Duncan's Explicated Four-Square House drawings. True to their sense of entitlement, they had picked up and moved the matted drawings from the adjacent flat file countertop, where Laura had been keeping them stacked together in plain sight as a reminder to herself to get one of them framed as a surprise for Duncan. Jinxy was just finishing laying all of them out on Laura's worktable. The pair of Ru ware bowls had evidently been put back into their box, which was now sitting on the flat file countertop where the architectural drawings had been.

"What a dear little house," Jinxy exclaimed, lifting aside the acid-free protective sheets Laura had sandwiched between the mats. "It's cunning!"

"Does the Gallery own these?" asked Dud. "Part of some collection, I suppose, or an archive of architectural curiosities of the past?"

"Actually, it's a house my husband designed," Laura said cautiously.

"Where *is* this adorable house?" Jinxy asked with animation. "I would love to see it. Dud and I are thinking about building a cottage for guests on our farm in Hallowell. We don't want anything too modern, but we don't want to just build something that's an imitation of the local American vernacular style, and we don't want to settle for something too ordinary, either." Laura had seen photographs of their fabulous nineteenth-century dairy barn that had been gutted and turned into a magnificent museum space, a perfectly climate-controlled home for their collections.

"You can't see it, I mean, of course you're looking at it, but that's it, that's all there is," Laura said. "It doesn't exist. It was never built. Not that I know of, anyway."

"Do you mean to say someone commissioned this clever house from your evidently very talented architect husband and then changed his mind?" Dud asked, bending down to scrutinize the axonometric drawing over his half glasses. Ottoline knew the command for pushing slipped eyeglasses back up someone's nose, Laura thought. Push up!

"No, I think it was a student project, something Duncan did a long time ago. I had never seen these drawings until I found them rolled up and stuffed on the back of a shelf, and I brought them in so I could mat them. I was thinking of framing one or two, to surprise him."

"I suppose your husband has designed many such houses in the intervening years that we could go and see?" Jinxy persisted. "Where have they been published?"

"Actually, no," Laura said. "Not exactly. He went to work for someone with a very different style, maybe you've heard of Billy Corrigan? So all of Duncan's houses are really Corrigan designs, pretty much. But he's not practicing right now, anyway."

"Has he retired?" Dud asked sharply. "Young men shouldn't retire when they're in their prime. They go to seed."

"Or is he much older than you, dear?" Jinxy asked in a semi-sweet tone.

"No, he's not working right now because he was in an accident." Laura didn't want to tell them too much about Duncan. She just didn't want to give them that information at this moment. "But would you really be interested in building this house?"

"Perhaps we would," Jinxy said. "Laura, I have to say I think we're beginning to understand each other. In fact, I'm sure we would like to build that dear little house. We could use our local architect in consultation with your husband, Duncan, did you call him? Would the fee help you both, if he's out of work because of an accident? But it does depend. Would you really be able to write that conservation report today?"

After the Cavendishes had departed with their three bowls and two satisfactory conservation reports, having made a commitment to Laura that they would be in touch within the next two days to come to an agreement about building the Explicated Four-Square House, what remained of Laura's afternoon had consisted of more ordinary tasks. She finished typing up her documentation notes from the previous week about a small bit of restoration work on a miniature Etruscan marble figure in the collection. Just before her workday ended, Laura got an email from a curator at the Yale Peabody Museum of Natural History, reminding her that she had not yet logged in the objects they had sent over the day before, a group of Pre-Columbian figurines. Laura loved objects from Tlatilco (Nahuatl for "the place where things are hidden"), which was the traditional name of a farming village on the edge of what is now Mexico City. It was only in the 1940s that these ancient representations of the human figure were first harvested from the earth by farmers who believed that they grew in the fertile soil.

The group of eight-centimeter-high female figurines Laura now had before her were all Tlatilco two-headed women, mysterious, disturbing figures, and Laura was uncommonly nervous about handling the fragile, dusty clay forms. While they were nearly identical at a glance, close inspection made evident the uncannily ferocious individual presence, as if each was a portrait of some specific being who had actually lived.

Nobody could say for sure why the Tlatilco people seemed to be obsessed with two-headedness or what it meant to them. Laura had seen some Tlatilco two-faced women in the collection as well, both on public exhibition at the Peabody and when they came in for repairs. Were these figures created to ward off birth defects or conjoined twins, or to document them? Laura had read that Tlatilco potters were thought to be women, judging from the size of the three-thousand-year-old fingerprints left in the clay.

Nine figurines had been sent over so that the conservation lab could fabricate exhibition stands to hold them securely to display them together in a lighted vitrine, and get them out of the drawer storage where they were currently housed. Having put on her Sure-Grip cotton conservation gloves again, Laura set about unwrapping each of the two-headed women, gingerly laying them out on a large velvet artifact tray. This day had grown impossibly long and was taking more time than she had meant to spend away from Duncan, and she was impatient as she began this final task. She had been alone in the lab since the Cavendishes left, and would have to lock up when she was done, a task she hated because there were so many procedures involving a sequence of locks and corresponding keys.

Eighteen heads stared up at her with grotesque bulging eyes, their paired, tilted heads reminding her faintly of Ottoline's flirtatious head tilts. Her documentation was nearly complete, each object getting its own page in the log, when Laura picked up the last figurine to confirm the India ink number on the label that was glued to its back by a museum curator fifty years ago, when such labels were routinely affixed to artifacts with no concern for the damaging consequences. She picked it up with one hand, so she could write with the other hand, though protocol required a precise, two-handed light grasp for objects such as this. The figurine slipped from her gloved fingers and hit the edge of the table, where it exploded in mid-air into a shower of clay dirt that scattered across the floor. In an instant, the object had ceased to exist. There wasn't one recognizable fragment.

It was smithereens, thought Laura (who often narrated to herself at stressful moments), as she stared at the reddish dust as it settled, from smiddereens, the Irish term for small fragments, which derived from the old Irish, *smidirin*, a diminutive of *smiodar*. Laura got a dustpan and a whisk broom and swept up. She removed the last page of the log, tore it to smaller and smaller pieces until it was confetti, bagged the paper bits in a specimen envelope, and tucked them into her purse to scatter in the kitchen trash at home.

Now just eight Tlatilco figurines had been logged in. Laura signed her name to the summary that documented the arrival conditions of the eight Tlatilco two-headed female figurines sent to the conservation lab in the Yale Art Gallery from the Yale Peabody Museum of Natural History so that exhibition stands could be fabricated to hold them securely for display in a museum vitrine case. She had never done anything like this before, not only damaging a work of art but then also covering up the loss. She was shocked at how easy it was to do both. Maybe spending a couple of hours with Jinxy and Dud Cavendish had loosened her sense of right and wrong. Laura thought about the visiting conservator from Florence saying that conservators were like doctors, and everyone murders at least one patient. Here it was at last, her inevitable murder victim. Then she locked up and went home.

The giraffes were gone, and a show about alligators living in the Everglades had begun. Laura reached for the remote on the blanket next to Duncan and turned off the television. Ottoline was curled asleep on his pillow, cuddled by his left ear, snoring slightly. He shouldn't sleep too much now or he would have a restless night, Laura knew from experience. But she didn't want to wake him just yet. She gazed at her unconscious husband for a while, and a wave of grief swept over her. Could she bear this? What else was there to do? She watched Duncan breathe. What if he stopped breathing right now? What if that was his last breath? What would she feel? She studied his face, imagining it in the still repose of death. Laura moved herself to some new place as she gazed at dead Duncan. Was she only shattered by grief or was she also lightened with relief? Ottoline opened her eyes and scratched her hairy inner leg at the junction of her diaper, which rustled, and Laura realized she was overdue for a change. Duncan heaved a deep breath and let it out with a sigh that fluttered his lips a little.

Laura made kissing sounds to attract Ottoline's attention, and Ottoline looked up at her, thought about it for a moment, and then accepted the invitation with a big springy leap across Duncan into her lap. They gazed at each other. Laura looked down at the dear wise little face and was moved by her uncanny near-humanness. What did she know, and how did she know it? Laura grabbed her and turned her onto her back, and began to tickle her while whispering, so as not to wake Duncan, "Who's my funny little monkey? Who is? You is?"

Ottoline flung herself back with her mouth wide open, keeping steady eye contact with Laura as she succumbed to her joy at being tickled. When Laura stopped for a moment, Ottoline grabbed her left hand and placed it back on her hairy waist, just above her diaper. Laura tickled her some more, and Ottoline convulsed in open-mouthed silent laughter. Every time Laura stopped, Ottoline demanded more tickles. "Are there enough tickles for Ottoline?" Laura murmured. "You need more tickles? Do you think I can tickle you forever?"

"She doesn't let me tickle her," Duncan whispered.

"Oh good, you're awake. That's because she respects you more than she respects me." She stopped tickling the monkey in her lap and Ottoline sat up and reached over to the rolling table next to the wheelchair and grabbed her sippy cup. She tilted it nearly straight up as she guzzled the water left in the cup before thrusting it in Laura's direction.

"Okay, more water for the monkey. Okeydoke, artichoke. And Dunc, do you want some soup, or maybe a toasted English muffin? Whenever I don't know what I want, a toasted English muffin is often the answer."

"That would be good," he said in the hoarse whisper that was often the best he could manage for a voice. "With cinnamon. Use the Vietnamese cinnamon on the top shelf, not the Ceylon, please. With sweet butter fully melted into the acclivities and declivities." Ottoline somersaulted out of Laura's lap onto the bed and climbed up onto his shoulder. "None of the PCAs know what to do with an English muffin," he said sadly. "Wendell puts the entire muffin in the toaster. And may I just say that his overcooked scrambled eggs are horrible. I think he uses oil instead of butter, and then he only scrambles the eggs once they're in the pan, on a very high heat. They're not scrambled, they're scried."

"You say that like it's a bad thing."

"It is! And while I'm complaining, Cathy slices English muffins with a butter knife, and then barely toasts them at all so they're still pale and floppy."

"Oh no, the horror!" Laura said, gently mocking him. Slowly, so as not to challenge Ottoline, she reached over and put her hand on Duncan's forehead, which was still damp with sweat. He was flushed and he seemed congested. Maybe he was coming down with a cold.

"It matters to me," Duncan continued. "And yesterday Darlene sliced my muffin with a knife so unevenly that the thin side was burned black while the fat side was underdone. Then she scraped the burnt one and thought I wouldn't notice. Even though Mounika tried to do better, she refused to use her thumbs, and insisted on splitting the muffin with a fork, so it still came out too smooth and flat."

"Not enough nooks and crannies," Laura said, trying to keep a respectful tone. "I promise a deeply scabrous, cragged, toasted muffin for you. I do understand." She herself had an atavistic appreciation for the smell of burnt toast and the sound of scraping. Her mother had been a chronic toast burner. Laura grew up believing that thoroughly scraping blackened toast over the sink, leaving a shower of charcoal dust, was the recipe for toast.

"I know you do," said Duncan wearily. "But I can't depend on you for everything. I even tried to teach Ottoline how to split a muffin with her little opposable thumbs, but she just kept taking bites and then she crumbled up the whole thing. I feel deprived and I get upset, and then I feel guilty, as if I'm being peevish and fussy with the PCAs about every little thing, and meanwhile, even when I am fussy, they can't get everything right. I give up asking. I don't care. It doesn't really matter."

"But Dunc, you do care! Nobody in the world cares more about how exactly he wants his eggs and his toasted English muffin! We haven't even begun to discuss your jam closet!

You should have things the way you want them. You have a right."

"I loved all my little details of daily life. When I was in charge of them. Now I'm supposed to be the patient patient, just accepting whatever comes my way without opinions or preferences about these things any more, but I still do care. Having a spinal cord injury doesn't mean you no longer care how your muffin is toasted or if your scrambled eggs are overcooked. This is just all too hard," Duncan rasped, his voice giving out. He was thinking about how earlier in the week Cathy had poured buttermilk into his coffee, mistaking it for Half & Half. After the first sip he had nearly burst into tears. Cathy started her mornings with a Diet Coke and had offered him one instead. "Everything is just too much for me I can't do it. I give up."

"I know," Laura said soothingly. "It's hard, and you're handling everything so well. You really are. And not everything is too much, Dunc. Is our little monkeypants too much for you?"

Duncan shifted to touch his jaw against the soft fur of Ottoline's haunch. "What do you think, Ottoline?" he asked. "What's your position on the English muffin question? Life's just a bowl of blueberries for you."

"Tell us, Ottoline," Laura said. "Tell us."

Ottoline chirped at the sound of her name, and gazed at Laura. Duncan made a clicking sound inside his mouth, and she chirruped back at him. She had her people.

"Is that thunder again?" Duncan asked. "In January? In the dark? It really was an evening all afternoon-ish day. If that's more rain you know it's going to soak into the snow on the roof and freeze and make the ice damming worse. I hope you moved the rest of the books from that shelf upstairs. All the rest of the M's and some of the N's, right?"

She would tell him about the Explicated Four-Square House and the Cavendishes in a week or two, when it was all arranged and he couldn't possibly object. She hoped he would be pleased. She wanted to be able to present it to him as a fait accompli when she presented him with the framed drawings of the house.

There was another rumble of thunder, followed a moment later by the clatter of rain against the windows. Ottoline cocked her head, listening, listening, curious, curious, everything in the world a question.

# THIRTEEN

## *Ottoline yanked the plastic bag*

OTTOLINE YANKED THE PLASTIC BAG DOWN OVER the musk melon, which wobbled on the table. "Good girl!" praised Duncan, "That was faster. Again. Pull it all the way in one fast move! Go! Good. Again. Down! Down! That's it! Good girl!" He held out a blueberry in his cupped hand, and she snatched it and stuffed it in her mouth, devouring it greedily while searching his hand for another treat. "You'll get another treat when you've earned it."

She dug her fingernails into the fragrant, soft stem end of the melon and scrabbled out a small piece of rind, which she ate, and then she straddled the melon to get a better grip so she could dig into the sweet flesh of the melon with both hands and excavate in earnest, now that she had found a way in.

"You look ridiculous, Ottoline," Laura said, passing through the kitchen with a basket of laundry. "What is this, a melon rodeo? Dunc, don't let her mount the fruit! We're eating that tonight. Let's at least pretend to be hygienic."

There was a scuffling sound at the front door, which made Ottoline sit up and cock her head inquisitively, and then a moment later the doorbell sounded.

"I'll get it," Laura called up from the laundry room in the cellar. Of course she would get it. There was an automatic opener that allowed him to roll out the back door and down the long straight ramp (made from economical cedar, at Duncan's insistence) to the open patch of grass in their yard, adjacent to the narrow driveway they shared with Jesse and Frank next door. But Duncan had no way to open the heavy old front door, as he knew well from the times he had been on his own, shouting instructions through the door to the United Parcel or Federal Express driver. Usually Ottoline alerted when her beloved UPS truck pulled up in front of the house, so it was someone or something else on this rainy Saturday afternoon in March.

Laura came into the kitchen with a bemused look on her face. "You have visitors."

"I don't want visitors," Duncan said irritably, annoyed by her constant intrusions on the training session with Ottoline. On the weekends, Laura was home all day and he had much less privacy. "You know that."

"You want these visitors," said Laura, unclipping Ottoline's lead from Duncan's chair. "They're in the living room. Let me put Ottoline in her cage for now and then in a while you can introduce them." She unclipped the lead from Ottoline's waist collar as she hopped onto the back of a kitchen chair. "Come on, honey, cage! Take a little break from assaulting the melon. Cage! Good girl." Ottoline leaped cooperatively into her headquarters and pulled the cage door shut behind her as she was supposed to do. Mystified and a little piqued, Duncan backed his chair from the table, turned, and rolled into the living room.

Ingie was sitting in an armchair, her head bent in devotion over her phone. Scout, Bailey, and Jackson McCarthy were sitting side by side on the sofa across from her. Scout's thumb was jammed in her mouth, while the boys sat with their hands clasped tightly in their laps, trembling with the effort of self-containment. Bailey was encased in swathes of brown paper Stop & Shop bags, held together with a lot of shiny packing tape.

"We came to visit!" he announced with a rustle as Duncan rolled into the room.

"Apparently! It's about time," said Duncan.

"The winter, it was so bad," Ingie said. "They have asked before now."

"Our mom said it was okay because we were getting on her nerves with school vacation all week and anyway Ingie is with us," said Jackson.

"And also even though you're a stranger you couldn't do anything to us," added his brown-papered brother, "because we're faster than you, because you're a cripple. So we can just run away from you."

Ingie looked up, startled. "Boys! Be polite to Mr. Wheeler."

"It's okay," Duncan said. "You guys, call me Duncan. So what's the story, kid, what are you, a grocery bag? A brown paper package tied up with string?"

"I'm a leaf."

"He isn't a leaf, he's a *re*-leaf!" said Jackson. "He was a leaf last Halloween! Now he's a leaf again! So he's a re-leaf, get it? His costume was all smooshed under the bed. He wanted to wear it just to show you so I taped him in. I went as a god-damned plumber."

"I would like to have seen that," Duncan marveled. "What does a goddamned plumber look like?"

"He had his Oshkosh overalls to wear and he carried a toi-let plunge," said Ingie. "We bought a new one so it had hy-giene."

"I was a wightning bug," said Scout, around her thumb. "I bwinked on and off."

"I'll bet you did," said Duncan.

"I followed them on the street," said Ingie.

"You gave out Milky Ways and Butterfingers," Bailey said approvingly. "That was cool."

"Did people understand your plumber costume?" Duncan had stayed in his room on Halloween with the television cranked up, his excuse being that he needed to keep Ottoline away from the excitement and confusion of children in costumes and the doorbell ringing over and over, not to mention the tempting bowl of candy. Halloween had made him inexplicably sad.

"So, you three were a leaf and a plumber and a lightning bug." Duncan was fascinated by the apparent existential depths of the McCarthy kids. He and Gordy had always been pirates or devils at Halloween. "Sounds like the beginning of a joke."

"Tell me the joke, tell me the joke," begged Bailey, crepitatiously bouncing on the sofa.

"I carried a ringing cell phone that I refused to answer," said Jackson. "All my calls went straight to voicemail but my mailbox was full."

"I think we have that plumber," said Laura, coming into the room from the kitchen, where she had been listening to this exchange. "Except for the hygiene. Would you kids like some hot chocolate and cookies, I mean, if you're allowed?" She glanced at Ingie, who shrugged.

"Yes, please!" Bailey said, jiggling on the sofa cushion, his brown paper crackling. "Where's the monkey? Where's the monkey?"

"Where's the monkey?" Jackson echoed. "When do we see your monkey?"

"Monkey, monkey," echoed Scout.

"I'll introduce you, after cocoa and cookies. But Bailey, you'll have to take off your leaf, excuse me, your re-leaf costume, because it might scare her. And everyone has to be much calmer and not so bouncy."

In the kitchen, Laura laid out a double fan of Mint Milano cookies (the only kind in the house—did children like mint?) on a plate and arranged mugs on a tray while the pot of milk (which was on hand only because she had planned to make rice pudding, which was the optimal way to surreptitiously dose Duncan with the Elavil his doctor had agreed to try) heated on the stove. Laura wasn't accustomed to having children in the house. It was nice. Ottoline, seeing the plate of cookies, bounced up and down and hooted, extending a hairy arm through her bars, holding out her empty hand in a gesture of supplication, give a poor starving monkey a crumb, please, kind woman.

"What makes you feel entitled to a Mint Milano, young lady?" Laura said.

Ottoline gestured impatiently, and then began to whine.

"Oh, stop it," Laura said. "See if you can behave as well as the McCarthy children. You don't hear them whining."

Over cookies and cocoa, the boys exchanged information with Duncan, while Laura and Ingie mostly just listened. They were clearly on best behavior, but even so, they sprayed a shower of cookie crumbs in a wide radius. Duncan heard about which girls in second grade had the most cooties. He was thrilled that cooties were still a thing.

"Did you have cooties when you were growing up?" Laura asked Ingie politely, attempting to draw her into the conversation.

Ingie turned red and said, "One very bad winter, in my family we all had the *löss*. We had to use *fotogen*, what is it, petrol, no, kerosene. "

"Lice?" guessed Laura. "Oh god, no, I wasn't asking about lice! Cooties are imaginary, not real insects, nothing like that."

"I do not know these cooties," Ingie said stiffly. "Those, we did not have them."

"Sorry, my bad," said Laura (though she detested people who said "my bad").

"My birthday is next week," announced Bailey. "We're having a clown." He leaned forward with a great rustle to take another cookie and then sat perched at the edge of the sofa, bouncing his sneakered heels against the tweed as he took bites of cookie and slurps of cocoa. Scout was asleep in the corner of the sofa cushions. Every now and then she sighed contentedly and nibbled on her thumb without otherwise moving.

"It's always good to have a clown," said Duncan.

"I *hate* clowns," said Bailey. "My mom said we have to have a clown or a pony or kids might not show up at the party. And my dad said a pony would shit on the driveway."

"Bailey, do not say a bad word," scolded Ingie automatically, without looking up from the cell phone in her lap.

"Everybody hates clowns," said Duncan. "It's just something you have to deal with when you're a kid."

"Did you have clown birthday parties?" asked Jackson, snatching another cookie.

"No, but I went to lots of them. With those stupid balloon animals, right? My brother hated clowns a lot more than I did. I think he was afraid of them."

"Is he older or younger?" asked Jackson.

"Younger," said Duncan, "By eight minutes. I'm a twin. I have an identical twin brother named Gordon. So we always had a shared birthday party and a shared birthday cake. We always blew out our candles at the exact same moment together."

"Does he have an identical wheelchair just like yours?" Jackson asked.

"No, no, he's not paralyzed like me. I was in an accident. Not that long ago. I guess you don't remember seeing me before I was in this wheelchair."

"So he's not identical," persisted Jackson.

"He is too," said Bailey. "You're the one who isn't identical anymore."

"I guess that's right," said Duncan.

While Ingie cut Bailey out of his costume with a pair of kitchen scissors (when Duncan said he was *relieved* that she would be *relieving* Bailey of his re-leaf costume, the boys giggled, and then giggled some more at Ingie's obliviousness to what they found so funny), Duncan showed Jackson the book on their coffee table, a glossy volume of dramatic, contrasty black and white photographs of the houses of William Corrigan. Jackson knelt in front of the table and leafed through the book at Duncan's direction. Duncan nearly instructed him to Page! the way he would command Ottoline, but instead he told him to keep turning pages, keep turning, again, again, there, stop, go back. The Waxman Dovecote had a page of its own. "See that?" Duncan said. "Now go look out that dining room window at our yard. What do you see?"

Jackson trotted obediently to the window and gazed out at the garden.

"Do you see the little toolshed by the fence?"

"Cool!" Jackson said, breathing against the glass. "It's the same, but different!"

"What's different?"

"It's really little. And it has ivy on it. The one in the picture is next to a big house and there's a blue watering can."

"Good observations. The one out there is half the size of the one in the book, but it's the exact same design. It's called a dovecote. It's a kind of building people made a long time ago for pigeons."

"Wow. Do you have pigeons?"

"No, I made it for my garden tools."

"That is so cool! Did you make the one in the book, too?" Jackson was amazed.

"Sort of," said Duncan. What was he doing, trying to im-

press a seven-year-old? "No, not exactly. I helped." Ingie, finished with her task, balled up the brown paper and stuffed it
into a wastebasket before plopping back down in the armchair.

"Okay, you guys," said Duncan. "Go sit over there, and
be really still, and don't wave your arms, and don't shout or
make any sudden noises, please. Can you be really quiet? Are
you ready to meet my monkey?"

"Should I have put the children into their helmets for
cycling?" Ingie asked anxiously. "I have responsibility. Do
they need a face protection?"

"Oh, god, no," Duncan reassured her. "Ottoline is a capuchin monkey, a smart little New World monkey, not a chimpanzee who could suddenly rip your face off."

"Duncan!" Laura warned from the kitchen.

"Face off!" echoed Scout.

"I am unclear," said Ingie.

"No, really, kids, don't worry! Ottoline is smaller than a
lot of cats, but she doesn't just sit around and think about herself like a cat. She has little hands that are a lot like yours, so
she can do things for me, like pick up stuff I can't reach, and
turn on lights, and turn the pages of a book. In a way she
takes care of me. She makes it possible for me to spend more
time alone."

"But if she's with you picking up stuff, then you're not
alone," Jackson pointed out.

"True," Duncan said, "I'll re-phrase, counselor. She makes
it possible for me to do stuff on my own without having to
ask another person to help me."

"Cool!" said Bailey.

"But do not let her on you, children," said Ingie.

"She'll be on a leash, don't worry," Duncan said. "Okay?
I'll go get her."

Duncan rolled into the kitchen, where Laura was washing the cocoa mugs and thinking about what to make for
dinner. Duncan used to do more than half the cooking, and

he often picked up groceries on his way home from work. He had always enjoyed taking charge of dinner most nights. Now, planning every meal was her responsibility, and she had to prepare just about every meal too, though the PCAs gave Duncan breakfast on some mornings. Eating in restaurants was such an elaborate production, and she missed the former ease with which they used to head out for pizza at Pepe's or a fancy dinner at Union League, without a lot of elaborate advance planning.

These days a meal out of the house involved finding a handicapped parking spot, getting out of the van and into the restaurant, situating Duncan at a table in the best spot for his chair, getting him out of his jacket if it was cold weather, figuring out what he could eat, setting him up with the long bendy straw, strapping on the utensil cuff and inserting the fork or spoon, clipping the dinner napkin onto his front with the bib clips—and then hoping that Duncan would last the entire meal without getting too tired, developing a headache, or going into dysreflexia, before it was time to reverse all these steps and get him home.

Cooking for Duncan at home was at times a pretty thankless task. Laura struggled to live up to Duncan's culinary standards, laboring with precision over dishes he would have thrown together casually with better results. On her own, she would have been content with a microwaved whatever. But having to cook for Duncan had led to Laura beginning to find pleasure in cooking, and she did like having more time in the kitchen on weekends.

Sometimes Laura just felt blank and out of ideas. But it was getting easier as she expanded her repertoire and confidence. Quinoa or orecchiette with the chicken tonight? Quinoa reminded her of miniature condoms. But then orecchiette looked like doll diaphragms. What was the matter with her, seeing tiny contraceptives in innocent carbohydrates? Some days everything seemed to have a sexual glimmer.

———

Duncan opened Ottoline's cage door and she leaped out onto his shoulder with a chirp that Laura thought of as her "ta da!" sound. Laura clipped one end of her lead onto her waist collar and said Ring! Ottoline, Ring! Ottoline nimbly grabbed the end of her lead and clipped it to the ring loop on the side of the wheelchair. Ottoline had developed a bad habit of seizing opportunities whenever she could to bolt up the stairs to roam around unfettered. She had done this a few times, after first slyly undoing the carabiner clip that linked her lead to the ring on Duncan's wheelchair, which she knew perfectly well was naughty behavior. Thus unhitched, she would wait for an opportunity and then suddenly make a run for it.

She chose her moments—afternoons when Duncan was alone in the house with her. Ottoline took her time obeying Duncan's instructions to come back down, too, though she always did mosey back downstairs, sometimes carrying a prize, such as Laura's toothbrush, or the gnawed remains of a miniature Say Howdy! still in its wrapper.

Duncan turned and rolled into the living room with Ottoline on his shoulder. Laura listened for the sound of excitement when the boys saw Ottoline. She heard both boys exclaim as Ottoline appeared; apparently Scout was still asleep. This was a nice change of pace from the quotidian woe around here. She really liked the gentle and funny way Duncan spoke to the McCarthy children. It was a side of him she rarely saw. He would have been a great father.

Though Laura's sense of her own possible babies had begun to recede, taking their Keller curly hair and Wheeler dimples with them, somehow their phantom Chinese daughter still hovered. She was real, of course, she had been born and she lived and breathed, only now she belonged to another family and had another life altogether, a life Laura had imagined so thoroughly, starting with the weeks of bonding in a room at the White Swan Hotel in Guangzho, where all the adoptive families stayed with their new Chinese babies for the nerve-wracking final days and sometimes weeks while the adoption approvals were processed through the Chinese courts. They had spoken of naming her Clementine. Clem, Clemmie. Did you finish your homework, Clemmie? Did those boys say you had cooties? Boys are the ones with cooties! Laura could hear shrieks of laughter from the McCarthy brothers, and some hoots and shrieks from Ottoline, too, sounds that were halfway between distress and excitement.

When Laura went into the living room, Ottoline was roaming across the coffee table, taking blueberries from the boys, who squealed with delight when she rudely grabbed a blueberry and shoved it in her mouth before sticking out her hand to demand another. She probably had three or four blueberries in her cheeks (more than were good for her in one day, but oh well), as it took her a long while to gum up a blueberry and swallow it down. Duncan looked amused.

Ingie, in the armchair, was oblivious, her attention entirely focused down on her phone.

She didn't notice when Ottoline, aware of Ingie's focus, hopped off the coffee table and proceeded to ransack her bag, which was on the floor beside her chair. First the monkey took a car key on a lanyard and flung it on the rug. Laura held her finger to her lips to hush the boys and Duncan so they could all play Let's see how many things Ottoline can remove from Ingie's bag before Ingie notices! Ottoline pulled out another key, this one on a ring along with a Stop & Shop bar code tag. Next came a little plastic pot of lip gloss with a clear lid, a wallet, a comb, a lipstick, an unopened bag of gummy bears Ottoline couldn't penetrate (though she tried for a moment), followed by a pen, a quarter, a mascara tube, a pony tail elastic, a Metro North train schedule, and a partly-empty pack of Nicorette gum. Ottoline seized a pair of sunglasses from the bag, which she held up to peer through, while Jackson and Bailey gurgled with glee. Next came a folding hairbrush that momentarily intrigued the monkey, who unfolded it thoughtfully and stroked it across her tail while the boys convulsed in silent giggles. She had fantastic deadpan timing.

Ingie continued to read something on her phone, and then she began to compose a reply, thumbs hurtling over her keyboard. Ottoline reached into the bag again and this time she pulled out a tube of moisturizer, a small bottle of hand sanitizer, a heavy, zippered, embroidered makeup pouch, a packet of tissues, an empty cardboard sleeve that had held sugarless gum, and, then, with a flourish, Ottoline extracted a pregnancy test kit. She gnawed on one end of the box for a moment before flinging it down onto the rug with the rest of her booty.

As the McCarthy children went out the door with their positively Delphic au pair (Laura and Duncan had been impressed with her placid and unchanged demeanor when she had looked up, discovered the monkeyshines, and had simply swept all her belongings back into her bag without a word of acknowledgment or explanation), Duncan said, "What did the crocodile say to the alligator?"

"See you later!" shouted Bailey.

"And what did the alligator say to the crocodile?" Duncan prompted.

"After a while!" Jackson supplied.

"After a while," echoed Scout, who was being lugged by Ingie. She had been woken when it was time to leave, and was not willing to walk the short distance home.

"Are alligators and crocodiles the same thing?" Bailey wondered.

"No," Duncan said. "They're not." The children and Ingie were halfway down the ramp, the zig-zag of which was one more attraction of the monkey house. They stopped and turned around. Duncan's soft voice didn't carry far. "They're similar, but not identical."

"What's the difference?" asked Laura, who was standing behind Duncan at the open door, intrigued that he knew something like this. (Duncan and Ottoline watched a great deal of Animal Planet.) With the little klepto primate stashed in her cage in Duncan's room, it was safe for her to put her hands on his shoulders, which she did, enjoying an Ottoline-free opportunity to touch him casually.

"Crocodiles are meaner," Duncan said. "And they have bigger heads. They live all around the world, while alligators are a little nicer, and they only live in the U.S. and in China."

"That's weird!" shouted Jackson from the sidewalk.

"I'm going as an American crocodile next Halloween," Bailey announced, before turning to his brother with a crocodile roar.

"I'll be a Chinese alligator!" shouted Jackson, roaring back at him.

Next October was a very long way from now, thought Duncan.

Duncan went to his room. He knew Laura wouldn't disturb him while she was making dinner. She hated being distracted or interrupted, as she was both insecure and not an intuitive cook, so she needed to follow recipes precisely. The radio was turned up loud so she could hear it over the gray buzz of the stove exhaust fan. The opening chords of the theme music for *All Things Considered* began. Ottoline was content in her cage, idly manipulating her colored plastic rings. He rolled over to his desk, and slid open the middle drawer. He fumbled for the polished mahogany cigar box which was pushed all the way to the back.

The box had once held fancy cigars from the Dominican Republic, and there was still a faint tobacco odor when you opened the lid. Owen Whitlock had given it to him a long while ago when Duncan admired the dovetailing when he saw the box on a bookshelf in Owen's office. Owen had kept drawing pens in the box, but he tipped them out and handed the box to Duncan on the spot, explaining that he had plenty more at home piled on a shelf in his garage. His brother had been a cigar smoker for many years, and the boxes were handy for nuts and bolts and picture hooks, but how many did a person need?

It was challenging for Duncan to get a grip on the polished wood. He managed to pull it forward in the drawer and then he raised the lid on his stash. Underneath the camouflage layer of several folded sheets of postage stamps were tucked: five twenty-one-milligram NicoDerm patches Ottoline had filched from Darlene's bag in recent weeks, a cylindrical prescription vial containing four thirty-milligram Adderall capsules that Ottoline had removed from Wendell's gym bag, a large plastic spring-loaded hair clip Ottoline had taken from Cathy's pocketbook, a prescription vial with three two-milligram Xanax tablets Ottoline had taken from the pocket of Ida Mae's jacket which she had left hanging on the kitchen doorknob when she was down in the cellar doing laundry, a nearly full tube of Nitro paste, six five-hundred-milligram Vicodin tablets saved from the final days of Duncan's burn treatment when he was first back home last October, five blue and yellow capsules of Fiorinal with codeine taken from the meds on the cart across the room (these were used judiciously to treat Duncan's headaches), and an Altoids tin holding thirteen little blue fifty-milligram Viagra tablets.

Laura had not known that Duncan had begun to use Viagra when they were trying to have a baby. He always filled the Viagra prescriptions at out-of-the-way chain pharmacies where he wasn't known, and he paid cash, so there was no medical insurance paper trail. Each time, he imagined that this must be how people who abuse prescription drugs operate.

Duncan would empty the blue tablets into the Altoids tin and dispose of the plastic prescription container before coming home with them. Once he started using it, Duncan had become fearful of going without Viagra, even as he felt increasingly guilty about concealing from Laura his dependence on the medication. They were supposed to be in this, in everything, together. But the longer he went without telling her, the more difficult it had become to imagine broaching the subject. He was embarrassed that he needed this chemical assistance when he wasn't even forty. But he did need the boost, just as he had become reliant on conjuring up mental pictures at those moments that had nothing at all to do with anything he had ever actually experienced. Duncan had only ever allowed himself in carefully controlled ways to long for those thrilling, tantalizing connections.

Laura would be hurt that he had kept the Viagra a secret all this time. Shortly before the accident, they had laughed together over a news article reporting that many people had started to spell Niagara Falls incorrectly, omitting the second a, because of the ubiquity of Viagra. They had relished the irony, given that the name Viagra had been derived from Niagara, invoking the classic honeymoon destination, not to mention the mental picture of gushing torrents pouring over the edge of the falls, combined with something that suggested vigor. That's when he should have told her. Instead, he quoted Oscar Wilde on Niagara Falls—"the American bride's second biggest disappointment."

They thought they had finally done it, last July. Duncan had been willing to let the realness of this baby be the turning point. He had sincerely hoped its birth would tip the balance—tip his balance—toward Laura. Toward the family they would become. If being a father shifted something fundamental inside him, it would be a relief. And then Laura discovered she wasn't pregnant after all, right after his accident. Yet another loss. It was better this way. Simpler.

Duncan added the Nicorette gum Ottoline had stuffed into the side of his seat cushion when she climbed back onto him while Ingie, when she had suddenly alerted to the trick being played on her, was busy shoveling all her private things back into her bag while the boys laughed at her. He studied the contents of his cigar box, taking inventory, something he found reassuring on the good days and on the bad days, though his plans were not yet entirely in focus, and then he slid the stamps back on top, closed the lid, and put the box away in the back of the desk drawer. Dinner smelled good.

"Did you hear about Adam Boxer?" Laura asked him as they ate.

Duncan could not quickly manipulate food onto the fork that she had wedged into the slot of his utensil cuff. In any case, he was at risk for aspirating bits of food into his lungs if he ate too fast, and his lung function was already compromised. The quad cough routine was not entirely efficient, brutal as it was at times. She could often hear Duncan's lungs squeaking with every breath he expelled. Laura had read that sooner or later there was a good chance that vigorous treatment would inadvertently crack one of Duncan's ribs. This would be the start of a spiral, with the risk of infection, pneumonia, dysreflexia.

Laura had to make a conscious effort to put her fork down and simply pace herself slowly through each meal with Duncan so as not to be finished ahead of him, which she knew discouraged him. She took a break while he continued to chase the cut-up chicken and orecchiette and broccoli with his fork, backstopping them at the raised rim of the special plate for people with compromised functions from which Duncan ate most of his meals. When Laura was little she had a Bunnykins dish with that sort of high rim. A Bunnykins dish might be more dignified than this heavy plastic institutional thing. Maybe she could find Bunnykins on eBay.

"Adam Boxer the pompous art historian? Didn't I just read something of his in the *New York Review of Books*? What about Adam Boxer?"

"He died on a Yale squash court today."

"What? He was only in his fifties. Seriously? Was it a heart attack?"

"No, it was a really freakish thing. He was playing squash with that guy we met at that dinner, remember, the one with the ridiculous mustache you thought might be waxed? Wayne Harris, the husband of one of the Garvan Collection staff, was playing on the next court, which is how I heard about it so fast."

"What the hell happened?"

"Apparently Adam was diving low for the ball and there was spilled water on the floor they didn't notice. Like many players, they had left their water bottles in the front corners of the court. Mustache guy, Fred? That guy he was playing, he's completely traumatized. Apparently a ball had knocked over one of the bottles a few points earlier. Adam slid into the front wall head first and broke his neck. I don't know if they figured out if he had a traumatic head injury, or if he just broke his neck, I guess it doesn't really matter which it was, because he died right there."

"Good bad luck."

"I wish you wouldn't say things like that."

"Shall I just think them to myself instead?"

"I just wish you didn't feel that way." Laura got up from the table and went to the front hall closet, where she had stashed two framed drawings of the Explicated Four-Square House. She brought them into the kitchen and leaned them against the cabinets in Duncan's direct line of sight.

"What the hell, Laura? Where did you get those?"

"They were on the bottom shelf in your study, and because I accidentally squished the tube when I moved your desk, I took them to work to get them flattened."

"I had put that house out of my thoughts," Duncan said, gazing at the drawings. He looked as if he might cry. This was not the response Laura had anticipated.

'Well, I love this house, Dunc. I've never seen this side of your work before."

"I loved it too, but nobody else did. It was a mistake."

"Well, somebody does love this house, in fact. I've got news. Those rich collectors I told you about, the ones with the Ru pottery, the Cavendishes?"

"Mugsy and Gramps?"

"Jinxy and Dud. You have got to learn their names. You know their Shaker collection. They probably have the most important collection of Ru pottery in the world."

"With rue their hearts are laden—"

"Anyway, they want to build this house. They saw the drawings when they came to the conservation lab a couple of weeks ago. I left them for a few moments when I was getting a bowl of theirs, and when I came back, they were admiring your Explicated Four-Square House. They want to build it as a guest cottage on their farm in Maine. Isn't that great?"

"Oh, Laura. I don't think this is great at all. I can't take that on, not now."

"There's nothing you have to take on. You don't have to be any more involved than you want. They'll bring in a local architect to do all the technical work and work with the builder to make it happen. You could consult!"

"It's too late."

"What do you mean? I thought you would be pleased."

"Really? You imagined that I would be pleased, and not upset that you showed my drawings to random rich people with silly names who make crazy decisions about building a house based on some vague, rudimentary drawings—"

"Not random people! Not vague! Yes to the silly names. It's your house! And it just happened, I didn't plan it. I really thought you would be happy to see your house built after all this time."

"I'm hardly going to *see* this house."

"I've already been thinking about how we can make the

trip to Maine. I'm sure we could figure it out. We'd bring along one of the PCAs. The Cavendishes would pay for everything. They're rich."

"We're rich too."

"Not Cavendish rich."

"I know you want me to want this, Laura. I get it."

"*I* want this! I want to see this house. And you're an architect, so where's your architect's ego? You know you want this too! Isn't there some little part of you that wants to see this house built?"

Duncan sighed. He so didn't want to want this. Ottoline shifted in her kitchen cage, waking from a nap, and peeped at him. "Okay. I'm not objecting. That's the best I can do right now."

Two weeks later, when winter had returned, it was again a Saturday when the McCarthy children came to call again, this time accompanied by their mother. She wanted to speak with Laura and Duncan, she said to Laura.

"Can the children come in and play with your monkey? Just for a little visit," Irene Jackson said, as she ushered the boys in the door. Scout trailed behind them. Duncan was in the kitchen, just finishing a late breakfast, and he chewed the last bite of a correctly-prepared toasted English muffin as her distinctly disagreeable voice carried through the house. He told Ottoline it was time for a time-out in her cage before she would be allowed to see what was going on. Ottoline rarely met strangers, and though she had liked the McCarthy children, her response was unpredictable.

"They can't actually play with her, no, that wouldn't be a good idea, but here, let me get them something to do," offered Laura. "Kids, here are some markers, and look, here are some number two pencils, and some of Duncan's graph paper. Let's clear off the coffee table so you have a lot of room. Why don't you guys draw something?"

"I'm going to draw a dovecote," Jackson announced confidently as he knelt at the coffee table and began to sketch an approximation of a hexagon.

"What, a little bird outfit?" his mother asked. "I don't know what ideas they get from those reality fashion shows."

"Number two pencils" Bailey chortled. "She said number two. Shit pencils!"

"Shit pencils," murmured Scout around her thumb.

"Don't teach your sister curse words!" scolded their mother. "So where's this monkey the boys told me about?" she asked, guardedly scanning the living room, as if she expected a wild creature to jump out at her.

Up close, she was startlingly older than Laura had thought from glimpses of her comings and goings across the street. And those Infomercials with her husband, with his big mustache and sideburns, must have been shot a decade ago. He was balder and clean-shaven now, Laura had noticed when she watched him as he came and went across the street. As she often did when she observed people and their children, Laura wondered if the Jackson children had been conceived naturally, or if there had been interventions, or maybe they were adopted. They didn't resemble either parent particularly, though it was hard to tell what Irene might have once looked like. She was wearing a black velour tracksuit, and even though it was a rainy Saturday morning, she wore makeup and shiny gold earrings that would surely attract Ottoline's curiosity.

"Did you have a good birthday last Saturday?" Duncan asked Bailey as he rolled into the living room. Bailey was kneeling at the coffee table beside his brother, both of them drawing intently. He nodded vigorously without looking up.

"I apologize for only staying a few minutes," Duncan said. "I wasn't feeling well."

"Oh, were you there? I didn't come downstairs until it was time for the cake," Irene said. "I was working on a brief. And

Ingie had it all under control. I'm Irene," she added unnecessarily. She held out her right hand to Duncan, though she had neither introduced herself nor offered a hand to Laura at the door, but then as Duncan started to extend his braced left hand, she switched to offer her own left hand. People were often flustered by Duncan's unavailable right hand.

"I missed the cake," Duncan said.

"Is it Ingie's day off today?" Laura asked.

"That's what I wanted to talk to you about," Irene said in a confiding tone. "Can we go in another room?"

Ottoline shrieked like a parrot at Irene as they entered the kitchen. Irene jumped back with her own little shriek. Ottoline scrambled up onto the sleeping shelf in her cage, where she bounced up and down, her ears flattened, her mouth open, staring at Irene while shrieking hoo-hoo-hoo, her pretend-stricken distress sound.

"Oh, knock it off," Laura said to her crossly, while respecting her judgment.

"The boys told me about how she can do things on command," Irene said, sitting down at the table and hoisting Scout, who had followed her, into her lap. "Very impressive!"

Laura stood with her arms folded, leaning against the fridge. She wasn't in the mood to offer coffee. Something about Irene made her enjoy being just a little rude.

Duncan had positioned himself beside Ottoline's cage.

"Do you have her trained to clean the house for you?" Irene asked, looking at Ottoline appraisingly.

"Hardly!" Laura tried not to laugh. "Monkey helpers do smaller-scale, more personal things, like fetch a phone or a television remote, or turn on a light, or put in a CD."

"Could she put your makeup on for you?"

Duncan burst out laughing, a rare sound that made Laura happy and grateful to Irene. (But she still wasn't going to offer her coffee.) "I am sure she would love to have the opportunity," he said, his laughter trailing off into coughing.

"If you let her, if she didn't eat your lipstick first, but the results would probably make you look a lot like that clown you hired for the birthday party."

"Clown!" crowed Scout, who had been staring fixedly at Ottoline, who had been staring right back at her. Scout jammed a thumb into her mouth, and Ottoline immediately stuck a long hairy thumb into her own mouth and sucked on it loudly. Laura struggled to keep a straight face. She didn't dare meet Duncan's eye.

"I fired Ingie yesterday," Irene said abruptly. "That's why I'm here."

"What happened?" Laura asked.

"I don't have proof, but I am pretty sure she was trying to seduce my husband," Irene said in a confiding tone. "I'm not going to go into details, but I just didn't trust her, and I didn't think she was a good influence over the children."

"So where is she now? Does she have to leave the country?" Duncan asked. "Wasn't she on a work visa tied to this job?"

"She's on her way back to Scandinavia is all I know," Irene said with a triumphant little laugh. "That's the end of that."

"But where is she from? I assumed she was Swedish," said Laura. "With a name like Ingie. What was that short for? Ingeborg? Ingrid?"

"Ingie!" exclaimed Scout, struggling in her mother's grasp, looking around the room expectantly.

"I don't remember. We just called her Ingie. She's from Scandinavia," said Irene, somewhat defensively, clamping down on Scout. "She has to go back to Scandinavia."

"Scandinavia is not a country," Duncan said in the quiet, even tone he used when dealing with an idiot. Uh-oh, thought Laura. "It's a region."

"Is she from Norway, or Sweden? Is she Danish?" Laura asked. "Did she ever talk about her family?" Laura pictured the Ingie family, all white blond and wearing primary color knitwear, plagued by their *löss* problem. She scratched her suddenly itchy head. In her cage, Ottoline scratched her own tufted head in mimicry of Laura, peeping and chortling and tilting her head. Sometimes Ottoline cracked herself up.

"Like I said, they told us at the agency that she was from Scandinavia," Irene repeated. "We prefer them to South Americans. The Icelandic ones are best. They're always very clean, even if they do have ridiculous names."

Laura and Duncan could hardly look at each other. What law school could she possibly have attended? Her nice clever children must take after their father. Or the series of au pairs who had raised them.

The sound of the television emanated from the living room. A football game. Did the McCarthy boys actually care about football? No, now the station had changed to something with a laugh track.

Seeing Laura and Duncan exchange glances, Irene said, "I let them watch whatever they want when I need them to stay quiet, especially right now, when we're between au pairs."

"How many au pairs have your kids known?" Laura asked. "Did they get to say goodbye to Ingie?"

"I know you judge me," Irene shot back, "but you don't have children. You have no idea what it's like."

"That is true," Laura said quietly, holding Irene's gaze for a long moment until Irene looked away.

"Anyway," she said. "I just wanted to ask you, since I get the feeling you're home all the time, I mean, I noticed your new handicapped parking spot, that must be so convenient, always being able to park in those handicapped spots, so did you ever see anything?"

"What do you mean, see anything?" Duncan asked, knowing perfectly well what she meant. "But no, I didn't," he added, not waiting for her to explain.

"Okay," Irene got to her feet, dumping Scout onto the floor, where he slid straight to a sitting position on her rubber folding legs. "That's really why I came over. Never mind. I thought you might—It's just that—"

"Nope! Didn't see a thing!" Laura said too cheerfully, and Duncan shot her a look.

In the living room, the boys were gazing contentedly at a Viagra commercial featuring a man on a beach lighting a bonfire.

"Reptile dysfunction!" shouted Bailey. "What is reptile dysfunction?"

"It's when alligators and crocodiles have eaten too many other alligators and crocodiles," Duncan informed them in an authoritative tone as he rolled into the room behind Laura and Irene. The boys scissored their arms wildly at each other, giant jaws devouring each other, as they roared in reptilian harmony.

"Let's go, boys," Irene said wearily, dragging Scout behind her.

"All facelifts turn people into a cat or a monkey," Laura said, watching the children run ahead of their mother across the street (there were no cars, nor warnings about the possibility of cars) and then scamper together up the steps of their house, forever Ingie-less. "That's what my mother always said. I think monkey."

"Don't insult our beautiful brown-eyed girl," said Duncan.

"Poor Ingie," said Laura. "And poor Scout especially."

"We owe Bailey a birthday present. Let's give the McCarthy kids a map of the world," said Duncan.

# FOURTEEN

## *After lunch, Laura set Duncan up in the living room*

AFTER LUNCH, LAURA SET DUNCAN UP IN THE LIVING room with *Rear Window*, which he never tired of watching. He dozed off in his wheelchair just as Grace Kelly was delivering the accusatory note (WHAT HAVE YOU DONE WITH HER?) to Raymond Burr, while Thelma Ritter and Jimmy Stewart watch anxiously. The movie ended. Duncan was snoring. Ottoline was ensconced on his chest, sifting through the whiskers on his unshaved chin. When Laura woke him gently, touching his face lightly with her fingers, Ottoline batted her hand away with a bossy cheep. "Oh stop it, you imperious little primate," Laura said crossly, and her voice woke Duncan.

"Megan Clark from the office is here. She said she just wanted to leave this bunch of revised Steiner drawings for you to look at whenever you like, but she said she would wait to see if you want to discuss anything. Do you want to see her? She's in the kitchen because I didn't know if you were up for it."

"What time is it? Let me wake up. For a loose wreck, I see an awful lot of people these days."

Megan Clark had been at Corrigan & Wheeler for about a year, so Duncan barely knew her. Todd Walker had been friendly with her. She had mostly worked with Dave Halloran, who had advocated for her hiring. Megan was a graduate of the University of Oregon, her home state. Pleasant and competent, if not thrilling, she was tall and thin and wore her hair in a single long braid. She usually dressed in what Todd had explained to Duncan was a deliberately gender-neutral way. Today, along with jeans and hiking boots, she was wearing a red checked flannel shirt over a blue broadcloth button-down shirt, over a black T-shirt. Shirts over shirts over shirts had been the look of Yale architecture students for decades, and when young architects come to New Haven they usually started wearing more shirts, a style Todd had resisted.

Duncan toggled his chair into a more upright position, and Ottoline hung on, scrambling up onto his shoulder to keep herself afloat. Then he motored across the living room into the kitchen, where Megan was sitting at the table. She smiled at Ottoline but didn't move a muscle. Ottoline hopped down onto the kitchen table and ran right up to her.

"Hello, monkey," Megan said. Ottoline studied her warily and then reached down to gingerly touch the freckles on the back of her wrist, trying to lift one with her fingernail.

"They don't come off," Megan said, and Ottoline scurried back across the table to Duncan, leaped onto his shoulder, and settled there with a chirp.

The Steiner drawings, which Megan unrolled on the table with the salt bowl and the pepper mill weighting the two far corners, were troubling to him. Laura brought him his reading glasses to swap for the distance glasses he had been wearing to watch *Rear Window*. Everywhere he looked on the familiar plans, Duncan could see elisions and compromises. There was no major change, and yet all the altered details added up to a dilution and a diminishing blurring of his original intention.

"Who's making these changes? These were all final locked drawings months ago. This is fucking unacceptable." Duncan didn't mean to speak so sharply to the messenger. She was just a kid. He liked her placid demeanor with Ottoline. She was bright and calm, two qualities he valued.

"Dave said the changes were necessary or we would be way over budget," she said. "Plus, there were some problems with this group that has a name like the Stony Creek Alliance—"

"The Stony Creek Coalition? Oh no, no, no, they're trouble. I thought we were done with them. We had all the town approvals and permits we needed. They have no actual power, but some people on various town boards are afraid of them. We satisfied them last summer. I took eight of those annoying, self-righteous people on a fucking weekend site visit myself last June!"

"There was a meeting," Megan said, "ten days ago. They came to the office to meet with Dave Halloran and a couple of the other people on the project."

"Were you at this meeting?"

"No, I wasn't, or at least I wasn't supposed to be," Megan said. "I was way over on the far side of our offices, in my workspace. I was staying late to finish the presentation material for the Altschul Lake House. But you know how sound carries in the office?"

"Tell me about it."

"So I could hear a lot of what they were saying."

"And?"

Megan bit her lip. "I really worried about this. To be honest, it's why I volunteered to bring you these revisions today. Dave said it could wait for your weekly pickup next Wednesday, but I really thought you ought to know about what's going on. Right now."

"I appreciate that. So will you tell me what you heard?"

"They kept using phrases like 'protecting and maintaining the unique character, charm, and balance' of Stony Creek and the Thimbles." She imitated the lock-jawed patrician tones very effectively.

"That's their slogan."

"Then one of them talked about trying to get a town referendum in Branford about designating a special zone or something for Stony Creek, based on some standards they want to establish. He said they wanted to 'reduce conflict' by creating a review board to assist the town commissions in making the best decisions. He kept using phrases like 'preserving the scale, rhythm, and architectural elements.' He sounded like maybe he's an architect."

"That was probably Roger Gallagher. He's an unimaginative and barely competent local architect who resents outsiders coming in and getting all the work—even though he benefits. Sometimes the big out-of-town firms throw him a bone and he's added to the project as the clerk of the works, especially since he knows his way around all the town boards and commissions. He may not have any new ideas about how to design and build, but he sure does have the skills to get shoreline projects approved."

Megan started to say something and then stopped.

"Was there something else?'

"Maybe it's not important. This woman who looked like a Sunday school teacher kept saying they were concerned about keeping out the influence of 'New York money.'"

"That's code. Do you know what that really means?"

Megan shook her head, puzzled. "It doesn't just mean that they don't want rich people from New York?"

"In my experience, Megan, when people like that talk about 'New York' anything, it means they're afraid of Jews taking over, but they know they can't just come out and say it."

"But the Steiners approved everything. All the changes."

"Really? Who met with the Steiners? Dave? I can just imagine how he sold the changes to them on the basis of cost and future good neighbor relations. Shit. Why am I only hearing about this now?"

"They announced in the office last week that you were off the project. They told us you weren't going to have an active role in anything from now on. Halloran said you had really tried to keep up, but you just couldn't do the work any more. He said it was your decision not to come back."

Duncan pored over the drawing some more, trying to make sense of what she had just told him. What the hell. The Corrigan & Wheeler credential box on the lower right of the plans listed Dave Halloran as the lead architect, where Duncan's name had been all along, from the first sketch of the Steiner house renovations and additions. Duncan's name was still on the project, but moved down to the top of the list of associates and assistants making up the Corrigan & Wheeler design team on the Steiner project.

"What are those drawings hanging on that wall?" Megan asked, suddenly, gazing past Duncan into the dining room. "Is that a Frank Lloyd Wright house?"

"No, it's mine, something I did a long, long time ago," Duncan said, secretly pleased by her error. She got up and went into the dining room to see them close up.

"This is fantastic!" she exclaimed. "The Explicated Four-Square House. Wow. This isn't like anything I've ever seen at Corrigan & Wheeler."

"Thank you. No, it isn't." Duncan waited at the table for her to come back into his field of vision. "It's actually going to be built this coming summer," he told her. "In Hallowell, Maine." He was glad of the opportunity to be in her eyes more than someone who used to be significant but now just needed to be eased out of the firm.

"I haven't seen that yet," she said. "I'd love to work on it."

"It's not going through the office, it's just this little project of my own, on the side. It's a strange thing, having something I designed when I was an architecture student suddenly come to life."

Duncan really had not wanted to want anything. But this house—the Cavendish Four-Square—had become important to him. It didn't really change anything about his situation, yet every day now when he woke up he found himself thinking about details of the plans instead of details of his own plans.

"I'm so sorry about Todd," Megan said suddenly. "Everyone misses him. We were friends. It was because of Todd that I applied for the internship."

"I was just thinking about Todd," Duncan said. "I would have loved to have him helping with the detail work on this house." This was partly true. Once the permits had been issued in Hallowell and bidding had started, Duncan had indulged in daydreams about what it would have been like to work on this house with Todd, if there had been no accident. Road trips to Maine, just the two of them. "Did you know him well?"

"I met him at overnight camp in Vermont when we were kids, and then we met again at an architecture symposium in London one summer. Since moving to New Haven, I was getting to know him better," Megan said.

"One night last May he took me out to Biscuit Island and showed me around the site. I know we weren't supposed to be there at night, but it was really thrilling for me. I had never been there. He brought a picnic. He was an amazing person. He talked about India all the time. He invited me to go to India with him next year." Her eyes brimmed, but she didn't actually cry.

"How did you get out there to Biscuit?" Duncan was trying to picture this. An ugly little jealous worm wriggled in his heart.

"We borrowed a dinghy with an outboard motor. Todd said it was okay. I don't know if it really was okay, but we put it right back where we found it moored at the public dock. I love the name Spartina. Why didn't we call the house Spartina instead of the Steiner House?"

"Most clients love to see their names on the plans, that's why," Duncan said, hearing an echo of Jimmy Corrigan telling him exactly this in exactly these words when he was the young architect sitting respectfully with the distinguished elder, asking respectful questions. "Clients love having their names on projects. It makes them feel important, and they can imagine becoming known as famous patrons, like Edgar J. Kaufmann and Fallingwater. Or Dr. Farnsworth. It really helps distract when you're way over budget and you can talk about the long view and posterity."

"That makes sense. But Spartina is such a great name—like Fallingwater. But I think I just figured out the name of my new kitten. She's going to be Spartina."

Duncan smiled. He was a fool for kittens. "Better than Fallingwater, for a kitten."

"Anyway, that night was one of the most wonderful experiences of my life," Megan said. "When I was there last week, now that all the subs are back on the site and everyone's cranking to get it finished on schedule, I got really upset." She hesitated and stopped. Ottoline hopped down onto the kitchen table to once again delicately pick at the irresistible freckles scattered on the backs of her wrists.

"They're really not tiny little bugs, monkey," Megan told Ottoline, without pulling her hands away. "Do you think I have fleas, or mites?"

"She's programmed to hunt for tiny insects on the undersides of leaves, so maybe she does," Duncan said. "You were about to say something. What upset you?"

"It was magic, that night on Biscuit Island with Todd. He was so proud of his work. He showed me all the window details, and how he had solved a problem with that placement of the new chimney, the way it tucks in with the line of the widow's walk. It was such a Todd Walker gesture! And now that's gone. It's so disrespectful of Todd."

Duncan nodded, thinking about how much he had enjoyed the feeling of his own talent sparking when that particular solution had suddenly revealed itself, as he sat alone at his desk in the stillness of the house on that spring morning, away from the hubbub of Corrigan & Wheeler. That was the moment he suddenly recognized with thrilling clarity how to tuck that chimney precisely into harmony with the existing features of Spartina. Todd had only been responsible for drawing the elevations for the presentation a few days later.

"But now it won't be Todd's design," Megan continued. "I mean, The Thimbles are a fantastic spot, and Biscuit Island is amazing, and Spartina, the Steiner House, it's a really cool project. I love the way you and Todd made it all work with such balance and integrity. When Todd took me out there he was so proud and excited about all of his work, everything he had created. It was going to be a huge portfolio piece for him, a really fantastic beginning for his career."

"I understand how you feel," Duncan said. He needed to see the Steiner House one more time.

# FIFTEEN

## *"The blood of horseshoe crabs is blue"*

"THE BLOOD OF HORSESHOE CRABS IS BLUE," GORDON said, leaning over the railing and peering down at the decaying, bleached carcass of a horseshoe crab bumping against the side of the boat. It kept rising and falling with the swell as if it were still alive. "It's a really beautiful blue, almost a haint blue like your porch ceiling."

"I can't see it from here," said Duncan, whose wheelchair was strapped into a position facing the fore end of the Thimble Island ferry. "Is it worth your taking a picture on my phone so I can see it?"

"Nah," said Gordon. "It's not bleeding. It's dead. I was just saying."

If you listened for it, Gordon's muted lisp rendered "saying" as "thaying." He crossed the empty ferry and sat down opposite Duncan on one of the bench seats that lined the boat. It was too early in the morning for most tourists, who were likely to be few anyway, on this cool weekday in the middle of May.

"It's ten past nine," Duncan said irritably. "I'm getting a little seasick sitting here. I feel trapped. I thought we had to hurry to catch this nine o'clock ferry. I made Wendell rush through everything in my morning routine so we could get on the road to meet you here. I had a banana in the van."

"I think I see a pair of tourists coming. They must be the ones he said he had to wait for," Gordon replied, shielding his eyes against the glare of the morning sunlight. A strong breeze pleated the surface of the water in the harbor, and the ferry knocked against the dock. The tourist couple scurried past Thimble Marine Service, past someone in coveralls in the doorway of the repair bay repainting an upside-down dinghy propped on two sawhorses. A forklift that was maneuvering a stack of plywood sheets, moving back and forth between a lumber truck and the top of the ramp down to the wharf, nearly ran them over.

"The Madison Beach Hotel reserved the ferry for them," Gordon said. "That's what he told me. I think they took that taxi down from there. Must have cost a fortune. See it?"

"No! I can't see anything that isn't directly in my line of vision, dumbass," said Duncan. He never mocked Gordy's speaking, though mentally he noted the "thee it?"

"Well, there's a taxi turning around that probably just left them off, and the guy said we were waiting for these people who were coming from the Madison Beach Hotel," said Gordon. "That's all I'm saying." ("thaying.") Gordon had bicycled the fourteen miles down the Post Road from Madison, and had in fact passed the Wharf Road turnoff for the Madison Beach Hotel, not far from his house. His bike was now chained to the handicapped parking space signpost where Wendell had parked the van on Indian Point Road.

Wendell couldn't swim and was fearful of boats and water, but he could drive the van. Gordon couldn't drive, but he was happy to go out with Duncan on the ferry to circumnavigate Biscuit Island so Duncan could see, from the water, progress on the Steiner House, along with any observable changes to his original designs. Laura, who could have both driven the van and accompanied Duncan on the ferry ride, was at a mandatory staff meeting at the Yale Art Gallery, where the agenda was a discussion of ways to develop better practices for managing their inventory and chain of custody documentation procedures.

Wendell had driven Duncan to the Stony Creek town dock, where they met Gordon. Wendell was a deft handler of all the mechanics of loading Duncan on and off the van, and he had helped them onto the ferry. He was now happily ensconced at a corner table at Thimbleberries for the duration of their outing, with coffee and a toasted English muffin and a medical text, studying for his next exam. He tried not to mind the bacon smoke coming off the grill. He was in an orthopedics module, and was devoting the morning to memorizing the twenty-six bones in the foot. He almost had them all, the tarsals, metatarsals, phalanges. When he looked up from his anatomy text to test himself, he was delighted to see that the boat had not even left the dock yet, which meant he would have that much more time to himself.

The tourists approaching the ferry were both bandoliered with camera and binocular straps. They wore sunglasses and straw hats. They were an elderly couple, Japanese. The husband was reading aloud from the open guidebook that he held reverently in front of himself, like a missal. He was far-sighted, and the new sunglasses he was wearing, purchased during a stop at the CVS in Guilford on their way to the ferry (which was why they were late), had ordinary lenses. His expensive prescription sunglasses had been left behind in their previous hotel in Watch Hill. He blamed his wife for this.

They processed up the footway onto the ferry, the husband first, the wife following, holding tightly to the handrail as she proceeded. Gordon stood up to offer her a governing hand as she teetered at the edge of the boat deck, but she didn't take it. She managed to keep her balance as she boarded, and then she followed her husband to the aft bench seat where he was already settling, still studying the guidebook.

Now the ferry captain boarded, and in a practiced motion he shoved the footway back onto the concrete pier and snapped into place the carabiner end of a dangling white plastic security chain. He swung himself onto the seat behind the ship's wheel and started the engine. As it chugged to life with a strong diesel smell, he came out of the pilot's cabin to collect fares.

Gordon explained that they wanted to circle ("thircle") Biscuit Island slowly if that was possible, seeing as how there weren't any other passengers, with the exception of the Japanese couple. Gordon paid their fares and went back to sit across from Duncan, who was trying not to think a lot of thoughts about a lot of things. Duncan watched his brother organizing the dollar bills he had received in change as he put them in his wallet. Duncan had given him the wallet for their birthday in April, though Gordon had said that he didn't want to exchange presents. The wallet, a simple, handsome, calfskin billfold, was actually something Duncan had bought for himself but never used. These days he didn't have much need for a wallet, and the old one that he kept in his desk drawer was sufficient.

"You still worry that Lincoln and Washington and Jackson are going to be kissing each other on the mouth unless you keep them all facing the same direction?"

"It just wouldn't be dignified," said Gordon, closing the wallet and putting it in his pocket. "Not a judgment, just not presidential." He loved the wallet, but felt terrible that he had nothing to give Duncan in return.

The captain cast off the lines that were looped over bollards fore and aft to snug the ferry to the dock, and a moment later the engine roared as he gave it full throttle. Soon they were chugging out into the harbor, following the meandering tourist route around the Thimbles.

"Remember that time we went out fishing for blues with that guy from Daddy's office on his Boston Whaler?"

"I guess so, yeah," Duncan answered. "We were what, eight?"

"Probably. We launched from this same dock. We went out into the sound past all these same islands. You really don't remember it?" Gordon persisted. "What was that guy's name, his salesman who had that boat, Dean something, Dean Dixon?"

"I think I do remember that guy. He was a retired football player or something. We went out on his boat that one time with Dad, right. Why?"

"We went out for the whole day and got sunburned. Mom was really mad about that when we got home. You and I were spinning for tinkers off the boat and then Daddy hooked a baby shark off the back of the boat, remember? With the big rod that was mounted on the back for blue fishing?"

"I think so, sure. Though our father wasn't exactly an avid fisherman."

"You really don't remember, do you?"

"Maybe not. So what? What about it?" Duncan said. "Is this going somewhere?"

"When Daddy reeled in the baby shark, that guy, Dean, leaned over with a big net and scooped it up, and he held it and told us to come near so we could see it up close, so we could touch it through the net. Then he hit the shark against the side of the boat to break its jaw and then he cut the line and threw it back in the water with that hook stuck in its mouth. He said there were too many damn baby sharks that would only turn into big sharks."

"I have no memory of that," Duncan said.

"I'll never forget it as long as I live," Gordon said.

They lapsed into silence. The ferry scudded along at a steady rate and then shifted up to an increased and louder rate of speed.

"See that house over there? On Halls Point Road, past Flying Point?" The boat had turned west and Duncan was in fact facing and could see what Gordon was pointing out on the far shore. "See that stone house? With the tree? Ayn Rand lived there for two summers."

"You're kidding," Duncan said.

"She told an interviewer she got the idea that Howard Roark should work in a quarry because of the Stony Creek quarry."

"How very autodidactic of you, knowing that," Duncan said. The boat slowed to circle Cut-in-Two, the island where General Tom Thumb courted his wife. Could the Japanese couple understand a word of the captain's scripted explanations of each landmark as they blared out of the loudspeakers? "What else you got?"

"Jack London wrote *Call of the Wild* in a boarding house in Branford," Gordon said.

"That is not strictly a Thimble Island fact," Duncan ruled. "What else?"

"General Tom Thumb and his wife don't interest you?"

"Actually, since my accident, I've been thinking a lot about freaks," Duncan said. "Diane Arbus said something that really interested me. She said that most people go through life dreading they'll have a traumatic experience. But freaks were born with their trauma, so they've already passed the test. That's how I feel. Not that I was born like this, obviously, but now I have joined the freaks."

"I don't see you that way, Dunc," Gordon said sadly, gazing at his brother's familiar face. "I don't think of you as having changed at all, really."

The boat sped up and zagged in another direction, and something was announced about the next island on their left. The Japanese couple stood up and began to take photographs.

"Wiryam Howard Taft?" the wife inquired of the Wheeler brothers. "He was important man?"

"He was very important," Gordon replied. "He was the fattest president in the history of the United States." She tittered nervously and uncomprehendingly, covering her mouth with the hand not holding her camera.

Duncan felt a headache blooming. The motion of the boat, the noise of it, the diesel stink in the air—it was all such a potent return to that day in July.

Gordon could feel Duncan becoming less and less present. Don't leave, he thought. Stay, stay here. Please stay. Stay with me.

"Hey, Hot Wheels," he said. "I think we're heading straight to Biscuit Island now. Doesn't he usually go the long way? Are we skipping Governor Island?"

"Maybe he's taking a shortcut for the pathetic cripple on the boat," said Duncan.

"No," corrected Gordon, "the pathetic freak. We'll probably catch Governor on the way back in."

"You know Doonesbury?" The tourists had moved up to stand at the bow for a better view. "We like Doonesbury very much," the husband said. "We have come to see his house on his personal island!"

Biscuit Island loomed ahead. The two small cottages that occupied the leeward side of Biscuit looked weathered and tired. They shared a dock that had taken a beating over the winter, and there was ugly yellow police tape crisscrossing the broken ladder that descended straight down one side into the water.

As they approached the island, the tourist couple took pictures of each other at the railing of the boat, with Biscuit and the outer Thimble Islands for a backdrop. Gordon offered to take a picture of the two of them together. They demurred, and the husband said, "We already have many selfies!"

The boat slowed, and the motor dropped down into a low-gear chug as the captain slowly circled. Clumps of spartina grass waved among the rough pink granite outcroppings of bedrock. Gulls nested along a barren stretch. They motored around the island toward the seaward side, the suddenly breezeless calm turning the movement of the boat into a glide on an unrippled lake. The Steiner House—Spartina— gleamed in the soft morning light. What a beautiful folly. Blooming rugosa roses dotted the dense green foliage at the water's edge with flashes of pink and white. The percussive echo of hammering and the occasional whine of a table saw, amplified by the water, sounded very near.

"Is this island house famous or culturally important?" the husband tourist asked, pausing his picture-taking.

"Eh," Duncan said, the verbal equivalent of the shrug he couldn't achieve.

"It's a Duncan Wheeler house," Gordon told them. "He's an important architect of the Rock Paper Scissors period. Note the full fenestration."

Ah. They both nodded eagerly. They took more photographs.

"What is full fenestration, anyway?" asked Gordon.

"Sounds pornographic, doesn't it? Just a window thing." Duncan looked at his hands that would never again win a round of rock paper scissors. He had always been able to tell Gordon's choice just a fraction ahead of the draw.

The boat floated past the Steiners' dock.

"That fucking gazebo," Duncan said.

"What's wrong with it?" Gordon asked.

"It's a piece of shit readymade crap fucking shit, that's all. Can't you see how crude and shoddy it is? It makes the cheapest Ikea flat pack look like Nakashima. The proportion is horrible. It's as well-designed as something built out of marshmallows by blindfolded toddlers. Would you serve a microwaved pizza in the middle of a three-star meal?"

"I would eat a marshmallow gazebo," said Gordon, after giving it a moment's consideration.

"If the clients had eyes or taste they would see how vulgar it is, but instead, it's probably the single thing they love most about Spartina, and it probably always will be. Christ, Gordy, don't get me started!"

"I think you've already started," Gordon said.

"I wish somebody would just burn down that eyesore."

The house itself was utterly enchanting from the water. The deep porches on every side seemed bare, but would look marvelous when populated by painted rockers and wicker settees and chaise longues. The external detail changes that had been made to Duncan's design for the subtle additions to the house were evident to his eyes, but the truth was that nobody else would ever know or care about the difference. His meticulous, painstaking attention to every detail of the plans had never really mattered. All the gingerbread trim—the pierced frieze boards, the scrolled brackets—and the six chimneys, the four bay windows, the three towers, the famously haunted widow's walk, the oriel windows embellishing every side of the house—that's all that most people would ever see when they looked at Spartina.

The trip back was uneventful. The ferry passed half a dozen more islands, with commentary, among them Governor. The excited tourists took turns posing for pictures of each other as they sped by. They searched with their binoculars in the hope of spotting Garry Trudeau or Jane Pauley in their natural habitat, but nobody was home.

"How's that doggess of yours, Madam Ferga?"

"She's fine." Gordon didn't want to cry.

"Good. How's the bookstore?" Duncan asked his brother, trying to defer, for now, his attention from the cold black lump of sorrow that was flourishing in his chest. He felt like cargo, strapped in this way, having the last boat ride of his life. He felt like crap from too much sun. He longed to be at home, in his room. As they neared the shore the sun shone on the rolling advertisement of a chronic medical emergency that was his white van, parked on Indian Point Road. He realized he had half-expected to see his old Volvo wagon. Where was it now? Compressed into a cube in some scrapyard, probably, with the last of Todd's blood anywhere on this earth.

"The bookstore's fine." Gordon looked sadly at Duncan. He could feel Duncan's energy receding, ebbing out of his reach. "Hey, Hot Wheels."

"Hey, Gords."

"The past, the present, and the future walked into a bar. It was tense."

"Nice. Hey, don't worry about me, Gordy."

The ferry slowed and then reversed with a roaring burst of diesel, and backed into its berth at the town dock.

"There's a red tide right now, you know that?" Gordon said, leaning over the side. "You could get paralytic shellfish poisoning if you eat any of those mussels down there."

After they docked, while the captain was hauling the footway with the handrail in place, Gordon undid the bungee cords lashing Duncan's chair to the wheelchair anchor points. As the last one was released, Duncan toggled the control to turn his chair. The tourists were going over the footway, apparently happy about their excursion. Duncan carefully motored up the ramp inside the lip of the boat and then onto the footway, which was just wide enough for his chair. He pondered the possibility of obtaining some of those poison mussels.

As he bumped down onto the dock, with Gordon following behind him, he saw that the cargo barge that had been moored at the open end of the dock an hour ago, loaded with plywood and sheetrock for the Steiner house, was gone. Presumably it was on its way out to Biscuit. The forklift that the building supply company used to unload materials from delivery trucks and deposit them onto the barge was gone

too, on its way to Biscuit with the construction materials for
the laborious process of unloading. His Corrigan & Wheeler
team—Halloran's team—would be out there later today; a
meeting with the clerk of the works would surely be on the
agenda for discussion of all the change orders.

Instead of turning his chair to the left, to roll toward the
street and the little village of Stony Creek in order to find
Wendell wherever he was waiting for them, Duncan toggled
the control to turn to the right, facing the empty end of the
concrete pier, looking out toward Burr Island. He was just
fifteen feet from the unprotected edge. The tide was going
out. His splinted hand hovered over the toggle control, cupping it. It felt warm from the sun. Rock paper scissors.

Please don't. Please. Don't. Don't do it, thought Gordon,
behind him. Please. Not yet. Don't go. Not yet. Too soon.

Rock. Duncan knew he would sink like a rock. Even
though the water was probably no more than eight or nine
feet deep, it was enough. He was strapped into the chair. The
combined weight was probably more than three hundred
pounds.

"Sometimes I let you take all the hearts on purpose," Gordon said, standing right behind him, bending down to talk
into his ear, "because I know you want to shoot the moon.
You're supposed to avoid hearts, you're always supposed to
go low, but when you go high and start collecting hearts you
think I don't notice. But I do. I let you shoot the moon."

Duncan rotated his chair to face Gordon. "Gordo, you
know why I always beat you at gin rummy? You always go
for the runs instead of sets, beyond all reason or logic."

"I like runs better," Gordon said. "They're nicer."

"I understand."

The brothers gazed at each other, each wanting to hold the
moment.

"I'm sorry I've been so unpleasant today, Gordo. You're a
good brother."

"So are you."

They looked at each other for a long moment. "Let's get out of the sun," Duncan said, finally. "I have reason to believe the ice cream at Thimbleberries is worth our while. You can treat, and when you pay, be sure to check that all the presidents are being dignified in your wallet."

# SIXTEEN

May 25, 2015

Dear Laura,

If you are reading this, I've died. You have found this document
on the desktop of my computer saved as DEAR LAURA
PLEASE READ THIS. We both know an infection could kill
me easily at any point. But if my death has been caused by my
actions, or if my actions have been contributing factors in my
life ending, then I hope this will help you understand. Voice
recognition software has made it possible to say much more
to you than what would otherwise have been a few inadequate
words laboriously pecked out with the stylus on the keyboard. I
should have thanked you more for setting me up with Bigstick
voice recognition software nine years ago when I broke my
right wrist skiing. I was only grumpy and irritable with you,
as I usually am with anything to do with technology, and for
reasons of pride I didn't tell you how much I have continued to
depend on voice recognition software ever since, for generating

drafts of work correspondence and memos to myself while driving or when I'm on a job site.

Since the accident, though, you had to catch me using it because I was such a child about not wanting to admit you had been right, Bigstick has been an essential tool that has allowed me to respond to work email without sounding like a feebleminded toddler, and it has kept my emails from looking like archy & mehitabel poems. This made my final efforts at Corrigan & Wheeler a little more graceful and a lot less pitiful than they might have been otherwise. Thank you.

Let me begin again, dear Laura. A week has passed since I wrote these first pages. I have become incapable of many things. Among them is my own distress. By this I mean I have been keeping company with my death for a long while now. The prospect of no longer existing doesn't distress me. It comforts me. It's staying alive that distresses me. I want you to understand how much I have looked forward to ending my life. This has become more than ambivalence. I am not as afraid of dying as I am of continuing to live this way indefinitely. Knowledge of my certainty about this, along with determination to find my way out, this has been like having gold coins jingling in my pocket, and has allowed me to endure life more easily these past few months.

Of course, I do recognize that you will have your own distress after my death, and I am truly sorry about that. Surely my consistent feelings do not come as a complete surprise to you. You know how despairing I have been since the accident. I hit rock bottom when I was back in the hospital because of that stupid burn. I told myself at the time that I would give it six months. In these six months, which were up a while ago, you and I have talked about, and have argued about, my reluctance to make the best of my new circumstance. You have insisted that I am depressed, and my faltering will to live is the depression talking. You have told me how lucky I am that I am not in any significant physical pain. We both know that many people with complete C6 injuries suffer terrible phantom pain below the level of injury—burning, stabbing, crawling pain. I have been spared that torment.

In certain ways, I envy the realness of pain like that. Am I lucky? I have been tempted to lie about this, to claim this agony was mine, knowing that if I was in excruciating physical pain then probably you would not have fought me so hard. I didn't lie about it mainly because pain meds might have put me into a fog that would have made it impossible to think and act clearly. The Elavil in my rice pudding you thought I didn't know about has been dizzying enough. And yet the antidepressant effect on me, if there has been any that signifies, has not altered my sense of the rational rightness of my choice to end my life now rather than wait. Perhaps I am less depressed, yet more certain. This should be proof enough to you that my death really isn't the ultimate depression symptom.

I am repeating myself when I say again that most people would understand my desire to end my life if they thought it was driven by unbearable physical pain, rather than unbearable mental anguish. Somehow that's harder for people to understand. My suffering is very small in the larger scheme of all the pain that all of humanity has endured through history, but it is suffering nonetheless, and it is mine.

But if it's easier for you, if it lets you off the hook and helps end intrusive, well-meaning speculative discussion, then please do feel free to tell people that I have had to endure terrible physical pain. They'll believe you, and it could ease a lot of minds. I mean that. If it's helpful, don't hesitate, without feeling for a moment that you are being in any way disloyal to me. People love a logical explanation for something that feels to them profoundly illogical. If someone tries to tell you that my choice was selfish or cowardly, please don't argue. You know me. You know that I may have many failings, but I am not making this decision out of cowardice, and I can only hope it doesn't leave you feeling that I have been selfish.

Ultimately, no matter how much love there is, each of us is alone inside our only body, and nobody can ever really know another person completely.

Last summer, when you were on a campaign to make me love my life, you also tried to make me feel that I owed it to you, and to Gordy, if not to myself, to stay alive. I said this then, and it upset you terribly, which is why I haven't tried to tell you again, but I will say it here, now: I believe with all my heart that you will have a better life without me. The first months after I die, whenever that is, will be terribly hard, but after that—a year after I'm gone, five years, ten years? I will be a sad story in your past. You can live a far more fulfilling life without me dragging you down. Surely you have allowed yourself to imagine your future without me? Haven't we both been imagining my death since the accident? When Robin Williams killed himself while I was still in the hospital, when I heard about it, I understood his choice in an instant. I know he had lots of issues, but if he was facing a life diminished by Parkinson's, and by encroaching dementia, how could he contemplate living in an increasingly un-agile body along with a diminishment of that frantic, agile mind?

Gordy will be okay. I know he'll have a hard time at first. But he'll manage. He does what he wants to do, he has Ferga (for now anyway, if only she were immortal), and I think he can keep living his life the way it is, though I worry about the bookstore staying in business, since it's his center of gravity. My Will, as you know, establishes a Trust for Gordy, with you and Sam Cooper as co-trustees. If the bookstore closes, if there is a way to buy some small, suitable business and install Gordy there on staff, with a sensitive manager to keep it all going, please feel free to do just that, even if it means going into capital.

Sam will help you sort out all the financial and legal stuff. I have tried to keep everything in order. Of course everything else I own in the world goes to you. On top of my life insurance, which will really set you up for life, you will have my pension fund, Social Security, and of course, our investments. The lump sum discounted payouts on workers' comp and the long-term disability insurance were a better plan for taking care of you, under these circumstances.

The mortgage is nearly paid off. Please stop fussing with endless repairs on our damned roof, though you have handled them so efficiently and (nearly) without complaint, and just replace the roof on our house before another winter comes. Ask the office for the best roofer in New Haven.

You should sell my share of Corrigan & Wheeler to the equity partners. I am sure Dave Halloran already has a precise structured plan in mind for just that eventuality. Don't let him railroad you. Let Sam negotiate terms.

You will only have to work as much as it suits you, perhaps just taking on a few of the more interesting conservation projects they offer you at the Gallery. Or maybe you will stop working, or do conservation work on your own. You have the skills. But I don't know if that's what you want. I am not sure I know what you will want to do with the rest of your life. I don't see you as a big world traveler.

Gordy is pretty isolated out there, especially in the winter, and I worry about how he'll manage in the future, as he ages to the point of not being able to just hop on his bike the way he does now. Who knows, maybe Gordy is finally ready to learn how to drive. After all, he didn't live on his own until our mother sold the house and moved to a condo when he was twenty-eight. I have never understood why he was content to live at home and sleep in that twin bed in our old room.

When I was a kid, I thought we had twin beds because we were twins, and I was disconcerted when I discovered that other children, even only children, slept in twin beds too. When I went off to college, I certainly never wanted to live at home again, even though I spent some summers there to save money. But he just didn't leave, until he had to. He doesn't have momentum. There's no name for whatever he's got, or hasn't got. Gordy Wheeler Syndrome. Of course our mother was partly to blame for Gordy's lack of development as a grownup. In her final years, I discovered that she had concealed from me how often she gave him money. More recently, in relation to my brother, you have called me an enabler. You're right.

When I'm gone, you will be all he has.

Please buy Gordy's cottage from his landlord. (I trust you to trust me that this is a good investment. I promise, I'm not doing a Floyd here!) The office can get you an honest and reliable contractor. They do exist. Please use all the resources of Corrigan & Wheeler for this project. I am sure they will take care of you. Have it winterized. Replace all the windows and doors with triple-glazing. Vertical cedar siding, rough side out, should wrap the house. Put a standing seam metal roof on it. That should solve the upstairs leaks from ice dams, and should also eliminate the source of the mold problems. Also, the knob & tube wiring desperately needs to be replaced and brought up to code. It's a firetrap right now. And the horrible galvanized pipes have to be replaced altogether. So this will be a gut reno. That furnace needs to be replaced, and you should switch from oil to propane. You may have to spend some serious money on remediation if the old buried oil tank under the front lawn has started to leak.

When I spoke with Mrs. Anastasio a few months ago about the roof problems, after her delinquent son had gone up there to fix the leaks with duct tape, it was clear that she didn't want to spend a nickel because she was getting ready to cash in and sell her family's property so she could move to Florida, and you should be able to persuade her to let it go for a good price if you point out that you would be willing to pay cash and close without the oil tank inspection that would be required for any kind of financing. I know you'll be able to handle this. You did a terrific job getting the work done to solve our roof leak this past winter (you know I am obsessive about roof issues), even though until now I have always taken care of everything like that over all our years together. I just always took over everything when it came to dealing with our house, making all the decisions without a second thought. But you have been in charge of just about everything since the accident. You'll be fine. I have faith in you.

Gordy docs love that ratty little Cape. Buy it and do the renovation and give it to Gordy if he's willing to take it. Otherwise, please just buy it and do the work and he'll keep living there. You'll have to find a temporary place for him and Ferga during the renovation, somewhere near the bookstore. I hope you will figure out a graceful way to check in on him from time to time in the years ahead, to make sure he has heat and lights, and enough to eat. If he agrees to take title to the house, you'll probably have to help him out with things like property taxes and homeowners insurance. Gordy is never really going to be a grownup. How strange it will be for you to be responsible for this genetic copy of me after I'm gone. The twin who stayed identical. At least with that beard we don't look much alike, though when we were kids most people couldn't tell us apart. And unless it is too hard for you to see him wearing my stuff, please do give him any of my clothing he wants.

Oh, dear Laura whom I love so much. Please forgive me. Nothing is your fault. I should have said that sooner. Nothing has ever been your fault. There is nothing you could possibly have done better than all you did for me.

So much has been my fault.

Todd's death was my fault.

The spaces between us were certainly more my fault than yours.

I know how right it is going to be for me to leave this life. This is not a careless fantasy, or an impulse. So many people have assumed that I am grateful to be alive. The truth is, I am grateful that I can make my own choice about being alive, remaining alive. You and I have argued about Primo Levi. You are certain that he clearly had a strong will to live and must have fallen to his death accidentally. I am just as certain that it was no accident.

How many times, over how many years, did Primo Levi climb that Turin staircase to his third-floor apartment and imagine flinging himself over the banister? At the news of his death, Elie Wiesel said that Primo Levi had died at Auschwitz forty years before that leap. What a comfort that plan must have been to Primo Levi! I am certain of that. Every day he didn't jump, he knew he could have. Please try to think about my decision this way. Think of me as having died in the accident. I will just be completing what began that day, when the moment is right. My plan has been a comfort to me. I have devoted a lot of time to finding my best opportunity. Unlike Primo Levi, I have not had the easy option of a hand on the rail, a leg over, a shift of weight, done.

Ottoline has been such good company. That amazing little primate has made a profound difference in my quotidian [a word Bigstick recognition did not understand and I have just spent two minutes on it! Quotidian! Not quote idiot!] existence. She definitely makes each morning a little more pleasant, when I wake up and hear her still snoring that delicate old lady snore she has, or find her already awake and cheeping at me impatiently because she is ready to begin our day together. She never saw me as broken, the way everyone else has. She thought I was in charge of the world!

I am deeply grateful to you for bringing Ottoline into our lives. And I am grateful to you for all that you have done for her, day in and day out, the baths, the diapers, the food messes, her cage maintenance, keeping in touch with the Institute people—all the monkey-minding! And you have done it all with few complaints, and your complaints were always justified! Ottoline's hardwired sense of hierarchy has imposed a lot on you. Your graceful acceptance of her imperious rudeness (and occasional nastiness) to you has been an act of love that I have probably not thanked you for sufficiently. She's an opinionated and high-maintenance little primate! Thank you, thank you, thank you, dear Laura, for bringing our little brown-eyed girl into my life, our life. She has given us some sweet moments.

And all that you have done for me, all the numberless kindnesses and efforts over these terrible months—of course I am truly grateful to you. You found the best PCAs and you managed their comings and goings. You have kept track of everything, managing so much, slaving over the endless medical and financial paperwork. Above all, as humiliating as many aspects of my daily life have become, you have always done everything you could to help me preserve my dignity.

I don't deny that there have been many moments when I was not in hell. Ottoline has of course touched me profoundly in unexpected ways. And I would never deny the ephemeral pleasures of your warm blueberry pie with vanilla ice cream, and late Beethoven quartets, and Lester Young playing "Honeysuckle Rose" (the 1937 Count Basie recording), and don't forget John O'Hara novels, and the wonderful sentences in Iris Murdoch novels (not counting her last two, and you should be sure to buy all new copies to replace the drowned books because I hope you will re-read Iris Murdoch from time to time, and please never forget her observation that religion is better off without God if anyone tries to console you by imposing religiosity), and of course we have spent some good hours together watching our greatest hits: "Rear Window," "Dial M For Murder," "Roman Holiday," "Bringing Up Baby," "Two For the Road," "Sunset Boulevard" (didn't we see Norma Desmond's relationship with that chimp differently the last time we watched it, you, me and Ottoline, our tribe, all together on my bed?).

But of course my deepest feelings for you are not about pie and our shared devotion to Iris Murdoch, and movies.

Nevertheless, since the accident, your strategy was a worthy effort, trying to sell me on the goodness of life by producing a touching sequence of my favorite things. Food, music, books on tape, movies, all the gizmos and gadgets and brackets and cuffs and grips and grab bars and the left-handed Easi-Grip scissors and all the other things you researched and obtained to make my life a little easier. The online Hearts game you found for me to play on my own, now that I can't hold a hand of playing cards to play another round of the eternal Hearts tournament with Gordy, though I do miss our cribbage and gin games. It just isn't the same if I spread my cards out on the table and you promise not to look. You know you can't help but look. I would look if I were you, and then I would use the information to win big, sprezzaturistically.

You invited people into our house even when I didn't want to see anyone. You encouraged the relationship with the McCarthy children, and you were so sweet and hospitable to them, because you saw how much they intrigued me. I hope you will let them keep coming over to visit Ottoline, and you. I am sorry you never got to be a mother. You would have been a great mother. I hope you have a chance to be a mother in the years that lie ahead. Really! I hope you find someone else. I want you to live a long and wonderful life, with people in it who love you as much as you deserve to be loved. Meanwhile, in the immediate future, I hope you will want to keep Ottoline, in the retirement she deserves at this stage of her life, and I hope the Institute lets you keep her.

And then there is the Explicated Four-Square House, which now, thanks to you, will be known to the world as the Four-Square Cavendish House. (I like the name. Makes me think of bananas.) You were right to know how much I would want the house built, despite myself, despite my intention not to want anything in this life. It bought some time. It took me out of myself even as it brought me back to myself, and I am touched that you made it happen. I am sorry I won't see it, and I am proud of that house, probably prouder of it than anything else I ever designed in my career, because it is really mine, every inch of it, the way nothing else ever was or ever will be. (Other than our dovecote toolshed.) It's a monument to the architect I could have been.

But I did overhear you telling Gordy about the deal you made to get them to build my Four-Square house—you were washing dishes together and you were talking louder than you might have realized over the clatter—and I felt terrible. What have I become that you would risk so much, not just your job but your reputation in your field, to aid those people by providing false documentation for their fake pair of bowls? You could lose your job, and they may have used you for some kind of insurance fraud, or some other corrupt tax dodge thing they're going to profit by when they donate those bowls to an institution. It can't just be an ego trip for them, possessing the only known matched pair in the world—though there's that, too. You allowed yourself to be manipulated by those corrupt people, and you manipulated them, for me. I know you made this deal with your eyes open. And I know too that you never wanted me to comprehend the connection.

You and I are both fascinated by the story of Edith Wharton inventing that fake literary award to bestow on her friend Henry James near the end of his life when he was pinched for money. She went to great effort, working through lawyers, to remain an anonymous benefactor. She knew how proud he would be, how proud he was, to have won this spurious prize which came with a large sum of much-needed cash. And she knew how devastated and shamed he would have been if he had ever learned the truth about it. And he never did. He would never have forgiven her, either.

So I wish I had not heard you telling Gordy about your scheme to get my Four-Square house built. I wish I had Henry James's obliviousness. Of course I am not angry at you. It was clarifying. Once again, after all these years, when I should have

known better, I was so easily persuaded to allow myself to feel
something about that house, and about myself as the designer
of that house, and once again I have found out how foolish that
was. The Four-Square Cavendish House was a momentary
diversion, a pleasant satisfaction. I thank you for that. But it's
over. My present reality is what remains, and my intention.

Pepe's white clam pizza does make life a little better. So
does Lester Young. So does rain on the roof. So do the cave
paintings in Lascaux. So does a coffee ice cream cone on a hot
summer night for you and a vanilla custard cone for me. So
does that ineffable unquantifiable smell of soil after rain—the
peculiarly harsh word I couldn't remember the other day when
we were having dinner—it's petrichor. But nothing is enough
to keep me here at the sidelines of the banquet, having to be
grateful for a few crumbs. Raindrops on roses and what Gordy
used to think were whispers on kittens are just not enough. Any
joy I feel at being alive is only the flip side of the despair coin.
I have hated the sunlight streaming in the window and making
a pretty pattern on the carpet, because it doesn't change
anything. That shining sun is a lie. I live in endless night.

You have tried admirably to persuade me that it is worth
my while to make a plan to stick around, to endure this
compromised life, trapped in my inert, damaged body that
I have come to despise more and more. I am tired of being
grateful for this life. I think you have just never really believed
me when I said that I just couldn't live with myself indefinitely.
I've been keeping an ugly secret: Each good moment you have
given me since the accident has only enlarged my sense of
everything I have lost. The Four-Square Cavendish House is
simply the most concrete example of what has played out in
a thousand other, smaller ways. Every pinnacle has given me
a view of the abyss. I know how melodramatic that sounds.
People call suicide a permanent solution to a temporary
problem. My problem isn't temporary. I will always be crippled

in mind and body. Todd Walker will always be dead. I will always be the reason.

There is no place for me in this world. I have to say it again: It was my fault. The accident that killed Todd Walker and put me in this chair was my fault. Every day I wake up is a day it was my fault.

When I was in the hospital the second time, for the burn, the same day I refused to talk with that rabbi, a social worker came to see me. Maybe the rabbi sent him. He wasn't just any social worker, but a really nice guy in a wheelchair. He gave me a pep talk about life with a spinal cord injury. He broke his neck diving into a pool when he was a teenager and he has lived his life in that chair. He went to college and graduate school and he became a social worker to help people like me. He told me that everyone with a spinal cord injury starts out miserable and suicidal. The secret to moving forward, he told me, was to set a goal for myself. When I reach that goal, then I'll know the accident is in the past. I took his advice to heart, but not in the way he intended. But he did inspire me. Ending my life is the goal I set for myself. When I have succeeded, the accident will indeed be in the past instead of the present, where it lives now, every day.

Everything I have read about suicide, and I have read a great deal, tells me that I have what it takes. Ability to overcome the instinct to survive? Check. Thwarted belongingness and perceived burdensomeness. (Let's not argue.) Check. The actual means to take my own life? This is where I have had the greatest challenge. I am marooned by my paralysis. It renovates every moment of the day. I think that's Blake.

I miss standing. I miss being taller than most people. I miss walking. I miss going up and down staircases without a moment's thought. I miss the upstairs of our house. I miss our room. I miss our bed. I miss you in our bed. I miss me in our bed. I miss you and me together in our bed. You are splendid,

Lauradora. You will never be unbeautiful. Even when you are a little old lady, you will be beautiful. I have always meant to love you the most, even when I haven't always succeeded. I haven't been fair to you. I have held back too much, not let you love me more, not let myself love you more. I'm sorry. You are the love of my life, and I hope you know it and will always know it.

I miss being able to make numberless small choices every day. I miss scratching my ass. I miss turning my head. I miss drawing, just picking up a pencil and drawing a line and another line. I miss that more than I ever thought I would. The kids use AutoCad, but I have never been able to design with anything other than a pencil. I miss believing that I was ever capable of designing something wholly original and entirely new, but that's been gone a long while.

I miss being spontaneous in a million ways. I miss cooking. I miss working in the garden. I miss yoga even though I hardly ever went to the yoga classes I signed up for. I miss signing up for yoga classes and not going to them. I miss riding on trains and planes. I miss shifting gears while accelerating, feeling the gears engage as I shift the stick hard into the top gear and ease off the clutch, timing it perfectly to mesh with the surge of power as I step on the gas. I miss stepping on the gas.

I miss getting dressed. I miss getting undressed. I miss turning over in bed. I miss using my hands. I miss using my hands to touch you without making an appointment first. (I miss being able to touch each other without first negotiating permission from a bossy little monkey.) I miss peeing on the grass in our yard, the pleasure of taking a piss with a full bladder, the pleasure of having a great bowel movement first thing in the morning. Farting! My body does these things without me now.

I miss walking. I miss running. I love my dreams of running but then I wake up in despair. Another pinnacle and another abyss. I miss biking and I wish I had biked more. I always

meant to. I miss the way it felt to play the piano when I was
a kid, and I miss having the option to play the piano again
some day, which I always thought I had. I miss coming home
from work, kissing you hello in the kitchen if it was a night
you were making our dinner, going out the back door with a
cold Blue Moon in my hand, walking down the two steps to
the terrace, hearing the theme to All Things Considered while
you clattered pots and pans. I miss wandering around the late
summer garden, drinking my Blue Moon and deadheading
the hellebores. I know we may not have been as profoundly
connected in certain ways as many couples are (as much as I
can ever know about other couples and how they really are), but
we were comfortable with what we had together, we loved that
life, and it worked for us, didn't it? It was a good life and I miss
it. And it's gone.

I have been thinking seriously about murdering myself since
last November. It's been a hell of a project. I agreed to go across
the street to Bailey McCarthy's birthday party in March neither
because I wanted to see inside their house—though I win
points for predicting that white piano!—nor because I longed
for time with the dreadful parents or the dreadful other over-
privileged, self-important parents of that rabble of amped-up
seven-year-olds. I didn't go in the hopes of experiencing the
undignified spectacle of being fed a few bites of disgusting
birthday cake (is there any other kind?). I went because I had
reason to hope for a clown with a helium tank. Sure enough,
I watched him arrive with it on a hand truck.

A helium tank and a plastic bag are the optimal equipment
for the do-it-yourself suicide kit, ideally but not necessarily
along with something sedating. (You can find anything on
YouTube.) I wanted to get close to the helium tank and get a
good look at the regulator valve, which I did, at the start of
the party. It was a huge disappointment when I immediately
recognized that I couldn't manage it. Even if I had somehow

been able to come up with a plausible explanation for ordering a helium tank rental from It's a Gas! without your becoming suspicious (and I never did think of a good way to do that), it was immediately evident to me in the middle of that hullabaloo, while all the screeching children were dueling each other with those idiotic light-sabre things (I vividly recall the moment during our first dinner together when you and I discovered our mutual antipathy for "Star Wars"), that I would not be able to turn the regulator and open the valve by myself. Not only was it out of reach at the top of the cylinder, but also it's a two-handed job for an able-bodied person, and even then, it requires some dexterity and strength. I really studied that helium tank that afternoon, watching closely each time the clown filled a balloon. So close and yet so far.

I had begun to imagine the various ways I could command Ottoline to perform tasks she already knew that would assist me in taking my own life. I tried to think through what would be involved to get her to turn the sillcock and flip the lever to start the flow of gas, and then I realized that it was out of the question, even if I solved all the logistical problems, even if I was ready with a plastic bag around my head that could be snugged sufficiently around my neck once the tube was inside the bag, because of the risk of exposing her to the helium, which would kill her along with me. That was when I decided I needed to leave Bailey's birthday party and asked Darlene to take me home.

I did not abandon every element of that option, however, and since then I have spent many hours in the afternoons when I am on my own, teaching Ottoline some skills with several different kinds of plastic bags. You have seen her sliding a large zipper bag over a cantaloupe or musk melon on the kitchen table or counter more than once, but you never questioned how and why I had been coaching this activity and rewarding her with treats for executing it quickly and completely. She's gotten very good at it. She was motivated after I moved on from rewarding her with blueberries to grapes (too sugary, according to the Institute) to Nutella (forbidden altogether) in recent times. The faster she could get the bag down all the way over the entire melon, the bigger the glob of Nutella. (I know, I know. Please let her have some Nutella from time to time, anyway. And let her bag the occasional melon, too. Why not?)

I encouraged you to believe that her constant bagging of objects was simply a funny artifact of some task from her previous placement. I let you think I was just enjoying testing her skills and intelligence, that it was a game. There were a couple of times when Ottoline slid a plastic bag over a melon right in front of you, and you didn't react and reward her, which made her really frustrated, and then she started whining and begging. You just called her a brat and gave her a time-out in her cage because you didn't know what we were up to. Everybody's got something to hide, including me and my monkey. (I couldn't resist that.)

I also experimented with dry cleaning bags on several occasions, going for simple suffocation, the very thing all parents are warned about right on the bag, but they were too big and unwieldy, and also flimsy. I tore bags to shreds just trying to get them off the hangers, and there were few opportunities, once I used up the bags on our winter coats in the front hall closet, since all our clothing closets are upstairs, where I will never again set foot—ha, me talking about setting foot. I had to move on from dry cleaner bags. I had concluded, in any case, that I couldn't really manipulate the bag on my own, with no ability to reach up over my head, and it was just too dangerous for Ottoline to be involved. The one time I tried having her handle a dry cleaning bag, she got her head wrapped up in it and I panicked until the two of us clawed her free.

My pursuit of a workable plastic bag continued. It was soon after Christmas when I noticed that each time she worked a morning shift, Cathy brought her lunch, in an old plastic drawstring bag from the Gap. I went to a great deal of trouble to make sure she had a day shift on an afternoon when I knew you would be coming home on the late side, leaving me at least a couple of hours of solitude with Ottoline. It was nerve-wracking work, getting the bag off the kitchen table, where it was nearly out of my pathetic reach, while Cathy was down in the basement tending to the laundry. I maneuvered Ottoline into smearing peanut butter inside and out, armed with her usual tool of choice, a Bic pen. She kept trying to lick the bag clean, undoing the mess when I wanted the mess. I let her take some handfuls of Quaker Oats right out of the cylinder (you know how she loves to do that) and this distracted her from the bag. Finally, with the bag sufficiently smeared and Ottoline engrossed in picking the oatmeal flakes stuck to the peanut butter on her hands, I dropped it on the floor just before Cathy came up the stairs with a laundry basket of folded sheets.

She saw Ottoline's naughtiness, and together we laughed over this typical little mess she had been made in an instant while my back was turned and Cathy was downstairs with the laundry. I was able to decoy nice, frugal Cathy (so funny how her sister Darlene is the spendthrift) into washing out the bag instead of throwing it away, and then I suggested casually that she could simply leave the rinsed bag hanging on the cellar stair doorknob in the kitchen. All that effort to get the damned bag, only to discover, when I had encouraged Ottoline, with liberal bribes of unlimited access to the peanut butter jar, to pull it snugly over my head just the way she had become adept at bagging a cantaloupe, that the bag had several rips in the bottom seam and was not remotely airtight. That was the day you wondered, as we ate dinner (you were so perpetually patient and kind in your attempt to cater to my needs without comment or caption as you provided the manageable bites of everything, the special ugly rimmed plate with the high sides, the Velcro slotted utensil cuff, the glass of water placed just so with the angled straw, oh God, how could you stand it night after night?), how on earth I had somehow not noticed all the peanut butter Ottoline had smeared in my hair and on the back of my neck.

I gave it all a rest for a while after that, most recently owing to time spent on the not unwelcome distractions of the Four-Square Cavendish House. But my body has been letting me down continually, and I am getting weaker. Each round of gut or urinary tract infection has been a potential turning point, as you know so well. A few autonomic dysreflexia events were instructive from the very beginning. Do you recall that unusually warm day in October, about a week after we got Ottoline, before Halloween, when you came home after some symposium and dinner at the Yale Art Gallery, and you found me shut in my room, which was quite hot, with the windows closed and the air conditioner turned off? I almost can't remember it myself. I know I was half-conscious, in my chair, my blood pressure going sky-high. You grabbed the Nitro paste and smeared it on my chest and I came around pretty quickly. You were understandably upset by how this had happened, and by the inexplicable gap in the PCA schedule.

It wasn't a misunderstanding. It was an experiment. I planned it. But I miscalculated. I told Ida Mae that she could leave at two that day because you would be home by three. I had told Wendell that we didn't need him at seven after all, and he could have the night off, someone else had the shift. Then I closed the door, and simply asked Ottoline, using the laser pointer, to turn up the thermostat in my room—Twist!—and she turned the dial all the way up, just the way she turns the lid of a jar when we ask her with that command. Pretty simple. And if you had not come home so promptly after that dinner I might have even died in that hot room. I wasn't worried about Ottoline—she can take the heat.

That was the first time I made it happen. Not every dysreflexia episode I have experienced was deliberately planned, though. It's a ghastly feeling—that sudden pounding headache, my head pouring sweat, my nose streaming, goose bumps, black spots in my vision, the room going dim. The miserable impacted bowel episode in January was certainly not something I planned. (Wendell is a saint.) Nor was the first time dysreflexia was set off by a kink in my catheter tube that blocked my bladder a planned event. But that was such a simple yet potentially dangerous AD trigger! Noted! After that, I experimented a few times, when I had the opportunity, each occasion like another spin of the chamber in a game of Russian Roulette. It wouldn't be a bad way to go, with no risk of harm to Ottoline. Several times, she helped me clamp one of Cathy's hinged hair clips onto my catheter line, out of sight. After a few hours, I could feel the early signs of dysreflexia, and I would skate along the edge for a while before pulling back, having her release the clip, which she understood quickly when I asked her to Push! And Flip! It was our secret game, and my secret thrill, knowing I had that power over myself. Nothing in my life felt as good as the plan for leaving it.

During the winter, when it was so frigid and relentlessly snowy and I didn't leave the house for weeks, I had a recurring fantasy of rolling out our front door without the protection of a coat or hat or gloves, heading down the ugly wheelchair ramp for which we lost half our front lawn along with the trellis that supported those wonderful old climbing roses (please have the ramp taken down as soon as I am gone and it is no longer needed, and perhaps some good use can be found for that expensive Ipe), navigating the zig-zag turns and then rolling down to the end of our front walk. In my mental escape I would head down the sidewalk towards Whitney Avenue until there was a cleared driveway and then I would roll into the street, and then I would accelerate to top speed and just go with the bitter wind in my face as I would start to feel lightheaded, and a little giddy, the first welcome sign of exposure hypothermia. I imagined rolling faster and faster. Sometimes I crash into a hill of plowed snow which cascades onto me and I succumb to the hypothermia, enrobed in snow, before help arrives. Sometimes I roll all the way to the end of Lawrence Street, right into the traffic on Whitney Avenue, where I die moments later in a fatal collision.

Do you remember our conversation just last month, during the big electrical storm that knocked out our power for a couple of hours, about that hiker who was struck and killed by lightning on the top of East Rock last November? Once you reminded me about it, I became obsessed with that story. I could only think about ways to get to the top of East Rock in the next thunderstorm. I have from then to now day-dreamed about rolling myself all the way up there every time it rains. I would go out the front door, and turn left on the sidewalk and go down Lawrence Street to the corner, turn left on Orange Street, and then (this is the impossible fantasy part) travel north on Orange and cross over the Mill River and somehow get myself onto the White Trail.

This was my morning route whenever I had the occasional burst of fitness intention and would go for early runs, which wasn't often enough. The trail is the shortcut to the big Farnam Drive loop road to the top, and of course it is not nearly wheelchair accessible. In my mind's eye I somehow navigate this and also manage the next impossible thing, a long uphill roll at the side of the road, still following my old running route, and then finally I reach the top. Sitting there at the summit, in my chair, in the rain, while thunder and lightning crack and roar around me, the water pours down, drenching me, runs down my face into my mouth, and I am exhilarated as I wait for the marvelous, deadly bolt of lightning that will surely come.

All pure fantasy, of course. As you know, I cannot even open our front door.

Several times in the last few months, I requested grapefruit juice instead of orange juice. Do you know why? Because of all the dire warnings out there about grapefruit juice interacting in deadly ways with medications! Bring it on! I tried drinking grapefruit juice at various hours of the day, with meds, before meds, after meds—but nothing happened. If it threw something off, it wasn't enough to matter. Maybe I didn't drink enough. How much would have been enough? With which meds? Somebody needs to figure these things out and post an instructional video on YouTube.

I almost rolled off the Stony Creek freight dock when I went out there with Gordy to see the Steiner house a couple of weeks ago. He knew. He knew how close it was. I couldn't go through with it with him right there. I wanted to have that perfect, effortless accident, but I couldn't do it to him. I couldn't do it in front of him. I knew he would always blame himself. Please do not blame Gordy for not telling you what I know he felt me thinking.

And about the Steiners' dock fire on Biscuit Island last week. I know the police think they're looking for stupid kids who vandalize things in the middle of the night just for the hell of it. And God knows the Steiner House has a lot of enemies at this point, starting with those Coalition reactionaries, so there could be a lot of theories of the crime. The fire won't have a high priority for investigation. There could be a deliberate looking the other way, in fact. Chances are, nobody will ever know who did it and why. But something tells me that Gordy knows exactly what happened to the Steiners' dock and that gazebo. I just hope he was careful.

I have come to realize that of course I cannot involve Ottoline in the ending of my life. Not only would I not want to risk physical harm to her, but also, I have come to believe that it would be a perversion of her life's work. It would be a terrible betrayal of the Primate Institute, too. They get enough grief about placing "exotic" capuchin monkeys in home settings. You and I have both debated a number of well-meaning and misguided people who are horrified by the idea of a capuchin enslaved as a trained monkey helper. I can make a case for the ethical use of a service animal like Ottoline. I can defend the training, even the extraction of those canine teeth.

I can, with all my heart, make the case for the value of monkey helpers living as singletons in captivity among humans in North America rather than in a big tribe of monkeys in their God-given habitat of the treetops of a cloud forest in Central America. But even though her presence seemed like the perfect solution to my personal pain, and I recognized how easily Ottoline's dexterous skills could be deployed this way, in the past months I have come to see how wrong it would be for me to use Ottoline as an instrument of my death. Not only would it harm the Institute and the monkey helper program, but also, more simply, I have come to see that the only moral thing for me to do is to protect this sweet, loving, loyal monkey from having anything at all to do with my choice and my action. I want to protect you, of course. I will choose my moment carefully in order to do that. Nobody should be blamed for my actions. You didn't know my plans. I am flying solo.

But I am done with experiments. I have a strategy, though I am not certain when the moment will be right. I have been writing and revising this letter to you for more than three weeks now, dreading and hoping all. So here it is at last, the expected thing.

I miss skiing terribly. I didn't know how much I loved it. I miss standing poised at the top of a double black diamond run, the tips of my skis already out over the void, gathering my nerve, giving myself over to that liminal moment of exhilaration and terror, standing tall, feeling fully alive in my body. Then I go over the edge.

Forgive me. Begin again, please. Keep the door open to let the future in.

Your Duncan

# SEVENTEEN

*Thirteen blue tablets of
pharmaceutical sprezzatura*

THIRTEEN BLUE TABLETS OF PHARMACEUTICAL *SPREZ-zatura* rattled in the Altoids tin as Duncan fumbled in the open desk drawer. He pushed against the cigar box with the wrist of his splinted hand, pressing it against the side of the drawer, and once he had it lifted up, he could lever it and rock it onto its edge, and then, using his braced grasp (thank you, physical therapist), he could drag it up onto the surface of his desk.

Duncan had four hours of privacy. He hoped it would be enough.

With Ottoline on his shoulder, he rolled into the living room and stopped in front of the window so they could look out together at the passing scene on Lawrence Street for the last time. He had his binoculars in his lap, for Ottoline. Duncan was all out of curiosity.

She hopped down onto the arm of his chair and snatched them, and he let her. She clambered into his lap and sat back against his chest, holding the binoculars tight in case he tried to take them away before she was ready for her turn to be over. Duncan let her look through the binoculars for a few minutes, gently stroking the back of her tufty head with the edge of his hand. It was beginning to feel like summer. Two people on bicycles came down the street, one in front of the other, their shouted conversation carrying ahead of their cicada whirr as they passed in front of the house.

When Ottoline got bored looking through the binoculars and began to gnaw on the eyecups, holding up the end of the binoculars with her feet, he traded her for the small, nearly full jar of Nutella he had stuffed down into the seat beside his leg. This she snatched avidly, binoculars forgotten, and in an instant she had expertly unscrewed the white plastic lid and flung it away. Duncan had stuck a dull drawing pencil in his shirt pocket when he was sitting at his desk, and this she plucked out, as he knew she would, to deploy as an excavation tool for shoveling globs of Nutella from the jar. She sucked the Nutella off the pencil as fast as she could, digging for more as she chewed and swallowed, her cheeks bulging with what she had already crammed into her mouth. A thread of drool hung from her lower lip. She had never before been given unlimited Nutella privileges, and she peeped happily as she dug into the jar with the pencil. Over and over.

After a few minutes watching her happy Nutella frenzy, Duncan took the jar from her grasp, which required only a few sharp words, and he left it on the dining room table as they rolled past it on their way back into his room. She clung to his shoulder, balancing easily, hanging onto his chest strap with one hand, like a subway commuter, while still holding the pencil with a final glob of Nutella in the other.

Duncan rolled over to her cage and instructed her, Cage! Cage! Good girl! Cage, Ottoline! Time for a time out. Out of time. She hopped off his shoulder and entered her lair agreeably, zonked on sugar, pulling the door closed behind her. The latch engaged. Now you'll be safe, my brown-eyed girl, thank you, my darling girl, my sweet angel, thank you, he whispered.

Thirteen hearts in the deck, each of them worth a point you don't want; the goal in Hearts is to have as low a score as possible. Thus the shiver of doom when the Queen of Spades turns up in all her horrifying glory, thirteen points in an instant. When she comes your way, is it always unlucky? Disappointment, the end of your plans? Or do you feel secret glee when the uninvited guest crashes your party? She sneaks into a diamond trick, or your King of Spades must bring her home. If you play your cards with care, you can hide in plain sight what it is you really want. But you have to be certain about what you really want. It's all or nothing.

Alone, Duncan fell down into the nothingness where this could happen. First, using the left-handed Easi-Grip scissors, he cut open three of the sealed NicoDerm patches, and then he managed to stick them on his neck and above his clavicles where he wasn't too hairy for the patches to stick.

"Don't take Viagra if you are using nitrates, as this may cause a drop in blood pressure. Talk with your doctor."

If you shoot the moon, going high instead of low, if you collect all the points, all thirteen heart cards and the Queen of Spades, your twenty-six points vanish in an instant, leaving you with zero points, and you are the winner of the hand. Which is to say you walk away empty-handed. You have achieved your goal of having nothing.

Thirteen Viagra tablets, one by one, down the hatch, sip from the long bent straw Ottoline had brought him when he asked, her last Fetch! Ottoline, Good girl! Swallow, sip, swallow, sip, times thirteen. Chased by four Adderall and three Xanax, sip,

sip, sip. Maybe just two of the Vicodin, and two of the Fiorinal, the pretty Fiorinal, so blue and yellow, like the flag of Sweden, like Ingie's knit cap that her grandmother knitted in Scandinavia, which isn't a country.

"Do not use Nitro paste if you are taking Viagra. Talk with your doctor."

Duncan picked up the tube of Nitro paste and raised it to his mouth so he could bite the cap to unscrew it from the tube by rotating the tube around and around. Done. He spat out the cap. Using the left-handed Easi-Grip scissors again, he cut into the neck of his T-shirt with a downward incision, and then he yanked down the wounded shirt to rip it more, to expose skin above his level of injury, where the Nitro paste would be most effective. He squeezed the tube hard against his bare chest and ejaculated a big soft glob of Nitro paste, which he rubbed all around with the back of his left hand, circling his left nipple, and then his right nipple. He loosened the Velcro of his chest strap to get it out of the way, but he didn't want to fall out of his chair, so he toggled to tip back just enough. This was comfortable. He squeezed the tube again and smeared one more glob of Nitro paste onto what he could reach of his right shoulder with his left hand.

He could hear his own breathing now, and something squeaking as he struggled to breathe enough, in and out, in and out, and it was the old familiar steady squeak of the porch swing, and as the room swayed back and forth Duncan let himself be rocked, he felt happy on the front porch as the tang of mildew wafted up from his cushion and he wondered how long he would have to wait, and he waited, he was always waiting on that swing for the next thing to happen in his life, not like Gordon who sat on that swing desperately not wanting the next thing to happen the way Duncan did, and now Duncan relaxed and let his life happen, and unhappen, happen, and unhappen, as he drifted back and forth on the swaying porch swing, breathing with its motion.

He couldn't really see now, but it didn't matter, and with his last strength he rubbed in the Nitro paste a little more, and it was soothing and smooth and nice, and he rubbed it in tenderly and slowly, and the headache that sprouted in his brain was red, the most beautiful red headache of his life, a single enormous chrysanthemum that took his breath away.

# EIGHTEEN

## *Primate Institute of New England*

**Final Placement Report**

Placement Date: 10.22.14
Name: NORMA JEAN, A.K.A. OTTOLINE
Tufted capuchin # PI06131028
Placement trainer: Martha Peterson
Recipient: Duncan Wheeler
127 Lawrence Street, New Haven, CT 06511

End Placement Date: 06.15.15
Reason: Death of Recipient Duncan Wheeler

Duncan Wheeler passed away in his home unexpectedly on Friday, June 12, as a consequence of his injuries.

Laura Wheeler has offered to foster Ottoline in retirement from service as a Primate Institute Monkey Helper and have her remain in the home. Given Ottoline's age (26–27?) and temperament, it would not have been desirable to attempt to retrain her for a third placement, and this is a very good outcome. As her Lead P.I. Trainer, I support Ottoline's retirement at this time, fostered in the Wheeler home.

Laura Wheeler has also offered to foster some of our young monkeys. This would be a highly suitable home environment for our young capuchins, and we have a number of possible candidates who are overdue for home foster placement for socialization. Ottoline was willing to interact with other monkeys in the Household Classroom during her retraining between placements in 2013–2014, so the introduction of young, junior status members of her troop should not trigger aggression on her part. In fact, knowing Ottoline for more than twenty years, I am confident that she will thrive on being the wise elder to young, apprentice monkeys. Given that our studies show that exposing young monkeys to the skill sets of our retired Helpers often causes a spontaneous adoption of those skills and responses, and if the alpha monkey is kept active and maintains her wide command vocabulary (Ottoline responds to 50+ commands), then the young monkeys have an opportunity to acquire some correct responses to recognized vocabulary as well. After home-fostered monkeys are exposed in this way to an older trained Helper, when they arrive for training they tend to excel in the A and B classrooms. It would be a win-win all around.

I urge the Director to accept this excellent foster home for immediate placement of two of our young female candidates for Institute training as Helpers. There is a pair of 36-month-old, laboratory-bred white-faced capuchins who have been raised together that would be a good match for this placement. They have not been officially named, and while we sometimes give this privilege to staff or donors, I suggest that Laura Wheeler be allowed to name them. In our experience, this helps in the attachment process that is the foundation of the bonding and nurturing that are key to successful home fostering of our monkeys.

MARTHA PETERSON<br>
SENIOR PLACEMENT TRAINER<br>
06.15.15

# NINETEEN

## *A bony, hairy little hand with long fingers*

A BONY, HAIRY LITTLE HAND WITH LONG FINGERS, A hand that was less than and more than a human hand, was thrust out at Laura for her attention. Ottoline gazed at the television screen, where motionless logs that were crocodiles lay in a bayou while viewers were instructed by a swamp guide that something might happen. She reminded Laura at this moment of Great-Aunt Stella, an old lady (who might not have been a true blood relative) whom she remembered from her earliest childhood in Ohio. She was somebody's great-aunt. Stella was very old and wizened, and on the one occasion Laura remembered being taken to see her, she was dozing in front of her programs with the same contented, toothless look on her face.

Laura moved the emery board gently across Ottoline's little index fingernail and Ottoline let her do it, settling with a happy sigh onto the soft fleece blanket in Laura's lap in a comfortable sprawl. She cocked her arm back up over her shoulder so Laura could trim the nails on that hand without disturbing her view of the television. Finished with the hands, Laura reached for a foot, and Ottoline swiveled around in her lap to lift her leg obligingly so Laura could tend to those nails too. Now she was watching the show upside-down. Laura filed away and thought about how Ottoline's feet and her hands were remarkably similar, with opposable thumbs and opposable big toes.

Molly leaped into Laura's lap, landing on Ottoline, who squawked and struck out at her. Now Molly was on the table next to the lamp, cheeping and carrying on in her usual victim fashion. She did it, she did it, she did it.

"You brought that on yourself, Molly," Laura scolded. "You know perfectly well that Ottoline was in the right here. You'll get your turn. Don't be a brat!"

Ottoline thrust her foot up into Laura's face to remind her that they had been interrupted. Laura took the foot in her hands and resumed her filing of Ottoline's toenails. She was faintly tempted to put pink polish on them, but that would be wrong.

"Where's your sister, go find Milly!" Laura did not keep the girls on leads at all times, and they had more freedom in the house on Lawrence Street than the trainers at the Institute knew or would have approved. Laura did not follow all of the protocols for socializing young monkeys, but in their own way they were highly socialized. The three monkeys slept in their cage at night, all together in a heap, the tribe that was two white-faced capuchins and one tufted capuchin dreaming a shared dream of treetops in a cloud forest, but during the day, when Laura was at home, she usually let them have a couple of hours at liberty, so long as they kept their diapers on and weren't exceptionally destructive. She was subversive, but not crazy.

It was a rainy afternoon. Milly and Molly sat together on the kitchen table watching Ottoline as she hopped across to the counter and stood up on her hind legs to turn the knob on the childproof kitchen cabinet, using both her hands to push and turn at the same time. The latch released and Ottoline quickly pulled the cabinet open and grabbed the cylinder of Quaker Oats from the shelf. She hurled it to the floor, where the lid flew off and the container rolled out a swale of spilled oat flakes. Watch and learn, youngsters. This is how it's done. Molly jumped down to the floor from the kitchen table where she had been grooming Milly's back. Left behind, Milly followed, more cautious about getting in trouble.

Nice nice nice, they hummed appreciatively as the two of them scooped hands full of oat flakes, chomping away as fast as they could, listening for Laura, who was engrossed in re-reading her favorite Iris Murdoch novel (*A Fairly Honorable Defeat*) on the sofa in the living room. The pleasant susurration of rain on the windowpanes drowned out the quiet mayhem two rooms away, and she had no idea what was going on out there. Ottoline remained on the counter, amused at the babies with their oatmeal flakes, quietly helping herself to her true objective in the locked cupboard, the bowl of rough brown sugar cubes that Laura liked to drop in her coffee.

It was evening. Ottoline slid the zipper bag down over the cantaloupe on the counter and held it tight. Milly hopped up beside her and Ottoline took the bag off the melon. Milly reached out to touch the sweet-smelling fruit, but Ottoline yanked the bag down again, trapping her hand. Milly hollered, and Molly jumped from the table to the counter to join her in the loud complaining about Ottoline, she did it, she did it, she did it. As the two of them tattled on Ottoline, she squealed her indignant denial, did not, did not, did not, and the noise in the kitchen was deafening.

Laura came up from the basement with a basket of clean laundry and scolded all the unruly monkeys. "Be a family, you three! Knock it off!" Milly and Molly cowered together and grinned in submission. Ottoline brushed it all off, wiping the back of her hand down her chest, and then again. She cheeped at Laura. Laura felt guilty for shouting at them. They were used to it, and they knew she loved them.

"Stop doing that, Ottoline, please." She picked up the cantaloupe and took the bag away from Ottoline. "You're retired," she said. She went over to the butcher block counter, where she opened the secure, cork-ended knife drawer, one of Duncan's best kitchen ideas, and she took out a knife to cut the cantaloupe in half. She scooped the pulpy seeds into the sink and then she sliced the melon into thin crescents.

The three monkeys watched her avidly from the counter across the kitchen, hooting softly in anticipation. Milly stuck her finger up Molly's nose, and Molly stuck her finger up Milly's nose, and they were calm again. Ottoline began to groom Milly's back. Milly groomed Molly's head. Molly stroked Ottoline's tail. Equilibrium was restored.

Laura piled a neat mound of diced cucumber in the middle of the Royal Copenhagen Blue Fluted dinner plate, one of the only unchipped dinner plates left from Laura and Duncan's wedding china, and then she laid the crescents of melon in a perfect fanned circle all the way around, reminding herself of the way methodical, precise Duncan used to love to organize his discarded artichoke leaves, a neat echo of the artichoke's original Fibonacci spiral, in a perfect nested sequence around the leftover hairy center choke. She scattered some blueberries neatly between the melon slices, and then she sliced a few red grapes in half and placed them evenly all the way around the plate, which she set before the hungry monkeys.

# A NOTE TO THE READER
## ABOUT MONKEY HELPERS

WHILE THE PRIMATE INSTITUTE OF NEW ENGLAND IS a fictional organization that exists only in this novel, Helping Hands, located in Boston, Massachusetts, is real. A non-profit organization that has since 1979 helped adults with spinal cord injuries and other mobility impairments to live more independent and engaged lives, Helping Hands provides, free of charge, highly trained capuchin monkeys to help recipients with daily tasks of living. The only organization of its kind, Helping Hands raises and trains these special service animals in "Monkey College" for several years before carefully matching them with appropriate recipients across the country. Helping Hands provides active support and care for the duration of each placement at no cost to recipients. Financial support of Helping Hands is always welcome. Monkey helpers change lives with the gift of greater independence, companionship, and hope.

www.monkeyhelpers.org
541 Cambridge Street, Boston, MA 02134
617-787-4419 | info@monkeyhelpers.org

The author will donate a portion of profits from the sale of this book to Helping Hands.

**KATHARINE WEBER** is the author of seven books, including *True Confections, Triangle, Objects in Mirror Are Closer Than They Appear, The Music Lesson*, and *The Little Women*; the last three were *New York Times Book Review* Notable Books. She is the Richard L. Thomas Visiting Professor of Creative Writing at Kenyon College, lives in Connecticut, and spends parts of the year in Ireland. She is married to the cultural historian Nicholas Fox Weber.

Photo by Corbin Gurkin

"In *Becoming Brave*, Dr. McNeil exercises uncommon courage. Part confession, part biblical reflection, part call to storm the gates, *Becoming Brave* declares that the Christian call to do justice cannot and shall no longer be guided, shaped, and defanged by sensibilities more loyal to white people's comfort than to God. McNeil has led two generations of evangelical Christians into the value and practice of racial reconciliation. With *Becoming Brave* she returns and calls her followers to gird their courage and engage like never before, for the sake of the gospel. This book is a must-read."

—**Lisa Sharon Harper**, founder and president, Freedom Road

"Brenda Salter McNeil has been a giant in the work of racial reconciliation among evangelicals. Like Tom Skinner and Bill Pannell in previous generations, she defines for this generation of evangelical scholars and pastors what real racial reconciliation means on the ground. There is simply no one who has worked with more thoughtfulness, theological precision, and faithfulness at this vital work than Brenda Salter McNeil. There is no one who understands more clearly what is necessary to move white evangelicals forward beyond their racial captivity than McNeil, and there is no more important book that must find its way into the hands of students, pastors, Christian activists, and all those who understand the urgency of this moment than *Becoming Brave*."

—**Willie James Jennings**, professor, Yale Divinity School; author of *After Whiteness: An Education in Belonging*

"This is a beautiful and courageous book about journeys. Brenda Salter McNeil takes us on hers, even as she invites us to newly understand Queen Esther's and—ultimately—our own. Real prophets lovingly criticize and truthfully energize. McNeil does both with clarity and with the kind of rare vulnerability that—when offered by a justice leader in it for the long haul and deeply responding to God's call—enables the rest of us to get quiet and ask again what it is that God requires of us.

This book will move your heart and compel your feet to move as well, with others, in response to God's call to do justice."

—**Jennifer Harvey**, author of *Raising White Kids: Bringing Up Children in a Racially Unjust America*

"During a time requiring moral clarity and moral courage, Dr. Brenda Salter McNeil calls any and all with ears to hear to be brave. Through a combination of personal reflection, cultural awareness, and biblical exegesis of the book of Esther, she provides a roadmap for leaders to become and to be brave."

—**Bishop Claude Alexander**, senior pastor, The Park Church, Charlotte, North Carolina

"Dr. Brenda Salter McNeil explicates that to speak about the centrality of justice in the story of God and in the gospel of Jesus Christ is to speak about the wet part of the ocean. A Christlike church cannot depart from Christlike justice. She urges the church to grow in the paradigm of racial justice and reconciliation into what the Spirit is calling the church to be now. For such a time as this: a just church that repairs broken systems. With over thirty years of ministry experience as a reconciler, she walks us through her own growth and development of a racial reconciliation paradigm with honesty, candor, challenge, and kingdom urgency using the courageous story of Esther. This book is light in our darkness and an urgent, prophetic wake-up call to a church that has lost its reconciling credibility."

—**Inés Velásquez-McBryde**, pastor, speaker, and reconciler; chaplain, Fuller Theological Seminary

"There is not a more credible, seasoned, and dynamic voice in the country that could speak to us about leadership and reconciliation than Rev. Dr. Brenda Salter McNeil. She has guided countless organizations and individuals through these choppy waters, and there are literally thousands of people who could bear testimony to the way she has changed their lives—including me. That is why I cannot recommend *Becoming Brave* strongly enough. In this book you will be equipped and moved to become someone different and better than what you've ever been before."

—**Daniel Hill**, pastor; author of *White Awake*

"Rev. Brenda illuminates a justice path for those seeking to be brave or simply responding to the times. With truth-telling, vulnerability, and profound scriptural insights, Rev. Brenda's work reflects the complex struggles that come from a long engagement in reconciliation work. In *Becoming Brave*, Rev. Brenda, one of the American church's great leaders of racial reconciliation, delves into the unexpected disruptions she has encountered during her journey toward deep reconciliation. She models and illuminates a path for others. A fantastic resource for advocating for and embodying justice."

—**Nikki Toyama-Szeto**, executive director, Evangelicals for Social Action at the Sider Center of Eastern University

"Brenda's reflections in *Becoming Brave* could stand in for countless numbers of people in the community of color. For many, the first years of faith disarmed the gospel of its resistance to injustice—the restoration of God's shalom—replacing it with the placating call to piety, to 'Just follow Jesus!' We celebrated soul salvation, our ticket home to a triumphant eternity, with the implicit expectation that earthly matters were important only inasmuch as they ensured we could 'occupy until Jesus returns.' This truncated experience of salvation meant that continuing injustice went unaddressed by many gospel-embracing believers. Clearly, a disarmed gospel is no gospel at all. If we are honest, most people of color can insert their names, stories, and journeys in the place of Brenda's. The gospel we initially responded to was about soul salvation and piety. Her stories, rooted in women of action in Scripture, inspire us to deepen our faith and take the whole gospel to the whole of creation. Paul admonishes us that 'the whole of creation awaits the revelation of the children of God.' Perhaps this is less about us being revealed than it is about us experiencing the gospel more fully. In *Becoming Brave*, Brenda challenges us to be woke!"

—**Terry LeBlanc**, director, NAIITS: An Indigenous Learning Community

"I want to be a leader for racial reconciliation. Dr. McNeil's book is an essential tool for my leadership education. It is not a book for the faint of heart. Dr. McNeil anchors her wisdom in the book of Esther. And while I was inspired by the wisdom of the book, it's going to challenge you. It pulls no punches. And for these reasons, it is an essential read."

—**Shirley Hoogstra**, president, Council for Christian Colleges and Universities

"For years, Dr. McNeil has been a pioneer in awakening churches to the biblical call to racial reconciliation. She is now taking a bold and courageous step forward into new territory. My prayer is that all who have received and appreciated her ministry will follow her into the wilderness—in a parallel journey to that of Moses and Miriam leaving Egypt. In this brilliant and powerful book, Dr. McNeil makes a case for recognizing this kairos moment when traditional reconciliation models don't go far enough to liberate us from fear and captivity. This book is a clarion call that cuts through the fog of our partisan arguments and blazes a path to abundant life for all. All of those who are suffering unjustly at this time need you to read this book and respond. This book will equip you to hear your equivalent to the call of Queen Esther—that you are who you are in order to speak out in your place for such a time as this."

—**Alexia Salvatierra**, Centro Latino professor, School of Intercultural Studies, Fuller Theological Seminary